Praise for *The Missing World* by Margot Livesey

"The sort of old-fashioned tale that Maugham would have admired—its thrills are understated, delicious and not to be missed . . . [Livesey's] style recalls the early, best Hitchcock, as evil unfolds in the most commonplace of circumstance."
—*The Washington Post Book World*

"An enthralling novel . . . that makes you feel as well as think."
—*The New York Times*

"In the skilled hands of Scottish writer Margot Livesey, the tale moves beyond the predictable mystery and becomes more a parlor game, full of chance meetings, questionable motives and possibly conspiracies, like the best of drama. And as with any good drama, we are left not only with a compelling plot, but also a complex portrait of human nature and the hazy line between virtue and self-interest."
—*The Philadelphia Inquirer*

"This is intelligent fiction, vigorous both in its observation of human foible and in its speculation on the role that memory plays in underwriting our sense of choice and direction in our lives."
—*The New York Times Book Review*

"In her first novel since the acclaimed *Criminals*, Margot Livesey makes a triumphant return, proving herself a master at revealing the complex, subtle emotional texture of seemingly ordinary lives."
—*Houston Chronicle*

PENGUIN BOOKS

THE MISSING WORLD

A native of Scotland, Margot Livesey lives in Waltham, Massachusetts, and London. She is the author of the novels *Homework* and *Criminals*, and of *Learning by Heart*, a collection of stories.

the
missing world

a novel by

margot livesey

PENGUIN BOOKS

PENGUIN BOOKS

Published by the Penguin Group

Penguin Putnam Inc., 375 Hudson Street,
New York, New York 10014, U.S.A.
Penguin Books Ltd, 27 Wrights Lane, London W8 5TZ, England
Penguin Books Australia Ltd, Ringwood, Victoria, Australia
Penguin Books Canada Ltd, 10 Alcorn Avenue,
Toronto, Ontario, Canada M4V 3B2
Penguin Books (N.Z.) Ltd, 182–190 Wairau Road,
Auckland 10, New Zealand

Penguin Books Ltd, Registered Offices:
Harmondsworth, Middlesex, England

First published in the United States of America by
Alfred A. Knopf, a division of Random House, Inc. 2000
Published by Penguin Books 2001

1 3 5 7 9 10 8 6 4 2

PUBLISHER'S NOTE

This is a work of fiction. Names, characters, places, and incidents either
are the product of the author's imagination or are used fictitiously, and any
resemblance to actual persons, living or dead, business establishments,
events, or locales is entirely coincidental.

THE LIBRARY OF CONGRESS HAS CATALOGED
THE HARDCOVER EDITION AS FOLLOWS:
Livesey, Margot.
The missing world: a novel/by Margot Livesey.—1st edition.
p.   cm.
ISBN 0-375-40581-X (hc.)
ISBN 0 14 02.9855 X (pbk.)
I. Title.
PR9199.3.L563M57   1999
813'.54—dc21   99–35785

Printed in the United States of America
Set in Garamond

For

Eric Garnick

the missing world

chapter 1

They were quarrelling on the phone when it happened, although anyone overhearing them might easily have failed to detect the fury that lay behind their pragmatic sentences. "I don't see why you need to bother Mrs. Craig," Hazel said, "about a leak in your study."

"But my hunch," said Jonathan, "is that the water's getting in through her roof as well as ours. No use fixing one without the other." He was standing beside the window, tugging at the dusty leaves of the indomitable cheese plant. Since Hazel's flight the other plants had, one by one, succumbed to his lack of care and now sat, brown and desiccated, on windowsills and tables. This monster, however, almost as tall as he was with its perforated leaves and hairy roots groping from the lower stems, had not merely survived his abuse but positively thrived. In the midst of his struggle with Hazel, he found time to apostrophise his old enemy. Die, you bugger, he thought, and shredded a leaf.

The brittle green flakes were still falling when Hazel's steady speech swerved, slewed across several lanes, hesitated at the guardrail, and plunged off into a dark field. "Elephants," she whispered. "Caracals."

"Hazel, is something wrong? Hazel?"

The receiver emitted a gurgling sound, then a thud. Jonathan held it away from him, glaring at the rows of holes, as if the machine itself might be responsible for this aberration. But the black plastic was mute. He dropped the phone, grabbed a jacket from the stand in the hall, his keys from the table, and ran. Miraculously, his beleaguered company Saab started on the first attempt. Only as he pulled away from the kerb did he realise he could see nothing; the windscreen was dark with snow. He climbed out again to wipe it clear with his bare hands.

The pillowed streets, rare in North London, had served as the pretext for his phone call. "Look at the snow," he had exclaimed, so exhilarated by the downy, festive weather that, briefly, he had forgotten he and Hazel were no longer looking at anything together. He had felt like an idiot when she replied, in a peculiarly quiet voice, that she'd had an accident on the way home. A car, unable to stop, had knocked her down in a zebra crossing.

"Oh, my god," he said. "Are you all right?"

"I think so. It wasn't going very fast. I just feel . . ." Her breath whistled into the phone. ". . . a little wobbly."

He offered to take her to the doctor, the hospital, but she said no, she'd have an early night; time enough to seek help if she still felt out of sorts in the morning. Then, eager to prolong the conversation, Jonathan had mentioned that he'd finally called the roofer about the damp patch in the ceiling and his belief that it was partly the fault of the next-door neighbour, who let everything go to wrack and ruin, and so they had drifted out of the calm waters of weather and health onto a familiar reef: his attitude towards Mrs. Craig.

Now Jonathan drove heedlessly, swearing at red lights. The deep-seated vexation, at Hazel, at himself, at the cheese plant, which a few minutes earlier had possessed him utterly, was gone. This is an emergency, he told himself; unbidden, the Latin *emergere,* to rise up, came to him. He was rising up to meet . . . he didn't know exactly what. Was Hazel under attack from someone? Some *thing*? He couldn't imagine what had produced those odd words—caracals, for christ's sake—or that gurgling. He turned off the Holloway Road. The car was still shimmying when, from between the parked cars on his left, a dark shape pelted into the street.

Dog? Cat?

A tiny interval existed during which Jonathan could have nudged the steering wheel or applied the brake. He did neither. The wheel jumped, and he was past it, whatever it was. The rearview mirror showed only the lights of other cars falling farther and farther behind as he hurtled down Camden Road. He leaned on the horn and overtook a taxi.

Pausing for a red light, he had visions of scaling a drainpipe to Hazel's second-floor flat, breaking down the door, and immediately doubted his own capacities; that kind of thing was much harder than it looked in films. Perhaps one of her neighbours had a key? Then it came to him: he himself had a set.

He had acquired them in a manner he could scarcely bear to consider, the complete opposite of that happy occasion four years ago when he'd given her the keys to his house. They were in a restaurant when he handed her the envelope. Hazel had peered at it, held it up to the light, and, finally, as the waiter put bowls of pasta before them, torn it open. At the sight of the Yale and mortice, still glinting from the locksmith's, her eyes widened. Shall we use them, she whispered. He had hesitated only a moment before taking twenty pounds out of his wallet and hurrying her home to bed. But last autumn, in the looking-glass world of separation, he'd agreed to pick up a light fixture for her flat—weeks of argument had reduced him to stony helpfulness—and she had asked if he could get some keys cut. For Maud, she explained. No problem, he'd said, dumbfounded once again at how poorly she understood his feelings.

For weeks he carried the extra set of keys in his pocket. Just knowing he had access to Hazel, that she couldn't keep him out even if she wanted to, made him feel better. Then one night, several Scotches to the wind, he ended up pacing her street and got as far as opening the outside door. After that, not trusting himself with such temptation, he put the keys in the glove compartment of the car and did his best to forget them.

In the one-way system of Kentish Town, afraid of a wrong turn, he slowed down. During the months before Hazel moved out, he had twice lost his way walking to the tube station and once, in a moment of fiercely lit, jostling panic, been unable to find his office. But now the same irradiating urgency that made him careless of the dark animal's fate guided him through these unfamiliar streets towards Hazel's shabby terrace. Skidding slightly, he double-parked and extricated the hateful keys.

The outside door was open. Rushing up the stairs, he pictured Hazel unconscious on the floor, clutching the phone. He would carry her into the bedroom and hold a cool cloth to her forehead until she opened her eyes and begged him to lie down beside her. As soon as he unlocked the door of her flat, Jonathan knew this was the easy version. Sounds he could not parse into sense came from the living-room. "Hello," he said, not loud enough to be heard.

He stopped to pick up the phone, beeping on the hall floor, and went slowly into the living-room. Hazel was lurching away from him across the carpet, as if her legs were of different lengths or different substances, one wax, one lead. A table lamp, directly in her passage, fell to the floor. She was wearing a black pullover and, surprisingly, a blue skirt he had given her.

"Hazel," he said.

She reached the wall but still she did not stop. She kept walking until she was pressed right up against it, her toes nudging the skirting board, her thighs moving in a parody of an exercise machine. She raised her hands and began to claw at the plaster, her fingers scraping the magnolia paint, over and over.

When at last she turned around, he would not have recognised her. The whole shape of her face had changed. Her cheeks were puffy; her eyes, always so large and luminous, were rolling back in their sockets; saliva frothed her lips, and even her jaw seemed to undulate oddly. Only her fine, feathery hair was the same. "Barasingha," she said in an unnaturally deep voice.

Jonathan fled. In the hall he seized the phone and dialled Emergency.

"Which service do you require: police, fire, or ambulance?"

"Ambulance," he shouted. And then he was speaking to a calm-voiced woman. Next to the phone was a bookcase, and as he recited the address he caught sight of the faded binding of Ovid's *Metamorphoses,* his second gift to her, squeezed between *The Poems of Rumi* and *A Guide to Seashore Birds;* at least she hadn't thrown it away.

"How long will it be?" he asked, but the operator was gone.

At the prospect of returning to the living-room, dread washed over him. Whoever was staggering back and forth, that person, that creature, was not Hazel. Barasingha? It sounded exotic: a small monkey, perhaps, or a complicated curry. He touched the spine of *Metamorphoses,* the gold lettering almost gone.

"Anything," he vowed, "I'll do anything to get her back again." His fingertips came away flecked with gold.

Hazel had sunk to her knees and was scrabbling at the wall, a desperate prisoner. Cautiously he knelt beside her and reached his arms around her, then almost let go. Deep, uneven zigzags were leaping through her, not like the vibrations of cold or grief but rather as if she were plugged into some wayward generator. He tightened his grip against the shocks. She continued to claw the paint. "Hazel," he pleaded, "stop it. Please, *stop*!"

Like the beginning of an answer came the faint seesawing of a siren.

At the hospital, there was an alarming sense of urgency. Last spring Jonathan had brought a friend here after an accident on the squash court. Steve was dripping blood, and they had both believed, mistakenly, that his nose was broken; yet an hour or more passed before anyone did more than bring him a towel. Whereas so many people converged on Hazel that by the time Jonathan arrived, only seconds behind the ambulance on whose coat-tails he'd flown through the icy streets, she was completely surrounded. Even as he rushed into the waiting room, the gurney disappeared through the double doors at the far end. He stared after her until a burly nurse tapped his arm. "Would you mind checking in with reception, sir?"

Following his downward glance, Jonathan discovered he was still wearing his maroon slippers; no wonder his feet were freezing. At the reception desk a plump-faced young man pried his gaze away from a portable television and typed Hazel's particulars into the computer. Hazel Ash Ransome, thirty-three, freelance journalist. Unthinkingly, Jonathan gave his address as hers and himself as next of kin. "I'll be right here," he said. "You'll call me as soon as there's news?"

The young man, his eyes once again locked on the glowing screen, nodded.

Across the counter, Jonathan imagined a red handprint springing up on one of those doughy cheeks. Then he gave in, he'd talk to a doctor soon, and retreated to the orange plastic chairs. His leather jacket creaked as he tried vainly to get comfortable. Another effect of Hazel's departure, besides the scourge of the houseplants, was the abrupt fleeing of his own flesh. Whenever he remembered, he wrote "sandwich" in his diary and, on the rarer occasions when he ate one, ticked it off.

Images flitted in and out of his mind: Hazel taking him to see the curse tablets at the British Museum; Hazel playing darts at the pub, scoring three bull's-eyes in a row; Hazel exclaiming over the honeycomb he had brought her, his first gift. She had insisted on baking bread. Hours later they emerged from bed to eat the warm loaf with honey.

"Blessed art thou amongst women, and blessed . . ."

Who on earth, thought Jonathan, was praying? Scanning his neighbours, many of whom had clearly come straight from the pub, he wondered if he had imagined the words, an attempt to conjure order from cacophony. The man next to him was singing inaudibly into his dirty white beard. Three seats down a stout woman was hectoring an even stouter one. "I told you," she said. "Didn't I tell you? I certainly did tell you." At last, in the row opposite, Jonathan located the unlikely source of prayer. A boy of maybe twelve or thirteen was saying the rosary. Every part of him, including his head, was long and narrow, as if he had passed through a vice; his jeans were secured with string at both waist and ankle.

Watching him, Jonathan lamented his own lack of gods. This room was saturated in waiting, no one merely read a book or held a conversation, but here was someone who could wait usefully. As a schoolboy Jonathan had gone to church hundreds, maybe thousands, of times and been left with nothing but a few hymns: "O Come, All Ye Faithful," "All Things Bright and Beautiful." Yet, standing in Hazel's hall, he had made his vow aloud.

"Amen," the boy murmured.

As for Hazel, in response to the receptionist's rote inquiry he had claimed her for the Church of England. In truth, all he could vouch for was a certain feyness. She sometimes checked her horoscope in magazines and periodically came home with flyers for Mrs. Sophia's Psychic Gallery. *Don't fail to come and visit this God-Gifted lady, for she has the power to heal by prayer. She will explain your past, present, and future fully. She will call out friends and enemies by name.* But he had several of these himself. Two slender girls in kurtahs handed them out at the tube station. Or they slid through the letter box.

The doors behind which Hazel had disappeared parted to emit an ample woman in a raincoat. The boy spilled from his chair. "Mama!" he exclaimed. How quickly his prayers had been answered.

"Hush, Louis." The woman patted his narrow head and led him serenely past the winos and bickering women.

A few minutes later the double doors opened again and a woman in a white coat strode to the reception desk. Jonathan's name came over the Tannoy. At once he was on his feet. "Hazel—is she all right?"

"Mr. Littleton?" The doctor signalled him to a booth. "I'm Dr. Schuler."

"How is Hazel?" he said, taking the proffered seat. "Can I see her?"

"Not just yet. I need to ask you a few questions." With her flaxen hair, her round face, her neat nose, the doctor reminded him of someone. And as she sat down, pen poised over a clipboard, he realised who: Hazel, the vivid, mercurial Hazel he'd met four years ago, a woman on such enviably easy terms with herself and the world.

"Ms. Ransome," the doctor said, "has suffered a blow to the head. She's unconscious at present. Have you any idea what might have caused this?" She gave him a quick, searching look.

Just for an instant, Jonathan wondered if he was being accused. Ridiculous. The only thing they both wanted was to help Hazel. As precisely as possible, he repeated what she had told him: the car, the zebra crossing, the wobbly feeling. "It didn't sound that serious," he said. "Then we were talking on the phone and she started speaking gibberish."

Dr. Schuler wrote all this down, or at least she wrote something down. "Does she have a history of epilepsy?"

"Not that I know of."

Did anyone in her family? Ditto. Was Hazel taking any medication? Ditto.

With each denial Jonathan felt his own guilt and uselessness. The doctor, however, when questioned, was equally uninformative. "She's in IC. We're still trying to contain the seizures."

Contain? "But Hazel," he said again, "she *is* going to be all right."

"We don't know yet, and we probably won't until she recovers consciousness." Now that Dr. Schuler was looking directly at him, he noticed that even her eyes were like Hazel's, showing white all the way round the iris. As if aware of his scrutiny, she blinked and gave a small, catlike yawn. "Sorry," she said, getting up. "We'll let you know as soon as there's a change."

Swiftly, silently, the doctor was moving away. What about Hazel? Why couldn't he see her? "Dr. Schuler," he called, but she was gone.

Dispirited, he returned to the ghastly chair. I'll do anything, he had vowed, but what if there was nothing? He went through his pockets, hoping for some forgotten piece of gum or chocolate, and discovered not even a scrap of foil. On the chair beside him lay a *National Geographic,* its yellow cover seemingly unchanged since he had given his father a subscription for Christmas thirty years before. Jonathan opened it to a picture of a black-and-white dog foraging in a meadow. *During the brief Antarctic summer penguins avail themselves of the chance to be herbivores.* He looked again and saw that the dog was indeed a penguin, a clump of grass in its beak.

At the time that he gave his father the subscription, Jonathan's closest companion was a black poodle. Flopsy accompanied him on bicycle rides, waited for him to come home from school, and slept at the foot of his bed. Besides him, her other great passion was cars. Given half a chance, she sneaked into his father's Morris Minor and accompanied him to his job at the knitwear mill. So when one October afternoon Jonathan arrived home to see neither Flopsy nor the car, he wasn't worried until he came into the kitchen and found his father drinking tea.

"Where's Flopsy?" he demanded, unzipping his anorak.

His father said something about a meeting in Glasgow.

"But what about Flopsy?"

His father puffed on his inhaler, a habit Jonathan hated, and stretched out a hand. "She disappeared. I'm sorry, Johnny, there was an accident, six cars in the fog. She bolted. I called and called but she never came."

"She'll be all right," his mother added quickly. She was at the sink, peeling potatoes. "She'll find a family who'll take good care of her. Would you like some cake?"

"We have to go and fetch her," said Jonathan, struggling back into his anorak. "She'll come if I call. I know she will."

"Our car's at the garage." His father kept looking not at Jonathan but at his mother.

"We can borrow one. The Dawsons will lend you theirs. We have to go now, before it gets dark. She'll be scared all alone."

But his parents had refused, stubbornly and absolutely, and at last grown so angry that they sent him to his room.

"It was the worst night of my life," he had told Hazel over supper at Standard Tandoori. "Every half hour I tiptoed downstairs to see if Flopsy was on the doorstep. In the morning, I pretended to go to school and caught the bus to Hawick and then on to Glasgow. I asked the driver to let me off at Sutra. Whereabouts, he said. The beginning, I said, the very beginning. So he set me down in this godforsaken place, bleak grassland as far as the eye could see, and I started walking, calling for Flopsy. After about five miles a policeman picked me up. . . ."

To his surprise and embarrassment, he had been unable to continue.

"You poor boy," Hazel said. "She was probably killed in the accident, wasn't she?"

"Killed?" Gazing into her clear blue eyes, Jonathan had thought, of course. What else could explain his parents' hardheartedness? They'd blurted out the lie to make him feel better and been too ashamed to take it back. Meanwhile, month after month, he had waited. He'd heard of animals finding their way home over hundreds of miles; why not his beloved Flopsy a mere thirty?

As he reached across the papadums for Hazel's hand, not only his parents and Flopsy and his younger self were illuminated by the light of her understanding, but also his older self, of whom, so often recently, he had despaired.

By midnight the crowd in Accident and Emergency had thinned. The bearded man had sauntered off, still singing, and most of the pubgoers had mysteriously vanished. Those who remained seemed to wait with neither hope nor expectation. When Jonathan tried to picture Hazel now, all he could see was her turning away as he entered a room; shrinking at his touch; muttering into the phone, I have to go, he's home. Better not to think of her at all, if this was the best he could do. Better to say multiplication tables or recite the names of rival insurance companies than to recall the aberrant Hazel of these last few months.

He was debating whether to check with reception again when the outside door opened. A gurney appeared, propelled by an ambulance man, followed by three policemen. Wheels squeaking, it swept past within a yard. Only the feet, clean and remarkably white, were visible beneath the grey blanket. Jonathan stared at the neatly cut toenails. My god, he thought almost aloud, those are the feet of a dead man.

chapter 2

Jonathan glimpsed a field, stone walls, and sheep before the present rushed in, obliterating the dreamscape. While he was dozing, something dreadful had befallen Hazel; his inattention had been fatal. The awful thought of never seeing her again paralysed him. Then another part of him emerged from the fear. They would have woken me, he told himself, if anything had happened. He struggled out of the orange chair and went over to the water fountain to rinse his mouth with the dirty-tasting water. Back in his seat, he saw that Accident and Emergency had filled up again, a greyer, quieter crowd than before. Only one other person from the previous evening was still there, a middle-aged woman in a puffy purple jacket. Unblinking, unyawning, she sat poker-straight, gloved hands clasped in her lap. Perhaps her vow, Jonathan thought, had been not to move until good news arrived. Her angular features suggested furious concentration.

The *whoomf* of the double doors interrupted his specu-lations, and a white-coated man headed for reception. Jona-than leaned forward—"Hazel," he murmured—but after a brief exchange the man loped away with a snort of laughter. In his wake, Jonathan approached the desk and discovered that the television watcher had been replaced by a woman his own age. A plume of frizzy brown hair waved over her formidable horn-rimmed glasses.

"Hazel Ransome . . . I'm afraid she hasn't recovered consciousness yet. Why don't you go and get a cup of tea?" Her plume bobbed. "I'll page the cafeteria if there's any change."

"Thank you," he said, relieved to be told what to do, and gave his name again.

Turning, he caught a trace of perfume and almost collided with the sleek-suited woman waiting to take his place. Her perfunctory smile, a mere twitch of the lips, brought home his own dishevelled state. His denim shirt and black cords, perfectly acceptable yesterday, were now not only crumpled from his night in a chair but also, mysteriously, ill-fitting. His slippers did nothing to help. And of course there was his fast-growing stubble, which in happier times Hazel had claimed made him look like an American film star.

In the cafeteria a slight, turbaned man presided over an immense teapot. Using both hands, he poured a cup and, after studying it, added more hot water to the pot, as if constant titration were the essence of his job. To his own surprise Jonathan asked if it was still snowing.

"I think not." The man lowered the pot. "Rain as usual."

"The papers claim we're having a drought."

"Drought," the man sniffed, suggesting a superior and very different understanding of the word.

Another customer appeared. Jonathan helped himself to a scone and moved on to the cashier. Most of the people in the low-ceilinged room were hospital staff chatting over what was either breakfast or supper. He chose a table with a single nurse, slender, mousey-haired, eating a yoghurt in tidy bites. Jonathan eyed her longingly; could he ask her about Hazel? He was poised to introduce himself when the PA growled—"Nurse Granger to orthopaedic . . . Nurse Bernadette Granger to orthopaedic"—and she was on her feet, licking her spoon and picking up her bag.

At last the sky began to lighten and the tea was gone. Jonathan stopped at a phone to dial Steve and Diane's number.

"Hello, Steve. Sorry to ring so early."

"Who is this?"

After nearly twenty years Steve still did not recognise his voice on the phone. It doesn't mean anything, Hazel used to say, but Jonathan could never quite banish the idea that this failure in his oldest friend proceeded from a secret wellspring of dislike. Now he identified himself and, cutting through Steve's exclamations, summarised the last twelve hours.

"Tell me again," Steve said. "You were talking and . . . did she have a stroke? This is terrible."

"Not a stroke. Seizures. They're still trying to find the cause."

"Poor Hazel—don't do that, Katie. Sorry. Have you rung her parents?"

"Her parents?" His gaze fell on a notice next to the phone. IN CASE OF FIRE DO NOT PANIC. DO NOT RUN. PROCEED CALMLY TO THE NEAREST EXIT, CLOSING WINDOWS AND DOORS BEHIND YOU. "Of course not. Hazel speaks to them twice a year and that's when things are going well. Besides, it's not like they could help, up in Kendall."

"Phone them," said Steve. "Don't be a martyr. I know you'd do anything for Hazel, but she isn't your responsibility. There might be decisions. . . . Hang on."

Jonathan watched the pence tick away: fifteen, thirteen. At nine Steve was back. "Sorry. Give a shout if we can help. Anything. Any time."

In his address book Jonathan turned to the Ransomes'

number. How happy he had been when Hazel gave it to him and urged him to call when she went to stay for the weekend. She had started, he remembered, to dictate the number but, eager to possess another small piece of her, he'd passed her his book. I have a terrible scrawl, she said. In China I would've been an old maid. During the last few months he had scarcely known whether to welcome or repudiate these memories, they came barbed with such pain. Now, gazing at her untidy 5s, her tipsy 7s, he thought life was once again making sense.

Back in the waiting room, the receptionist shook her head. He sat down in the nearest chair and picked up a discarded newspaper. Satellite observation showed that spring in the Northern Hemisphere was arriving a week earlier. What effect, he wondered, would this have on his bees? An insurance scam was likely to give some of the frauds he dealt with fresh ideas. But after a couple of paragraphs his concentration fizzled. All he could think of was Hazel clawing the wall, her skin jumping beneath his touch. Surely there would be news soon.

At nine o'clock, desperate to pass five more minutes, he went to ring his office. The manager, an elfin woman he'd never seen without a cup of Earl Grey, answered. Even the syllables "Com-et In-sur-ance" seemed to carry a whiff of bergamot. Over the years he had watched her listen to countless tales of ruin and disaster with implacable calm—You need to fill out section 18c, sir; That's dealt with in the appendix to G6—but as soon as he said that his wife had been hit by a car, she burst into a flurry of commiseration. He started to explain about his appointments and she chased him off the phone.

Then he went to the bathroom. Wife, he thought, I've got a nerve. But she hadn't called him on it. He was not, as Steve suggested, pursuing martyrdom—quite the contrary. The Hazel who tore at the walls, foamed at the mouth, and said "caracals" was closer to his beloved than the harsh, strident woman who had moved out of their house and threatened to get an unlisted number if he didn't stop calling. As he rubbed the soap between his palms, Jonathan allowed himself to hope that at long last the cloud of rage which had settled over Hazel, distorting everything he said and did, was lifting.

A few miles away, in another part of the city, Charlotte stared at her visitor, aghast. Ever since her sister dropped in last autumn, she'd had a firm rule about uninvited callers, but at least she need not compound the error of opening the door by allowing her landlord even one step inside. Barely taller than she was, with a belly as high and round as if he'd swallowed a beach ball, Mr. Aziz was smiling in a way that made her clutch her coat more tightly over her nightdress.

"Miss Granger," he said with a little bow that somehow did not involve his belly, "there seems to be a problem with the post." In his hand he held a stack of envelopes, presumably collected from the ledge in the hall where mail for Charlotte, and the house's three other tenants, piled up.

Ignoring the envelopes, Charlotte began to babble. "I've been away, doing the Christmas pantomime in York—*Peter Pan*. I was Wendy. Didn't you get my note?"

"Oddly, no, but here we are. It's four months since you paid rent. Am I to assume"—his small brown eyes grew even smaller—"that you are moving out?"

Would crying help? Or was the high road of indignation better? Her heart was pounding so violently it was all she could do to hold her ground. "No," she managed, and louder, firmer, "No, I'm not."

"So I will have a banker's cheque by the end of the week?"

"I swear." Then, as her hand closed around the letters, she

realised the recklessness of her promise. "The end of the month," she amended. "When the theatre pays me."

Mr. Aziz, frowning, reached into his pocket and produced a diary. "Three weeks. You are asking me to wait three weeks for four months' rent, five by that time."

"Please, I've been a good tenant. No fuss, no repairs. If I get the money sooner, so will you. But by the end of the month, for sure." Cross my heart, she almost added. Instead she concentrated on parting her lips and letting her coat fall open, just an inch, a damsel in distress.

For a long moment Mr. Aziz continued to regard her. Then, with the briefest of sighs, he closed the diary. "I suppose I've waited this long. But I warn you, Miss Granger—"

"No need," Charlotte interrupted gaily. "Thank you, thank you. Now, if you'll forgive me, I was about to take a bath." In one swift movement, she stepped back, closed and secured the door. Heart still pounding, she pressed her ear to the wood and listened to his footsteps, oddly light and regular, descend the stairs.

An hour later, having skipped the bath but fully dressed, Charlotte had something that resembled a plan. All this kerfuffle, she thought, reaching into her bag, past a National Theatre brochure, a free sample of soap, an apple core eaten down to the pips, and a hairbrush, was simply a matter of sums. In the seam of lint at the bottom, her fingers rooted out a coin, several coins, but not, alas, the pleasant chubbiness of a pound. She laid the two fifty-pence pieces and a ten on a corner of the futon. If she sublet her flat to a student—better still, two students—and moved in with her sister, just until summer, she would be able to catch up on the rent, get a good haircut and new publicity photos, pay off her debts. Well, not the bank maybe, but interest rates were down, and surely the manager could see his way to extending her loan. Amortising: it had such a nice solid sound.

Picturing Bernadette, Charlotte felt some of her satisfaction slip away. Bernie would lecture, she would scold, she would carve out her kilo of flesh, but Charlotte, for once, would hold her tongue. With Mr. Aziz at the door and Bernie her only living relative, what choice had she? Not my only living relative, she corrected. She had, once again, forgotten not merely their impossible parents but the rug-rats. That Bernie's bonking Rory had somehow created two new people with a claim on her was hard to keep in mind. Aunt. The very word was a wail of pain.

But weren't the rug-rats grist for her mill? She picked a pair of tights off the floor by the television and draped them along the bookcase. She could hear herself telling Bernie, in crisp Oxbridge tones, what a good thing it would be for Oliver and Melissa to have their aunt around during this difficult time. Stability is so important for children. She would take them to museums and matinees, encourage their artistic pursuits. Oliver, at eight, was a bit of a bully, but Melissa, six and a half, had real dramatic talents and, so far, seemed to have escaped Bernie's suffocating neatness of spirit. "Order," Charlotte announced to the cluttered room, "is the enemy of art." She turned her attention to the armchairs, in whose crevices the odd coin sometimes lurked.

The bus for Oxford Circus was pulling away as she reached the stop. Bollocks, and all her own fault for being seduced by a cushion in the skip at the corner: red embroidery, African looking, probably thrown out by the tasteful lawyer couple two doors down. Not daring to leave it until later, Charlotte had dusted it off and carried it home. Now a good ten minutes passed before another bus came shouldering through the traffic.

Only to Marble Arch, but on she hopped and, good news, the conductor was upstairs. Maybe everything did have meaning. At first there seemed to be no seats. Then she spotted one next to a schoolgirl.

The girl gave a little sigh and drew close to the window. Nicely making room, Charlotte chose to think. She settled her capacious bag on her lap and glanced over at the notebook the girl was holding. *Why does Iago hate Othello?* was written across the top of the page.

"Are you doing *Othello?*" she asked.

"Yes." The girl leaned even closer to the window.

"So what's the answer?"

"I know it," the girl said sharply. "I just can't think how to put it." She twisted the point of her Biro into the page.

My younger self, thought Charlotte. The bus braked abruptly and jerked forward. "If I were answering," she said, "which, thank goodness, I'm not, I might say, 'Iago claims to hate Othello because of a rumour that Othello has slept with his wife, but that does not entirely explain his vehemence. There is an unreasoning quality to his hatred, perhaps inspired by Othello's nobility.' "

The girl was scribbling furiously. "A what quality?"

"Unreasoning. You might mention race, but I'm not sure I remember what Iago says about that. Are there more questions?"

"Two. 'Why does Othello believe Iago's lies about Desdemona?' And 'What does Othello realise after he's killed Desdemona?' "

"Who on earth gave you these? They're pathetic."

"Miss Groper. Do you have the answers?"

"Groper!" Charlotte stifled the jokes everyone else must have made. "I can certainly come up with something." As with many plays, she was much more familiar with the second half of *Othello* than the first, owing to her habit of slipping into theatres at the interval and settling herself, sans ticket, in an empty seat. "The real reason Othello believes Iago is that that's the plot and Shakespeare needs to get on with the play, but Groper would probably have a fit if you said anything so postmodern. Maybe, 'In spite of Othello's protestations that he is not jealous by nature he experiences twinges almost as soon as Iago hints at Desdemona's infidelity. He is subsequently convinced of her guilt by seeing Cassio with the handkerchief.'"

Before she could launch into a disquisition on Act V a cry came: "Fares, please. Fares." Charlotte sat very still, but as the conductor approached she felt the girl's eyes upon her. Caught between the two, she handed over a precious fifty pence.

"What handkerchief?" the girl said, closing her book. "This is my stop."

Charlotte quickly listed the handkerchief's various owners. "Can you remember all that?"

"Of course." With a shy smile, the girl squeezed past and was gone.

Alone, Charlotte allowed herself and her possessions to sprawl across the seat. A cushion and *Othello* before ten in the morning; surely such good fortune justified the dearer coffee-house. Then she remembered Mr. Aziz, his absurd belly and small brown eyes, his diary ticking like a time bomb.

On their rare previous visits to London, Hazel's parents had struck Jonathan as out of their depth. Brisk, upright country people, the pointless busyness of the city stymied them. What was it all for, this huddling together amidst noise and litter, they seemed to ask. They endured the activities Hazel organised—an exhibition, a play—dutifully expressing pleasure but never losing the air that the zenith of their visit would be the moment at Euston when they boarded the train back to the Lake District and their useful lives.

Now they were surprisingly self-possessed as they joined him at Hazel's bedside, to which, after a long morning of shuttling between the cafeteria and the waiting room, he had finally been admitted. Stout, red-faced George asked intelligent questions over the unconscious body of his only child; forty years of farming had educated him in medical matters. Nora held Hazel's hand and smoothed her hair. The seizures were still coming with alarming frequency. Various machines registered them with jumping lines and small beeps, but no dials were needed to detect their presence. They passed over Hazel like wind over water, twisting her face and limbs, rattling her breath. Sometimes she spoke in that odd, deep voice. George identified several of her remarks as referring to India—a barasingha was a kind of deer—and Jonathan wrote down whatever he could. Once she mentioned him. "Jonathan, did you pick up the potatoes?" Not exactly oracular, but at least not embarrassing.

Between his phone call to George and Nora and their arrival, his sole respite from worrying about Hazel had been to worry about their reaction to him. Everything was terrible, yet here he was at the hospital as her next of kin; the advent of her parents could only spell demotion. What would they have made of Hazel's complaints against him, her moving out? Up popped a memory of her shouting, "Don't you understand? There are things you can't apologise for. They change who you are, and you can't change back." And that, Jonathan thought, was before his slip-up.

So when George and Nora tiptoed into Hazel's room and behaved as if he were the ideal son-in-law, he felt an immense, billowy relief. Nora embraced him and George pumped his hand. "Thank goodness you were there," they both said. What the hell had Hazel told them?

On the morning of the second day, a doctor paused long enough to listen to their questions. Why wasn't Hazel conscious? George demanded, puffing out his chest.

The doctor, a tall, solid woman, smiled chidingly. "Mr. Ransome, we're still trying to find out. The CAT scan is negative, which"—she coiled and released her stethoscope—"is good news, and the EEG is fine."

What does that show? Jonathan wanted to ask—George, too, was shaping the words—but the doctor, enunciating as if for non–English speakers or the hard of hearing, swept on. "The next step," she said, "will probably be a spinal tap, to check for infection, even though at present we see no signs of trauma. Meanwhile, I'm afraid you're learning why we use the word 'patient.' " She was still nodding at the familiar joke when her beeper sounded.

The hours stuttered by. Later that afternoon, following an especially severe seizure, Hazel was taken away for yet more tests. George stared after the gurney. "I feel so helpless. Nobody's giving us an honest answer."

He sank down on the empty bed, Nora joined him, and they both turned toward Jonathan. A single night at the hospital had aged them a decade. George's eyes were bloodshot, his chin flecked with stubble. Nora's hair had slipped out of her usually neat bun, and her skirt was askew.

Don't look at me, Jonathan wanted to say. He yearned to break something, hurt someone. Instead he summoned his most authoritative manner. "They're doing their best. Everyone seems to agree that they won't know what's causing this until she wakes up."

The empty bed, the two elderly people—it was unbearable.

With nowhere to go in the small room, he retreated to the window. In the car park below drivers jousted for spaces, their jerky U-turns and reversals mirroring his muddled thoughts. He wanted Hazel better, of course, but wasn't that like desiring his own banishment? What he really wanted was for her to recover not merely from the accident but from the delusions that had carried her away from him.

"Yes, they're not keeping anything from us, George," Nora chimed in. "We'll talk to the neurologist tomorrow. Get up for a minute." Behind him, Jonathan heard them moving. "I was wondering," she continued, "about Maud."

"Maud?" Why on earth would Hazel's mother ask about Maud? Bewildered, he turned to discover her straightening the bed.

"You mean," Nora paused, a taut sheet in one hand, "you haven't told her?"

As a longtime inhabitant of the hospital Jonathan had learned to avoid the phone beside the fire-drill notice. Instead, he waited for a woman in overalls to finish using his favourite, near the X-ray department. "No, no peas," she was saying vehemently. The receiver, when at last she ceded it, smelled of cleaning fluid.

Unlike Steve, Maud had no trouble recognising his voice. As soon as he said hello, she burst out, "Jonathan. How are you?"

Bizarre, she sounded almost friendly. "I'm calling about Hazel," he said, and launched into his by-now-practised speech.

"A seizure," she said. And then, "Thank god."

Thank god? Only after he'd given directions and hung up did he realise he must have led her to expect something even worse. Well, why should he be the only one to suffer?

But as he neared the room this petty triumph faded. Although matters had worked out so surprisingly well with Hazel's parents, he had no illusions that this would happen with her best friend. Maud knew every item on the charge sheet, all those crimes large and small, true and false, which Hazel held against him; she'd probably suggested a few entries herself. Several times after Hazel left, he had met Maud for a drink, hoping she might act as peacemaker. On each occasion she'd offered further arguments as to why he and Hazel were doomed. No, he thought, he could expect no mercy from that quarter.

In 407 Hazel was back from the tests, arms bruised and lips very pale. Even in her unconscious state she conveyed an extra dimension of exhaustion. He was filled with pity and a wild desire to rescue her.

At the news that Maud was on her way, Nora exclaimed, "Oh, good."

"Why don't you two get a cup of tea?" Jonathan said, trying to sound casual. "I'll watch Hazel."

Alone, he grasped her hand, the one without the IV, and implored her not to let Maud come between them. "Hazel, I'll do anything to make things right."

She uttered a small moan.

Thirty minutes later, he was trying to explain, again, what really had happened with Suzanne, when the door opened and Maud appeared. Rising to greet her, Jonathan was struck by how rapidly the rest of them had been worn down by the hospital. With her glowing cheeks and dark hair, Maud was a messenger from a more vivid world.

"Oh, Jonathan." She flung her arms around him and he smelled the cold air clinging to her outdoor clothes. Despair, he thought, makes strange bedfellows.

After a long moment, his neck was straining, she released him. "Why is she still unconscious?"

"They don't know. At first they said it was a good thing—the brain resting—but now they're getting worried."

He stood on the far side of the bed. The shadows beneath Maud's eyes, which he'd always considered a sign of sulkiness, were even darker than usual. He saw that she was crying.

"Do you talk to her?" she said at last.

"Sometimes."

She put her hands on her hips. "We have to talk to her. I mean, if we give up . . ." She left the threat unfinished.

He nodded, both annoyed and relieved. Maud was her usual high-handed self, but at least she didn't seem antagonistic. Years ago, when Hazel introduced them, he had failed to understand the force of the phrase "best friend." Over drinks Maud had grilled him—what, exactly, did a claims adjustor do?—and, at Hazel's urging, he repeated some of his best stories: the couple who faked a burglary; the man who pried the slates off his own roof.

"Don't you ever worry about making mistakes?" Maud asked. "Depriving some little old lady of her immersion heater?"

"Of course," said Jonathan, then thought to add, "Don't you?"

"All the time." She described how she had sent a bouquet from the deceased to the widow, rather than vice versa. "She was convinced her husband called Interflora with his last gasp. I didn't have the heart to charge her." She shook her head. "Everyone assumes running a florist's is laid back, but most people buy flowers at times of crisis: death, love, a new job. They expect a dozen roses to change their lives."

"If only," said Hazel, who had worked at Plantworks for a year and still helped out on weekends and holidays.

Maud herself, as far as Jonathan could see, was well beyond

the reach of even the most lavish bouquet. The week after he met her, she and her husband threw a divorce party, but despite all the jollity Hazel insisted Maud was lonely and often invited her along on their dates. Or did Maud invite herself? He wasn't sure, but grew adept at booking tickets to sold-out shows, reserving tables for two in popular restaurants. Once he even asked if she was gay. Why on earth would you think that? said Hazel. She seems to enjoy your company so much, he had said. *Our* company, said Hazel, patting his cheek.

As for George and Nora, their one encounter with Maud had devolved into a fierce argument about veal calves and battery hens. Now all feuds were forgotten. The Ransomes were grateful for her devotion to their daughter. This is the best place in the country for head injuries, she told them. They'll have her conscious soon.

On the afternoon of the third day Hazel sprang a fever and was back in ICU. The four of them sat hopelessly in the waiting room until a soft-spoken Turkish nurse sent them packing. "I'll phone if there's a change," he promised. "You go home. Sleep."

Outside, the foggy air slapped their cheeks. George remarked that it was close to freezing. "Be careful on your bike," he admonished Maud.

Beside him Nora, pulling on her gloves, said, "Maybe tomorrow . . ."

"Absolutely," said Jonathan. "She just needs rest. She . . ."

His truisms were lost in the rip of sirens; from opposite directions two ambulances raced towards the hospital. Probably the end of their shift, he was thinking, when something made him glance at Nora. She was watching the vehicles as if each contained her nearest and dearest. They tore through the gates, and before the sirens died away, George had taken her arm and was leading her down the street towards their bed-and-breakfast.

Jonathan turned to Maud, who was fastening her bicycle helmet. "Do you fancy a drink?"

"I thought you'd never ask."

They walked to the pub on the corner in silence save for the clicking of her bike. Maud chained it to a railing and they entered a savagely lit room wreathed in smoke. Fewer than a dozen men were huddled at tables and the bar.

"What a shithole," said Maud. "I'll have a Bloody Mary."

She headed for a corner banquette. Jonathan ordered her drink and a Scotch, both doubles, then realised he didn't have the cash and contradicted himself. The bartender grunted.

"Cheers." Maud raised her glass. "Alone at last."

"Cheers." He gulped, hoping the alcohol on an empty stomach might induce wooziness. Beside him Maud seemed committed to studying every inch of the banquette. "I just thought," he said, "it would be good to have a chat about Hazel."

"Oh, Hazel," said Maud. Across the room, a man in a mac had begun to kick the cigarette machine. "Only a week ago we were talking about a cycling holiday in the spring."

A knife in his jugular, plans without him, but no time for that now. "All I wanted to say is that I hope we can let bygones be bygones. I know you can't be exactly thrilled to find me at the hospital, but Hazel and I have been together for four years."

"After which she couldn't wait to leave you."

He clutched his glass, blind for a second. "I've always had her best interests at heart," he choked out.

"I must say you have an odd way of showing it. Fuck, Jonathan, what were you thinking of?"

Finally she was looking at him, her stare like a hundred bee stings. "I saved her," he said. "If I hadn't got her to the hospital, she might've died."

Maud held his gaze a moment more. "To be honest"—her eyelids dipped—"I'm glad you're here. Apart from anything else, I couldn't handle George and Nora."

He took the olive branch and offered his own. "I thought they'd be angry with me too."

" 'Fraid not. From their point of view you've always been the knight in shining armour, rescuing Hazel from her hippie ways. They were so upset when she moved out that she ended up telling them it was just a trial separation." Someone bumped their table; the man in the mac lurched towards the gents'. "Want another?"

He nearly said yes, but something in her shadowy face stopped him. This wasn't peace, he reminded himself, only an armed truce. "Thanks, I'd better be going." To his surprise, she leaned over and kissed him on the cheek.

Leaving Maud to make a phone call, he stepped outside to discover the earlier fog had turned to freezing rain. Damn, he thought, recalling the study ceiling. Tomorrow he'd phone the roofer again. He zipped up his jacket and jogged towards the bus stop.

Maud invented rules. They must behave as if Hazel were already conscious: greet her on entering the room, report daily news, include her in their chatting. At first it was hard to publicly address this unconscious being, scarcely a woman anymore, though Jonathan had learned from the chart at the end of the bed that she was having her period; but soon it became surprisingly natural to offer her a cup of tea and remark on the weather.

His own particular contribution was reading aloud, intimacy without revelation. He chose a history of bee-keeping, which they'd read to each other one rainy Easter in a caravan near Windermere; ever since, the misty greenness of spring had been inextricably connected with the slow growth of cells, the uses of honey, lovemaking. Now Jonathan sat by her bed narrating the life of Frances Huber, the blind beekeeper who, in 1792, invented the leaf hive. Like a book, he explained, the leaves were the pages with the outer leaves, or covers, made of glass so that Huber's sighted assistant could observe the bees and describe them to his master. Even in this bleak room, the words cast a spell.

Late on the afternoon of the fifth day, Maud whispered, "Look."

Jonathan jumped up from the chair where he was dozing. George and Nora dropped their newspapers. Hazel's eyelids were fluttering. She opened her eyes and gazed up at the four of them. The colour of her irises had deepened, as if the long twilight of the last week had taken up permanent residence in her brain. "Who will pay?" she said. And then, unmistakably, "Oh, what time is it?"

Such a common question, but one Jonathan had never heard her ask before. Soon after meeting Hazel he had noticed she always knew the time. When he praised this ability, she protested. You couldn't praise something involuntary.

"On the contrary," he'd said, "that's the Calvinist in you, equating virtue with struggle. Aristotle believed the reverse." He explained the theory of innate virtue, and charmed her by turning all the clocks to the wall.

"A quarter to twelve," said Nora gently. "How do you feel?"

"Thirsty."

Maud helped her sit up, and Nora held a glass of water to her lips. As she sank back onto the pillows, Hazel caught sight of the tubes feeding into her arm and frowned.

"You had an accident," said Nora. "You're in hospital."

Hazel blinked. She turned to Jonathan, eyebrows arched, lips parted. What does she want, he thought. Suddenly he realised he had forgotten to be afraid. Was he about to be hurled into outer darkness?

"She doesn't know us," Nora said quietly. "We're strangers to her."

Now he could read the question in her face: who are these people? He stepped forward and took her hand in his. Her uncut nails pricked his palm.

"Jonathan." Slowly she closed her eyes.

chapter 3

Freddie Adams was suffering a not unfamiliar restlessness of spirit. In spite of the hour, nearly midnight, and the weather, raw and cold, he had borrowed a bike from the flock in the front hall—Kevin's, he was pretty sure, the only one unchained—and set off to pedal the streets of Canonbury and Highbury. He had not cycled for months and even the small hills made his side ache. Beneath him the bike creaked ominously and the gears threatened to slip.

What had set him going, woken his demon? The morning had been a breeze. He had fixed a gutter at the house across the street in exchange for lunch, a nice steak-and-kidney pie. He was barely home, however, settled on the couch with Agnes, than the phone rang. The caller introduced himself as Mr. Early: an emergency, water pouring in. Freddie listened vaguely, planning at the first pause to recommend his former boss, Trevor. Then Mr. Early said, "My mother always claimed it was bad luck to open a brolly in the house, but if this keeps up I may have to ignore her." Picturing this guy and his family, each with his or her own brilliant umbrella, Freddie had found himself promising to arrive within the hour.

"Heavens to Betsy," he'd said to Agnes. "Why am I such a marshmallow?"

Agnes pricked her ears and nudged her dish meaningfully.

Thirty minutes later, when he discovered the tall houses and steep roofs of Mr. Early's street, Freddie berated himself all over again. He parked outside number 11 and sat there, hoping for a sign. If I see two magpies, he thought, or one black cat, I'm off to the nearest pub to phone and say the van won't start. But there were no birds to be seen, nor a cat of any colour, only two white women in jackets and jeans coming down the sidewalk.

Resigned, Freddie got out of the van, secured his scarf, and opened the gate. The front garden was the usual scruffy flower bed, but the stretch of mosaic leading to the door was superb, a diamond pattern of black-and-white tiles interwoven with ochre and blue. And, equally rare, not a single tile was missing. Often a section had been ripped up to lay pipes—vandalism, to Freddie's way of thinking.

He reached approvingly for the dolphin knocker. One of the pleasures of life in London, as opposed to Cincinnati, was the many methods of announcing your presence. In his various jobs Freddie had become acquainted with old-fashioned bellpulls, shrill chimes, and the many brass knockers: dolphins, wreaths, lions, hands, heads. These last were his favourite, though the thud they produced made him feel like a bill collector. He knocked twice for good measure and peered into the wavery, unrevealing glass.

Nothing. No cry of "Coming," no footsteps brisk or shuffling, no light. A bubble of relief took shape in Freddie's gut. He was off the hook. This wasn't some old geezer who might've suffered a fall. Mr. Early had sounded safely middle-aged. Knocking again was beyond the call of duty, but he'd give it another thirty seconds. He stepped back to study the nearest rosebush, the crooked branches shoulder high. If he ever talked to Mr. Early again, he might recommend Kevin, his downstairs neighbour and a knockout gardener. Last summer he'd taken Freddie on a tour of the back garden, introducing him to the creamy white Winchester Cathedrals, the many-petalled Brother Cadfaels.

Without warning the door swung wide and a voice streamed out. "Mr. Adams, I am so sorry. Inexcusable, really, especially in this sodding weather. I was doing the eyelashes. The glue dries in ninety seconds. Do, please, come in."

In the doorway stood the most immaculately bald man Freddie had ever seen. His entire head was a beautiful, shapely, shining pink. Freddie stared, knowing he was staring, until Mr. Early motioned him inside. "Upstairs, upstairs," he urged, and Freddie climbed.

On the first landing he stepped into an amazing room. Everywhere, in serried ranks along the walls, were heads and their components: trays of eyes, piles of wigs and hairpieces, drawings of lips, sets of eyelashes and ears. And as Freddie stood there, taking in these proto-humans and feeling taken in by them, Mr. Early came up beside him. "May I get you something? Tea? Coffee? Horlicks?"

"What are these? I mean, what are they for?"

"Shops, films, telly, the police, whoever needs a head. I should apologise for the overwhelmingly Caucasian nature of my work."

At the word "Caucasian," Freddie turned to look at Mr. Early and found his gaze met by a pair of mild blue eyes behind dainty circular glasses. Mr. Early was looking at Freddie as if he saw not the external thing that most people got caught up with—a six-foot-two black American, arguably good-looking, possibly threatening—but the secret, complicated, surprising homunculus that Freddie considered his true self. "Coffee, please," he said.

As Mr. Early padded away, Freddie wandered across the room and sat down at the long worktable. His arms were trembling; beneath his clothes tiny hands were brushing the skin. He recognised the old feeling, deeply buried, dormant for nearly two years, undiminished; and beyond the feeling, a fact that neither time nor words could alter. The hands were all it took to thrust him out of his state of quasi-contentment with his job, with London, with himself. They were what had driven him to skip his graduation at Stanford, to quit four jobs in Silicon Valley, to flee Cincinnati first for Paris and then south to Lourdes, where he'd worked, if that was the word, as a stretcher bearer, an occupation that made everything else tolerable until it, too, became intolerable.

Here in London, before becoming a roofer, he'd had a perfectly decent job as a locksmith, part-time, okay money. One day he'd had a call from the council: a social worker needing entry to a basement flat in Dalston. As he dismantled the old-fashioned lock, a faint mewling came from behind the door. "Perhaps they have a dog," the social worker said hopefully.

"Perhaps," said Freddie.

Finally the lock yielded, but not the door. Something lay against it. "Push gently," said the social worker, and Freddie did.

He quit the next day. The hands were everywhere. After lying on the couch for three weeks, until there was nothing left to eat in his apartment save a bag of rice, he phoned Trevor, a friend of a friend, and asked if he could apprentice himself as a roofer.

"An apprentice," said Trevor. "Crikey. I've never had one before, but I don't see why not."

In person Trevor turned out to be a bouncy, talkative man, wearing the cleanest hightops Freddie had ever seen outside a shop. "Oh, you're black," he said when Freddie appeared at the foot of his ladder. "That's nice." Freddie could only agree.

At thirty-seven, Trevor still shared a house with his mother in Stoke Newington. Freddie, invited for tea, found the two of them awash in antimacassars and aspidistras, not to mention three Scotties, one pregnant. They questioned him about America—was it true you could get married at twelve, buy a gun at thirteen?—and made him point out his hometown in the atlas. The huge distance between London and Cincinnati had prompted Trevor's mother to give him Agnes. "Your family are so far away," she said.

For six months Freddie followed Trevor around, carrying ladders, passing tools, learning how to diagnose problems and fix them. Then he'd phoned home to ask for a loan. "Oh, Freddie," said his mother, "not again. Talk to your dad." And there was his eighty-year-old father growling into the phone that he wasn't made of money. "All I need is five thousand," Freddie protested, "for a ladder, tools, and a van." "Why would anyone hire you to fix their roof?" his father said. Freddie explained that the roofs in London were trash, fixing them was easy, and he was good at it. "People trust me because I'm tall," he said. "Not me," his father said, and hung up. Ten days later the cheque had arrived, accompanied by a form promising repayment, at prime interest, within two years. Freddie still had it in a drawer somewhere, along with Agnes's pedigree.

Mr. Early returned carrying a tray. "Milk? Sugar? Help yourself." He followed his own advice and took the wicker armchair beside the tiled fireplace.

Maybe, thought Freddie, taking the opposite chair, if he just kept moving, chatting, he could stay ahead of the devils this time. "Nice stuff," he said, holding up his cup. "Pooleware? Most people keep a chipped mug for the roofer. Did you fix the eyelashes?"

"Sufficiently. It is amazing how much one can do in ninety seconds. How do you know about Pooleware?"

"When I first came here, I helped out at an antique store. I once saw a William Morris tea set in somebody's kitchen. Old guy, dead wife, didn't have a clue."

"And?" said Mr. Early, tweaking the knees of his trousers.

"I suggested a trade: the repairs on his roof for the set. He agreed, then changed his mind. Said Mildred wouldn't like it and gave me a rubber cheque. Let's hope he finally made a killing."

Mr. Early was nodding. Behind him a row of heads, some with features, some without, mirrored his gleaming pinkness, pate after pate. "One of those sad cases when virtue must serve as its own reward. I expect Oscar has some trenchant remark about that." He waved an airy hand as if this Oscar might be lurking among the heads. "Do you like taking risks?"

Oh, Wilde, thought Freddie, glad he hadn't asked. "No way. I'm a cautious, cross-at-the-crosswalk kind of guy."

"Me too, in most respects. I read a book, *The Day Before Yesterday*. Maybe you've heard of it? The author claims that every twenty-three million years, roughly speaking, the earth is hit by a meteor so large it changes the entire climate. Everything. That's what happened to the dinosaurs. They weren't stupid. In fact, as a species they were quite highly evolved. Then this meteor showed up and . . ." He shrugged.

"Curtains?" Freddie offered.

"Curtains," Mr. Early agreed gravely. "I found it quite helpful: fear of meteors. For a while all my other worries seemed irrelevant." He raised his cup, lowered it untasted. "How old are you?"

"Thirty-four—no, thirty-five," said Freddie, struggling to

recall both his birthdate and the last time someone who didn't want to get him horizontal had asked about it. Was this guy a fag? He checked out his host's neatly crossed ankles, his black trousers and dark green cardigan. Could be.

"I would have guessed late twenties." Again the blue eyes regarded Freddie. "I don't mean appearance."

"About your roof," Freddie said.

They put down their cups and Mr. Early led him up another flight of stairs to a back room the colour of honey, a room so restful that Freddie had to fight the temptation to sit down again, and pointed to a stain the size of a frying pan. "I thought," Freddie said, "you were practically using an umbrella in the house."

"Forgive me." Mr. Early spread his hands. "Exaggeration in the face of emergency. I was worried you wouldn't come if I said a small leak was driving me mad. Do you need something to stand on?"

Freddie didn't. In this attic room he could touch the ceiling without even stretching. The plaster was damp but still firm. He opened the window. Happily there was a paved patio.

He went on automatic pilot, carrying the ladder around, setting it up, thinking all the while about the room of heads. He pulled on his gloves and started to climb. Just past the first floor, something happened. The ladder began to dip and sway, as it always did around this height, but suddenly Freddie was afraid. A few feet in front of him the dingy bricks of the house blurred; the mossy pointing vanished. He stopped and clung to the next rung. Something was falling out of the sky. Something was smashing him down to earth.

Then, from the same window where he had reconnoitred, Mr. Early's shining head appeared. "You know it's a beastly day for this. Are you sure you're all right?"

Though the ladder still swayed like a willow, the bricks

grew solid and the sky, while grey and lowering, was again empty. "Cool," Freddie said firmly.

He continued climbing and was delighted to find two broken slates in the gutter. These were the easy jobs: the problem inside matched by a clear cause outside. Often enough he mounted the ladder to be met with row upon row of smug slates. The water was getting in somewhere and trickling down until it came to a weakness in the plaster. Lucky he'd never had to work on thatch.

Back inside, he couldn't help noticing a letter on the hall table addressed to Donald Early, Esquire—unopened, in spite of the month-old London postmark. So Mr. Early too, thought Freddie, has his dark corners.

In the upstairs room he was bent over the head, steadily punching in copper-coloured strands of hair. "I'd forgotten," he said, "that I don't like people on ladders. I always imagine them falling and feel guilty."

"Yes, well, you've got two broken slates." Freddie gave his standard warning about how once the nails started to go, it was downhill until the whole roof was redone. "I only guarantee the work I do, and that's void if you let anyone else up there."

"Stern words. What's the damage?"

"Forty-seven pounds."

Mr. Early reached for another lock of hair. "How did you arrive at such an odd sum, Mr. Adams?"

Freddie was used to having his estimates queried, but not with such calm curiosity. "Call me Freddie. Three pounds fifty for each slate and forty for labour."

"And when might this labour occur?"

"The day after tomorrow, if the weather holds. Around three?"

"Good, you'll be able to admire Bethany."

"Bethany?"

Mr. Early waggled the head.

So it was settled, and now, pedalling around the drab expanse of Highbury Fields, Freddie asked himself, What the heck am I going to do? A speed bump appeared in front of him. Slowing, he caught sight of a street sign. The name rang a distant bell. Did he know someone who lived here, or someone he'd worked for? Then it came to him, the message on his answering machine a few days ago. The caller, Littleman, Littleton, had been unusually precise, a back extension of Welsh slate, possible party-wall problems; he was sure to be a pain to work for. If I *can* work, Freddie thought. The couch beckoned.

He stopped, straddling the bike, to scan the street. No way to tell which house contained his potential customer. In the darkness, except for a couple of sagging ridge-poles, the roofs were all perfect. Glancing from chimney to chimney, he remembered his fit on the ladder. Stuff like that came and went, but could he have had an attack of vertigo? He started pedalling again. If only, he thought, slipping into second gear. What he wouldn't give for a decent, ordinary phobia.

They had been waiting for so long for Hazel to regain consciousness, through so many tests and drugs and consultations, that without anyone precisely saying so, Jonathan had become convinced this was the key to recovery. Once she was conscious, the seizures would stop. So the day after she opened her eyes, when he felt her hand tremble, his first thought was that she was moved by his reading; he had reached the chapter on swarming. Two summers ago, he and Hazel had followed the inhabitants of one of his hives down the street and across the railway line only to watch the small, dense cloud settle impossibly high in a horse chestnut tree. "Do you remember," he said, "when my bees swarmed?"

The muscles in her neck grew taut, her eyes rolled back, a gurgling sound came from between her lips.

"Hazel," he said urgently. "I'm here. Are you all right?"

And then all he could think about was one of those horror films where something lunges from the depths of a lake to drag its prey beneath the surface. Hazel vanished and he was left clutching the hand of this struggling body. The IV lines swung back and forth. "Call the nurse," he shouted. "Hazel, Hazel, stay still."

But already she was far away, the nurse holding her arm and calling for more help. Jonathan stood back, trying not to watch. Even his presence could not save her.

After Hazel was wheeled away to the ICU, Nora suggested an early night. As usual George demurred; the two of them should leave, he would wait. But Jonathan added his voice to Nora's. Waiting helped no one, especially Hazel. What they needed was a decent meal and a good night's sleep. "You can always phone," he added. Out in the street, worried they might ask him to join them for supper, he bade a hasty good night and strode off towards the bus stop. The orderly chaos of the hospital had left him starved, greedy. He buttoned his coat against the wind and drew in deep breaths of bad London air.

He and Hazel had woken to a wind like this their first New Year together. I know what we should do, Hazel said. Walk the Pilgrims' Way. They drove south across the empty city and in less than an hour were tramping along a muddy lane, struggling to recall the opening lines of Chaucer. Presently signs led them to Coldrum Barrow; a beech tree hung with ribbons and garlands marked the entrance. For the solstice, Hazel said. Side by side, caught in the absolute oldness of the place, they watched the ribbons dancing in the wind, the standing stones circling the grave. How many journeys had begun or ended here, thought Jonathan. He took off his scarf and tied it to the tree.

Perhaps this memory, or perhaps a sudden influx of teenagers on the bus, made him get off two stops early and head for Steve and Diane's. By the time he turned into Jackson Road, he was half hoping they would be out, but Katie, their two-year-old, kept them close to home, and as usual the lights were on. Now that he was here, it seemed stupid not to say hello.

Steve answered the door, holding a dish towel, his long face uncharacteristically stern. "Jonathan." The towel slipped from his grasp. "What's the matter? Is Hazel . . . ?"

"No, no. I was just passing." He bent to pick up the towel, which had landed neatly on his shoes. "Any chance of a drink?"

"Of course, come in. I thought you were a Jehovah's Witness. Diane's getting Katie to bed."

In the sitting room Steve turned off the television and went to fetch wine. Jonathan studied the familiar surroundings. For several weeks after Hazel left he'd come here almost nightly, unable to bear his empty house; twice Steve had had to drive him home and guide him up the stairs to bed. Now, at the sight of Diane's photographs and Katie's toys piled in the corner, he understood his hesitation in the street. These walls and their inhabitants were a reminder of all that he was eager to put behind him and forget.

Steve came back with a bottle. "Plonk," he explained apologetically. Katie made a brief appearance; she giggled when Jonathan said hello, and refused to speak. Then came Diane's voice from the bedroom, reading:

"Unfortunately she's into repetition," said Steve. "We both know 'Three Little Pigs' by heart. How's Hazel?"

"Not so good," Jonathan said, and could not utter another syllable. He sat there, holding his glass, picturing her eyes losing their moorings, her limbs writhing. From a great distance he heard Steve say, "I'll get Diane."

Alone, Jonathan breathed and did battle. He would not look at the fear or give it words; he would neither touch nor breathe it. Hadn't the nurses said Hazel was on the mend? Hadn't she opened her eyes and spoken to him, to no one else?

"Jonathan, are you okay?" Diane knelt beside him, patting his thigh.

His first instinct was to swipe away her hand; the only touch he wanted now was Hazel's. Instead he fidgeted, as if in search of a handkerchief, and stood up, forcing her to release him. Diane leaned back on her heels, watching as he blew his nose. "I'm fine," he managed, and risked sitting down again.

Beneath their anxious scrutiny, he gave an account of the last twenty-four hours: Hazel's brief escape from the underworld and her terrible return.

"How awful," said Diane, her beaded earrings swaying. Even Steve, the optimist, was frowning.

Now that he was talking, Jonathan could barely contain himself. He was longing to tell them that Hazel had recognised not her parents, not Maud, only him. That afternoon he'd overheard a nurse assuring George and Nora that Hazel's forgetting them was nothing personal. "It's just electrical," she had said, "like a fuse going." Nonsense. What could be more personal than whether someone remembered or forgot you?

Diane, however, had embarked on a story about her uncle, a bus driver who'd made a miraculous recovery from a stroke. "Last month he helped me service the car," Steve said, his maddening cheerfulness back in full force. "I'm sure Hazel will be fine."

Across the hearth rug, Jonathan was glad to see that the bump in Steve's nose was still visible. "Would you mind if we talked about something else?" he said.

"Of course," came their parroting reply.

In the awkward pause, Jonathan could almost hear them picking up and discarding subjects. He was doing the same himself. What *did* people talk about? What did he and Steve talk about? They'd been at York together and shared a house in London until Diane moved in, bringing with her a cooking rota and meticulous recycling. For years Jonathan had kept in touch, intermittently; then he met Hazel and played them as one of his trump cards. He might work in insurance, but look at his friends. Over Sunday lunches, she had laughed at Steve's bicycle-shop jokes and shared Diane's interests in the environment and women's issues. That autumn Steve and Diane had gone to Vancouver Island to help his brother build an eco-house. When they returned, Diane was pregnant and the force lines were irrevocably altered. He and Steve met to play squash, Hazel and Diane to do whatever women did, but meetings of the four of them were rare.

Now Jonathan found himself remembering why: he couldn't stand his best friends. Steve's everything-will-be-fine comment was simply a reflection of lifelong stupidity, and Diane's expressions of sympathy were a little too practised. He was about to mention the leak in his roof, always a safe topic, when Steve volunteered that some neighbours had a fox den at the bottom of their garden. "They've tried everything short of murder to get rid of them: loud noises, the family dog. Then they discovered lion droppings. Apparently the smell frightens them away."

"Where on earth," said Jonathan, "do you get lion shit in London?"

"That's the snag. They had a contact at the zoo—tiger droppings work, too—but demand is soaring. They're looking for another supplier."

When this gambit faltered, Diane asked how Comet was responding to Jonathan's absence.

"They're being terrific." He reported his boss's admonition to take whatever time he needed. "They sent the most gorgeous bouquet. Maud said it must've cost a fortune."

"That's great," said Diane. "Steve and I were worrying they might be a bit sticky. I mean, the situation is irregular."

Jonathan glared at his glass, at the green walls, at every-thing in the room save Steve and Diane. He saw himself career-ing amongst the toys, hurling stuffed animals into the air, grinding Lego blocks underfoot. As if to reinforce his vision, from the bedroom came a cry. Steve started to rise. "Give her a minute," Diane said.

They both sat forward in their chairs. After a brief cre-scendo Katie lapsed back into silence, by which time Jonathan had decided to leave. He'd always known they were less than partisan. Diane in particular was given to infuriating remarks. You have to try and understand Hazel's point of view, she would say. Thank goodness he had not told them about the precious moment of recognition.

"Well," he said, getting to his feet, "one for the road."

He went over to the mantelpiece, refilled and drained his glass. As he set it down, he saw Steve and Diane exchange glances. Did no one, other than Hazel, ever forget anything?

"Why didn't you phone?" Bernadette's lips tightened and even her ponytail seemed to grow rigid with annoyance. Melissa and Oliver stood on either side. Together the three of them filled the doorway not, Charlotte had to confess, like a welcoming com-mittee but more like an army protecting its flanks. That they were all in uniform—school for the children, nursing for Bernie—intensified the military effect.

Charlotte opened her own arms wide—look, no weapons—and smiled. "I tried," she bluffed. "It was busy. And I found these books that I thought would be perfect for Mel and

Oliver." After years of Bernie's squeamishness she knew better than to explain that she had quite literally found them in a box outside the Rumanian Relief Fund shop in Lamb's Conduit Street.

"They're in the middle of their homework."

Bernie's posture yielded not a centimetre, but Charlotte caught the slight shift in tone—her sister no longer sounded exactly like an answering machine—and rushed into the breach. "I won't interrupt. I could supervise them, or maybe they need to be tested. That way you can get on with whatever you need to do."

"I suppose you want to stay for supper."

"Lovely."

"Oh, Mum," Oliver exclaimed. "She always eats everything."

"I do not." Charlotte glared, though it was true that on her last visit she had inadvertently taken a massive second helping of stew that precluded anyone else, including Oliver, from having more. But Bernie was already moving away, and she hurried inside to cut off further unwelcome disclosures. As she hung her coat on the rack, she noticed a row of milky splotches running down the front of her blouse. Bugger it, just the sort of thing that drove Bernie berserk. Had she any idea what a stick she looked in that nurse's uniform? Charlotte draped her scarf across her chest and planned a visit to the bathroom at the first opportunity. Sometimes it seemed impossible that she and Bernie were related, but then one of the few things they did agree on was how ill-suited their parents were, battling through forty years of marriage as if Henry VIII had never existed.

In the kitchen, Bernie was chopping onions to the chatter of Radio 4. "Can I help?" Charlotte said. She made a great show of rolling up her sleeves. Without even glancing up, Bernie shook her head.

"Fine." God, she could be a drag. "Give a shout if you change your mind."

Melissa and Oliver were huddled in the living-room, goading each other about homework. Bernie had some stupid rule that the television couldn't be switched on until they both had finished. Still, it gave Charlotte an opportunity to show what an excellent addition to the household she would be. "Can I help?" she asked again, settling herself in an armchair.

"I'm done," Melissa said.

Oliver brought over his notebook. "We're doing sums."

"And very nicely, too." Charlotte nodded at the numbers lurching across the page. Was Oliver growing up to be Mr. Aziz?

"Have I got the right answers?"

"I think so."

"Don't you know?" he said, sounding like his mother.

"Of course I know. I was just being polite, unlike some people." But she had another look. If she was going to see the children every day, she'd have to be more careful. It was not enough to burst into their lives, be wonderful, and trust that any errors would be forgotten by the time she reappeared. Meanwhile, sitting in a warm, clean room with a single newspaper lying on the table was remarkably pleasant.

Alone with Bernie, Charlotte said she'd make the Nescafé and stood humming nervously over the kettle. She'd been waiting for the rug-rats to retire to mention her plan. Now the important thing was to stress that in three months Aunt Charlotte would be history. And she would pay for her keep by babysitting. God knows how much Bernie was shelling out these days. At the same time, the children would be spending time with one of their nearest relatives, which had to be a plus. As they trailed off to bed, she had offered to read them a story, to which their mutual response—polite in Melissa's case, less so in Oliver's—was that they preferred tapes. She set the mugs, still frothy, on the table.

"Thanks," said Bernie. "Forgive me for cutting to the chase, but I have an interview at a nursing agency first thing tomorrow. So if there's something you want, you'd better spill it out."

"I just wanted to see all of you," Charlotte said reflexively. "Why are you going to an agency? Are you quitting the hospital?"

"Not unless they give me the sack. This would be in addition. People are always telling me how lucrative private nursing is. Even a couple of afternoons a week would help."

"Doesn't Rory send money? That would be typical, stiffing you all the way to kindergarten."

"The children are in primary school. Actually, he's pretty good about paying his share, but I have lots of expenses—babysitting, treats, you know."

Charlotte blew on her Nescafé. With anyone else this would've paved the way for her request; Bernie though would think she was taking advantage and become even more acerbic. "You're a terrific mother," she said bracingly. "You should see my neighbours' kids. Real brats. They've never heard of 'please' or 'thank you.' "

"Oh, I hate that. No, Oliver and Mel are good about manners. Their school may be a bit free-form, but it's excellent on the basics."

"Brilliant." Christ, the inexhaustible subject. From bitter experience she knew Bernie could hold forth for hours about Melissa tying her shoelaces or Oliver's numerical skills. Panic-stricken, she plunged. "I went to see my accountant last week."

"Your accountant?" Bernie wrinkled her nose. "What on earth does he or she account for?"

"Not much so far. But Mr. O'Grady—he's Irish—is helping me get things sorted. We're drawing up a five-year plan."

"Maybe that will include getting a job."

Here it comes, thought Charlotte, not fooled for a second by the seemingly casual tone. Her sister was of that antlike tribe for whom the mere prospect of a less-than-forty-hour work week was anathema. "Bernie, acting isn't like nursing. There's no point in my pulling pints at three quid an hour and not being able to go to auditions. Parts for someone my age, no longer an ingenue, are as common as lunar eclipses. I have to be ready when they come along."

"In fact, lunar eclipses may be a sight more common." Bernie shook her head. "Listen to yourself. If parts are so scarce, then it's even stupider not to have a job. I haven't seen you in anything since that play in Battersea. When was the last time you even went to an audition?"

"I sent my resumé out on Monday to the Royal Court." Charlotte drew herself upright, the picture of wounded dignity. She remembered, distinctly, finding a photograph in the rubble on her floor; she was almost sure she'd put it in the post. "All that's going to change. I'm getting a new agent, someone who appreciates the sort of work I do, and then, you'll see, the auditions will start pouring in."

"But meanwhile," said Bernie, "you do need a job, don't you? I'm not crazy about bedpans, but . . ."

Stupid cow, thought Charlotte. With her neat ponytail, her tidy gold earrings, Bernie really did exemplify the phrase "po-faced." No wonder Rory had bolted. A few weeks ago Charlotte had run into him in a pub off Dean Street. "Hey," he'd said, "if it isn't the sister-in-law from hell. What are you drinking?"

For half an hour they had a fine, bantering conversation. Then Rory grew maudlin. He'd already been well oiled,

Charlotte realised, before the two pints he drank with her. "Your sister's a pain," he said, "but I can't help missing her."

"You were the one who was a pain," Charlotte said. "Bonking your way through the entire office."

"One small misdemeanour is not the entire fucking office. I *know* I shouldn't have. She tempted me and I fell. My big mistake was telling Bernadette. I hated the thought of deceiving her. And she went nuts. This from the woman who made us exchange a list of lovers on our second date."

"She did what?" The poor bloke was so far gone he was confusing Bernie with some bimbo.

Rory nodded. "She made us each write down who we'd slept with. Said it would clear the air."

"Clearing the air" was one of Bernie's expressions; still Charlotte doubted. "You mean Bernie had a list? I thought you were it, besides her weedy nursing-school boyfriend."

Rory laughed. "What an innocent you are. While you were poncing around doing *Romeo and Juliet,* your sister was carving a swathe of safe sex through the hospitals of North London."

"I'm gobsmacked," Charlotte said, and she had been, though not so much as she was now, sitting opposite Bernie in that awful uniform. Who on earth would want her neat, dull sister?

As if reading her thoughts, Bernadette stood up.

Charlotte realised she was about to be shown the door. "Bernie," she blurted, "I need a favour."

"Surprise, surprise." She carried her mug to the sink and turned, arms folded, to face Charlotte. "Well?"

"I need to rent out my flat, just for a few months, and I was hoping I could stay with you. As you said, parts are scarce. And even with a new agent, it's going to take a while for the tide to turn. I'll collect the children from school, babysit, shop, whatever you want. Mr. O'Grady"—she dwindled—"thinks it's a great idea."

Throughout the day she'd been acting out scenarios in her head, but the basis for all her scripts was her superiority to Bernie: the artist versus the drone. Suddenly Charlotte understood that her sister was an opponent to reckon with. Sweat trickled between her breasts at the prospect of rejection.

"Who would rent your flat?" Bernie said. "It's a pigsty."

"Students. I'll tidy it up. I'm sure I can get seventy pounds a week each. Sixty, anyway."

"I suppose people are desperate."

"Exactly," said Charlotte, overlooking the insult. "So I'll spruce it up, rent it out for three months, get caught up on my bills, and really focus on my career."

"That sounds fine, so long as you can find somewhere else to stay." She stepped over to seize Charlotte's mug, still half-full, and put it in the sink.

"But you haven't even thought about it," Charlotte said above the noise of water. "Only a minute ago you were saying how hard it is being a single parent. Of course I'm not a parent, but I could help. Think how much you'd save on babysitting."

"I'm going to bed now," Bernie said, drying her hands.

"I don't expect you to answer right away. Just please say you'll consider it."

Bernie left the kitchen and returned with Charlotte's coat. "Did you know there's something on your blouse?" Her finger pointed at the trail of splotches.

Demon nurse, thought Charlotte, tyrant. She could see Bernie taking positive pleasure in gouging a needle into someone's veins. And that surge of anger prevented her from pleading further or from asking to borrow the bus fare home. Forget Mr. Aziz, she'd sooner starve. She hitched her bag onto her shoulder and set out to walk. Barnsbury to Kilburn couldn't be more than a couple of miles, maybe three. Crossing the Caledonian Road, she remembered visiting a squat here; the walls of the living-room had been lined with geraniums, row upon leafy row. Where did you get all these? she'd asked. Cuttings, her friend Una replied. One big incestuous family. Too bad she didn't know any squatters now.

She was waiting at a red light, the wind whipping through her threadbare coat, when a taxi pulled up in front of her, FOR HIRE sign glowing, and she opened the door to ask if the driver would take a cheque. A moment later she was being borne through the streets of London, discussing the importance of children studying foreign languages. The driver's daughter was in her third year of French and his son had started Russian—not as useful as a few years ago, but still a major language.

Charlotte confided that she'd spent the evening babysitting her nephew and niece. "We decided to have a French night. We made crêpes and spoke French all evening."

"What a great idea. I wonder if the wife and I could manage."

"You don't need to be fluent. The children enjoyed correcting me."

The driver said he could see that and she was welcome to babysit for him anytime. Reluctantly, he agreed to drop her at the corner. "I hate to leave a young lady on the streets this late."

But she insisted there was no place to turn around, and wrote the cheque with a flourish, adding a pound tip. "Thanks, love. Hope to see you again."

For a few seconds watching his taillights dim, Charlotte felt buoyed by the ease and comfort of her journey. As she started walking, however, her spirits sank. Though the driver wouldn't know her exact address when the cheque bounced, what the hell was she going to do? What did people do when they had no money? She opened the door of her flat and stumbled over the red cushion, still propped against the wall. Several unpleasant answers presented themselves.

chapter 4

"Think of her," Dr. Hogarth suggested, "as having fallen off a mountain. In the Himalaya, for example." He nodded towards the photograph of white peaks and blue skies which hung beside a certificate from the London School of Neurology. "Or even a hill in your Lake District. The descent is swift, the climb back proportionately arduous."

From his seat near the door of the office, Jonathan followed the doctor's gesture. Julian Hogarth had appeared at Hazel's bedside the day after she opened her eyes. No relation, he had said cheerfully when he introduced himself, as if a Kashmiri neurologist might easily be mistaken for a descendant of the polemical printmaker.

"The good news," he said, smiling at the three of them in turn, "is that the subdural hematoma has gone down. We hope to see steady improvement to the point of full recovery."

George and Nora were bobbing, but Jonathan scratched his palms. Hogarth was so indefatigable, always another drug, another test, and so cheerful, that only the bitter experience of Hazel's continued seizures had enabled Jonathan to discern the guarded nature of his predictions. Wasn't hope a matter for him and for her parents?

"As you're well aware," Hogarth continued, "Hazel's memory has been affected. Some degree of amnesia is fairly common in the case of head injuries. Often it proves to be temporary, passing off by degrees. Hazel, as far as I can determine, has lost the last three years. Like a large suitcase, she just put it down and walked away. Or, more precisely, she put it down and a thief came by." Again a smile for each of them. Other things, he went on, were missing too—her parents, for instance, and Maud, though clearly she was fond of these people who hovered over her bed. She remembered the emotion if not its origin.

While the doctor launched into a disquisition on memory —the hippocampus was crucial but memories were stored throughout the brain; erratic losses, as with Hazel, were not unusual—Jonathan stared at the golden seal on the School of Neurology certificate and willed himself to stay in his seat. Now he understood that moment when Hazel had opened her eyes and claimed him. If she had lost three years, then their rows, his slip-up, her moving out were all gone. Only harmony and happiness remained. What was the last thing she remembered, he wondered. Might it be their making love? He tried to recall what they had been doing three years ago. Was that the winter they went to Lanzarote and came back to learn Hazel's article on the railways of southern India had been accepted?

Then Hogarth invited any questions and Nora was speaking. "We did want to ask you, Doctor, should we tell her who we are?"

Christ, thought Jonathan. This was the sort of thing that happened when he drifted off. From the way Nora's voice wavered, he knew she was fighting back tears. Several times in the last few days he had come upon her and George arguing over whether to reveal their identities. His own position was icy clear: Hazel had already remembered everything essential. Please, he thought, scratching furiously.

A bar of light from the neon strip bisected the doctor's glossy hair. "I think"—he tapped his fingertips together— "you're the best judge of that. You're her parents, you know her better than anyone. What I would urge is not to deluge her with information. Her brain has experienced a series of tremendous shocks. We can't expect her to recover all at once."

Nora and George nodded. Jonathan let his fists relax. Again he was forced to admire the doctor's diplomacy: strongly indicating the appropriate course of action yet leaving it up to them. He could see how glad they were to have their importance to Hazel acknowledged and, just for a moment, he shared their pleasure.

George cleared his throat and asked, as one of them always did, if there was a proper diagnosis, and Hogarth, as always, retreated into medical jargon. How variously people responded to apparently similar injuries. How crucial it was to proceed slowly with the different drugs. Same old shit, Jonathan had remarked to Maud after their last meeting; now he listened almost fondly to the litany.

"So," said Hogarth, "we hope to discharge her shortly. I don't need to tell you that she's precarious, but with this kind of situation we often find a familiar environment works wonders."

George and Nora were exclaiming as Jonathan shot from the room. In the corridor he collided with two men in wheelchairs, a mass of wheels and arms. "Shite," he said, grabbing a handle.

"No worries, mate," the older of the men replied with a flash of yellow teeth. They wheeled cheerfully on.

Jonathan set off, almost running, in the opposite direction. He had been so exhilarated by the news of Hazel's missing suitcase that he hadn't stopped to think what her improvement might mean. Coming to the hospital every day, sitting by her bed, reading to her, playing cards and dominoes with George and Nora, eating in the cafeteria, going home only to sleep— this had become his life. Now everything he had yearned for, worked for, was once again in jeopardy.

He stopped beside a window and pressed his forehead to the cold glass. In the car park below a man and a woman emerged from a blue minivan and walked towards the hospital, the man's tie flapping, the woman's coat billowing. Jonathan pictured himself rushing back to Hogarth's office and seizing the doctor by his lapels. He couldn't even discover what was wrong with Hazel, let alone cure her. And here he was proposing exactly what the newspapers complained about: throwing a seriously ill woman out on the streets.

Steady, lad, he murmured, steady. It was a phrase his father had used at critical junctures on the golf course and, later, when his emphysema worsened, leaning towards the television; Jonathan sometimes found himself uttering it as he slid the supers in and out of the hives. The hardest part of bee-keeping, he'd explained to Hazel, was not learning the various seasonal tasks but how to perform them calmly. The bees responded badly to anxiety and were hard to fool. The first summer he'd been stung almost daily. Didn't it hurt, she had asked. To start with, he said, then one day I was watching a bee sting my hand and I realised all I felt was a little pinch. My body had adjusted to the poison. Like Mithridates, she said. Only less organised, he agreed, and went on to describe the victim's complicity, that the muscle spasm drew the poison deeper into the bloodstream and, at the same time, killed the bee by pulling off the stinger.

Now, staring out at the grey landscape, he longed for the buzzing orderliness of his hives. The mere thought of them, squatting at the bottom of the garden, soothed him. Nothing terrible has happened yet, he told himself.

He continued to walk, more slowly, past the linen room and the nurses' lounge, trying to sort out the implications of Hogarth's decision. This, after all, was what he was trained to do: evaluate possibilities and rank them. Hazel could not return to her flat alone; that was a given. George and Nora would want to take her back to Kendall, but he could make an argument for proximity to the hospital. As for Maud, her third-floor flat would turn Hazel into a virtual prisoner. Did she even have a spare room? Then it came to him. As far as Hazel was concerned, there was no flat. The terraced house they had shared for four years was her home, her only home.

The swish of wheels interrupted his exultation. The two men were rolling towards the orthopaedic ward. "And so all hell broke loose," said the older one.

"Blimey," said the younger. "What a fiasco." Guffawing, they wheeled into the ward.

Would he be capable, Jonathan wondered, of joking around if he were crippled? Hazel used to pose those kinds of questions: If you had to lose either sight or hearing, which would you choose? If you had a year to live, what would you do? Once, in bed, she said, if the house caught fire and you could rescue one person, your mother, your father, or me, who would you save? You, he had answered. That's awful, she said. You didn't even hesitate. In his dreams that night, his parents had cried out.

In 407 the bed was empty. Hazel was taking a bath, but George and Nora were waiting. Obviously they'd been discussing him: what to do with the grouchy son-in-law. As he crossed the threshold, George raised his life of Wellington. Nora drew him over to the window. "I know it's upsetting," she said. "After all these tests they don't have a firm diagnosis."

Jonathan watched a seagull approach a rooftop across the street. Claws outstretched, it glided down onto the ridge-pole, a perfectly judged landing. If only he could muster such skill in putting forward his case. But Nora was speaking again. "Hogarth said that if all goes well, touch wood"—she reached for the sill—"she can come home on Friday."

The gull minced towards the chimney and loitered at its base, studying the pointing. "Home?" Jonathan burst out. That double-edged word.

"Isn't that marvellous?" She smiled, radiantly, and became businesslike. "We know the two of you have had some upsets, this nonsense about her subletting a flat, but there's no way Hazel can go back there. Besides, she's clearly come to her senses. Look at how she asks for you." She gestured at the bed as if this sight were presently visible. "So we were wondering if we could stay with you while she convalesces? Hogarth was very firm that she mustn't be left alone."

Save for Hazel's amnesia, he thought, Nora had laid out his argument as well as he could ever have hoped to, and now she was looking at him, head cocked in a manner reminiscent of her daughter, though really it was the other way round. "Absolutely," he said. "Of course. Whatever's best. . . ."

He was still pouring out agreement when Nora's hand alighted on his arm. Before he could stop himself, he flinched. He saw her eyes widen, another of Hazel's mannerisms; then, just as clearly, he saw her push the doubts away. "Thank you." She patted his arm. "We're just so glad the two of you are back together."

"Did you know," said George, lowering his book, "that Wellington owned five busts of Napoleon and a life-size statue?"

On the pretext of a phone call, Jonathan excused himself. Do not panic, do not run, walk briskly to your nearest exit.

The phrase came to Freddie while brushing his teeth and seemed so apt that he went into the kitchen to tell Agnes. "Agnes," he said, squatting beside the table, "I am beset by bitches. What do you think of that?"

Agnes, however, as so often these days, chose not to reveal her cognitive processes. She simply lay there, looking remarkably like an astrakhan pillow. Soon after he brought her home, Freddie had joked to Trevor she was becoming his I Ching: two wags of the tail, go ahead; a flick of an ear, forget it. Full of surprises, Trevor said he knew the feeling, though he himself was more a Book of the Dead kind of bloke.

"Okay." Freddie prodded her lightly. "Be that way."

Back in the bathroom, he finished his teeth and stepped back to examine his reflection in the mirror. Swivelling his head from side to side, he tried to imagine his hair shaved. No way he'd look as good as Mr. Early, and he might turn out to have one of those little slabs of fat at the back of his head. Still, he was getting a tad wooly. Time to visit the barber but, like almost everything else, that meant leaving the house. He was wondering whether he could ask Kevin to take him, when the phone rang.

"Oh, I caught you," said his mother. As if, at two in the afternoon, he was about to rush out. "Guess what loony tune your father's gone off on now? He's convinced I've got something going with the man at the service station."

"Have you?"

His mother giggled. "Freddie, you know me better than that. No, I was thanking him, and your dad saw me pat his arm."

"Sounds like a good move, Mom. Maybe he'll take the car in for a change."

"Maybe. Meanwhile, every time I put on a nice blouse he

gives me grief. Says I'm getting all dressed up for my boyfriend. But how are you? How's the weather?"

"Rain. I've got customers queueing round the block."

" 'Queueing'! Aren't you English? It's too early to say what kind of day we're having here. Yesterday was very nice. Sunny with a little breeze." His mother, who'd owned a washer and dryer for as long as Freddie could remember, still judged weather in terms of wash days. Then she asked about Agnes, in whose condition she was keenly interested, and Felicity, about whom Freddie sensed she had some reservations, though none she would divulge.

After their love-yous and goodbyes he stood staring at the bookcase, momentarily amazed to find himself in the hallway of a run-down London flat rather than his mother's cosy kitchen in North Avondale. One of these months . . . For now, wanting to do something that would please her, he headed for his kitchen and last night's dirty dishes. Beset, he murmured again as the sink filled, especially by Felicity. When they met last spring, at a lecture on socialism in the nineties Kevin had dragged him to, she had seemed the ideal girlfriend. Her wrist was broken from a rollerblading accident and, drawn to her cast like a turtle to water, Freddie offered her a ride home. On the way to Bethnal Green, she talked about her dissertation, on the Brown Dog Riots of 1907, and he happily succumbed to her tales of the battles between medical students and antivivisectionists, which— and this was Felicity's real area of interest—often included the suffragettes. For months they'd had fun, going to movies and exploring the neighbourhoods in Battersea and Southwark where the riots had taken place. Recently, however, more or less since Christmas, Freddie thought, she'd been flying off the handle for any reason, or none at all.

A few weeks ago, for instance, one rainy afternoon in bed,

he was trying to tell her about Lourdes. Life there had been simpler, he said. Underneath the bullshit, people knew what they wanted and weren't afraid to ask. Prayer refined desire.

"Lourdes." Felicity had popped up like a jack-in-the-box. "The whole thing makes me furious. People who are ill need doctors, not mumbo-jumbo."

"No, you don't understand." He nuzzled her shoulder, hoping to coax her back into that dreamy state she entered only after lovemaking. "This isn't the Dark Ages. These people have seen doctors and been told they're incurable. They don't have anything to lose, except hope. I never meant to get involved. I was just passing through. Then this miserable old guy on crutches needed help. While I waited for him to be blessed, I noticed the stretcher bearers and I knew I had to be among them. That's why I was there, six foot two and able-bodied."

"Freddie, you're six foot two and well educated. You could do something a hell of a lot more useful than cart invalids around—or fix roofs, for that matter."

"Fixing roofs is useful," he said. "We all need shelter."

And just when he thought the storm was lifting, another arrived. Felicity had made it clear that, in lieu of an immediate career change, more horizontal activity would be welcome. Had he finked out, feigning sleep, or performed? Thankfully, memory failed.

As for Agnes—he began to dry the wineglasses—at least her fussiness in the final weeks of pregnancy had a clear cause. Trevor had lured him into breeding her by mentioning that a purebred Scottie could fetch over four hundred quid. Easy money, Freddie thought, but from the moment the dog mounted Agnes he had had qualms. She seemed to get so little pleasure from the coupling, and then the vet lectured him about the dangers of letting her gain too much weight. Awful things could happen if the puppies got too big during a first pregnancy. Unfortunately, Agnes showed not the slightest instinct for these possibilities.

He raised the glasses to check the shine and decided to take her for a walk. Since his visit to Mr. Early she'd had to settle for a turn around Kevin's rosebushes, but in the aftermath of his mother's phone call, he thought, if he moved fast, he could get to the corner and back. He pulled on clothes, grabbed the leash, and announced the drill. Predictably, Agnes showed zero interest.

"Okay, baby. Time for matter over mind." He hoisted her into the air and headed downstairs. Once he reached the sidewalk, he set her down—there was no denying she smelled—and clipped on the leash. Agnes scanned the wet streets, peed, sniffed, retreated several steps, peed again.

"I wish I'd gotten a greyhound," Freddie told her. "You'd fit right in at Lourdes." Me too, he thought. *Malade imaginaire.* Still, so far, so good. He was in the next street, Agnes was waddling ahead, and the sky was empty.

"God it's freezing," said Felicity. "Where can I put my jacket?"

Bending to kiss her, Freddie discovered, as usual, that she was smaller than he remembered. She was wearing his favourite red pullover, a black skirt, and her ever-present combat boots. Sitting at the kitchen table, she began to clean her glasses. He'd been asleep when she rang the bell. Now he put the kettle on and watched her fondly. Barefaced, she had an endearingly helpless look. "Can I make some toast?" she asked. "I missed lunch."

"Sorry, I've run out of bread."

"A biscuit?"

To be sure, he checked the cupboard again. Maybe something had materialised since last time. "I didn't get to the store today," he explained.

Felicity stopped polishing. "That's what you said yesterday. Were you out on a job?"

"Just hanging around. You know I don't work in the rain." He handed her the tea. "No milk."

"But"—she slipped her glasses back on—"how can you do nothing all the time?"

"I've told you, I'm a nothing kind of guy. I wake up, have a cup of tea, sleep, look out the window, count the clouds, nimbus, cumulus, cirrus, mackerel, sleep some more."

"Sugar?"

"That we can do." He brought her the jar and urged her to heap it in.

"I still don't get it," she said, taking a modest spoonful. "You're thirty-five. You owe your dad twenty thousand dollars and you're totally broke. Aren't you tired of having no money?"

Freddie sighed. More and more conversations with Felicity took this form: her demand for explanation, his attempt, her incomprehension. She had even grilled him about his not swearing. Some Catholic thing, she concluded so definitively that he could only nod. Now he said, "Sure, I'd like some dough, if it was handed to me on a plate. I'd have some shirts made, buy a good tennis racquet, eat at the Savoy. The question is, am I going to bust my ass working for that junk? And the answer is—" he did a drumroll on the table—"no way. So, what did you do today?"

Felicity, however, was in rottweiler mode. "But just last week, the day we went to Southwark, you were going on and on about adopting children. How you'd rent a house in the country, here or Brittany, with a big garden. You had everything organised."

"You're great." He squeezed her arm. "Doesn't all this remembering wear you out? Yeah, if someone gave me a few hundred grand, I'd be scouring the orphanages tomorrow. I think I'd make a good father, so long as I wasn't genetically involved."

"Genetically involved? Do you know how old I am?"

What's come over people, thought Freddie. First Mr. Early, now Felicity. "Thirty-two?" he guessed, trying at least for the right decade.

"Thirty-seven. I'm a thirty-seven-year-old woman." Behind her newly polished glasses, her eyes were suspiciously bright.

"Who doesn't," he said quickly, "look a day over thirty-two." He jumped up, as if he'd just noticed Agnes noodling over her bowl, and pretended to be absorbed in measuring dog food, getting fresh water, until Felicity gave up and went to the john.

When she came back her mood, or whatever it was, had lifted. She told him she'd finished the footnotes for a new chapter that morning; in the afternoon there'd been a crisis at work. Freddie listened and asked questions. He liked hearing the details of her day, though he was powerless to describe his own. That he could do nothing better than most people was true; still, his current hibernation was extreme, and he had no idea what would constitute spring this time around.

The morning star was hanging over the elderberry tree when Jonathan drew the bedroom curtains; surely, he thought, a good omen. His conversations with Hogarth and Nora had left him stunned, incredulous. I'll do anything, he had vowed—and here he was, being allowed to do it. He and Hazel would have their life together over again, the good parts without the mistakes, yet with the benefit of those mistakes. You can't change back, she had said, but you could, you could. Once again he would be the man she'd fallen in love with. And vice versa. This was the ultimate second chance.

By the time he'd washed and dressed, the dense night sky had thinned and the star was gone. On impulse he decided to visit his bees. Spending every day at Hazel's bedside, he couldn't remember when he had last checked the hives. He mixed sugar and water while making coffee. Then, pulling on his jacket and grabbing the smoker, he opened the back door. The air was so crisp he blinked. The bees were only sixty feet away, but as usual the short walk cheered him. How can you keep bees in the middle of London, Hazel had asked. Easily, he said. The houses around here have long gardens and I pick docile breeds. If they show any signs of hostility, I replace them.

He set his coffee on the ground, lit the smoker, and gave a few puffs in the entrance of the nearest hive. He would have to figure out how to work at home, he thought. As for Hazel, happily there seemed no immediate prospect of her returning to journalism. Perhaps he could steer her back into the more predictable world of teaching ESL. The first skirmishes between them, he recalled, dated from her having an article in a major newspaper. Well, they needn't make that mistake again. He lifted the lid off the hive and found the bees gorged and barely stirring. The smoke made them greedy for fear that their food was about to go up in flames.

"I can't stand it," George was saying, his weatherbeaten face an even deeper shade of red. "This isn't some comedy where you test your loved one by concealing your identity."

Nora shook her head. "We're not testing her, George. We're nursing her back to health. She had three seizures yesterday. Whatever we can do to lighten her load is a good thing."

They were standing on either side of Hazel's empty bed, so absorbed in conversation that neither of them noticed Jonathan's arrival.

"Won't it lighten her load to know she has parents?" George asked, his arms flailing like those of a tired swimmer aiming for a distant shore.

"Not if she's forgotten you." As he stepped forward, Jonathan sensed rather than saw Maud come up behind him. "Sorry," he said, striving to sound diffident, "I couldn't help overhearing. I know this is hard for you, both of you, but we have to remember what Hogarth said. Hazel's had a tremendous shock. Every day she's a little better: she's eating, walking, able to follow a conversation. I'd hate for us to do anything that might set her back."

He did not dare to look at Maud, standing only a few feet away, but when George appealed to her, she too sided with Nora. "We mustn't be selfish," she said.

"Selfish?" George's arms collapsed by his sides. Still muttering, he allowed Nora to lead him towards the cafeteria.

Jonathan followed with Maud. "I feel so sorry for them," she said quietly. "Nora told me yesterday that George is convinced Hazel will die without recognising them. You smell of something. Smoke?"

Now he caught a whiff, lingering in his clothes and on his hands, the fragrance of honey. "Hazel's not going to die," he said, and explained about the bees. Was it possible, he wondered, that for once Maud actually approved of his behaviour?

Later that afternoon, for the first time since Hazel's arrival, sunlight filled the drab room. Jonathan sat by the window, going through the papers his secretary had forwarded. In his absence most of the cases were progressing smoothly, claims awarded or denied, estimates queried; even several tricky subsidence claims, dragging on since last summer, were moving towards resolution. Near the bottom was a blue envelope. *McLusky— any thoughts?* Alastair had written.

Pushing back his sleeves, Jonathan remembered the unusually bleak day of his visit to Evelyn McLusky. Standing in the front garden of her unmodernised four-bedroom house off the Ball's Pond Road, water trickling down his collar, his shoes soaked, he had stared at her tattered lace curtains and thought his life could sink no lower. Then the door opened and, briefly, he was startled out of his gloom. Mrs. McLusky was made up as if for a nightclub: mascara, rouge, lipstick were all in evidence and oddly at variance with her flowery apron, almost identical to one his mother had worn. "Thank you for coming," she said. "I'm afraid things are in a bit of a state."

Her accent was unexpectedly foreign: Eastern European? Greek? She led him down a dank corridor. While she put the kettle on, Jonathan glanced around the kitchen. A single lightbulb glinted off the yellowing paint. In one corner was an old-fashioned porcelain sink and next to it, on a sideboard, an electric kettle and a two-ring cooker. Apart from the calendar on the wall, nothing in the room looked less than thirty years old.

He took the forms from his briefcase. Ah, now it came back to him. Mrs. McLusky was trying to sweep into the twentieth century on the strength of a burst pipe, claiming not just for the plumbing but also for rewiring and a new floor. The estimates totalled nearly fifteen hundred pounds.

"Could I take a look at the damage?" he had said.

"Here." On the far side of the table several floorboards had been ripped up, one broken. Between the joists ran three pipes. Jonathan bent down. "My son-in-law, Laurie, said he'd fix it after your visit. Now I go next door with a bucket for water, like the old days."

Her voice was anxious, but that was true of almost everyone he dealt with. People had so little idea of what their insurance covered that invariably they behaved as if they had something to hide. The hole was on top of the middle pipe, an unlikely place to spring a leak. Across the room her apron fluttered as she moved back and forth, making the tea.

What do you do when people lie to you? Hazel had asked. If I can prove it, deny their claim. But what about when you're actually talking to them? I nod, I take notes. So you don't even give them a chance, she said.

The memory of these words, plus the apron, had prompted him to comment to Mrs. McLusky, "A lot of damage for one little hole. Like that poem: for want of a nail a kingdom was lost."

Two painful spots, not exactly matching the circles of rouge, appeared in her cheeks. She mumbled something about Laurie, and Jonathan, unable to bear her embarrassment, said there was no accounting for elderly plumbing.

Now, reluctantly, he bent his eyes to the blue paper.

Dear Mr. Littleton,
        I am writing to say I am sorry. The house is old
and Ivan took care of it. He was very handy. Could
mend almost anything with a coat-hanger. Now he is
gone, I muddle along. Really things are not too bad.
The place will see me out.

Her writing, childish in its rounded clarity, reminded him of his boyhood letters—*Thank you very much for the book token/ handkerchief/model train. It's exactly what I wanted*—the same phrases for every gift. Mrs. McLusky went on to say she was withdrawing her claim. *Sorry for the inconvenience. Yours faithfully, Evelyn McLusky (Mrs.)*

He was staring at her signature when from behind him came the sound of George clearing his throat. "Hazel," he said hoarsely, "I'm your father, your dad, and this is your mother."

"And I'm Maud, your old friend."

In a shower of papers Jonathan leapt from the chair. For a moment, the struggle not to hurl himself on George rooted him to the sunlit floor. Mad, idiotic, to have trusted the old fucker. Slowly he took a step towards the bed, another. Would the memory of her parents bring back all the terrible memories as well?

He reached the foot of the bed in time to see her gentle smile. "I knew I knew you," she said, as if this were a triumph and her forgetting a mere triviality. She turned to Maud. "Your hair looks different."

"How do you feel?"

Hazel, frowning, seemed to take an internal inventory. "Some orange juice would be nice," she concluded, "if it's not too much trouble." She shifted against the pillows, searching the room.

Jonathan held tight to the bedrail and closed his eyes. Behind his lids, the darkness sparkled.

Then he heard his name, a question. "Jonathan?" Still he kept his eyes sealed, in the vain hope that that thin membrane might shield him from Hazel's wrath.

"Will you read to me?"

chapter 5

Charlotte was lying in bed, which meant lying on the futon she'd discovered leaning against a wall in Priory Park Road last Halloween, and persuaded a surly Irish cabbie to squeeze into his taxi. The futon in turn lay on the six months of newspaper that layered her living-room floor. These, as Charlotte liked to remind herself, were not merely a source of current events but excellent insulation. In fact, until she found the futon, she had slept directly on top of the papers, between two quilts. Her old boyfriend, Walter, had taken the bed when he moved out, and nearly everything else besides. Charlotte had come home at midnight—she was playing Mrs. Linde, Nora's friend, in *A Doll's House*—to find the flat empty except for her clothes and books, heaped carelessly on the floor. Walter had left nothing, no note, only a pair of crumpled black socks and his keys.

Charlotte had stood in the empty rooms, beyond feeling, looking at the outlines, marked in light and shadow, dirt and cleanliness, of the vanished furniture. She'd come into the wrong flat; it was an elaborate joke; this was not happening at all. She hurried out again and took a taxi to Soho. Walter frequented a number of after-hours clubs around Dean Street, and she had gone from one to another, upstairs and down, none of them were ever at street level, asking for him in what she hoped was a casual manner. People welcomed her, bought her drinks, talked about her current show, and no one vouchsafed one iota of information about Walter. Her sole glimpse came from Jerry, the bartender of the dark green upstairs room that had served as Francis Bacon's local. He leaned over and patted her cheek—by this time she was quite drunk—and said, "Charlotte, love, you ought to be home getting your beauty sleep. Take my word for it, Walter isn't out on the town tonight."

But there was no question of going home. Drink by drink Charlotte had refurnished the rooms, reinstalled the bed and the table, hung Walter's clothes in the wardrobe, put his tooth-brush back in the bathroom. As long as she stayed away, he was there and nothing had changed. She spent twenty-four hours on the streets and, when she showed up at the theatre the following evening, gave one of the best performances of her life.

Walter, it transpired, had moved in with an American actress, a tall blond bimbo without an ounce of talent or a penny to her name. Somehow, though, she brought him luck. During his years with Charlotte he had landed a series of thankless parts, from Malcolm in the Scottish play to the other husband in *Who's Afraid of Virginia Woolf?* A month after leaving her, he appeared in a comedy which allowed him to display a sly sexi-ness, previously concealed, and by the autumn he was playing second lead in a West End hit. Charlotte had perfected a look of keen interest when people insisted on telling her how well he was doing.

Now, since the dustbin men woke her with their clatter, she burrowed into the futon, trying to figure out yet again exactly when Walter had decided to leave. Was it the previous week, when they were discussing holidays; or the week before, when they'd gone to Habitat to buy towels; or a few days earlier, when she heard him on the phone promising their friend Alex they'd both be at her wedding with bells on? As usual, she was unable to detect the slightest fissure in their relationship. Walter had seemed his normal, irascible self until the moment she left for the theatre. It still gave her vertigo to consider how adroitly he had lied: his best performance ever. What could she do with these unblemished, fraudulent memories except trample them underfoot?

Pulling the covers higher, she turned determinedly to planning her day. Get up, dress warmly; the weather had grown bitter. Then she must go to the office on Oxford Street to pay the phone bill; a threatening red form had arrived in Tuesday's post. She remembered her father brandishing such letters over the breakfast table and explaining that this was not where the expression "red-letter day" came from. But what was the origin? Something to do with saints, she thought. She must ask Bernie.

Once again she had blundered; these days her sister was no safer a topic than Walter. Hastily, Charlotte retreated to the minor anguish of the bill. The pressing question was not the mechanics of payment but the means. The hole in the wall had twice refused her money and on the next attempt would probably seize her card. She'd bought a lottery ticket yesterday, but since a tenner last October she'd had no luck with that. A stupid system, Jonah at the corner shop claimed, too impersonal. Charlotte would agree, while pointing out that the lottery did support the arts; more theatre, she'd say, more parts for me. And Jonah would flip back his braids and praise her numbers. When you win, he said, we will move to Jamaica, meaning, Charlotte knew, not just the two of them but his wife, his three children, his parents, his parents-in-law, and his brother's family. You will like Kingston, he added.

She fished the bill from beneath her pillow and checked again: within seven days, the unyielding capitals announced, her phone would be disconnected and she would be liable for both the account and a reconnection charge. Quickly she stuffed the envelope back out of sight and reviewed her prospects for a loan.

Cedric, in his expensive leather jacket, strutted into view. From her first glimpse of him, behind the bar of the Trumpet, Charlotte had recognised a fellow thespian; an actor, she assumed. But no, Cedric said, tossing back his thick, dark hair, he was going to be a designer/director. Over several slow evenings they'd grown thick as thieves. He couldn't get enough of her gossip and advice; she'd even introduced him to the stage manager at the local theatre. Last Wednesday, though, when she'd dropped by the pub, he had seemed less than overjoyed. Bringing him back here one frosty night, shortly after New Year, had been a mistake, Charlotte thought. And then she'd let slip—well, he was pressing her—that she was no longer on speaking terms with her agent. No, forget Cedric; he was strictly pleasure.

Maybe Brian was a better bet. They had studied acting at RADA together but, surprisingly early on, he had recognised his own lack of talent and become an estate agent. I do one-man shows, he boasted, about built-in wardrobes and forty-foot gardens. On numerous occasions Charlotte had acted as hostess for him and got him into plays for free. Wasn't all that worth something? Yes, but probably no more than the long weekend she'd spent at his flat last month when her electricity was cut off.

What with one thing and another, it was nearly noon before she left the house. Nothing on the skip today, and no money for the bus. She set out, walking briskly past the Trumpet and the bakery only to be halted at the newsagent's by the date on a paper; she was meant to do something today. Lunch, or a drink? Suddenly she recalled the audition her friend Ginny had arranged, a Jacobean drama at a theatre above a pub in Richmond. I told the director you'd be ideal, Ginny had said, for the housekeeper. A compliment to my acting, Charlotte thought; after all, who knew less about housework? And she had fully intended to go, had even plucked her eyebrows last night. But the auditions had begun at ten down in Richmond, and the housekeeper's part must already be long gone.

"Excuse me," said a voice, and Charlotte ceded the pavement to a woman with a double pram. Never mind; the venue was tiny and the play sounded dull as ditch water. As for what to say to Ginny, perhaps she could claim the bus had broken down. No, Ginny would see that as yet more evidence of hopelessness. Trust Charlotte to choose a decrepit bus.

She was looking in the window of a travel agent—skiing in the Pyrenees versus scuba diving in the Canaries—when inspiration struck. Just as she was leaving for the audition, Struan had phoned—remember, he'd been a year ahead of them at RADA—to talk about a film he was producing, set in Gloucestershire. Charlotte was one of the first people he'd thought of for the second female lead. Or maybe a cameo, she nodded at the Canaries. She didn't want to make Ginny jealous.

Happily elaborating, she scarcely noticed as the clutter of Kilburn High Road gave way to the reticence of Maida Vale. Even the sign PADDINGTON 2 MILES, which normally made her want to sink down on the nearest doorstep, today carried a different message. Wasn't Paddington where one caught the Gloucester train? She passed two women in chadors cleaning a car and turned into the Marylebone Road. She saw the cameras rolling, herself delivering heart-rending scenes in a single take, improvising speeches that reduced the director to tears.

Not until she was standing in line for the salad bar at the Baker Street Pizza Hut—all you can eat four ninety-five—did she remember the phone bill smouldering at the bottom of her bag. Perhaps she ought to go and write them a cheque just before five, when it couldn't clear that day. Then tomorrow she'd have a talk with the bank manager about her famous financial overhaul, how she was going to rent out her flat and live with her sister until Struan's film got under way. Or maybe—she helped herself to beetroot—something would come through at the Royal Court.

She was sitting at a window table, eating as slowly as possible, when someone said her name. A slender, extremely good-looking boy was bearing down on her. Now who is this? Charlotte thought, beaming at him and surreptitiously adjusting her scarf.

"Jason," he said helpfully. "We worked together at Books Etc. a couple of years ago during the Christmas rush."

"Of course." How nice to be recognised. That'll show you, Bernie. "We used to divide the customers between us. You serviced the twin sets and pearls while I took the toy boys."

"What a team." Jason laughed. "So you've discovered my little secret. I thought I was the only ordinary person who ever came here. All my naff colleagues go to Pizza Express. May I join you?"

"Lovely. In fact I was about to have a second round."

Leaving her bag to hold the table, Charlotte followed him to the salad bar and they chatted their way through the choices. Once they sat down, Jason said, "Well, this calls for a celebration. Red or white?"

"Just what I was thinking, but I'm totally broke."

"My treat. I'm working these days." He ordered a carafe of red, and they toasted. It turned out that Jason, an aspiring actor when they met, had moved on to radio and now helped to produce an arts programme. "Basically I'm a glorified dogs-body, though I do get to make suggestions. Hanif Kureishi was on last week—what a thrill! I fetched him Perrier."

He asked if she had any ideas for guests. Charlotte mentioned an actor she knew who was now starring in a soap, and Jason said they'd done him. "We need ought-to-be-famous, rather than actually is."

"Oh, I've got the chap for you." She flourished her wine-glass. "Donald Early. He was my tutor at RADA. He used to be a designer, now he does heads and stuff for TV, but he's worked with everyone—Gielgud, Olivier, the Redgraves," she improvised. "And he's a great talker, touch of the blarney, besides being awfully nice."

"Sounds perfect." Gratifyingly, Jason produced a Filofax and made a note with an asterisk.

"I expect recognition and ten percent," Charlotte joked. She took a bite of pasta salad. "So how's your love life?"

"Grim. I've been seeing this older man, and from being a kind, intelligent person he's turned into a possessive monster. Maybe I'll say I had lunch with Charlie just to wind him up. How about you?"

"Still with the toy boys, I'm afraid." She described Cedric. "A babe in arms, so utterly ruthless. He's looking for an older woman to teach him bedroom manners, and I seem to have volunteered."

"And is he a good student?" Jason fluttered his dark eyelashes.

"A for effort, B for execution. Interested?"

"Absolutely not. It's bad enough putting up with myself. I can't stand anyone else under twenty-five." He refilled their glasses.

The new shift of waiters was arriving by the time they wandered, flushed and exuberant, out into the street. Jason had

ordered a second carafe, then coffee, and paid for everything.
They'd played desert-island sex and discussed his screenplay,
and Charlotte had told him about Struan, the film for Chan-
nel 4, and promised to recommend Jason to him. "Well, I'm
off to see the older man," Jason announced, bussing her cheek.
"And you?"

"Errands," Charlotte said firmly. She headed down Baker
Street.

She was standing in front of the flower shop at Selfridges—
where did they grow such beautiful lilies in February?—when
the phone bill surfaced again. It was already too late to get to
the office today, but it might be worth giving them a call. No
point in being an actor if you couldn't persuade people to do
what you wanted.

One of Freddie's small extravagances was never to go out at
night, even in summer, without turning on several lights.
When Felicity scolded him about waste and the environment,
he argued that her habit of leaving on only the hall light was
like putting a sign BURGLARS WELCOME in the window. In
truth, his own behaviour had nothing to do with security; he
simply hated coming back to a dark apartment. So when he
pedalled down Mr. Early's street and saw his house lit up like a
Christmas tree, he both recognised a kindred spirit and was
fairly sure Mr. Early was at home, awake. He dismounted, leaning the bike against a lamppost across the road.

A fine drizzle filled the air and as he stood, staring up at
the room of heads, droplets clung to his face and hands. Why,
he wondered, this evening of all evenings, had he suddenly
been able to leave the couch? He was stamping his feet, feeling increasingly dumb, when a figure appeared at the window.
Mr. Early, pate glowing, was looking towards the lamppost—
indeed, seemed to be looking right at him—but Freddie,

confident of his own invisibility, did not budge. When I was a kid, he'd told Felicity, the three things about being black were: people picked you first at sports; they assumed you had all the rhythm moves; and they joked about running over you in the dark. Same in London, she'd said.

Mr. Early raised his hand. Darn, so much for being one with the night. Across three thousand miles of ether Freddie heard his mother's voice: Get your lazy butt over there right now, Frederick Lewis Adams, and apologise to that poor man for being crazy as a loon. Miserable, embarrassed—only yesterday he'd phoned to say he was too busy to do the roof—Freddie was nearly at the gate when he realised Mr. Early had been wiping the glass, not waving. A cat meowed in the next garden. He retreated to the bike and was poised to depart when he saw Mr. Early's lips moving. Perhaps he was singing to himself.

For a minute, maybe two, Freddie watched, entranced. Then Mr. Early moved away and his senses returned. We are freezing, came the message from fingertips, feet, ears. As he mounted the bike, the front door opened and a woman stepped out, hefting a large box in her arms, and headed to a nearby car. Pedalling past, it occurred to Freddie that the box contained Bethany and then that Mr. Early hadn't been singing but talking to the woman.

Back at the house, Kevin popped out of his apartment the moment Freddie came through the door. In the shadowy hall light his afro, the best Freddie had ever seen on a white boy, hummed with indignation. "Freddie," he said softly, "you can't keep borrowing my bike without frigging well asking. I wanted to go to the off-licence and by the time I walked there, it was closed."

"I'm sorry." Freddie leaned the bike against three others. "Why didn't you take one of these?"

"The same reason you didn't. They're locked. How would you like it if I kept using your van without permission?"

"Plenty, if you filled the tank, but then I never claimed to be an anarchist. I'm just a fellow traveller."

"Oh, bugger off."

Poor old Kev, Freddie thought, climbing the gloomy stairs. Not a happy camper. As usual, it didn't pay to take people at their word. When they met, during Freddie's locksmith days, Kevin had preached against the evil of keys. "We have to trust each other," he said. "It all comes back." At the time he was leaving his flat unlocked, an experiment he abandoned after his second CD player was liberated. Freddie, who shared Kevin's taste in cookies and beer, had lamented the erosion of his ideals. And look at him now. You could hardly tell him apart from an ordinary, grubby socialist.

Inside his apartment all thoughts of Kevin vanished. Agnes was gone. She was not mooching in the hall or under the kitchen table. She wasn't napping behind the couch. Heart pounding absurdly, he searched the three rooms, calling her name. At last he found her in the closet where he kept his clothes. "Agnes," he said, "is this it? Are you about to drop?" She pushed her hot nose against his hand and gave a single wag of the tail. Fire on the mountain. The Lord is coming. He sat beside her for twenty motionless minutes before going to bed.

The four of them divided the tasks of bringing Hazel home. While George and Nora took care of paperwork at the hospital, Maud borrowed Jonathan's car to go to Hazel's flat, and Jonathan organised what they all referred to as "the house," as if the definite article could expunge his ownership. Walking home that Thursday evening, he made a mental list: clean sheets, groceries, a quick flick with the duster. The prospect of

Hazel once again beneath his roof was like sliding into a warm pool of bliss.

As he turned into his street, a figure shambled towards him through the gloaming: the Tourette's boy. The young man, faintly Oriental in appearance, with a crest of black hair and a ragged backpack, had been a fixture in the neighbourhood ever since the summer after Hazel moved in. They'd diagnosed him from his odd method of locomotion; he could walk no more than thirty paces without turning in a circle.

"Good evening," said Jonathan.

The boy spiralled beside him, mute, and continued on his way.

Jonathan woke an hour before the alarm—Hazel, he thought—and could not linger in bed another second. Downstairs, he filled the kettle and, reaching for a mug, found every last one of them piled in the sink, along with whatever dishes he'd used since the accident. The kitchen, he now saw, was filthy, the counters rimmed in dirt, the floor mossy with crumbs. Even the stain on the wall, where a glass of tomato juice had landed, seemed more livid. In the months before she moved out, Hazel had ceased to clean, and he too had abandoned his normal tidiness. Carrying his coffee from room to room, Jonathan discovered that the entire house had become a grubby shrine.

Furiously he began to scrub and hoover, polish and dust. He gathered up the dead plants from the living-room, lining them up in the garden, and hung last year's Amnesty calendar over the tomato stain. He made Hazel's bed, their bed, with clean sheets and put the dirty ones in the washing machine. Later there would be time to organise the spare room for her parents, the study for himself. He turned on the heat and extravagantly opened the windows.

Then he set out to Sainsbury's and bought food for lunch

and dinner as well as everything he could remember Hazel liking: mozzarella, olives, Camembert, raspberry jam, avocadoes, oranges, cream crackers, tuna, olive oil, wine, apples, and three large bars of chocolate. The cashier's announcement—"Eighty-eight pounds twenty-six pence, sir"—filled him with satisfaction; too often recently his purchases had barely dented a ten-pound note. Sitting in the taxi, however, he fell prey to a mysterious anxiety. Had he forgotten something, he wondered, eyeing the bags at his feet, but the market round the corner was open until midnight. The shabby houses of the Liverpool Road with their lovely fanlights flashed by. Maud, he thought, scratching his palms. He remembered her face when Nora broke the news that Hazel would convalesce at his house. Really? she'd said.

Years ago, at an exhibition on the Spanish Civil War, he and Hazel had seen the Orsini bomb. Orsini, the placard explained, was an anarchist who had risked his life to hurl the bomb at an important personage in the Madrid opera house only to have it roll under the skirts of a nearby lady and fail to explode. Side by side, Jonathan and Hazel had studied the gleaming silver sphere, no bigger than an orange, and speculated as to the fate of the unnamed woman. Was it possible to recover from such a spectacular intertwining of good and bad luck? Yes, Hazel had argued; she had gone on to have two beautiful daughters and become a famous portrait painter. No, said Jonathan; she fell into depression, her husband left her, her dog was run over, even her mother found her boring.

He was trying to recall the date of the exhibition, more or less than three years ago, when the cab pulled up outside the house. The driver apologised for not helping with the shopping. "I slipped a disc right after Christmas. Bloody murder."

He's lying, Jonathan thought, and perversely tipped him a pound rather than the fifty pence he'd already sorted from his change. Once inside he went through the fridge, dumping two frothy pints of milk and a seething carton of yoghurt down the drain, before installing fruit juices, wine, hummus, gleaming dairy products. Then he moved on to the fruit and veg. He was pondering whether a bunch of rubbery carrots might still be good for soup when the doorbell rang. He raised his hand as if to ward off a blow. He wanted Hazel across his threshold more than anything, but not yet, it was too soon, he wasn't ready.

"Sorry," said Maud. "I didn't realise packing would take so long." She held a suitcase in either hand.

"No problem." He tried to exhale quietly. Even his apprehensions seemed unreliable today. "Is there more?"

"Lots."

While she carried the cases inside, he set the carrots on the radiator and went out to the car. At the sight of the back seat full of bags and boxes, his hands unclenched. For five minutes he and Maud trotted back and forth. "That's it," she said in the kitchen, handing him the car keys. "Thanks."

He was about to comment on the amount of luggage but superstitiously caught himself. "Can I get you anything? Tea? Coffee?"

"A glass of water. Maybe tea in a minute. You've been busy." She indicated the piles of groceries on the table and the floor.

"Sainsbury's. The cupboard was a little bare. I took a taxi," he added, answering her unasked question.

She drank the water in slow, steady swallows. The shadows beneath her eyes were even more pronounced than usual; most evenings after leaving the hospital she had gone back to the florist's to place orders and check the accounts. It was on the tip of his tongue to make some euphemistic plea, don't rock the boat, let sleeping dogs lie. Instead he said, "You look tired."

"You too." She turned the glass round and round as if it were a crystal ball. "I have something to tell you."

Carefully, not taking his eyes off her, Jonathan sat down at the table. He pushed aside the jars of jam and boxes of pasta, not so much to make room as to remove temptation. Whatever happened, he must not lose his temper. Maud went to the sink and refilled her glass. As she stepped back, the blood rose in her cheeks; her hands trembled and water splashed onto the newly washed floor. "I've sublet Hazel's flat," she said. "A friend of Graham's—you know, my banker friend—needed a place for four months."

"Four months." If Maud had floated up to the ceiling, he could not have felt more astonished, or more delighted.

Her colour deepened. "I should've asked Hazel but the businesswoman in me took over. Hopefully, in the not too distant future, she'll be well enough to worry about her finances again. This way her flat is safe and paid for until the end of June. As soon as she's better, she can come and stay with me."

Across the crowded table her eyes glowed at Jonathan. He stared back, a cautious incredulity mixing with his relief. Surely she must know she'd given him exactly what he wanted. "Thank you," he said, but she was speaking again.

"It felt so strange being there this morning. Everything is as she left it, her notes on the desk, her swimming costume in the bathroom, yet she has no idea the place exists."

Her hand reached towards him and her eyebrows rose. She was asking for something, if only he could figure out what. He glanced down at the jam. As a boy he had gone raspberry picking, spending whole days gathering the soft fruit, whisking away flies. "Hogarth did say one step at a time. All we're trying to do right now is get her well again. The less stress, the better." What else, what else could he invoke on the side of discretion? "George and Nora," he concluded, "will be very relieved the flat's taken care of."

Maud made a gesture of assent. Her hand slid back across the table. He watched warily—had he said enough?—then as she raised her glass again he risked pointing to the clock. Tempus fugit, carpe diem. They both stood up. In the hall he seized two of the suitcases and headed upstairs. Maud followed. With a rustle of plastic, she laid several carrier bags on the bed.

While he adjusted the radiator, she opened the first suitcase and lifted out a grey pullover he recognised, a blue one he didn't. "Where do these go?"

And suddenly, in the aftermath of getting everything he wanted, he was dying to say, Maud, aren't we making a terrible mistake? What will we do if she does remember? In most cases, Hogarth had said, the memories did come back. But Maud was lifting out neatly folded sweaters, one after another.

He abandoned the radiator and walked over to the chest of drawers. The faint odour of sweat rose from the bottom drawer. He picked up his squash clothes and threw them in the laundry basket. "Here," he said, and went to make tea.

In the kitchen, while the kettle throbbed, he watched the sparrows fussing in the elderberry tree. He'd been wrong to attribute his anxiety wholly to Maud; it was simply easier to worry about her than about Hazel. Once, on Hampstead Heath, they had come across a holly tree with several condoms impaled on the thorns. The holly and the condom, Hazel had said, and told him about a guru in Bombay who blessed condoms because they slowed down reincarnation. Who would you like to come back as? she asked. You, he said, and she burst out laughing.

He was already in the hall when he realised he'd forgotten about Maud. He doubled back, made a second mug of tea, and carried both upstairs. "Thanks," she said. She had emptied one suitcase and was at work on another. "There's not much room in the wardrobe."

As he carried an armful of shirts to the spare room wardrobe, Jonathan allowed himself to re-enter the pool of bliss. Hazel was coming home, that was all that mattered. He noted with admiration that Maud had brought not only clothes but books, jewellery, photographs, papers. She moved a stack of newspapers from the chest of drawers. "Can you remember what she had here?" she asked.

"A hairbrush, a photo of George and Nora in the garden. Oh, good, you got it. Some earrings. Kleenex." He paused, trying to visualise the room as it had been up until a few months ago and found that instead he was thinking of Hazel. This was what it must be like to be constantly searching for missing words, objects, experiences. Even the things he recalled—the photo, the brush—grew hazy. Had they been here; or there? No firm place to stand remained.

"Jonathan?"

"Sorry. That's all I can come up with."

She handed him a bag of Hazel's toiletries and went downstairs to hang up the coats. In the bathroom he gave the taps a final polish and arranged shampoo, toothpaste, face creams. We're doing the right thing, he repeated. She's getting better. He was folding a towel when he caught sight of the dent in the wall beside the light cord; it dated from a fortnight after the tomato juice. No way to conceal this. You couldn't put a picture right behind the cord. As he fitted his fist into the depression, he heard a taxi in the street outside.

None of them knew what to do. For the first half hour they sat awkwardly in the living-room, every attempt at conversation interrupted by Hazel exclaiming over some change, getting up to look at a picture, a chair, the VCR. She was wearing a dress Jonathan was particularly fond of, dark blue and low waisted. "Why did you get rid of the old sofa?" she asked. "What happened to the red curtains?" The familiar room, rather than jogging her memory, made apparent the full force of what was missing. At one point she paused in examining the cheese plant and turned, eyes widening, to regard the four of them. "So it's true I have lost my memory. When Hogarth told me, I didn't really believe him. But Jonathan couldn't have made all these changes while I was in hospital."

This is it, he thought, glancing at his companions. If they keep silent now, they'll never speak. Maud, after this morning's conversation, seemed safe, and Nora was invariably discreet. George, though, with his red-rimmed eyes and his fear of mortality, was a loose cannon. Before he knew what he was doing, Jonathan was standing over him.

At the same moment Nora crossed the room. "Don't worry, dear." She put an arm around her daughter. "It will come back, piece by piece."

"I'm not upset." Hazel shrugged off her embrace. "I'm just trying to understand."

"Can I get anyone a drink?" Jonathan said. "George, a dram?"

"Not for me," said George. The others, too, refused. Then Maud suggested lunch and everyone seized on this as a stroke of genius. As they ate quiche and salad, Hazel was almost incoherent with pleasure. "Hospitals are awful," she said. "And the food is a joke."

"Some of the nurses were very nice," said Nora. "June and Laetitia, they were lovely."

"You know, Laetitia told me her mother was the first woman in Yorkshire to wear a bikini. Her father bought it because he thought anything connected with the atomic bomb was a good thing."

"Am I being dense?" said Maud. "What do bikinis have to do with the bomb?"

"That's what I asked." Hazel smiled. "Apparently the man who invented the bikini named it after the site of the first nuclear tests." She tapped her fork, a bird seeking escape from the egg. "I thought it might make a good article: bombs and bikinis."

"Ridiculous," growled George. "Not you, dear—I mean this inventor chap."

At the end of lunch Maud produced a surprise: a cake with WELCOME HOME, HAZEL written in red letters on the white icing. Hazel clapped her hands and laughed.

This was the sound, Jonathan thought, that had been missing from his life. He had a dreamy, pastoral vision of the two of them living happily ever after. Hazel would cook while he read to her; he would tend his bees and she would garden; she would write her articles and come home and tell him stories about the people she'd met and the things they'd done; she would peel away his layers of reserve and show him how to be present in the world.

Yet even as he imagined these cosy scenes, a shadow passed over Hazel. Carefully, she set aside her cake. "I think I'd better lie down."

She rose to her feet and stood looking around uncertainly as if everything in the room, including herself, had grown strange. Nora took her arm and led her upstairs. Jonathan, George, and Maud remained at the table.

"Well," said George at last, reaching for the knife, "no use letting a perfectly good cake go to waste."

chapter 6

Something in his familiar landscape had shifted. Freddie paused in the hall, rocking back and forth on the balls of his feet, wondering if he was simply sensing the aftershock of his prolonged absence. Since meeting Mr. Early, he had left the house only briefly until today, when he had gone to help his former boss the antiques salesman move a wardrobe and stayed on for supper. But no, he thought, standing on tiptoe, listening as hard as he could, it was presence he was sensing, not absence. Had Kevin come to borrow something? Unlikely. Although they still shared keys, their easy camaraderie was gone. Had a burglar, undeterred by his lavish use of lights, paid a visit?

Then he heard a low noise from the direction of the bedroom. A sort of sobbing, it stopped and started and stopped again. Agnes. He dropped his jacket and strode across the hall. In the clothes closet, her chosen refuge, she lay panting. "Agnes," he said, falling to his knees. "Are you okay?"

Ignoring him, she moaned and pushed herself around in a circle. She had made a nest out of what, after a moment, he recognised as his blue bathrobe. Served him right for leaving it on the floor. As she moaned again, Freddie was overcome by panic. What the heck was he supposed to do? He thought of phoning Felicity. More usefully, he remembered Trevor. "I'll be right back," he assured Agnes. Her haunches quivered.

Trevor's mother answered. "Freddie, how are you?" she said, as if he were ringing at noon, not midnight. "I hope you've been taking care of yourself in this bitter weather."

"Agnes is in labour. I don't know what to do."

Mrs. Jackson laughed. "Fortunately she does. Where is she?" He told her that Agnes preferred the closet to the pen he'd built, and Mrs. Jackson said that was often the way, but now was the time to put her in the pen. "You want her somewhere warm and enclosed so she can't wander off. Don't worry, I'm sure everything will be fine."

"How will I know if it isn't?"

Mrs. Jackson explained that each pup was born in its own sac. Agnes would break the sac and bite the umbilical cord, thus enabling the pup to breathe. If for any reason she failed to perform these duties, then it was up to Freddie. "Snip the cord a couple of inches from the belly. And be sure that the placenta comes out after each pup. If it doesn't, or if she's in labour for too long with no results, that's when you should call the vet. I usually keep a bottle of Scotch handy. For myself," she added.

Freddie hung up feeling slightly better, although the reference to instinct was not reassuring. Agnes hadn't had a clue about the dangers of overeating, so why should she grasp this much more complicated process? He was in the kitchen, rinsing the scissors in hot water, when he heard the click of nails and turned to see her waddling into the hall. By the time he caught up with her she was head-butting the outside door.

"No," he said. "Good girl. We'll go out later."

A small, dark lump popped out and fell to the floor.

Agnes turned. She looked at the lump, then at Freddie, her amazement mirroring his own. This is it, he thought. What had Mrs. Jackson said? Break the sac, snip the cord. "Agnes! Do what you're supposed to."

He dashed into the kitchen, grabbed the scissors, and ran back to where Agnes stood, still looking blank. Trying not to think about it, he knelt down, gingerly tore open the sac, and snipped the cord. The puppy made a mewling sound. Agnes bent to sniff the tiny body without enthusiasm. The placenta lay on the floor.

"Jeepers, Agnes. Don't be such a retard."

Carefully he scooped her up, carried her into the kitchen, and set her down in the pen. Then he went back for the puppy—so slippery he almost dropped it—and nudged it against one of Agnes's teats. At last someone knew what to do. The puppy latched on, and Agnes began to lick it clean.

Freddie sat on the floor, wishing for the whisky Mrs. Jackson had recommended. For half an hour nothing happened. The pup nursed blindly and Agnes fussed over it. He was beginning to nod off when the panting started again. He sat up, scissors ready. Again the dark lump popped out, seemingly with no effort, but this time Agnes was all business. No sooner had it landed on the newspapers than she turned around, tore the sac, bit the cord, and began washing the newborn puppy. All Freddie had to do was guide it to the teat.

"Agnes," he said, "you've got it. You're a bona fide mom. Number two and counting. Go for it, baby."

Within forty minutes another puppy appeared. Freddie put on *The Magic Flute,* drank tea, cheered Agnes on. "No pain, no gain," he admonished. After the third birth came a pause. An hour passed, ninety minutes, nearly two hours. He eyed the clock, paced the apartment, studied the dog. Was Agnes through? Three was a perfectly respectable first litter, the vet had said. Cautiously he reached to feel her belly, but she growled and snapped. A few minutes later the panting started again.

After a noticeably longer period, a fourth sac slid out. Agnes simply slumped to one side, allowing the three pups to reattach themselves. Even as he broke the sac, Freddie knew the puppy was dead.

His first thought was to get the body away from Agnes and her brood. He carried it over to the table. Under the light he studied the small being. At the sight of the neat ears, the unmistakable paws, Freddie's eyes watered; he hadn't seen a fatality since the day he forced that door in Dalston. With one finger he stroked the sleek fur. In the morning he would bury it near Kevin's Brother Cadfaels. For now he wrapped it in a clean tea towel and laid it in the airing cupboard.

By the time he came back from washing his hands another surprise awaited him. Agnes was panting again, sounding bored rather than pained. A few minutes later a fifth puppy appeared. Agnes performed her duties with brisk efficiency, and somehow Freddie knew it was over. He brought her a bowl of milk, which she lapped greedily. She settled to rest and he arranged the puppies along her teats. Only when they were all suckling did he at last turn off the light and get into bed. In the darkness he held his breath. Four new beings were sharing his apartment, but they were doing so in utter silence.

"Prick," said Hazel.

The word emerged distinctly through bubbles of saliva. For the second time since breakfast her heels were drumming the floor, fortunately in the carpeted living-room. Jonathan was doing his best to keep hold of her head and arms. Meanwhile George tried to restrain her legs; already he had let go twice.

"Hazel, love," said Nora. "Relax. Take a deep breath and relax. We're all right here."

"Gooseberries. Top and tail. Top and tail."

Her head whipped from side to side, and just as Jonathan was about to lose his grip, the seizure ended. Hazel's limbs grew heavy, her breathing slowed. He cradled her head while Nora brought a cushion. Together they covered her with a blanket. George hurried from the room; he would be making an entry, Jonathan knew, in the notebook where he detailed each seizure, searching for a correlation with weather, exercise, diet, household events. Sometimes Nora followed him but today, no such luck. She knelt in what Jonathan regarded as his rightful place, next to Hazel. He resigned himself to the nearest armchair. "That was terrible," he said.

"Really." Hesitantly, as if the lightest touch might offend, Nora began to stroke her daughter's hair. "You know, the year she ran away from home, I slept fourteen hours a night. I couldn't bear to be awake. After twenty-seven days she sent a postcard saying she was okay." She looked up at Jonathan and he saw on her cheek the bruise where Hazel had struck her during yesterday's seizure. "It's awful to admit, but the first few days at the hospital I thought, this is easier."

He had heard Hazel's version of running away, the excitement and the boredom. Now he glimpsed those adventures from her parents' point of view; like him, they had been abandoned. "She is getting better," he said, "just not as steadily as we would like."

"Oh, Jonathan. You've been splendid. You know, when Hazel told us she'd sublet that flat, well, I haven't seen George so upset in years. He was sure it would be right back to the old days. No word for six months, then a call at two in the morning, from god knows where, over some crisis. You're so good for her."

He stared at the cheese plant, trying to hide his pleasure. The truth was, since he'd learned what to do, he found the seizures more fascinating than distressing. After ten days at home Hazel was still having at least one, sometimes several, a day. A few were so minor as to be barely perceptible: she would put down her cup, blink, and continue with what she had been saying or doing. Others, like this afternoon's, were a force of nature. And it was during these, while she foamed and thrashed, that she made her odd pronouncements. Much of what she said was gibberish, but Jonathan sensed an ancient power seeking a conduit. He understood why, in other times and places, epileptics were regarded as prophets.

For him the hardest part of Hazel's illness was how seldom he had her to himself. When friends and colleagues phoned, he lowered his voice. Lovely of them to call, he'd pass on their good wishes, yet at the moment, as he was sure they could understand, a visit was out of the question. Still, no matter how many well-wishers he fended off, her parents were always around—where else would they be?—and in the evenings Maud often dropped in. She would read Hazel to sleep and after George and Nora retired, they kept farmers' hours, settle in to watch television. The best way to get rid of her, Jonathan discovered, was to go to bed himself. Once there, he fell asleep promptly, only to wake, an hour or two later, to the semi-gloom of a city night.

What occurred then he at first called thinking but soon conceded could scarcely be dignified by that term. Here was the first quarrel, the cross words uttered and never, quite, forgiven; the first lie, uneasily offered and, to his amazement, blithely accepted.

Sometimes he tried to drive out the memories by summoning his bees. Was the middle hive sufficiently insulated? Had he glimpsed wax moths in the third hive? But even the bees led back to Hazel. During their courtship, he'd told her that the Egyptians used honey in embalming the pharaohs and that the bees themselves understood this property of their food. If a mouse climbed into the hive and died, they would coat the corpse with honey to prevent it from spoiling their home. Magic, Hazel had said, nibbling his ear. Last November she'd accused *him* of being embalmed, "like your precious bees."

The night Hazel said "Prick," the memories circled until Jonathan gave in and switched on the light. From the pillow, the damp patch on the ceiling winked at him. Tomorrow, he vowed, he would call the roofer again. In the meantime he debated turning on his computer, and instead opened a book on memory he'd borrowed from the library. An American study showed that witnesses remembered events quite differently, depending on how questions were phrased. Perhaps his silence about the past was a mistake. What he ought to be doing was mentioning their difficulties—well, at least some of them—in such a way as to adjust Hazel's memories.

He set aside the book and at last succumbed to the impulse that had been tugging at him since he opened his eyes. On the landing he paused to listen. Reassured by the silence from her parents' room, he slipped into Hazel's. As usual after a major seizure, she was sleeping deeply; it was as if she had left her body, sloughed it off like a selky her sealskin, and gone elsewhere. In the amber glow of the nightlight, Jonathan bent down. Except for the faint rise and fall of her breathing she lay motionless, but when he tried to take her hand, she pulled away. "Hazel," he whispered. "Please."

"My sister," Charlotte explained, "is flat on her back, some ghastly virus. And her husband, wouldn't you know it, has done a runner. So"—she leaned closer to the window—"I'm looking after the kids. I've barely been home in the last month, except to change my clothes."

The woman, she had the waxen skin and garish lips of a vampire, tapped the computer keys. "Our most recent printouts show a high level of telephone usage, many of the calls late at night. And"—she raised her hand like a policeman—"many to numbers that frequently appear on your bills."

Who was it, Charlotte wondered, who had invented the computer? Babbage? How she hated him and his descendants, the overlords at IBM and Apple. Ten years ago, even five, however sceptical, the woman would have been alone with her doubts. Now these machines, like huge spiders, spun their webs, trying to ensnare Charlotte at every turn. The bank was the same. Life had been much pleasanter in the old days, when a cheque took a week to clear and her manager begged to inform her that she had an overdraft. "I didn't say I hadn't been there at all," she said, going for patient long-suffering. "Of course I occasionally dashed over for a few minutes."

Behind her, two men, a woman, and a small girl stirred restlessly. In the confined space of the basement office, they were privileged to share every syllable of Charlotte's performance. At first she had assumed they were cheering her on—lone woman versus capitalist giant—but, minute by minute, it was becoming apparent that they didn't give a toss. All they wanted was for her to surrender the window.

"A seventy-minute call to Greenwich last Monday? Eighty-three minutes to Victoria?"

"I told you, I've had family difficulties, and I myself am unemployed."

"Perhaps then"—the red lips curled—"it would be better to wait until you are employed to have the phone reconnected."

"But I'm an actor," Charlotte burst out. "I can't work without a phone. People need to be able to call me about TV and films."

Even these magic words had no effect, on either the queue, newly joined by a man in a duffel coat, or the ghoul behind the glass. "I'm sorry, Miss Granger. British Telecom does take hardship into account, but frankly I find no evidence for this in your case. In the last year most of your bills have been paid at the final notice."

"This is outrageous." She drew herself up to her full height and beyond, standing on tiptoe. "My sister's doctor will be phoning your supervisor later today."

The woman, seemingly unaware that she was being treated to a West End performance, flicked a speck of dust off the screen. "All right. If you bring in cash or the equivalent within forty-eight hours, we'll let the reconnection charge go."

Even as she spoke, the man at the head of the queue stepped forward, waving his cheque book like a flag. No arguments here, thought Charlotte, hastily gathering up the contents of her bag. Think family silver, she murmured as she stalked up the stairs. Think servants and bad plumbing.

Back in the swirl of Oxford Street she walked to the corner as Lady Granger and managed to make it across the road and through the narrow darkness of Christopher Court, but as soon as she reached the pub on Wigmore Street and the bartender said "What'll it be, love?" she was returned to her plebeian, heavily indebted self. Mr. Aziz loomed. Bernadette, far from being bedridden, was obstinately refusing to let her move in. She once again had not won the lottery. The phone was gone. She ordered a half of lager, all she could afford, and began to draft her advertisement on the back of an envelope. *Spacious, furnished flat to sublet. Feb–June. Suit couple, students? £100 p.w. inc. Deposit.*

She broke off. Now, who had an answering machine and wouldn't mind getting calls? Her first thought was Jason, who'd sprung for lunch as if it were the most natural thing in the world, but she felt reluctant to muddy the clear waters of his enthusiasm. As for Ginny, in their last conversation, just before the phone was cut off, she had let fly a volley of reproaches about Richmond. "I recommended you over all these other people and you didn't even have the decency to show up. I don't know why I bother. The same thing happened at the King's Head."

When at last Charlotte managed to tell her about Struan, Ginny, far from being mollified, had reacted like Bernadette. "Films," she snorted. "I mean, if it works out, great, but you need a job right now."

The conversation had left Charlotte with a sick, shaky feeling. She paced back and forth amongst the newspapers until she remembered the bottle of vodka jammed at the back of her fridge. Armed with a glassful, she climbed onto the futon and, a stroke of luck, *A Man for All Seasons* was on the box. By the time she fell asleep, her own struggles were subsumed in those between church and state.

"Do you have a light?"

Charlotte looked up to find her face mirrored in an absurd pair of rose-coloured spectacles which exactly matched their wearer's velvet coat. "Probably," she said.

"Do I know you?" said the second girl. Unlike her vivid companion, but like Charlotte and almost everyone else in the pub, she was dressed in black.

Fans, thought Charlotte, feeling what could be a box of matches. "Maybe you've seen me in something." No, a sewing kit. Then came the familiar questions, and she was all becoming modesty, explaining that she was the person having a haircut in *Pie in the Sky* or the third patient in *Casualty*.

"I was sure I knew you," said the one with ridiculous glasses. "I never forget a face."

"Bollocks," said her friend. They began to argue about each other's mnemonic powers just as Charlotte's fingers closed around a box of matches.

"Here." She handed it to the nearer girl. "Can I ask your

advice?" For a moment they looked uneasy, as if she were turn-ing into a Scientologist before their eyes, until she told them about her flat and showed them the ad so far.

"Whereabouts is it?" said the first girl.

"Why not say you're an actress?" said the second.

An hour later, as Charlotte rode the bus north, both the enve-lope and the final bill were covered with their suggestions. Per-haps it was their youth that had reminded her of Cedric. She had been neglecting him lately. True, she'd left several messages on his answering machine, but of course he couldn't call her back. Briefly she considered phoning now, from the call box at the bus stop, then decided to take her chances. Her optimism was rewarded. As she turned into his street, a light shone in the window of his bed-sit, like a good deed in a naughty world.

"Who is it?" called a muffled voice.

"Charlotte." A prolonged silence greeted her name. "Come on, Cedric. It's bloody freezing out here." She jiggled from foot to foot, wondering if he might have someone with him. No, more likely he'd been asleep or doing some drug he didn't want to share. Cedric had a dog-in-the-manger side she was finding increasingly hard to ignore.

The door opened and there he was, looking ravishing in a red silk dressing gown. He had the longest neck Charlotte had ever seen and a coltish, Modigliani body. He can't possibly be straight, her friend Luke had insisted. Well, she'd said, he cer-tainly goes through the motions with enthusiasm. Now she smiled warmly, wondering if he would kiss her.

"Why the hell didn't you phone like a normal person to say you were coming?"

"I didn't know," said Charlotte, breezing past. "I was at the bus stop and the first one came right by your door. I took it as a sign."

"No bus comes right by my door." He followed her into the room. "Here." He moved some books off the sofa and straightened a cushion. She took off her coat, sat down in one corner, and stretched her toes towards the gas fire. Lovely. Cedric's room, though not much larger than hers, was so warm and tidy. She waited eagerly for him to offer her a drink. He usually had a bottle of plonk on the go.

"So." Cedric stood over her, hands in the pockets of his dressing gown. "How are you?"

"Oh, the usual. Hectic. I've been offered a small part in a film and I'm auditioning for a couple of plays."

"Sounds good."

Why was he still standing, not budging or offering her a glass? "Yes, the film will make a huge difference. That was one reason I wanted to see you. But were you in the middle of something? I don't mean," she offered cheerily, "to be the man from Porlock." Cedric had pretensions to write poetry, although Charlotte would not have used that word for the verses he'd read to her one slow afternoon at the pub. Still, far be it from her to discourage anyone in artistic pursuits.

"I was writing a letter, actually, but I can take a short break." He pointed to the desk and at last focussed on Charlotte and his responsibilities as host. "Would you like a cup of tea? I just put the kettle on."

"Lovely." She tried to keep the disappointment from her voice.

He disappeared into the alcove that served as a kitchen, and she glanced around the room for telltale underwear or surprising publications. A heap of coins glinted on the mantelpiece. She listened to a cupboard opening and closing, then sprang up and helped herself to three pounds, a small gesture towards repaying the many drinks she'd bought for him in palmier days. By the time he reappeared, she was back in her seat. He put the tray on a table between them and settled himself at the other end of the sofa. This was more like it, she thought, eyeing the plate of biscuits—chocolate-coated ginger snaps, if she wasn't mistaken. She ate three without thinking and was reaching for a fourth when she felt Cedric's gaze. "I didn't have lunch," she said.

"*Comme d'habitude.*"

Quickly Charlotte drew back her hand. She'd forgotten how sharp-tongued Cedric could be. "So how are you?" she said, accepting her tea. "I haven't been into the Trumpet in ages."

"Same old same old. Louis is a drag, but he does let me have the hours I want. I've been sending out resumés as hard as I can."

"Me too," said Charlotte, looking longingly at the biscuits. "What we both need is a good agent."

"I don't think stage managers use agents, at least not at my lowly level."

"Did you talk to Luke? He's great on the business angle."

Cedric gave a little nod and said Luke had indeed been helpful. Charlotte said she was glad, that he was sure to find work soon; in fact, that was really the reason she'd stopped in. She told him about the film, set near Gloucester. If he gave her a copy of his c.v., she'd be happy to pass it on to Struan.

"Thanks." He peered into the teapot and said something about hot water. While he was out of the room, Charlotte ate the fourth biscuit and rearranged the remaining two to look less lonely. Then she straightened her leggings and smoothed her hair. If he asked nicely, she wouldn't be averse to spending the night.

Cedric returned. Gazing up at him from the sofa, Charlotte thought his neck seemed even longer and his jaw, as Luke had pointed out, was admirably firm. When he had poured them both more tea, he announced he wanted to ask her something. At once she felt little pricklings of alarm. Perhaps she shouldn't have mentioned the film; suppose he wanted a loan?

"Why did you tell Luke that we slept together?"

"Oh, he's such a gossip." Charlotte giggled. "I certainly didn't say that. Or at least not intentionally. He'd been trying to reach me one night and I told him I was with you. You know I don't believe in lying about these kinds of things."

"That's not what Luke says," said Cedric. "But the point is, we didn't. Twice you've been too drunk to go home and, rather than put you in a taxi, I've let you stay."

"We shared a bed."

"Both fully dressed. Listen, you can tell any cock-and-bull story you like about yourself—you're screwing Charles and Camilla, for all I care—but leave me out. Okay?"

He was still speaking as Charlotte retrieved her shoes. In an instant, she was slamming the door, fumbling her way down the dark stairs. On the first landing she stopped. Wasn't that Cedric calling her name, asking her to wait? But no, there was only the echo of her own footsteps. Stupid, she thought, hurrying on, stupid to trust a twenty-three-year-old. Of course he had to impress Luke. How else could a nancy boy like Cedric get anywhere in the theatre, except by the casting couch?

chapter 7

Nora was rambling on about their dogs. From across the table, Jonathan eyed the fading bruise on her cheek. He was trying to pin down the colour—olive, ochre, sepia, mauve—when the sense of her words reached him.

"Of course," she said, "we hate to leave." Her hands fluttered above her plate like large moths, as she explained, at arduous length, all the reasons that drew them back to the Lake District: the aforementioned dogs, a frozen pipe, lambing. "We really do have to go," she concluded. "More chicken?"

"Not yet, dear."

"No, thanks," said Jonathan. His palms were tingling. Recently he had been afraid Hazel's parents might never quit his spare room; his vow had been answered—he had got her back—but in the company of two full-time chaperones. Now, like a swarm out of a clear sky, happiness descended. For a moment he was simply dazzled. Then he heard the familiar throat-clearing.

With the air of a man facing an unpleasant duty, George cast aside his silverware. "Frankly, Jonathan, it isn't just the practicalities. We have neighbours who would help, but neither of us can handle Hazel. Any fool can see we get on her nerves."

"George." Nora's hands beat frantically.

Only that afternoon Jonathan had overheard Hazel berating her. "Why do you have to pretend everything's all right? I'm ill, for god's sake. No one even has a diagnosis." "Darling," Nora protested, "you walked to the end of the street today." Hazel muttered something he couldn't catch, then: "This is like when I failed O-level biology and knew I'd never be a vet. You just wouldn't admit that I'd messed up. You kept pretending it was a clerical error." Whatever came next was lost as Jonathan stepped into the bathroom.

Now he emptied his glass and hastened to support their decision. "You've been terrific, absolutely marvellous. I'm sure we can manage, though. Hazel is much better. And Maud will help."

"That's the other thing," said George. "Nora and I have talked this over. We'd like to pay for a private nurse, two days a week."

Christ, thought Jonathan, they haven't even left and they're suggesting a substitute. He promised, vaguely, to look into it. But when Nora remarked that he didn't want to depend on friends, he glimpsed the alternative: an endless parade of people coming by on the pretext of helping. Inevitably, sooner or later, someone would mention the breakup. He could just imagine Diane's fake solicitude: *Hazel, there's something I think you ought to know. . . .*

"Of course," George continued, "this all depends on Hazel. If she doesn't want—"

"Want what?"

Hazel, wearing yellow pyjamas, stood in the doorway, arms

braced to either side. Since the accident, Jonathan had noticed, she held on to things, a doorframe, a chair, as if either she or the world needed steadying. He went to her. "Your parents have to go home," he said smoothly. "Back to Kendall. We were figuring out the arrangements."

Behind him he heard Nora's gasp and George's shush, but his attention was on Hazel. A little crease appeared between her eyebrows and was gone so quickly he doubted his vision. She let go of the doorframe. "Funny," she said, "today I was thinking this is the longest we've spent together since I got back from India. Or"—she clasped her hands—"that's what I remember. Is there more chicken?"

"Plenty," said Nora. Hazel could have given her no better gift. "Potatoes too?"

"Please." She slid into the fourth chair. Jonathan reached to pour her wine, then substituted apple juice.

"You're right," said George. "You stayed with us for a fortnight after India."

"Oh, good."

"Cheers," said Jonathan. "Here's to more soon." With varying degrees of hesitation and enthusiasm, they drank.

After the taxi turned the corner, Hazel released the garden gate and allowed herself to be led back inside. At the last moment she had clung to George and Nora, her face wet with tears. Thank goodness, Jonathan thought, they already had their tickets. He closed the front door as delicately as the lid on a hive and followed her into the living-room. Seeing her standing in the window, her hair glinting in the light, he wanted to shout for joy and fling his arms around her.

"Well," he managed, "they're in good time for their train. Would you like to go for a walk?"

"Not yet." She fingered the cheese plant. "Maybe later."

For the remainder of the day, their first alone together in several months, Hazel was restless and fretful. Nothing he could say or do seemed right; she left the room while he was reading to her and apologised, shook off his embraces and apologised, refused again to take a walk and half an hour later insisted on doing so immediately. He was almost relieved when Maud showed up with an Indian take-away.

"What did you get?" asked Hazel, prying open the containers.

"Your favourites," Maud said, quickly adding, "prawn korma, sag paneer, aloo gobi, nan, pilau rice."

"Prawn korma," Hazel repeated. "Aloo gobi. Sag . . ."

Jonathan looked over from the cupboard, where he was searching for mango chutney; he still hadn't mastered Nora's reorganisation. "You might have different favourites now. You can change your mind."

She didn't even glance in his direction. "Sag paneer," she exclaimed. "Green mush with lumps of cheese. Of course I remember that."

"So." Maud began to divide the rice. "Day one without the parentals."

Reaching for the nan, Jonathan heard the muffled threat. I'm here, Maud was saying, and I haven't forgotten. Please, he wanted to say. I'll do anything, only please don't rock the boat. "Would you like a beer?" he offered.

"Thanks," said Maud, and to Hazel, "Do you miss them?"

"I do. The house seems empty. But the thing I realised is that they weren't helping me get better, because . . ."

As he set the beer on the table, he saw her eyes widen.

"Because," she went on, "they're not part of my adult life. It's you two who know me, who know I like prawn korma." She turned first to Maud, then to him. "You have to tell me about the lost years, you—"

The phone cut short her next imperative. "Aren't you going to answer?" Maud asked after the fourth ring.

Reluctantly Jonathan rose and went to the living-room. George was on the line. As he described the snow, so deep the taxi hadn't been able to get up the drive, and the lambs wobbling in Doughty's fields, Jonathan heard in his voice something that had been missing for weeks. George was back on his home ground. "Let me fetch Hazel," he finally interrupted.

The following afternoon he was deep in e-mail, dealing with a query about a burglary, when the doorbell rang. Right on the dot, he noted approvingly as he went to answer; he'd asked the agency nurse to come during Hazel's nap. On the doorstep, he found a fair, slender woman dressed in crisp slacks, a white shirt, and dark coat.

"Bernadette Granger," she said, offering her hand.

He shook it, wondering why she looked familiar, and ushered her into the living-room. As she listed her qualifications, he realised where he'd seen her before: Hazel's hospital. He must have glimpsed her in a corridor or waiting room. "I don't know how much the agency told you," he began. "My girlfriend—fiancée—has had an accident."

"Something about seizures?" Bernadette said helpfully.

Her posture, he observed, was admirable. Sitting a little straighter, he described Hazel's condition, the treatment so far. Bernadette knew Hogarth. She praised his skill and, producing a notebook and pen, asked about medicine.

Jonathan recited the list. "None of them entirely stops the seizures. And of course, she sometimes gets in a state about this memory business." He stopped, alarmed at the gusto that had crept into his voice. Lulled by Bernadette's attention, he had forgotten his mask of grief.

"Memory business?"

"Excuse me." He pointed to the door as if he'd heard something.

In the hall he sank down on the first stair. He hadn't meant to mention Hazel's amnesia, but maybe this blunder was for the best. After all, he couldn't control every syllable she uttered. Absentmindedly he plucked a piece of fluff off the blue carpet, one of their last joint purchases for the house.

Back in the living-room he was pleased to find Bernadette still seated. Such docility seemed a good sign. "False alarm," he said, resuming his own seat. He explained Hazel's memory lapses. "Hogarth is very clear that she mustn't be troubled with questions."

"And her short-term memory?"

"Fine. Occasionally she gets in a muddle but"—Bernadette turned to a new page of her notebook—"that's probably as much the drugs as anything else."

"This must all be very worrying, Mr. Littleton."

"Jonathan."

As she described a couple of patients who, like Hazel, had suffered head injuries and gone on to make tremendous progress, he studied her long neck and small breasts. Not bad, he was thinking when she asked if she could meet the patient.

"The patient?" For a moment he had no idea who she meant. "She's asleep," he stammered.

"What a pity."

Was that a note of sarcasm, or incredulity? Once again he reminded himself Bernadette was only an employee. They arranged for her to come two afternoons a week, from two to six. "I'll need to leave promptly," she said, "to be home for my children."

"Does your husband look after them?"

To this straightforward question, she responded like one

of his clients when asked the exact date of the storm damage, fiddling with an earring, patting her ponytail. "My sister."

Aha, something here. Might be useful, he thought, getting to his feet.

She followed his example. "You know, this is more like being a companion than a nurse. I'll do my best, but a lot will depend on whether Hazel likes me."

"I'm ninety-nine percent certain she will. We have very similar tastes."

As Bernadette ducked her head and moved towards the door, he realised what he'd said. "If there's any change of plan, Mr. Littleton," she said, sounding very businesslike, "please get in touch as soon as possible."

Upstairs Hazel was awake after all; he found her reading. "Who was that?" she said.

"Who was what?"

A year ago his response would have upset her; six months ago she would've raised her voice; last month she would've slammed down the phone. Now she simply repeated her question. "The doorbell. Whoever you were talking to."

"Mrs. Craig. I was just telling her about the roofer. I didn't want her to be startled when a man on a ladder appeared outside her house."

Why am I doing this? he wondered, sitting on the edge of the bed. The answer perfumed the air, sweet as violets: because I can.

It had happened like this before, Charlotte thought. When only disaster lay ahead, when the horizon was dark in all directions, when she understood why people jumped from high buildings or into deep rivers, at that very moment some long-forgotten source of help, or at least distraction, would appear. She stumbled out of Cedric's, back to the Marylebone Road. Not a single friendly face rose before her; home, never a refuge at the best of times, was out of the question. Then a bus bearing the legend ARCHWAY pulled up, and at once she had a destination. She clambered aboard, proffering one of Cedric's pounds. She wished now she'd taken every penny and eaten the last biscuits too.

She took a seat halfway between an elderly couple and a tired-looking woman in a suit. "Lovely upholstery," the man of the couple was saying loudly. Charlotte spotted the pink knob of a hearing aid. "Fabric like that will see you into the next century. Goes with anything."

"Very easy on the eye," his companion agreed.

He's not worth my little finger, Charlotte thought. Ginny and Luke had tried to warn her. Ten years younger, Ginny had argued. He'll just take what he wants and throw you over. But Charlotte had told her she was being fuddy-duddy. Hadn't Ginny heard younger men and older women were all the rage nowadays?

The man had moved on to webbing: "the heart of a good chair." Like it or not, Charlotte thought as they slid into the underpass, men did act their age. And how old was Donald Early? When he was her tutor at RADA, he already seemed middle-aged, which probably meant between twenty-six and thirty-nine. Since then, she'd run into him periodically at the theatre. And last year they had met at the Chelsea Flower Show. She'd been there with Bernie and Rory, still a couple in those days. They were arguing over a blue rose—"Unnatural," Rory claimed—when a voice said, "Ms. Granger?"

She and Bernie both looked up to see Mr. Early in a white linen suit, standing beside a white rose. Charlotte made the introductions. "Enchanted," said Mr. Early. "This is magnificent, isn't it? Sometimes I think it's the single great sorrow of my life that I don't have a green thumb."

Rory said he was the same. Charlotte, not to be left out, made a joke about nursing the inner green thumb. "I like that," said Mr. Early. "Do come to tea sometime. I have open house on the first Sunday of each month." And then—Rory said afterwards it was too camp for words, but she and Bernie had defended Mr. Early's sense of style—he produced a silver case and handed her a card.

A couple of months later, at loose ends one Sunday, Charlotte had knocked at his door and been welcomed to jasmine tea and cucumber sandwiches. She enjoyed the odd mix of Mr. Early's neighbours, designer friends, and, thank god, only one other actor. An elderly opera singer made up a limerick in her honour, predictably rhyming Charlotte with harlot, and a hairdresser had lectured her about selenium, four brazil nuts contained all one's daily needs; but what had stayed with her and now drew her back was a conversation with her host. They were in the kitchen, waiting for the kettle to boil, when he remarked, sotto voce, "I used to believe there were no criminals in love, but the older I get"—he dipped his glowing head—"the more certain I am that there are some people, not many but a few, who ought to be shipped off to a desert island where they can torment one another and leave the rest of us in peace. Earl Grey, or more jasmine?"

"Jasmine," Charlotte said. Walter, she thought.

Now she couldn't remember the house number or even the name of the street, though she knew it was off the Holloway Road with a garage on the corner. Once the bus passed the Nag's Head, she went and stood beside the driver. Normally she would've joined in his rendition of "Brown-Eyed Girl." Tonight she simply peered out of the window until a BP sign came into view. "Safe home," he said, launching into "Yesterday."

As the bus pulled away, doubt washed over her. What on

earth was she doing turning up on some acquaintance's door-step at eleven at night? Wasn't Cedric a warning against sur-prise visits? But she had no choice. At whatever cost, she needed company. She set off down the right-hand pavement, studying the drawn curtains and shadowy front doors, certain it was on this side. Some of the houses were entirely dark, or lit only by the blue god. Others emitted thumping, raucous music, which seemed to rule out Mr. Early. Then she was at a side street and knew she'd gone too far.

This time she examined both sides of the road and, halfway along, was rewarded by a wrought-iron gate on the left. Yes, that looked familiar, and the upstairs windows were reassur-ingly bright. Without hesitation she marched up the mosaic path and seized the dolphin knocker. Presently the hall light came on. "Who is it?" called Mr. Early.

"Me. Charlotte Granger." At her back a car grumbled. Everything hung in the balance. After her long days, long weeks, of rejection, here she was, her entire self, on this doorstep seeking admission. If Mr. Early sent her away, she could not imagine what she would do.

"Ms. Granger. What a pleasant surprise." He kissed her cheek and showed her upstairs to the room whose window she had seen from the street.

Charlotte registered the clutter, nothing like hers, and that the room was even cosier than Cedric's. Then Mr. Early was helping her out of her coat and offering Horlicks. "I'd rather have a drink," she confessed.

"Certainly. I have the usual wine, gin, Scotch, those Christ-massy drinks like amaretto and Bailey's. Name your poison."

"Scotch, please."

Alone, she sank into a wicker armchair and surveyed her surroundings. A few minutes before, she might have regarded the heads as part of that condemning chorus—you lazy freak, can't act your way out of a paper bag—but now they seemed to be nodding approval of her many and generous talents. What was she going to say when Mr. Early asked why she was here? For once, nothing came to mind and it didn't matter.

He returned with a tray: a bottle of Scotch, two tumblers, a bowl of ice, a jug of water. "I forgot to ask how you like it," he said.

She settled for one ice cube and a splash so as not to seem like a lush. Mr. Early, unabashed, had his neat. "Bottoms up."

"Bottoms up." To her horror, as the first sip slid down, her eyes grew watery. She stared fixedly at her host's elegant ankles, trying to listen as he talked about the rush job he was doing. "Twenty heads in six weeks. I feel like a factory. I keep focussing on my Umbrian holiday. The church at Orvieto, I tell myself with the eyelashes. Todi, I say over the hair."

"I've never been to Italy," she managed.

"Oh, you should. It's glorious. Whenever I come back, I'm struck all over again by what an ugly city London is, poor old thing. No wonder we're not better people. Another?"

Charlotte looked down in surprise. Her glass was empty. How had that happened? "Please," she said. "Neat."

Mr. Early stood up, poured her a generous measure, and sat down again. As if the second whisky had been an invitation, Charlotte began to talk: about Mr. Aziz and the woman at British Telecom, about Bernadette's stinginess and how cross Ginny was that she'd missed the audition, and her plan for renting out her flat. Mr. Early kept nodding and saying the right thing— how ghastly; oh, I am sorry; good for you—until, quite suddenly, she was telling him about Walter and not crying, not a tear, but yelping with high-pitched laughter.

Then he was shaking her gently. "Stop. Take a deep breath and think of Queen Victoria." Gradually she subsided into breathless hiccups. When she could once again speak, she explained she hadn't eaten today, which was true, save for Cedric's biscuits.

Instantly Mr. Early was all sympathy and self-reproach. He hadn't even asked if she was hungry. And then they were in the kitchen, Charlotte minding the toaster while Mr. Early beat eggs and sizzled butter in the pan. Suddenly she remembered Jason and his radio programme. "I recommended you as a guest. Can you pass the butter? I think you'd be brilliant. And Jason was very interested. I'm sure he'll be calling soon, if he hasn't already."

"How kind. Shall we have a dash of Parmesan in the eggs?"

"Please," said Charlotte, her mouth full of freshly buttered toast.

At the table there was an awkward moment when she was about to set the plates down on the white cloth and Mr. Early quickly whisked mats into place. Who does he think I am, she thought, Eliza Doolittle? But when he spooned almost twice as many eggs onto her plate as his own, all was forgiven. Unlike everyone else in her life, here was someone who didn't judge her, which in a way was even better than Jason's admiration, with its fragile demands.

Across the table Mr. Early balanced eggs on the back of his fork and talked about how much easier it had been for him to negotiate mad cow disease than the egg scare a few years ago. "Sometimes I think there's nothing left on the planet that's safe to eat. I mean," he explicated neatly with his fork, "here we are, feasting on free-range eggs and organic bread, and I still worry that I'll open the paper tomorrow and discover it was bad for us. I can't get over the shame of living in a country where the water isn't fit to drink."

Reaching for another slice of toast, Charlotte offered her own theory about maintaining a certain level of toxicity;

keeping yourself too pure made you vulnerable to every chemical that came along.

"You have a point," said Mr. Early. "One doesn't want to become too rarified." His glance slipped over her shoulder. "This has been a treat, our midnight feast, but I'm afraid I must get back to work." So, her rival was a clock. "I hope it won't seem inhospitable if I call you a minicab."

"Oh." She gazed at her empty plate, shining from a last vigorous pass with the toast. Why can't I stay, she wanted to ask. You've got plenty of room. I'll be no trouble. See how nicely I made the toast. How little space I take up.

"A tot for the road?" he offered. "Another cup of tea? You must let me pay for the cab. It's understood between us artists that whoever is in work picks up the check."

"More tea would be perfect." Even as she spoke, Charlotte was rising gracefully, moving towards the kitchen. Lady Granger to the rescue. She would leave not a second sooner than she had to. She filled the kettle to the brim and was back in her seat, saying gaily, "Don't you get tired of working alone? Head after head?"

"Sometimes, but I do have a couple of assistants. One of them would be here now if she hadn't caught a cold. Besides, I like having time to myself. Really, that was one of the trickiest aspects of theatre for me: all the socialising."

Charlotte was focussing on her character. Charm, she thought, not sex. Were all the buttons of her blouse secure? She held up her hand—hark, the kettle—and, following her gesture out to the kitchen, made tea meticulously. Back at the table she announced with a flourish, "I'll be Mother." A splash landed near the jam, a brown comma punctuating the snowy cloth; no reason to think he'd notice. "Milk? Sugar?"

"Let me rinse the cups," said Mr. Early hastily.

When they were seated and poured, Charlotte raised her

brimming cup. "Thanks for rescuing me." She had meant to talk about Struan and the film; instead she found herself asking if she could help Mr. Early. "I was always good at crafts. I made a papier-mâché vase that my mother kept for years. And I don't mind being a dogsbody. I can go to the shops, deal with the plumber, anything. You won't have to pay me. Just food and the odd fiver."

Mr. Early hitched up his glasses, pushed his cup aside. "My dear Charlotte, you're much too talented to be anybody's dogsbody. I couldn't possibly permit it, and to be frank, what I do, although not exactly complicated, does take a while to learn. You already have your skill, and thank goodness it's not lolly-gagging around with dummies.

"I know the last few months have been dreary, but that is the nature of the artistic life. We all have our periods of appreciation and depreciation. Let me tell you a story."

His voice was mellifluous, respectful, courteous, and, inside, Charlotte was screaming, *Stop!* But as he spoke, sentence by sentence, her grief and rage ebbed until she was able to hear his words.

"So Orlando went mad," said Mr. Early, "and his friend Astolfo made the first space journey on his behalf. He travelled to the moon and there, in the valley of lost things, he discovered everything that had gone missing on earth: umbrellas, gloves, tempers, dogs, reputations. He even came across some of his own wits, which he'd never noticed were gone. Deep in the valley he found the vial containing Orlando's lost wits, and brought it back to earth. Thus Orlando was restored to sanity and able to woo his lady fair."

Before Charlotte grasped what was happening, Mr. Early had picked up the phone and was ordering a cab. Then he left the room and returned, her coat in one hand, the bottle of Scotch in the other. He handed her the former and poured a stiff measure from the latter. The door knocker sounded as Charlotte drained the glass; tears came again to her eyes.

"Thanks," she said, struggling into her coat.

Heedless of the cold, Mr. Early showed her into the cab. "I have an account with them," he said, and pressed something into her hand.

Charlotte gave her address and, leaning back against the lumpy seat, asked the driver to turn up the radio. Wailing music engulfed her: Kurdish perhaps? With every yard they travelled, the Scotch grew more potent, until the streets and houses and other cars were rising up and flipping over and over. Doing cartwheels, thought Charlotte. Oops-a-daisy.

On the fourth attempt, her key opened the door of her flat. Lurching across the threshold, she spotted a postcard of Trafalgar Square. One of her neighbours must have brought it upstairs. *Charlie, where are you? I've been trying to phone. Please come to supper tomorrow. Bernie.*

chapter 8

A stupid door, Freddie thought, eyeing the brass numbers screwed crooked above the letter box. Instead of the graceful Victorian doors of the rest of the street, two arched panes of glass set in neat panelling, number 41's was a slab of meaty wood, with one of those little rectangles of wavy glass at face level. No knocker, of course, just a plastic bell that shrilled beneath his finger. He backed across the street.

The roof was not among the swaybacks he had noticed on his nocturnal visit. In fact, considering the original Welsh slate, it was in remarkably good shape. And next door, number 39 wasn't bad. He and Trevor had prolonged debates about artificial versus natural slate. Usually I'm with you, Freddie, Trevor said, but real slate is a hassle. It weighs a ton and breaks if you sneeze. Against such pragmatism Freddie offered aesthetics and durability. Now he felt vindicated by the two roofs, both bearing up gracefully, whereas the house across the street, the victim of a particularly nasty fake slate, looked like a great-aunt wearing her niece's hat.

He was still tut-tutting when he realised the bell had produced results—a woman in blue pyjamas was peering up and down the street. "Hey," Freddie called. Not pyjamas, he thought, walking towards the gate: sweats. She watched him approach with a secret, dreamy expression quite different from that with which most women greeted his appearance on their doorsteps. In the cloudy afternoon light her skin glimmered, like the abalone shells he used to come across on the beach near Stanford.

"I'm Freddie Adams," he said, feeling strangely breathless. "The roofer."

Her eyes, and he would not have thought it possible, widened still further. With one hand she held tight to the ugly door. "Are we expecting you?"

"A Mr. Littleton phoned and said there was a problem with the roof at this address."

"I don't know anything about that. At least"—she tilted slightly—"I don't think I do. You'd better come in and wait. Jonathan's on the phone."

"Will he be long?"

"I don't know."

A small movement of the head suggested she was just as annoyed by her ignorance as he might be. He could not help noticing that her hair needed washing. "Can you . . ." he started to say and, seeing her face, fell silent.

"Please." She let go of the door and stepped back into the hall.

Many of the houses Freddie entered were in this state, half renovated, as if both owners and workmen, often the same, had pricked their fingers and forgotten even the possibility of finishing. Here the hall walls had been left stripped. That no immediate change was expected seemed indicated by the pictures hung on the scarred plaster. The kitchen, an immaculate yellow, was a pleasant surprise.

The woman sat down at the table. "If you want to make tea, go ahead. Jonathan is upstairs."

"No, but thanks." He sat across from her. The light above the table made her less pale. Her hair when clean would probably be the colour of straw. "Are you sick? I mean as in ill, not as in throwing up."

"Yes," she said simply. "Something happened and now I have seizures. That's why I can't go upstairs alone or make a cup of tea."

"You don't look like you have seizures. What's your name?"

"Hazel. Is there a seizures look?"

"I'm Freddie," he said, forgetting his earlier introduction. "There certainly was when I was at Lourdes. You could tell the people who went in for them. Everything had gotten shaken loose. They didn't know their heads from a hole in the ground. One old guy, Matthieu, was convinced I was his father. Am I a good boy, Papa? he kept asking. Then he'd start rocking like a Holy Roller."

The word "Roller" had barely left his lips when a sense of his own tactlessness hit him. What was he *thinking*? Hazel was staring towards the floor; he wished he knew her well enough to squeeze her hand or tell her a joke. "That was different, though," he said firmly.

"Why?"

"Because most of the people were either lifelong sufferers—they'd never had a chance to get their minds organised—or very elderly. The seizures were another part of the body breaking down. You're neither."

"I got hit on the head." She mimed a blow, fist to forehead, and again glanced down, just long enough for Freddie to wonder if she was still upset, then back up, and instead he wondered if there was a name for eyes like that, with the white visible all the way around the iris. "What were you doing at Lourdes?" she asked. "Do you have seizures?"

"Only the ordinary kind," Freddie said, charmed by her readiness to include him. He was in the middle of telling her about the stretcher bearers when footsteps sounded in the hall.

"Hazel?"

As Mr. Littleton came through the door, Freddie's hackles rose. He recognised the kind of guy who claimed to be six foot when he was barely five-ten. The lower part of Littleton's face looked as if it had been dipped in iron filings. But that wasn't the problem. Nor were his clothes, a trendy black turtleneck and cords. No, it was his eyes, the complete opposite of Hazel's, so guarded that he might as well have been wearing shades.

"Who are you?" he demanded, fists muzzled by his sides.

Again Freddie accounted for his presence. "Hazel let me in," he added, and watched in amazement as the man's eyes clicked like a combination lock. Was it because he'd used her name? "Could I see the roof? I'm on a pretty tight schedule."

Littleton laid a hand on Hazel's shoulder. "Are you all right, darling?"

Beneath his touch she seemed to shrink. "I think so."

Freddie followed Littleton into the hall and up the blue-carpeted stairs to a room at the back of the house—a study, judging by the books and computer. "There," said Littleton, pointing to a corner where the wallpaper dimpled and peeled.

"How long has it been like this?"

"Since Christmas." For a second he sounded like a normal person. He offered a chair to stand on.

"Thanks. You may need new plaster. Once it gets this soggy, it doesn't always dry out right."

"Not your problem."

Why am I here? thought Freddie, slipping his hand
through the seams in the paper. The answers lined up neatly.
Because Trevor had recommended him while he and his mother
were visiting cousins in Newcastle, and because Felicity had
been there when Mr. Littleton phoned again. Since the empty-
cupboards fiasco, he didn't dare turn down jobs in her hearing.
But surely even she wouldn't have wished Littleton on him. He
had a sudden flash of his father's reaction when he quit his summer job bagging groceries. The trouble with you, Frederick, is
you don't know how to take orders.

"What's your opinion?" Littleton was leaning on the
windowsill; against the light all Freddie could see was the black
of his turtleneck and the sheen of his jaw.

"My opinion," said Freddie, hopping off the chair, "is that
I'd better have a look outside."

This time, the first since Mr. Early's, he had no problem
with the ladder. He carried it through the side door, propped it
against the back wall, and climbed steadily. No slates missing
or cracked. No nails gone, as far as he could tell. The rear roof,
like the front, was in surprisingly good repair.

On the ground again, he tried the back door and stepped
inside. "I'm going to have another look upstairs," he called in
the direction of the living-room. Silence. She's sick, he thought,
and he's a jerk. Then he reminded himself that he was no longer
a stretcher bearer—Hazel and her seizures were none of his
business—and headed up the powder-blue stairs.

Without Littleton's glowering presence, he felt free to take
in his surroundings. On the desk were stacks of files with dates
and categories on the spine: December 1993, January 1994,
plumbing, roofs, subsidence. Perhaps the guy worked in con-
struction. The damp patch was farther over than he'd remembered, and the wetness, he saw now, was worse by the party

wall. Outside, back up the ladder, he discovered the flashing loose in several places; on the other side, at number 39, it was virtually flapping in the breeze.

With some people he'd have bid low to get the job, worked almost for nothing, but with this guy he guessed that would be a mistake. He carried the ladder round the house and stayed there, leaning on the wall, until he had a diagram and a list of figures. Then he rang the bell.

"Found the problem?" Littleton said, hands in pockets.

No way, Freddie thought, he was going to be invited in again. He reported the faulty flashing, and Littleton responded with a barrage of questions: how much, when, would Trevor guarantee his work? Freddie gave his estimate, explaining the variables.

Littleton nodded. "That sounds in line with Trevor's prices. When could you come?"

"Tuesday?" Another gamble—he might have said tomorrow—but a workman with no work is suspicious, and Littleton grudgingly agreed.

Although he had sworn not to offer one more shred of advice, Freddie mentioned it might be worth checking whether the insurance would cover the damage. Most of his customers were glad of such suggestions, but Littleton simply said, "See you on Tuesday."

As the door shut behind him, Freddie started to recite Reds scores under his breath. Reds 5, Braves 3; Reds 1, Dodgers 4. He was almost at the corner when he heard a shout. "Your ladder," called Littleton. "You're not going to leave it, are you?"

"No, just getting the van." Reds 2, Giants 6. Reds 3, Cardinals 2. He hadn't been so rattled since that day at Mr. Early's when the sky was falling.

· · ·

"I suppose that's a good idea." Hazel tweaked a couple of dead fronds off a fern; an editor she worked for, Jonathan forgot which one, had sent it along with a get-well card. "Assuming she's not some vixen. You could do with a break from me."

He couldn't see her face, bent over the plant, but he could tell from her sullen tones that she was less than thrilled at the news of Bernadette. "Of course she's not a vixen," he said, "and I don't need a break from you, silly goose." Odd how endearments that would once have made him cringe now sprang from his lips. "But I do have to start showing up at the office. If you don't like her," he added, "we'll find someone else. Nothing that you don't want is going to happen."

"Is that a joke?" She turned to look at him and, tossing the fronds into the air, left the room.

Jonathan watched her go. He couldn't be sure when he had begun to think of sex all the time. After Maud left the night before, he had, scarcely daring to breathe, climbed into bed beside Hazel. She was already asleep, in one of her quiet phases, and he hoped that instinct would prevail, but when he pressed his lips to hers she lay motionless and when he touched her breast she shrugged his hand away. He stayed for an hour before getting up to prowl the house and, eventually, bring himself off in the spare room. Now, as she returned with a jug of water, he found himself scrutinising her thick green jumper, wishing her jeans were less enveloping.

"Sorry," she said, drenching the cheese plant. "Wobbly moment. What time do we have to be at the hospital?"

"That's not until tomorrow, ten a.m." He spoke unthinkingly. Then he saw her lips quiver. "Darling, it's all right. Hogarth just wants to see how you're doing. There won't be any students." Towards the end of her stay in hospital, Hazel had grown to detest the medical students who flocked to her bedside, asking the same questions over and over. I feel like an exhibit, she'd said. The world's craziest woman. You ought to charge admission.

"No, it's not that." She clutched the jug. "I was so sure the appointment was today. I know I've lost part of the past. What I can't bear is losing the present too. It makes me feel there's nothing I can count on."

He came over and put his hands on her shoulders. "You can count on me. I may have made a mistake when I first told you. You shouldn't assume you're the only one who gets things wrong."

Slowly, as if the air between them had thickened, she leaned against him. He stroked her hair, longer now than he had ever seen it.

Later that afternoon, when Maud arrived, Jonathan visited the hives. In the cold weather he took his veil and gloves but decided against the smoker; the poor beasts had enough to put up with. He felt his usual reluctance at leaving the women together, but walking to the bottom of the garden he was glad to be outdoors, and alone. Lighted windows glowed in his neighbours' houses, and in the lint-coloured sky a waxing moon hung paper-thin. He heard the sharpness of his own footsteps and, from the Holloway Road, a hundred yards away, the undifferentiated throb of traffic. Dimly he recalled the charts in some schoolbook showing how sound waves alter with temperature.

At the hives he pressed his ear to each in turn, like a doctor listening through his stethoscope. All three emitted a faint, reassuring hum. Not exactly a buzz, he had explained to Hazel, but the sound of the bees clustered together, wings rubbing, legs touching. And when he lifted off the lids his confidence was confirmed. A few bodies on the floor of the middle hive, but fewer than last week, and almost none in the other two. He filled up the sugar and water and checked the insulation. The last month of winter was often the most dangerous; the bees might be tricked by a brief spell of warm weather, or exhaust their supplies of food.

By the time he turned back the moon had gained weight, and in his yellow kitchen the two women were talking. He loitered for a moment beneath the elder tree. Hazel was speaking, Maud nodding and listening. Then she spoke, and Hazel laughed and raised her hand to pat her chest.

As he came in, silence ruled. Hazel sat down, like a schoolgirl caught frolicking out of her desk. "Everything all right," said Maud, "down at the hives?"

"Fine. What was the joke?"

"What joke?" said Hazel.

"I saw you laughing." He gestured behind him. "From the garden."

"Oh, nothing. We were just talking."

Before he could question her further, Maud jumped in. "We were saying it would be useful to get one of those wall calendars. That way you can keep track of the nurse, doctors' appointments, whatever."

Jonathan hung up his veil. Keep calm, he told himself, it's only a calendar. But it was a glimpse of what he dreaded: the women forming an alliance that would steal Hazel away from him again, bit by bit. Suddenly he realised they were both watching him, waiting. "Good idea," he said. "I'll bring one home from the office."

They had also planned the evening. The three of them would make risotto, and Maud had rented a video. "Now that George and Nora are gone," she said, "we can revert to our old, bad ways." She left the kitchen and music filled the room. Jonathan paused in peeling an onion. He couldn't name the singer but he recognised one of Hazel's favourites and, after a few more bars, that it dated from the missing years. Christ. He set down the onion. Could he plead a headache or claim he wanted to hear the news?

"This is what we used to do," Maud said cheerfully. "Listen to music and cook. Do we have any wine?"

"Red or white?" said Jonathan.

"Whatever's easiest. You know me—I'll drink anything." She launched into an account of her first wedding anniversary. Her husband had bought vintage wines for each course of the dinner they'd planned, and she and a friend had polished off two of the bottles the night before. "It was like Vesuvius when he found them in the dustbin next morning. Looking back, I think that was the beginning of the end. I never recovered from him being so snotty, and he never recovered from my lack of penitence."

"How was the wine?" Hazel was slicing mushrooms.

"Okay, as far as I recall. Jan and I were having a heart-to-heart. We weren't worrying about tannin and body."

A new song started. Hazel stopped slicing, head cocked. "What is this music?"

"Michelle Shocked," said Maud. "You used to like her."

He watched Hazel's eyes, the corners of her mouth. She sat very still and then, praise be, the knife fell from her hand and she was gone, a good neck-locking, heel-drumming, all-out seizure. He held her head while Maud rushed to pull chairs out of the way.

"Who will pay?" Hazel asked. "Stupid bugger."

"Oh, god," said Maud.

"Fetch a blanket and a flannel."

The seizure was the worst since the hospital. Foam dabbed her lips. She kicked frantically. "Shall I call an ambulance?" asked Maud, offering the flannel.

"Not yet. Turn off that damned music." She scuttled out of the room again. "Hazel, it's all right. I'm here. Don't fight it. Relax. You're quite safe."

He wrapped his arms and legs around her, a straitjacket of affection. But the seizure went on and on. Her limbs thrashed, and he could feel his grip weakening. Maud hovered anxiously. Maybe she was right. "Give it one more minute," he said. "She'd hate to end up back in hospital."

As if she heard his threat, Hazel began to kick less strongly; her breathing slowed; soon she was barely trembling. Maud suggested they carry her up to bed. They tucked her in and he managed to give her her eight o'clock pills.

Back in the kitchen, Maud poured them each a brimming glass of wine. He dragged the chairs over to the table, and they collapsed. "Hell's bells," said Maud. Beneath her red shirt her breasts moved rapidly. "Just when it seems she's getting better, something like this happens. I can't imagine how she feels."

"Exhausted, for one thing." He himself felt a shaky exhilaration, as if he'd won a race or a fight.

"You were great." She smiled. "So calm. I'm sure she can sense what's going on, and people panicking only makes it worse."

"I've had a bit of practice these last few weeks."

"This was a bad one, though, wasn't it?"

He nodded. He was longing to ask if she thought the music might have been a factor, but hesitated to utter even a syllable that would break their unspoken truce. "I'm starving," he said.

"Me too." She sounded surprised. "I can make risotto if there's a recipe. Did you finish the onion?"

"Almost."

Half an hour later they were on the sofa watching *Truly, Madly, Deeply*. Jonathan had been to check on Hazel twice. Each time she was sleeping soundly, with no sign of the disruption that had knocked her to the floor. He switched on the monitor he had bought and set the listening device on the table.

Around nine they paused. Maud cleared the plates and he opened a second bottle of wine. When they sat down again, the distance between them, he noticed, had narrowed; during the next twenty minutes, he could not have said quite how, they edged closer and closer until, ineluctably, their bodies adjoined from shoulder to ankle. A single whimper came from the monitor and, as they both turned to listen, was supplanted by the soft, oceanic sound of breathing.

At the end of the film, Jonathan pressed rewind, drained his glass, and let his arms encircle Maud. We're old friends, he was thinking; she slipped her hand inside his shirt, he reciprocated, and they were falling upon each other.

"Come," she said, and they moved to the hearth rug.

Jonathan's brain, the thinking part of him, seemed to have taken a leave of absence. This ought to have been one of the most astonishing events of his life, fucking Maud on the living-room floor, the TV glimmering above them, but he was all skin and blood, tongue and prick. Even more astonishing, Maud was in the same state, so naked, so unabashed, he could scarcely believe this was Hazel's dour friend. Who would've thought she could utter such groans as he ground himself against her?

Afterwards, the room roared with silence. Now surely, thought Jonathan, I'll know I've done something mad, unforgivable. No such sentiments, however, came into view. Instead he felt calmer than he had in months; at last he'd acted with his whole self. As for Maud, whom he expected any moment to raise the flag of propriety, she nuzzled her head against his shoulder and murmured his name. It was quite possible, he thought, his breathing lapsing into time with the monitor, that neither of them would ever move again.

When he opened his eyes, Maud was saying something about the bathroom and slowly unwrapping herself from him. She stood over him, naked. Come back, he thought. But she was pulling on her clothes, clever girl, and leaving the room. Alone, he gazed up at the odd W-shaped crack he had filled both times he painted the ceiling, and which always reappeared within a month. Cassiopeia.

Maud was back, holding out a glass of water. "You'll get cold."

Sitting up to drink, he realised he already was and that his ardour for Maud had cooled too. While he swallowed half the water, the last glimmerings died away. He was desperate to be rid of her. The transformation was over, for both of them. She perched on the sofa, knees primly together, hands clasped in her lap. As he reached for his trousers, she said, "I'll kip here, if it's all right with you."

No, he wanted to say. Absolutely not. Just the thought of her under the same roof made his palms itch. He'd happily have bought her a room at the Ritz. But she overruled all suggestions: a cab, a lift.

"I'm afraid I'm not up to cycling," she said coyly, "and I don't want to leave the bike, because I need it in the morning."

"Oh, do what you want," he said at last. "You know where everything is." He turned away but not before he'd glimpsed, with pleasure, her shocked expression.

chapter 9

Charlotte lay back, enjoying the spectacle of her small breasts cresting the foam. A nymph, Walter had called her once, a wood nymph. No, think instead of herself and Bernie, aged eight and ten, standing at the ends of their beds, swinging their arms, chanting, *I must, I must, develop the bust.* This isn't working, Bernie had declared after their third evening. You have to do it for ages, Charlotte had said, months and months. But she soon followed Bernie's example and returned to bed. Later, to their mutual fury, their father had begun to refer to them as his nubile lassies. Old goat, thought Charlotte, closing her eyes and sinking beneath the surface.

In the warm, underwater world a dull drilling sound reached her. She was running out of breath when she recognised it: her alarm clock reminding her that her two prospective tenants were due today, Renee at noon, Mike at one. She was out of the bath in a flash. No time for primping, just a squeeze of toothpaste and yesterday's clothes. Then she turned on every possible light, unfurled the roll of black rubbish bags, and set to work.

She had only herself to blame for this crisis. In the days since her supper with Bernie she'd thrown out the odd newspaper, sprayed Mr. Sheen on the bathroom mirror, but after five minutes, ten at most, she would put aside the duster, find her coat, and head for Kilburn High Road. Stupid even to start, she reasoned, until she had a stretch of time.

From the moment Bernie had opened the door that evening, dressed like a normal person in jeans and a sweatshirt, and poured her a glass of wine without being asked, Charlotte had known that the wind was blowing from another quarter.

"Cheers," said Bernie. "By the way, there were some calls for you." She pushed a notepad across the table.

Charlotte started to apologise—at her wits' end, she'd listed her sister's number in the advertisement—but Bernie simply shrugged. "What can you do when your phone's on the blink?"

More and more mysterious. She put the pad aside and smiled cautiously. "Something smells wonderful. I hope you haven't been slaving."

"Chicken cacciatore, like Mum's." Bernie moved the salt shaker half an inch to the left, an inch to the right. "You must be thinking I've lost my mind. Last time you were here you suggested we do a deal and I told you to piss off. Well, now I'm desperate."

Watching her unfurrowed brow, Charlotte thought, she could never be an actress. Look at the way she said "desperate." Totally unconvincing. "What happened?" she asked.

Bernie ticked off items: Rory was doing overtime; the woman who collected Melissa and Oliver from school had found a new job, plus a highly unsuitable boyfriend; and she herself had been offered a private job twenty minutes away. "So," she gave a pinched smile, "how about you move in for three months. You'd promise not to make a mess or run up the phone bill. And you'd collect the children from school four afternoons a week and mind them until I got home."

"What about shopping?"

A happy vision of herself buying trolley loads of goodies with her sister's money was wiped out by Bernie saying she would take care of that. "I know we're like chalk and cheese," she went on, "but I do think we can help each other. In fact, I was going to suggest we write everything down and both sign it so there can't be misunderstandings later."

Charlotte nodded. As if an agreement ever solved anything. But that was Bernie for you: brittle and bloodless. And she was the smelly old cheese. "Where will I sleep?"

"Oliver's room. He and Melissa can double up."

"That'll make me popular." She scrunched up her face in imitation of Oliver, and they both laughed.

"Who's this?" Wineglass in hand, she paced the kitchen, shoulders hunched, jaw jutting.

"Rory, Rory to a T."

"He's an easy one." And then—the words flew out of her mouth—she asked why Bernie didn't take him back. "He loves you, he loves the kids, his not being around is making everything complicated. I know he behaved badly, but he is sorry. I don't understand why you can't forgive him."

She stopped, horrified. At last Bernie was doing what she wanted, and here she was trying to talk her out of it. Not daring to see the effect of her words, she stared at a picture on the cabinet, a blue cow towering over a red house.

"One," said Bernie, "it's none of your business. Two, you may think you know the whole story but you don't. Three, not everyone is a doormat. Four, I'm considering it. Your being here would mean I could see him without telling the kids."

A blue cow and a red house, thought Charlotte. *I must, I must, develop the bust.* She turned, doing her best to smile.

"Charlie, I'm sorry. If you're frustrated about me and Rory, then you're getting a glimpse of how I feel about you and almost . . ."

Some small, imploring gesture must have escaped Charlotte. Instead of launching into what was clearly an exhaustive list, Bernie went to check on the chicken and Charlotte excused herself. In the bathroom she scrubbed her hands and redid her eyeliner. Her fantasy about Bernie was coming true, so why did her heart, or was it some other organ, feel so heavy?

What took time, she discovered, was sorting. By eight-thirty she had filled only two bags, and if anything the mess was worse. Sipping her second Nescafé, Charlotte reconsidered. She must streamline. The newspapers, every last one, would go into rubbish bags. As for the clothes, they too deserved to be bagged, a first step to the long-awaited encounter with a washing machine. Everything that wasn't a newspaper or a garment would go into a third set of bags: miscellaneous.

Only the threat of Renee and Mike—ten-ants, ten-ants— kept her from climbing back onto the futon and pulling the covers over her head. At ten o'clock, on her fourth Nescafé, she finally forced herself to enter the bedroom; she hadn't so much as touched the doorknob in six months. Now what met her gaze was a pale, musty, utterly empty room. Not utterly empty; what was that little grey heap in one corner? Cautiously she approached, fearing something dead, and recognised, beneath a layer of dust, another of Walter's socks.

Back in the living-room, she seized the futon, dragged it into the bedroom, and dumped it on top of the sock. She piled on the duvet and pillows, swept the floor, and, choking on the swirl of dust, opened the window and swept again. A quick spray with Mr. Sheen and the air took on the plasticky smell that most people equated with cleanliness. Stepping back to survey her handiwork, she noticed for the first time that Walter had failed to take the curtains, which was somehow almost as upsetting as the sock.

By eleven the floor was clear and Charlotte was surrounded by a flock of bulging bags. She tried lining them up against a wall in the hope they might pass for sixties furniture, but even to her biased eye they remained, obdurately, rubbish bags. Then, as if some hitherto forgotten storage space might reveal itself, she scanned the room. Her gaze stopped at the window. Grey sky, not actually raining. She picked up the nearest bag and headed for the stairs: rubbish to the left of the door, clothes and miscellaneous to the right. After a dozen trips she counted nineteen bags along the pavement.

Upstairs, she wished she could experience triumph or at least satisfaction at the sight of the clean floor with the two rugs, the two armchairs covered with bright shawls, the row of posters, the bookcase filled with books, the several lamps, their scorched shades turned towards the wall. Instead, grief grabbed her. The place looked so nice, nicer than at any time since Walter left, and now here she was, handing it over to strangers and going back to live with her sister, like a child or, more precisely, an old maid. And what did it mean to have most of your possessions in rubbish bags on the pavement? You didn't have to be Madame Curie to know it meant your life was not in tiptop shape.

At five past twelve Charlotte opened the door to two immaculate, pale-skinned hand-holders, both dressed in black. Briefly she lurched again into the past: Walter and herself when they came house hunting years ago, although neither of them had ever been this small or this neat. Then she went into full hostess mode. "Charlotte Granger," she beamed. "Welcome. I hope you didn't have any trouble with directions."

Renee held out her free hand. In the clarion tones which on the phone had led Charlotte to expect someone taller and stouter, she introduced herself and her companion. "This is Ian," she boomed.

Ian mumbled something, certainly not hello, and kept his hand firmly in Renee's. They had, Charlotte noticed, identical sandy eyelashes. "Come in, come in," she said, flinging open the door in *Merry Wives of Windsor* fashion.

As they crossed the threshold, the phrase "pied-à-terre" died on her lips. She saw the flat for what it was, a tip. All the more reason to sparkle. "My humble abode, but I think you'll find it has everything you need." She pointed out the TV, the kitchen area, the armchairs, the lamps.

"Where do you eat?" asked Renee.

Pizza Hut, Charlotte wanted to say, the Trumpet, then realised Renee was enquiring about the lack of a table. "I loaned it to a neighbour, for his daughter's birthday party. He'll bring it back this evening."

"And . . . where . . . you . . . ?" said Ian.

"Mostly in Gloucestershire. I'm doing a film for the next few months. Otherwise I'll be with my sister in Barnsbury. She's a single parent, and I've promised to help out when I can."

Like the woman at British Telecom, Renee seemed impervious to the word "film." "So what exactly do you have in mind?"

"I'd like to sublet from this Sunday until the end of June. I'll pay the utilities, except for the phone." She faltered and went on to detail rent, security deposit, and the importance of forwarding mail and messages.

"We need a few minutes."

"Of course." Charlotte settled back in one of the armchairs

only to catch Renee's pointed stare. Already they were taking over. She huffed into the bathroom and leaned on the edge of the bath, absentmindedly arranging bottles of shampoo and bubble bath, blue and pink, amber and snow. Now, who could she borrow a table from? Maybe Louis would lend her one from the Trumpet.

"Ms. Granger," called Renee, and dutifully she trooped back to her own living-room.

"We'll take it," said Renee. "It's a bit primitive, but the dates are perfect." She got out her cheque book. "Who shall I make it payable to?"

Hastily Charlotte explained that given how soon they were moving in, she would need the security deposit and at least part of the rent in cash. "It's not that I don't trust you," she said, and it wasn't. For Renee to bounce a cheque was as unthinkable as for Bernie to wear an unironed blouse, but offering a cheque to her overdraft was like spitting into the Thames.

So it was decided. Charlotte put on her coat and walked with them to the hole in the wall, where they each received enviable wads of fresh notes. Whoopee, thought Charlotte. She was slipping the money into her purse, already planning lunch, when Renee asked for a receipt.

"A receipt?" She seemed to be surrounded these days by people who believed in pieces of paper. "I was going to do that on Sunday, but of course if you'd be more comfortable, I can scribble something now."

"We would," said Renee. Ian murmured a few words which she translated as a suggestion to go into the nearest pub.

While Charlotte leaned on a sticky table, Renee dictated a monotonously explicit account of their agreement. Each of them signed and Renee pocketed it, claiming she'd make a copy for Charlotte. Outside on the pavement, another murmur from Ian interrupted their handshakes. "About the phone?" said Renee.

And there was half the money gone as Charlotte assured them that it would be back on by Monday. "The whole street's complained, but you know British Telecom."

Walking home, somehow she had lost her desire for lunch, Charlotte caught sight of the row of rubbish bags and, pacing beside them, a tall, thin man in a bobble cap and anorak. Of course, Mike, the other would-be tenant. She stopped, wondering whether to introduce herself and buy him a consolation drink. He could be sex on legs, from this distance it was hard to tell, though the bobble cap was not encouraging. Just as she rehearsed her opening lines—"The daughter of a friend, I couldn't say no"—he bent to prod one of the bags. Charlotte turned and fled.

"Lovely," Hazel said. "If it's not too . . ."

From the landing Jonathan assumed she was talking to herself, perhaps practising a conversation she planned to have later, with Maud or with him, but as he crept down the stairs, hoping to hear more, the rhythm of her remarks alerted him to another possibility. He hurried into the living-room and found Hazel holding the phone. Since the hospital it had been an unwritten rule that she did not answer calls.

"No, no one can say for sure if it's permanent. I do get . . ."

Not Maud, not Nora. Diane, perhaps, or a colleague? An editor named Lucy had called twice in the last week. He strode across the room, hand outstretched. "Who is it?"

"So you'll come about four," said Hazel. "Yes, I'll tell him."

She replaced the receiver and, misunderstanding his gesture, reached for his hand. Her lips parted when he snatched it away, then she grasped the arms of the chair and said nothing.

"Who was that?" he insisted. "Who's coming at four?"

"Mrs. Craig." She looked deliberately past him.

He felt his eyeballs grow hot. "This afternoon isn't convenient."

"Did I forget something?"

Her gaze swung back to him, defiance gone, and again he thought, this is easy. He noticed her hair straggling over her shoulders. "You're having your hair cut," he said.

Before he could elaborate a time and place, Hazel was on her feet moving towards the door. Well, it wouldn't be hard to get an appointment on a weekday. His hand closed around the still-warm receiver and, to his surprise, Mrs. Craig's number appeared in his head. He had phoned her once from the hospital, to ask if she could take in some files the office were sending, and blurted out the plans for Hazel's convalescence. Poor Hazel, Mrs. Craig had said, but is that wise, after last year? Furious, he had explained that her return was her parents' suggestion and hung up.

Hazel reappeared. "It's not on the calendar."

"What's not?"

"The hairdresser. Maybe I didn't forget after all. Maybe you forgot to tell me." Her smile was somewhere between appealing and accusing. As Mrs. Craig's answering machine came on—"You have reached the Golden Road"—she shook her head. "If you're calling Mrs. Craig, she's doing massage this afternoon. We can rearrange the hairdresser. Anyway, I might like to let my hair grow. I could braid it again."

Massage, christ. He gave up and went over to the window. The sky was the colour of the pavement, bitter grey, and so was everything in between. Hazel had said rain was forecast, but no rain fell. Who knew what Mrs. Craig's jibe about last year referred to—he wouldn't put it past Hazel to have told her everything—yet, as their immediate neighbour, she was certainly privy to the crucial fact: Hazel had moved into her own flat. He had done so well with her parents, with Maud. Were his hopes about to founder on some indiscreet middle-aged woman? He stared at the pavement, fissured with dead grass, wondering if he could intercept her. But Hazel might catch him. And you couldn't dodge a visit from someone next door indefinitely.

A red trolley rolled into view, followed by the postman, a spindly, ginger-haired boy racing through the second post. That was it. He could write Mrs. Craig a letter and slip it through her door, even better than talking; no interruptions, no contradictions. He turned from the window meaning to be jolly, apologetic—"You know how she gets on my nerves"—to find Hazel gone.

The light was off in the kitchen, but he walked down the hall to be sure. The yellow walls, normally so welcoming, had succumbed to the universal gloom. The new calendar lay on the table. Under today's date, Hazel had scrawled, *Mrs. Craig— 4 o'clock.* She must've gone upstairs, another bad sign: Hazel venturing the stairs alone.

The bedroom, too, was empty. He touched the sheet, as if it might hold a trace of her. Then he checked the bathroom, chilly from an open window and smelling faintly of sandalwood soap and shit, Hazel's. How startled he'd been, when they first lived together, by her lack of embarrassment about such matters. Give it a minute, she would say. Gas-mask time. In the spare room, the bed was neatly made save for the hollowed pillow. For one dreadful moment Jonathan thought she had gone outside. Scratching his palms, he stepped back into the hall. And there she was, in the study, sitting on the floor, a book open on her lap.

"Hazel," he said gently. "What are you doing in the dark?"

"Oh," she shrugged, "wandering. Sometimes I feel so

cooped up. Were you reading this?" She held up the book about memory.

Odd how one became inured to danger, like a fireman whom only a raging inferno can startle into fear. He nodded. "I thought it might give me ideas how to help you. Anyway, shall we go for a walk? We could stop at the bakery and get something for tea."

"Crumpets," she closed the book. "We haven't had those in ages. Crumpets with honey."

Dear Mrs. Craig,

I'm sorry I wasn't available when you phoned. Much though we'd love to see you, I would certainly have said that Hazel isn't up to visitors yet but I know she'll be disappointed if you don't come in for a quick cup of tea.

I do want to explain that her condition is precarious. She still has frequent seizures and stress is a major factor. In view of this we (her doctor, her parents, and I) have been at pains not to bring up our difficulties of the last year. Like many couples, we've had our ups and downs, but I can confidently say our affection for each other is stronger than ever.

Please keep this in mind for the duration of your visit.

Jonathan Littleton

Not bad, he thought, rereading his briskly typed words. Firm and not neurotic, the cadences echoing one of his insurance reports: claims of subsidence at number 41 are greatly exaggerated. Doors and windows still function. The reference to the doctor was inspired. And if Mrs. Craig did let something slip, he'd be there to practise damage control.

At ten to four the bell rang. "Sorry to be early." Mrs. Craig held a jar of something purple in one hand and what he identified, at second glance, as a ginger root in the other. "For once all my appointments were on time." Her silver hair was pinned up in the style that Hazel claimed made her look especially like Virginia Woolf, though he'd never seen the resemblance.

Before he could ask about his letter, Hazel appeared from the living-room. "Mrs. Craig," she exclaimed.

Her hands full, Mrs. Craig inclined gracefully into Hazel's embrace and made the little humming sound Jonathan remembered as one of her most irritating habits. "You look radiant," she said, and, including both of them, "I see you still haven't finished the hall."

"Still?" said Hazel.

"Come in. We're in the kitchen." He gave Hazel a nudge in that direction. "Didn't you get my letter?" he muttered.

"Yes, I got it," Mrs. Craig said in a normal voice. She regarded him calmly until he turned away.

In the kitchen he put on the kettle and tore open the packet of crumpets, not a minute to lose. Hazel and Mrs. Craig sat down. "It's so good to see you," gushed Hazel.

"I should've come sooner," said Mrs. Craig, "but I worried about intruding while your parents were here. Tell me how you are. That's the important thing."

To the thrum of the kettle, the little pings of the toaster, Hazel described her seizures, her memory loss, her unsteady convalesence. "Wretched," said Mrs. Craig. "One minute you're walking down the street and the next—"

"I can't even make a cup of tea."

"Do you know when a seizure is imminent?"

"Sometimes." Jonathan watched her uneasily. "Last week there was a moment, a millisecond, before everything disappeared, when I understood what was happening."

"You saw an aura?"

Hazel reached for the sides of her chair. "Not exactly, but I could see the drip on the faucet, the filament of the light bulb, the whoosh of gas in the cooker." Her hands thrashed up and down. "That's not quite right, either. Seeing things separately wasn't so important. It was the connections between them." She gave a nervous laugh. "Whatever that means."

"More than most of us ever get," said Mrs. Craig. "That's what I tell my clients who've been injured: there *are* compensations. Illness shows us the world from a new angle. We can't dismiss that."

"I don't dismiss it. I hate it. Not the seizures so much, I could live with them, but the forgetting."

"But there's lots you do remember," said Mrs. Craig, "because here we are."

Knife pressed to crumpet, Jonathan froze. Should he stage a distraction, maybe drop the plate? All his anxiety had been focussed on what Mrs. Craig might say. He had not thought to worry about confidences in the other direction. Looking up, he found Mrs. Craig's eyes upon him; she raised a finger to her lips.

"That's true," agreed Hazel. "Nowadays I live in three worlds. There's the world I do remember. I can tell you about the Christmas I spent in Bombay, the day I met Jonathan, no problem. Then, the world I don't remember but where people and events linger like shadows. It's as if I'm wandering through one of those surrealist paintings with the wrapped statues, only I can't lift even a corner of the wrapping. Awful. But worse, much worse, is the notion of a third world where everything has vanished. The missing world."

Her hands had fallen still. She drew a shaky breath. Was she about to cry, Jonathan wondered. Please.

"I remember," she said softly, "lots of things. Just not the ones that matter. Sorry, minus ten for self-pity. When I'm better, I'm going to design a board game called Convalescence, a cross between Snakes and Ladders and Monopoly."

"I'd buy that." Mrs. Craig hummed. "My son gave me Therapy for Christmas. We won't speculate why."

"Have a crumpet," said Jonathan. They busied themselves with passing jam and honey, last year's crop. "If you pay attention," he told Mrs. Craig, "you can taste the lavender from your garden." She asked after his bees and nodded at his account of how well the hives were wintering.

"I bought you some beetroot," she said to Hazel. "It fortifies the blood, and the ginger will help with dizziness and nausea. Grate half a teaspoon to make tea. Do you have a good doctor?"

"He's doing his best." Hazel took another bite. "Sometimes, though, I can almost see him contemplating the article in the *BMJ* that will clinch his reputation. The Elephant Man, the Seizure Woman."

"Well, if you do decide you need a second opinion, I'm quite nicely connected, medically speaking."

"Mrs. Craig." He was amazed his voice could emerge from his choked throat. "Would you come and look at the study ceiling?"

For a few seconds he thought she was going to give him a cool glance and say no thanks, but she wiped her hands and got to her feet. Upstairs, he closed the study door. "What on earth do you think you're doing?" he whispered. "You come here without so much as a by your leave, you press Hazel to talk, you suggest her doctor isn't good enough."

"Jonathan."

Looking down, he saw he had seized her shoulders and was shaking her back and forth. "Hazel loves me," he said, letting go.

Mrs. Craig made her humming sound. "No one's saying

you haven't been terrific. From all accounts you saved her life. But that doesn't mean—"

He pushed past her, out of the room. I wouldn't save you first from a burning house, he thought. I wouldn't even save you last. Without knowing how, he was down in the hall, and face to face with Hazel.

"I need to lie down," she said. "Will you help me?"

The high-pitched squeal tapering to a breathless moan was Virginia, Freddie guessed, sounding off as usual. Over the last two weeks it had become increasingly hard to forget that he shared his apartment with five other creatures. At first he'd responded to every yip and whimper, and on several occasions had caught Agnes about to crush one of her tiny offspring. Was this also part of the Jungian archetype, he wondered, the mother as Medusa, or Moloch? But as the puppies grew, they learned to avoid Agnes and he in turn learned to ignore their outbursts and indeed remembered all the reasons he wasn't wild about dogs: smelly, demanding, omnivorous.

Virginia squealed again and fell silent. There might, he calculated, be as much as forty-five minutes before her siblings woke, demanding breakfast. Felicity, however, asleep beside him, was less predictable. At any moment she might bob up, ready for vigorous conversation. Fingers crossed, he turned towards her, hoping the small puffs of her breathing would carry him away from this apartment and the imperatives of the day. Imperatives . . . imperious . . . and then his father was teaching him to drive in the high-school parking lot. "Mirror, signal, manoeuvre, dummy," his father kept saying, but no matter how hard Freddie tried, he couldn't manage. "I'm doing my best, Dad," he pleaded. "So why are you always broke?" said his father.

Something tickled his nose. Opening his eyes, he found his

irascible parent replaced by Felicity, offering tea. "Thanks, sweetie. How long have you been up?"

"Two minutes." She slipped back into bed. "It's like a zoo in there. Yesterday I was thinking we could use some of the proceeds from the puppies to go to Paris for Easter."

"Neat. I'd love to be at Sacré-Coeur on Good Friday."

Felicity had long ceased to comment on his churchgoing, but now protested that she'd been thinking *pain au chocolat* and the Louvre, not choirboys and incense. "I never have grasped how you can go to mass and still be such a bad Catholic."

"Everyone's a bad something," said Freddie, pleased with the notion. "Kevin's a lousy anarchist, locking his door and hoarding personal property. You're a wobbly feminist, struggling with women in the workplace. Trevor's an inept Romeo, living with his mum."

"My difficulties at work have nothing to do with a failure of feminism," said Felicity, and began to describe the hotel in Montmartre where she'd stayed a few years ago.

A little hammer went tap, tap on Freddie's skull. Wake up, it said. Pay attention. Bitter experience had gradually taught him that what he regarded as pleasant conversation—we could do this, we could do that—was for Felicity a blueprint for the future. "Let me talk to Trev about selling the pups. We can't go anywhere until I get rid of them."

With perfect timing, fresh cries rose from the kitchen. "My turn for crowd control," said Freddie. Next door, the dogs were piled into one corner of the pen. Meanwhile, Agnes was ignoring them, as usual, and nudging her dish.

"Bad boy." He grabbed Connecticut and set him in the centre of the pen, separated the other three, and continued to the bathroom. While brushing his teeth, he caught himself, unawares, thinking of Hazel. Do you have seizures, she'd asked, her amazing eyes opening even wider. Maybe he should give her one of the puppies, for company. The day he was due to fix her roof had brought some of the worst weather of the year, rain and driving wind. Even Mr. Littleton had been cordial about rescheduling. Now, drying his hands, Freddie pictured a glowing head. He was ready, at last, for Mr. Early's roof. No big deal, just replacing a couple of slates. He could hardly remember why he'd gotten so bent out of shape.

Back in the bedroom, Felicity glanced up from her tome about the Pankhursts. "What are you doing?" she said, as he stepped into his underwear.

"Off to work. Another day, another dollar."

"You're joking."

He started to make a speech about not letting Trevor down; after all, he recommended most of Freddie's customers. Felicity was still staring, unconvinced. As a girl, she once told him, she'd wanted to be a detective.

"The truth is"—he pulled on a T-shirt—"it's either haul ass or starve. My father's a softy but, barring World War III, he's maxed out. Besides, my being broke is messing everything up. We don't have fun like we used to."

This was what he hated about love. You barely had to breathe the word before you were wriggling like a snake in the grass. The worst part was, it worked. Felicity was nodding, trying not to smile. "I'll feed our investment," she said.

Only when he heard the shuffle of slippers and saw Mr. Early standing in the doorway, radiant and bleary in an orange silk bathrobe, did Freddie realise that a phone call might have been a good move. The urge to action had been so strong he'd assumed Mr. Early felt it too. "I could come back later," he said, picking up his toolbox.

But Mr. Early after a slow start—"Goodness, Freddie," he fumbled with the sash of his robe—was looking more cheerful.

"No, no, I'm delighted to see you. For some reason I'm having a spate of unannounced callers these days." He led the way inside, not to the room of heads but to the kitchen. "I'm making porridge. Would you like some?"

"If there's enough."

Soon they were both sitting at the table, Freddie in the sturdy chair meant for guests, eating porridge with milk and brown sugar and drinking tea. "Typhoo," said Mr. Early. "I don't believe in anything fancy first thing. Forgive my being a simpleton, but to what do I owe this honour? Rain seems likely, and last week, when it was much pleasanter, you adamantly refused to come."

Beneath his benign blue gaze, Freddie struggled for an answer on the wavering line between truth and falsehood. "When I was here last time something happened"—well, that was true—"and ever since I've had a hard time leaving the couch. It was too dopey to tell you, so I kept making ridiculous excuses." He reached for the milk. "Sorry."

"You did seem a trifle out of sorts." Mr. Early ate a spoonful of porridge. "Jane came to collect some heads one night and reported that a man was watching the house. From her brief description, forgive me, I wondered if it might be you."

"Darn, and I thought I was invisible." He caught himself. "I hope I didn't scare her. Or worry you."

"Not worry, exactly. Puzzle. Here you were, always claiming to be about to fix my roof, never actually doing so, and at the same time making nocturnal expeditions to spy on my house. Well, it is eccentric to say the least."

Heavens to Betsy. Freddie stared at the remains of his porridge. Confronted by this account of his own behaviour, he was struck dumb. If he'd acted like this in Cincinnati, he'd be in the morgue.

"Let me tell you a story." Mr. Early gave his spoon a final

lick. "I'm feeling avuncular today. Years ago, in a repertory thea-tre, two young designers were jockeying for position. They'd each been asked to produce designs for Max Frisch's *Andorra*—an odd play about anti-Semitism and chauvinism, not often done these days. The director was based in London, and a day was chosen for him to visit the theatre, hold auditions, and decide between the designs.

"The morning of his visit, both the young men rose, washed at least minimally, dressed in their trendiest clothes, and pre-pared to leave for the theatre. But one of them discovered that the door of his room wouldn't open. It was on the fourth floor of a boarding house. Needless to say, no phone. He banged and shouted in vain. His room overlooked the garden. Eventually he lay down and fell asleep. When he woke up and tried the door again, it opened."

"And?" said Freddie. "I hope he ran all the way to the theatre, collared the director with his brilliant designs, and got the job."

"Alas, no. The designer who kept the appointment was given the commission. I was one of those young men, though probably not the one you think. I hate the idea you might resort to illegal methods out of some feeling that you can't ask for what you want."

As he spoke, Mr. Early reached for their bowls and, before Freddie could question him, stepped out to the kitchen. But which one was he? At first Freddie assumed he was the poor stooge on the bed; after all, he seemed to know his every move. Then, given his cautionary words, he thought he was the crook. So if Freddie thought he was the crook, did that mean he was the good guy? But if he really thought about it, he would've fig-ured Mr. Early for the good guy all the way, which of course meant he was the bad guy.

He was still tossing around the alternatives when Mr. Early sat down again. "Dare I enquire about my roof?"

"About your roof, I've been a doofus. The only time it felt okay going out was after dark, and one night I came here."

"And what changed?" said Mr. Early. "If you can talk about it without retiring to the sofa for a fortnight."

"Agnes had her puppies. Don't get me wrong. I'm not a sucker for animals, but somehow the whole business made the sky seem empty. And"—he fingered the milk jug—"I met a woman."

"Cupid's dart?"

"No, I have a girlfriend. This is something else." But what? Salvation? A reprise of Lourdes? "I don't know her very well," he ended lamely. "Can I do the dishes?"

"Dishwasher. Right now, what would raise my spirits is for you to have a go at the roof while I take a bath. If you're finished by lunchtime, I'll make you a sandwich. How's that for a deal? Breakfast and lunch, plus forty-seven pounds and a free confession."

"You're a peach."

As they stood up, Mr. Early said, "At the risk of being horribly impertinent, let me offer yet another word of advice. Guile is not your strong suit. You may think you're invisible, but you're the reverse."

"Crown Derby?" Freddie pointed at the milk jug.

"Worcester. They stole the pattern."

On the hall table Freddie saw the letter addressed to Donald Early, Esquire, still unopened.

chapter 10

"He says I'm getting better, but I always feel worse after seeing him." Kneeling on the floor, surrounded by playing cards, Hazel pressed her fingers to her temples as she described Hogarth's endless, probing questions. "I wish," she concluded mysteriously, "I had a brother or a sister."

Jonathan knelt on the other side of the cards. Above them, the Cassiopeia-shaped crack zigzagged across the ceiling. "You always used to say that you were glad we were both only children, that it meant we understood the peculiar pressure of our parents' undivided attention." Surely no harm, he thought, in one innocent memory.

"The trouble is, friends can disappear." Hazel let her hands fall. "That's what I've realised. I mean, look at Maud and me. We've been best friends for nearly six years, but if something came between us, if we quarrelled, we'd never see each other again." She turned over an eight of hearts, frowned, reached for another card.

Jonathan kept very still. She couldn't know what he and Maud had done on this very carpet only a few nights ago; just for a moment, though, he felt as if his head were transparent. Hazel had simply gazed in with her wide blue eyes and seen everything. Then he realised she was speaking again, asking him something. "Sorry?"

She repeated her request: to invite Steve and Diane for supper. "I didn't do so well with Mrs. Craig, but I have to keep trying."

"I'll give them a call," he said, and added that he thought Katie might have chickenpox.

When he had come downstairs that evening, long after Mrs. Craig let herself out, a note lay beneath the beetroot jar.

> Jonathan,
>   Sorry if I tired Hazel. Do let me know if there's anything I can do to help. I'm at home most days. Remember, Hazel isn't alone in the world.

Sanctimonious bitch, he'd muttered, and, turning on the cooker, held the note to the flame. Now, watching Hazel uncover the eight of spades, he cursed Mrs. Craig all over again. This was what always happened. Everything was fine between him and Hazel until something, someone intruded from the outside world; then difficulties sprang up like varroa mites, devouring the sweetness between them.

"Poor Katie," Hazel said and, to her cards, "Pathetic." She flipped them face down and swished them into a pack. Although the drugs made her fingers clumsy, her knack for shuffling had returned. "I had this idea," she went on, "we could make a timeline for the last three years. If you give me the main facts, I can learn them, like swotting for exams. And other people, Maud, Steve, and Diane, people at work—" she faltered—"will help to fill in the blanks."

Instantly he was on his feet, muttering about the hives, and out of the room. He had never left her alone; now, not bothering with the smoker or the veil, he strode through the kitchen and out of the back door. His blood rushed with doubts. He'd been living in a fairy tale of second chances. Things were surfacing beyond his control. *Hazel* was surfacing. He stood beside the hives, too miserable even to bend down and listen. Instead he found himself remembering Suzanne. How carefully she'd helped him check the supers for extra queens, how good she was about straining the honey. One of his hives that year was particularly docile. On an early date he drew out a frame and showed her how to stroke the bees, gently passing her hand over their many downy backs as if they formed a single beast. Do they enjoy it, she asked. Who can tell, he said. For the first time he wondered if he might have treated her badly. To be honest, he had known all along that she was in love with him.

And then, when Hazel learned the truth, her lips had turned pale. She had been in the study using his computer and, for reasons that remained murky, flipped through one of his old cheque books and discovered the monthly stubs marked S.B. Why didn't you tell me? she shouted. It isn't important, he repeated. Your having a child isn't important? Well, you didn't tell me about all your old boyfriends.

She kept bringing it up for days, weeks. If anyone had deceived anyone, he explained, Suzanne had deceived him. He'd never made any secret of his feelings about her, or about children. What if it had been the other way round, if I'd forced her to have a child? You'd think I was Genghis Khan.

You could still love the child, Hazel said. I send money, he protested, and knew at once that in her eyes this diminished him yet further.

In the corner of the garden by the wall he caught a flash of purple and gold, crocuses pushing up through the mat of drab grass. He turned to see Hazel walking towards him. She'd slipped his leather jacket on over her dress and was carrying something white. "Here," she said, holding out his veil. "I'm sorry."

"What for?"

"Jonathan, please."

And, wasn't this the miracle he always hoped for, his anger was gone, a red mist blown away. He had her, that was all that mattered. Looking down at the veil, it came to him: a way to secure his ownership. "I'm not angry. I had an idea, too, but I'm worried you won't like it."

"Try me." She smiled. A drop of water—a tear, he supposed—ran down her cheek.

He passed the veil lightly from hand to hand. "Let's get married?"

For a moment he thought she was having a seizure. She gave a small gasp; he felt her tremble. He started to say she didn't need to answer this minute but she was grabbing his hands, all over him. She had been so afraid he was losing patience; that was why she sometimes pushed herself. Now she'd be more careful. She couldn't wait to tell her parents. "They'll be beside themselves. We must fight off my mother's grand schemes. I can bake a cake. And Maud will do the flowers."

Maud, Jesus. Briefly he was back again on the living-room floor, the carpet scratching his thighs. Then Hazel was asking about the bees. Was he finished? Did he need to feed them?

"They're fine so long as we don't have another cold snap. They've been on a roller-coaster these last few months."

"Like us."

Seeing her smile, he risked, "We've had our rows."

"You'll have to tell me about them. We'll put them on the time line. Come on, I want to phone my parents."

She was already tugging him in the direction of the house

when he spotted movement at the entrance to the middle hive. Two workers had emerged and were perched on the sill. How bright the world must seem after the winter darkness. "Look," he said. "The first bees of the year." Together they bent down.

Watching the bees air their wings, Jonathan recalled a long-forgotten fact. This was not the first marriage proposal to pass between him and Hazel, nor the first acceptance. The second year they lived together was a leap year, and on February twenty-ninth, over dinner, Hazel had proposed. He had said yes and that same night woken her to say he couldn't; the word "husband" made him feel like he was drowning. Hazel had shushed him. No pressure, she said. Just an idea. Later, of course, his refusal had become another rod to beat him with. He'd had his chance. You didn't want me, she said tauntingly, triumphantly. Now, seeing her face as she watched the bees, he began to urge her inside. They should call her parents. Let the die be cast.

In the living-room, Hazel stopped and pointed at the window. Following her gesture, Jonathan saw the Tourette's boy in his blue anorak and dark trousers, circling in the street outside. He turned once, took a hesitant step, and, as if some spring in the mechanism had broken, circled again. His spectacles were tied to his head with a thick black cord. Someone—the boy himself, or his mother?—must put them on every morning and take them off at night. The effect was that of a headband, making his thick dark hair stand up, like a cock's comb.

"He frightens me," said Hazel.

Jonathan put his arm around her. "He's quite harmless. In all the years he's been around, I've never heard him say a word to another person."

"Years?"

Once again he'd crossed the threshold into that world without echoes or shadows. "Come," he said quickly, "let's tell George and Nora the good news."

He installed her on the sofa, dialled the number, and was about to leave the room when she reached for his hand. Presently he was talking to his future parents-in-law.

"We couldn't be more delighted," Nora said, and promptly burst into tears.

"Splendid," said George. "A spring wedding."

He passed the phone back to Hazel and made his escape. In the hall he leaned against the radiator—in spite of numerous drainings, it had never worked properly—and allowed her remarks to flow over him. "As soon as possible," he heard her say. The floor was a mass of footprints; he really must wash it this week. "I don't care about a big wedding. . . . Of course I have something to wear. . . . No fuss, just family."

For a moment, picturing Nora's gentle smile and George's blustering common sense, Jonathan was abashed; how much he owed to their kindness. He was tempted to rush back in, retrieve the phone, and thank them profusely. Instead, he held tight to the tepid radiator and fixed his gaze on a fragment of wallpaper that had escaped the steamer, a white flower, right at eye level.

chapter 11

By ten-thirty, in spite of slowing at every crosswalk, letting taxis and delivery trucks cut in at every intersection, Freddie was inexorably approaching Littleton's. He couldn't understand the nature of his unease any better than he had been able to describe it to Mr. Early, but something about Hazel and her situation—sick, alone with a man whose eyes snapped at the least provocation—haunted him. He turned into the street and, just his luck, there was a parking space two houses down from 41. I'm fixing the roof, he thought as he undid his seat belt, not playing Robin Hood.

Littleton answered the door, wearing a shirt that had to be expensive, the dark blue fabric fell so softly. Freddie was suddenly aware of his baggy jeans, cement-spattered sweatshirt, and Reds jacket. The way Littleton's eyes flicked over him, as if a piece of garbage had landed on the doorstep, did nothing to help.

"At last," he said, although no definite time had been set.

To his own disgust, Freddie began to dribble out excuses. "The builders' supply was nuts. I don't keep Welsh slate on hand. And the traffic . . . I'd better let number thirty-nine know I'm here. Can I ask how you'll be paying?"

"I suppose you're going to say cash only?" Littleton said, and launched into a tirade about workmen on the fiddle. "You pretend to do me a favour, letting me off VAT, actually you're none of you registered. All I'm doing is helping you to cheat on your income tax."

Freddie listened calmly. Abuse was far preferable to the cold shoulder. In fact, just for a second, Littleton reminded him of his father, ranting about the city council. When he could get a word in edgewise he said a cheque would be fine, that he'd been asking about how the bill would be divided with number 39.

"Mrs. Craig. She gets her own bill. Separate roofs, separate bills."

"But I didn't give her an estimate. What if she refuses?"

Littleton blinked and, for an instant, his expression acknowledged the blunder. "I did speak to her when we had to reschedule. If she wanted an estimate, she could've told me then. Well, maybe you should have a word with her before you start. Let me know if there's a problem." He closed the door, not quite slamming it.

If this were home, Freddie thought, eyeing the ugly orange wood, I'd call him a bigot. He walked round the dividing wall to 39 and, good news, Mrs. Craig had the original door, the stained glass set in curved wooden panels, and a perfectly acceptable wreath knocker. The door opened and Freddie found himself engulfed by a pair of yellow eyes. The cat craned into his hand, purring.

"This is Lionel. As you can see, shameless. I'm Mrs. Craig. You must be the roofer."

Freddie's gaze travelled over bare feet, up flowing purple trousers and a purple tunic to a long, mobile face of the kind he unthinkingly classified as very English. Mrs. Craig's silvery hair, piled on top of her head, matched the cat's. He guessed her age at between thirty-five and fifty-five. "Freddie Adams. He's cute. Is he something fancy?"

"A long-haired silver, not pure-bred."

"Maybe all the better," said Freddie, recalling the indignities of lineage and pedigree to which Agnes had been subjected.

"Do come in. Would you mind taking off your shoes?"

She led the way into a room that reminded him of an ashram he once visited in Santa Cruz. The walls and ceilings were a deep rose, the floor thickly carpeted, with large cushions and low chairs scattered around. Two small drums and a sitar stood in one corner. On a table by the window, a vase of white tulips paid homage to a photograph of a man in a white turban. Cool, thought Freddie. "I'm sorry I didn't call last week," he said. "I got railroaded by Mr. Littleton."

"That can happen," she agreed, sinking cross-legged onto a cushion. "The main thing is there's a problem and you're going to fix it."

He took an adjacent cushion and, seeing an opening, headed towards it. "Have you been neighbours for long?"

"A decade. He's ideal in practical terms—knows all about houses and how to take care of them—but no warmth. First there was him, then him and Suzanne, then him, then him and Hazel, then him. And now she's back again."

"She's been sick. I mean ill."

"Yes. I took round some ginger and some beetroot. I hope she's using them." She nodded in the direction of the photograph, as if invoking the guru's aid.

"I'm very fond of Hazel," she went on, "though our friendship has had its phases. When she moved in she'd been living in India, so we had lots to talk about." She spread her arms, whether an exercise or a gesture he couldn't tell. "Later she got busy with her journalism, putting her energies into that, and we drifted apart. It can happen more easily than you'd think, living side by side. The last time we spoke was the day she moved out. She couldn't even say his name. I tried to tell her she had to let go. That kind of anger only hurts you."

"But she's living there again?"

Mrs. Craig flexed her toes. "Illness brings you to a new place. Marianne Williamson talks about that. Have you heard of her? Friends tell me she's extremely popular in America."

"I haven't. I don't spend much time stateside these days." The cat, who had been rubbing against his cushion for several minutes, suddenly keeled over. Freddie obediently patted its stomach.

"You have a strong body," said Mrs. Craig, "yet you sit badly. You're impeding your natural flow. That makes it hard to get things done."

"You're right about that." She was sitting straight as a plumb-line. "Look at me, fooling around with Lionel when I ought to be up a ladder."

"That's not what I mean." She shook her head. "If you want to correct the problem, I can help. I give classes on Tuesdays and Thursdays, sliding scale."

From somewhere she produced a card and handed it over. *The Golden Road,* he read. *Let me help you walk part of the way.* "I teach a combination of yoga and Alexander technique which many people find helpful. You don't have to believe to benefit."

"Thanks. I'll keep it in mind." His concern about Hazel had been replaced by an odd contentment. If he wasn't careful, he could spend the whole day chatting to this supple woman about ley lines and energy fields.

"Now"—she dipped into a full lotus—"if I understand correctly, you need access to the back of the house and you'll be working on the roof fairly noisily, for several hours."

Freddie explained that he'd have to cut away the old slates, fit the flashing, then hammer in the new slates. "You'll know I'm there."

Mrs. Craig listened attentively. "This is a nuisance," she said. "Since I spoke to Jonathan something's come up. I simply can't have you working today. What about Thursday?"

The question had only one answer. What about an estimate, Freddie asked. She made a humming sound, low and sweet, and said if she trusted him to do the work, she'd also trust him to charge a fair price. "Thursday," she repeated. "In many respects it's a better day."

"Fine with me, but Mr. Littleton might get bent out of shape. His work is useless until yours is done."

"And vice versa. If he can comprehend that." She smiled brightly. "Today is no one's fault. Thursday, you'll see, it will all come together."

In one fluid movement she stood before him. Freddie, trying to emulate her, stumbled. She was right, he did use his body badly. With a final obeisance to the cat, he pulled on his boots and was back on the sidewalk. Get a grip, he thought. Slate, flashing, pointing. Toolbox in hand, he again approached number 41. Looking towards the bay, he saw a face at the window.

"You're back," said Hazel, when she opened the door. "Freddie?"

"That's right. Finally we got an okay day for the roof." Her eyes widened, exactly as he'd hoped, and her hair, clean now, was the flaxen colour he'd guessed. She was dressed more formally than last time, in black trousers and a dark green sweater. "How are you feeling?" he said.

She gave a lopsided smile. "Better. The seizures seem to be slowing down"—she patted the doorframe—"touch wood. I haven't had one for nearly a week."

"That's great. I was just talking to Mrs. Craig. She hopes

you're taking the beetroot and ginger she brought you." He was about to say more, about Hazel living in India and Mrs. Craig's guru, when he caught himself. "Where's Mr. Littleton?"

"In the garden. He said you were to go round."

"Finish telling me how you are." He spread out his attention like a mantle on which she might walk.

"I've been making a chart with Jonathan and my nurse, filling in events for the last three years. There are still gaps, but I get glimpses."

"Gaps?"

She ran her fingers up and down the doorframe. "Maybe I didn't tell you, the accident made me lose part of my memory."

"No, you didn't tell me." He put down the toolbox, as carefully as if it contained a dodo's egg, and, reaching into his jacket pocket, drew out his notebook and pen. Turning to a clean page, he began to write.

"What are you doing?" said Hazel. "Did you have an idea?"

"Sort of." He tore out the page and held it towards her.

After an uncertain moment, she relinquished the door and took the paper. " 'Freddie Adams,' " she read. " 'Twenty-one Mayville Gardens.' "

"My address, and my phone number." He lowered his voice. "I know this is weird, but if you ever need anything, call me anytime. Even if it's the middle of the night, or something stupid, like . . . like you want to go to the aviary in Regent's Park. Just call me."

A little line appeared between her eyebrows, and with her free hand she reached for the door again. He worried she was about to ask the impossible question—why was he doing this? Then the line disappeared and she smiled, not as before but hugely, brilliantly. "Thank you, Freddie." She slipped the paper into her pocket.

He balanced the ladder through the side door and around to

the back. As he was heaving it into place, Littleton appeared from the bottom of the garden. "Got Mrs. Craig organised?"

"She wants me to wait until Thursday."

"But we chose today because it suited her."

"Something came up." Although he too was irritated with Mrs. Craig, he couldn't help defending her. "At least I'll get a chance to check the work I do for you. This kind of job, with a lot of pointing, can be tricky."

"Ridiculous," Littleton said, and stalked off towards the back door.

Watching him go, Freddie heard his father again, no longer a resemblance but a growling complaint: there goes a planta-tion owner if ever I saw one. And buried under that, some other, deeper resemblance he didn't care to examine. He tied the lad-der to the fascia board and hooked the ridge-pole ladder into place. He still could not quite believe the events of the last few minutes, being so bold, writing out his name and address. As he began to cut through the first set of nails, he worried that Hazel might tell this man what he'd done. He had a vision of Littleton's fists leaving their pockets. The slate came away and he caught himself. Just because a guy was an asshole over his roof was no reason to assume he'd go for the jugular. He was simply one of those anal Brits that Felicity complained about: too many cold showers and suet dumplings as a schoolboy. Besides, Freddie thought, remembering Hazel's smile as she pocketed the paper, she won't tell.

In his mind, Jonathan had gone over and over the details of the wedding: the registry office, with Hazel's grateful parents and, perhaps, one or two of his colleagues; the meal, a quietly festive lunch at a local restaurant; the honeymoon, a weekend in Cam-bridge of walks by the river and a visit to Ely Cathedral. But he had entirely failed to consider what it would be like to sit around the table with Hazel and Maud and hear Hazel say, "Jonathan and I have something we want to tell you."

At once he was on his feet, bending to inspect the contents of the fridge: white, orderly, and absolutely no comfort. He studied the cheese, opened the vegetable drawer and, when he could not stay down a moment longer, retrieved a bottle of Pinot Grigio. The Orsini bomb was flying through the air, and all he could do was wait for it to land, harmless or fatal. Finally, sensing Hazel's expectant gaze, he edged over to stand behind her, his free hand on her shoulder.

"Jonathan and I," she said again, and with those three words Maud's face underwent a terrible, subtle transformation, as if beneath the skin a host of tiny muscles were tugging and pulling in different directions, "are getting married."

Maud was perfect. Her mouth split into a facsimile of a smile. She jumped up and flung her arms first around Hazel and then—he had stepped back slightly—Jonathan. As she came towards him, he braced himself to feel christ knows what and felt . . . nothing, neither temperature nor fragrance. He knew that Maud was hugging him, pressing her cheek to his, but no sensation reached him.

Then she was back in her chair and he was opening the wine and pouring them each a glass, even Hazel. "Here's to you," Maud said.

"To us," they echoed.

Maud reached to lift her glass and instead, as if it were overly full, lowered her head to drink.

"Only a little for me," said Hazel gaily. "I don't want to end up on the floor."

At the same instant he and Maud burst out laughing, raucous cries. Hazel watched, baffled. "It isn't that funny," she protested.

"Sorry." He caught Maud's eye, and they both fell silent. As she asked about dates and plans, he excused himself. What the fuck, he thought, am I doing? In the bathroom that question, along with Maud and her eerie embrace, gave way to an image of Hogarth. Picturing the doctor tapping his fingers, talking about the long climb back to health, he realised here was another person he would prefer not to know about the marriage. Once or twice he'd caught the neurologist glancing at him suspiciously. Had he guessed that Hazel and Jonathan were not quite the happy couple Jonathan advertised, or had she said something during one of her seizures? The faint braying of a car alarm brought him back to the present. Quickly he completed his business and returned downstairs.

In the kitchen, the situation seemed unchanged. Maud's cheeks were still burning and her glass was full again. Hazel was talking about the nurse. "She's nice. Our age, with two kids. Not scary."

"Anyone for pudding?" said Jonathan.

"Pudding," said Hazel. "You didn't tell us."

From a box on the counter he produced a Linzer torte and served them each a slice. Hazel tried a mouthful and asked where he'd got it.

"At the bakery near the office, Patisserie Jacques."

A tremor passed over Hazel. "It just opened a couple of years ago," he said gently.

She gripped the table. "Sometime soon I'd like to come to your office. Bernadette suggested I should revisit the important places in my life, make a kind of map."

"That's a good idea," said Maud. Seemingly by accident her gaze fell on Jonathan. "You can start with my flat."

Abruptly he reached to refill her glass.

All this, though, was easy compared to what came next. Hazel went off to bed, and he was alone with Maud. He dived into the washing up. She dried and put things away. Go home, he thought. Please, go home. But she had no intention of leaving. Quite the contrary. He could feel her purpose filling the room. He washed a plate, rinsed it, held it to the light, and, catching the slightest smear, began again. Finally, when not even a teaspoon remained, he drained the sink and sat down. Maud scraped a chair over the floor to sit opposite.

"May I get you something?" he asked. "Tea, coffee, more wine?"

"No thanks." Chin in hand, she studied the table.

In his confusion Jonathan adopted the same position while his thoughts leapt from one possibility to the next. Should he apologise, throw himself on Maud's mercy, beg her to keep quiet? Let them talk, Alastair, his boss, always said about their clients. They'll hang, draw, and quarter themselves if you only let them. But this time, he thought, emptying the glass before him, his or Hazel's, he was the one approaching that desperate trinity.

"What about Daniel?" Maud said at last.

"Daniel?"

"Hazel's tenant."

So that was how she was coming at it. Not their faux pas on the living-room floor, not him taking advantage of Hazel being ill, but the simple fact that a few months ago she'd been so determined to get away from him that she'd rented her own flat. A sudden crack and a flare of pain made him jump.

"Oh, my god," Maud cried.

Blood sprang up across his palm. Unwittingly he had crushed the glass he was holding.

She was by his side. "Let me help. Do you need a bandage?"

Ignoring her, he stood, swaying slightly, light-headed, and walked to the sink. Cold water, he thought, remembering his mother's homely remedies. His hand numbed while the water flushed and ran clear.

When he was again seated and Maud had stopped asking if he was all right, she announced she would have that drink. She left the room and returned with a bottle of Scotch and two squat tumblers. "Now don't break this one," she cautioned, and poured the whisky as if it were wine.

"It just isn't very sensible," she went on, "to try to keep such a large secret. Even apart from her memory coming back, there are too many ways she could find out: George and Nora, friends, people at work."

"Well . . ." He stole a glance at his beekeeper's veil, the white folds slightly soiled, hanging on its hook by the door. "What would you recommend?"

"I think"—her voice gathered speed—"you should tell her. Tell her more or less what she told her parents, that you had a row and she moved out, temporarily, to give you both space while you came to your senses."

"And what would the row be about?"

Maud drank some Scotch. "I've been pondering that. At first I wondered if a version of the truth might be easiest." She raised her eyebrows and the yellow walls seemed to fall towards him. She knows, he thought, my god, she knows everything: Suzanne, my slip-up. He dipped a finger in the Scotch and ran it along the cut, craving the sting of pain.

"Then," she continued, "I thought, better to be more ordinary. Perhaps you were busy at work, the threat of redundancy, you couldn't give Hazel the attention she needed. This flat came along for a few months, a sublet, and it seemed like a break would be best for both of you."

"Will that wash? Moving out is pretty serious."

"Which is precisely why we don't want to attribute the motivation to Hazel. If we say it was her decision, then she'll try to figure out what would drive her to that. Whereas if it was your idea, you're the obvious person to ask. Of course"—again something odd happened to the muscles of her face—"I'll back you up."

Of course? thought Jonathan. Am I losing my mind? He wanted to lean across the table and shake her. He understood his own behaviour: however convoluted, he had one clear and radiant motive. But why would Maud aid and abet him against her best friend? What had Hazel done to deserve such treachery?

"Maud," he said. His tongue thickened. Instead he found his uncut hand sliding towards hers. She stood, kissed him open-mouthed and open-eyed, and went into the hall. He followed, hopeful, only to see her putting on her bicycle helmet.

"Not tonight," she whispered. Then she was out of the door, her bicycle clicking down the pavement.

chapter 12

The only solution, thought Charlotte, gazing bleakly at the saucepan dappled with baked beans, the slice of bread, one small, crooked bite gone, the plates and cups, cars and crayons, was to pretend she was in a play. Mother Courage does the dishes, or that downtrodden woman in *Look Back in Anger*. After a prolonged struggle Melissa and Oliver had retired to bed, leaving the house looking more like her home than Bernie's, a change for which, Charlotte knew, she would be held solely responsible. Since the afternoon her sister had returned early to find the kitchen awash and herself asleep in front of the television, she had made a rule to use only one set of dishes a day, but serving first tea, then supper to the children seemed to have dirtied every piece of crockery Bernie possessed.

With an imaginary audience and a male lead—You no longer love me. Of course I do. Look how beautifully you washed that plate—cleaning up proved less intractable. Might this strategy work, Charlotte pondered, tackling the frying pan, in other areas? If she invented scripts about earning money, going to auditions, would she suddenly be able to accomplish these tasks? Meanwhile, Bernie could not have come home at a better moment. By the time the key scraped in the lock, she had finished the dishes, wiped the counters, and was sweeping the floor.

"Charlotte," Bernie exclaimed. "Are you all right?"

"Ace. Doing a spot of housework." She moved the chairs to make a final pass under the table and manoeuvred the little pile of crumbs, cereal, apple fragments, green beans, and baked beans into the dustpan. "There," she announced. "All done." Arms akimbo, she turned to examine her sister. As usual, even in civilian clothes, Bernie gave the impression of being ready to wield a thermometer at a second's notice. I should never have let her wear that beige cardigan, thought Charlotte. "How's Rory?" she asked.

Instantly Bernie lost some of her starchiness. "It's hard going on dates with your husband," she said, slumping against a pristine counter. "We say good night and don't know what to do with ourselves."

She sighed, and Charlotte saw their mother at the end of a long evening, the last drunken customer newly departed and their father staggering around singing "Over the Sea to Skye." She had always regarded Bernie as the opposite of their parents, firmly keeping chaos at bay, but it never worked, did it? "Would you like something?" she said. "Tea? Cocoa?"

"I don't think we have cocoa, unless you bought some."

Still in her domestic role—one of those Irish matriarchs, perhaps—Charlotte made tea, rinsing the pot as she had at Mr. Early's and using two of the nicer mugs. "So," Bernie asked, "did everything go all right?"

At first Charlotte didn't get it. What was there to go on her part? She'd been here the whole evening. Oh, of course, the rugrats. "Fine," she said firmly. "Oliver did his homework and Melissa laid the table and they went to bed within sight of the usual time. I did lose the battle of the bath, though."

"We can fix that in the morning." Bernie swallowed a yawn. "Listen, I wanted to ask you—Hazel, my private patient, was saying she'd like a reader. Especially if she's tired, she finds focussing tricky. I told her about you, your being an actress, and said you'd phone tomorrow."

"Why did you do that?" Already her life had dwindled to childcare and housework, and now her sister planned to add reading to the sick to that scintillating list.

"For god's sake, Charlie, you can't lie around on the sofa all day."

They glared at each other. For a moment they were back in their bedroom above the pub, Bernie scolding Charlotte night after night into whitening her gym shoes, learning her lessons, while from below rose the babble of voices and the stink of beer. Then Bernie relented. "She sounded so beleaguered. I thought you'd cheer her up. You are good at that, you know, when you put your mind to it. And they'd pay five pounds an hour."

"I don't lie around all day." She was about to embark on an explanation of the creative process—Struan, the search for a new agent, the notion of writing her own play, which had occurred to her only yesterday—but suddenly she felt exhausted. Why was she being such a cow? She could read a couple of times, then quit. No big deal. And the extra dosh would be nice.

At least, Charlotte thought, she doesn't *look* ill. Hazel was sitting cross-legged on the floor, wearing a blue pullover a shade or two darker than her eyes and surrounded by large sheets of paper. If Charlotte had run into her, at the theatre or in a shop, she would've found an excuse to talk to her, to see those amazing eyes up close and how her face changed when she spoke.

"This is Charlotte," Jonathan said. "Bernadette's sister. She's come to read to you."

"If you like," Charlotte added. Typical of Bernie not to

mention that her employer was terrifically handsome in a dark, intense way; she was glad she'd worn her new leggings and put on makeup.

Now he smiled, which oddly made him less attractive, and said he'd be working upstairs. Hazel pressed the point of a pencil against her finger while he fiddled with the doorknob, until Charlotte understood it was up to her to release him. "Thanks. We'll give a shout if we need you."

As the door closed behind him, the room seemed to grow lighter. Charlotte glanced around, searching for the source, but the sky beyond the bay window was the same leaden grey; the standard lamp next to the fireplace gave off the same steady glow. The mysterious change, she realised, emanated from Hazel. "What are you doing?" she said, crossing the room to kneel beside her.

Hazel explained she was drawing a map of her parents' farm, or at least that was the objective; she kept spilling over from one piece of paper to the next. Scale was the problem: the duckhouse was bigger than the bier. Charlotte nodded, as if following this rigmarole: where was the farm?

"North of Kendall, in the Lake District."

"Oh, I went to Dove Cottage a few years ago." Vainly she tried to summon the documentary she'd seen last summer. "Great scenery."

Hazel looked at her narrowly. "You can't live on scenery. Or at least I can't. It was fine when I was six or seven and liked baby animals, but as a teenager I thought I'd go mad."

"And did you?"

"No, I ran away with a lorry driver."

"Brilliant." Charlotte couldn't help giving a little bounce. "What was he like? Were you in love?"

Hazel laughed. "Colin was gorgeous. I met him at the pub. He had a weekly run through Kendall, up to Glasgow, and back. I went to live with him in his flat in Preston. That turned out to be the opposite of romantic, too. The place was filthy, his feet smelled, and neither of us gave a toss about housework. I lasted four months before I got tired of take-aways and went home. What about you?"

"Me?" said Charlotte, filled with regret for her well-behaved childhood. "We lived near Northampton, and I started coming to London to see plays. I'd get student tickets or sneak in at the interval. Afterwards I'd hang around the stage door, hoping some actor would buy me a drink."

"Jailbait," Hazel said appreciatively.

Charlotte shook her head. "At the time, I was sure people just wanted to chat about perfecting their art."

"Maybe they did. Did you have a boyfriend?"

Boyfriend, thought Charlotte, such a nice, innocent word. No, she'd never had one of those. Then Toby's freckled face and lanky frame popped up. "I'd forgotten all about him," she offered. "I only got interested because of Bernie. She had a mad pash for him."

"Imagine your sister having mad pashes. Did you go all the way?"

"Certainly not." Now it was Charlotte's turn to laugh. She could still picture herself in the ghastly school uniform, even the knickers labelled, and the contortions she and Toby had gone through at the back of the gym. "You're a journalist, aren't you?"

"In other words, I'm being nosy. You can always tell me to shut up."

People often made this sort of remark—tell me if I'm being a nuisance—but Charlotte could see that Hazel actually meant it. "Why are you drawing the farm?" she said.

Once again the room changed, and this time she was close enough to watch a kind of scrim fall over Hazel's brightness. "I had an accident," she said, "that wiped out part of my memory. Your sister thought making a map of places I do remember might help me to reach some of the ones I don't."

"What would you like to remember?"

"Everything."

Charlotte stared, dumbfounded. "You would? There are so many things I'd love to forget." She struggled for a safe example. "Once I closed a door in a set and it wouldn't open for the rest of the play. Another time I skipped two scenes in *Tooth of Crime.* Half the actors skipped with me and the rest didn't."

"But you have the choice. What if you really couldn't remember? Wouldn't you feel other people had an advantage over you?"

"They do anyway." Charlotte shrugged. "I know all this Santayana stuff: that which we do not remember, we are doomed to repeat. As far as I'm concerned it's the other way round. We repeat what we remember. Only forgetfulness sets us free."

Hazel was frowning, a sign of disagreement, Charlotte assumed, until she saw Jonathan peering round the door. She'd heard no footsteps, she now realised, since he left the room. Might he have been loitering, this whole time, in the hall? "I came to see if you wanted anything." He smiled in his disquieting fashion at Hazel, and raised an eyebrow at Charlotte. "I thought you were going to read."

"We are. I was just telling Hazel about a play I'd been in." Did her salary depend on so many pages per hour?

He withdrew again and this time, seeing the door ajar, she stood up and, without checking, closed it. Together, they sketched the farm. In Melissa and Oliver's company Charlotte had rediscovered a knack for drawing, and now she happily followed Hazel's directions to mark the stone farmhouse with its orchard on one side of the road and the farm proper on the other. "What was here?" she asked.

"An old Land Rover, where we put the hens when they were sick or broody."

"And here?"

"The bier where we kept the cows. The muscovy ducks used to roost in the manger."

"You know," said Charlotte once several sheets were full, "you remember an astonishing amount, at least compared to me." She recalled a radio programme she'd done on the rise and fall of memory palaces. Had Hazel heard of them? "It was a trick the Roman orators used. You stored the paragraphs of a speech in a familiar house. Then, when you had to give the speech, you walked through the rooms and there were your sentences, all nicely lined up in atriums and frescoes, waiting to be uttered."

"What if you were poor and didn't have a house?"

"You had to find one. Apparently young men used to wander the Forum, memorising it column by column. The farm would make a terrific memory palace. You'd put first love in the duckhouse, your first job in the midden."

"India in the stable. Running away from home in the granary. Boris in the water trough." Hazel was gesturing at the pages as if moving the events of her life to the different locations when, suddenly, mid-sentence, she fell silent.

"Are you all right?" said Charlotte.

With a small shake of the head, Hazel leaned against the sofa. Charlotte spotted a rug on one of the armchairs and spread it over her. She could see the tendons standing out in Hazel's neck. "Should I fetch Jonathan?"

Somehow, again, she understood no. Hazel indicated a book on the sofa, a guide to India's flora and fauna. After five dreary pages about irrigation in Goa, hard even for Charlotte to read eloquently, the door opened and Jonathan appeared with a tea tray. "Refreshments," he announced.

"Good timing," she said.

As he approached, his eyelashes were fluttering. He's nervous, she thought, absolutely on tenterhooks. She turned to Hazel, who was smiling up at him, broadly, fiercely. The ground had shifted. Who's in charge here, thought Charlotte.

"This is the stable where we kept Ginger, the gelding," Hazel said. "And this was where the cats lived, far too many of them. Sometimes they ate their own kittens."

"Here's the tractor shed," said Jonathan, pointing to a shaded area along one side of the bier. The actress—she'd left an hour ago, smiling coquettishly as he paid her—had done a surprisingly good job with the map. "The farm was one of the first places you took me," he added.

"Have I ever been to your home?"

"No." In the last week or two he'd stopped worrying that such questions, either in the asking or the answering, would precipitate a landslide of memories. "We talked about going when we went to Edinburgh, but Denholm isn't really on the way. And there's absolutely nothing there."

"Except your mum and dad."

"We'll visit them one day, after we're married."

"Won't they come to the wedding?"

Jonathan had a sudden, appalling picture of his parents in London, his father in his baggy, old man's trousers and worn cardigan, gasping like a fish, his mother in her apron, constantly offering to help. "It's too far for them to travel. My father can't go anywhere without an oxygen cylinder. What's this?"

"Two old carts. They had wooden shafts and wheels with iron rims. I used to climb on them and pretend I was going places."

"Prophetically. What did you think of your reader?"

"Nice. More fun than her sister. Bernadette is okay, but it's always clear I'm just a job. She told me about memory palaces."

"Cicero. Fancy her knowing that. Did she mention Simonides?" He described the early Greek poet who had first understood the link between spatial order and memory. Hazel nodded happily; she'd always relished his stories, those random bits of information which—apart from his affection for her, for his bees—seemed to occupy most of his brain. Seeing the smooth curve of her ear, he wanted to say your body is my memory palace. At last he knew what he must do. No wonder things were messed up when they still weren't lovers. She was well enough now; the seizures had dwindled and, of course, there would be no more nonsense with Maud. That had never happened.

"I've been meaning to ask," said Hazel, "does Maud seem different to you? She was so odd about us getting married. And I often have the feeling she's avoiding me, even though she's here every evening. Did I do something when I was ill?"

He stood up and walked around the room, twitching the curtains, straightening a card on the mantelpiece. This was like the old days: Hazel glimpsing the shape of his thoughts almost before he did. Steady. Here was a chance to reinstate one small piece of the truth and to be less at Maud's mercy; he mustn't waste it. "When you recovered consciousness you didn't recognise her. She found that upsetting." He eyed the cheese plant. Barasingha. "Also, I'm not sure she entirely approves of me, of us."

"Why not?" It was her journalist's voice, curious but dispassionate.

"Partly—" he pretended to consider—"chemistry. You know, *I do not love thee, Doctor Fell, but why it is I cannot tell.* Partly she thinks I'm a bit stuffy, a claims adjustor, that I don't appreciate you sufficiently. You used to go out with these arty types."

"Like Boris and Paul."

"You remember?"

She nodded. "I don't need a memory palace for everything. Boris thought he was Sartre. Unfortunately I wasn't de Beauvoir. And while Paul was sweet, he turned me into Boris. I suppose, in the final analysis, I wasn't in love with either of them."

What happier words? He bent to nuzzle her cheek.

Hazel gathered up the drawings. "Isn't it time for my pills? Should we start supper?"

Not until he heard Maud saying "Plantworks" did he realise he couldn't simply tell her not to come round. Quickly he blurted out the first excuse that occurred: he and Hazel were going round to Steve and Diane's. Oh, said Maud, that'll make a nice change. Back in the kitchen, he confessed what he had done, another step towards veracity.

"Jonathan—" Hazel was sorting vegetables for a salad. "You said Katie had chickenpox."

He apologised, even offered to phone Maud back, and she relented. "Actually I'm glad. I could do with a break from her."

As he put on water and peeled garlic, he told her about his visit to the registry office the day before. A boxy room in the Town Hall, the tall veiled windows overlooked Rosebery Avenue. "What I didn't expect was all the babies."

"Of course," Hazel exclaimed. "It's where you register births too, isn't it?"

"And deaths. But everyone seemed pretty cheerful."

"So what happens next?"

"We show up and say 'I do.' I filled out a form with our particulars, ages, occupations, etc., and handed over the money. We're all set: eleven-thirty on Tuesday, March nineteenth."

He lifted the lid off the saucepan and studied the barely steaming water. There had been babies, half a dozen of them, but what he remembered was the woman who'd interviewed him, opening Hazel's passport and saying, "Oh, she's lovely." At the sight of the passport in her hands—he'd retrieved it from Hazel's flat on his way—he had felt like a thief twice over, stealing first the document, then its owner.

He didn't know how to do it. That pullover really brings out the colour in your eyes, he said. I like your hair this way. When she announced she was going to bed, he wanted to say me too, but the prospect of refusal stopped him. He took her upstairs and returned to the kitchen to drink a whisky, then another, before daring to make his approach. In the bedroom doorway he stood listening, until the soft sough of her breathing reassured him. He retreated to the spare room, undressed, and padded down the corridor. Hazel did not stir as he slid in beside her. He lay shivering, checking himself for warmth.

Recalling her map of the farm, he began in his own mind to make a map of Denholm. Here was the house where they lived, 8 Riverside Drive, beside the Teviot; there the primary school and, beyond, the village green with its monument to some war—Crimean or Boer or maybe the Great War? In all his years there, he'd never looked. Nearby was the playground. From the swings, the shops around the green were visible, including the newsagent's run by Stephanie's father.

A crush, people called it, meaning something light and ephemeral, not realising how utterly weighed down he'd felt as he followed her home from school, made excuses to go into the newsagent's, sent her elaborate cards for Valentine's Day and Christmas. Once Stephanie had dropped a glove, and he slept with it under his pillow, until his mother threw it out. In eighteen months they spoke barely a dozen times, banal exchanges about the weather, a teacher being ill. When her father sold the shop and the family moved to Glasgow, Jonathan expected to plunge into an abyss. Instead he found himself whistling as he walked to school; he missed her, but he wasn't entirely sorry to be weightless again.

Hazel sighed in her sleep, and he reached towards her. If only he'd thought to put out a nightdress. Now he faced the intricate aggravation of pyjamas. He unbuttoned the top and fondled her breasts. Another sigh. He kissed her neck and whispered her name, then held back. He didn't want her awake, not yet. Clumsily, carefully, he removed her trousers, easing them down her legs and over her feet. She would wake up with him inside her, surrounded by his love, and they would be inseparable, soon to be married. She would never leave him again.

He stole from the bed and found a tube of lubricant in his washbag. Diminished by the cold, he was back beside her, heart racing. Hazel, he thought, I'm coming home. In the same meticulous way as he had removed her pyjamas, he edged her legs apart.

For one ineffable moment everything made sense. His head swam with happiness, and the fragrance of honey filled the room.

A cry rent the air.

He tried to tell himself it was pleasure, a shriek of pleasure.

"Stop. Get off me."

"Hazel, I love you. Don't be afraid."

Her screams rose. He lowered his weight, pressing down against her breasts, her hips, her thighs, to keep her safe. If only she wouldn't keep tossing her head, he would slip his tongue into her mouth to taste the sweetness. He wanted this to last forever—to keep moving slowly, inexorably, inside her—but the more she struggled, the fiercer his own movements became.

The first time she bucked beneath him, he didn't know

what was happening. The second, he understood: she was having a seizure. Now he was fucking her at the deepest level, like the Pythian and her priest. The electricity that ran through her was coursing through him, too. As Hazel bucked once more, he came.

chapter 13

In what respect, Freddie wondered, was Thursday better. The day was chilly in that sneaky London way, windy but not enough to justify cancelling; cars lined both sides of the street; and worst of all, number 41, when he drove past, was dark. His excuse for seeing Hazel, checking their side of the roof, might easily come to nothing. After circling the block twice, he pulled over to dump the ladder and supplies on Mrs. Craig's doorstep—if someone wanted to steal them, fine—and resigned himself to parking around the corner. And they hadn't even agreed on a price, he remembered as he stumped back. Well, no favours on this golden road. He was going to do everything by the book: so much for materials, so much per hour.

Some of his crankiness faded at Mrs. Craig's warm greeting. "Oh, good, Mr. Adams. You know, I realised last time we didn't even check whether I had damage inside."

"And do you?"

"I was waiting for you to take a look. No point in rushing to meet bad news."

"That I can understand," he said, bending to unlace his boots and fondle the cat. She led him upstairs to a room the mirror image of Littleton's study but so different that it took him a moment to recognise the similarity. The only furniture was a canvas chair and a long padded table. "My massage room," she said. The walls were lined with posters of the body and with wooden shelves holding books and bottles of oil: rosemary, lavender, jasmine. He could see why she hadn't noticed the problem. The room was softly lit and the leak was hidden by the shelving. When he removed the bottles the damp patch was markedly larger and wetter than next door.

"Tut tut," said Mrs. Craig. "The gremlins have been at work. You're here in the nick of time."

Downstairs, she shut the cat in the living-room and told Freddie to shout if he needed anything. He carried the ladder through the side gate and, breathing hard, propped it up against the wall. Of course she would have a beautiful garden. A large herb bed was already green; clumps of lavender grew along the path and green spears—daffodils maybe—were shooting up. He stared at Hazel's windows, dark on this side too. She hadn't actually said she was too sick to go out; he'd simply wanted to believe her a princess in a tower.

Once he got the ladder and ridge ladder in place, he could see the extent of the damage: the flashing had lifted in half a dozen spots and several slates had slipped. He barely needed the dog to pry out the cement; in no time at all he was levering up the old flashing and measuring for the new. He was getting better at this business, if he did say so himself. The idea was both pleasing and alarming. He didn't want to be a roofer all his life, for Pete's sake. Though when he thought about the jobs his classmates had—lawyer, broker, consultant, internist, junior professor—there wasn't one he coveted. Better to earn an autonomous living by the sweat of his brow than to take orders and meet schedules eight days a week.

He worked steadily for almost two hours, then came down

to beg a cup of tea and cut the slates. The first broke in his hands—so much for his newfound skill—but there was enough left to make an eaves slate and the others parted sharp and clean. A thrush, seemingly unfazed by his activities, was trundling a snail along the path. Following its passage, he noticed a light had come on in the kitchen of 41. Back up the ladder he began to hammer noisily, a message. *Ha-zel, I'm here.* Since giving her his address, he jumped every time the phone rang.

He was dressing the new flashing, cutting and bending the lead, when he heard a tapping sound. Hazel was at the study window. Through the glass her face shone even paler than before, though white people often did strike him that way, blanched as if they lived underground and never saw the sun. "Hi," he called. "How are you?"

She shook her head. What did that mean? "I'm coming to check your roof later."

Again the small shake. Suddenly her hands went to her face. Littleton appeared behind her. Freddie waved cheerfully. "Sorry about the noise."

It was like watching a pantomime. Hazel turned her back to the window, Littleton scowled, and they both disappeared, leaving Freddie alone with the flashing.

He measured the next section, notched and cut the lead. The more he thought about it, the more worried he felt. On his previous visits Hazel had seemed ill at ease in Littleton's company; just now she had looked genuinely afraid. If there was any chance of seeing her, he'd ring the bell at once, but the curmudgeonly Littleton would only have her hidden away. No, he must bide his time. Later, when he'd finished Mrs. Craig's roof, then he would make an attempt. Back up the ladder, he wedged the flashing between the bricks and was moving to the next section when he ran out of cement. A yard to go, and not so much as a scraping left.

Inside, Mrs. Craig appeared from the living-room. Briefly he thought of telling her what he'd seen, then realised how intangible it was: Hazel looked pale, she acted surprised when Littleton appeared—so what? He confined himself to the cement and she suggested the DIY shop on the Holloway Road. "Or there's a builders' supply place five minutes up from the tube station."

An hour later, he was done. Mrs. Craig offered him a tofu sandwich and asked if he would mind checking the front bay. "I've had my eyes on other matters." She showed him the cracks along the cornices and Freddie said probably due to subsidence caused by the recent hot summers, but he'd be happy to take a look. The sandwich was totally tasteless. Had Felicity's curries ruined his palate? Mrs. Craig ate hers with every sign of pleasure.

He was up the ladder at the front of the house, pulling clumps of leaves from the gutter, as he'd suspected no sign of a leak, when a woman—all he could see was her neat ponytail and dark coat—rang the bell at 41. She disappeared inside. Five minutes later, he was on the other half of the bay, the door opened again and Littleton stepped out, wearing a suit, overcoat, paisley scarf, and, quite unnecessarily, sunglasses. He stopped to stare darkly up at Freddie. "Is everything all right?"

"Fine. I'd like to check on your side before I leave."

"I suppose," Littleton grunted, "as you're here. The key to the side door is under the nearest geranium."

You'd have thought I was offering to rob him, Freddie thought, not do him a favour. As soon as the car rounded the corner, he was down the ladder and on the doorstep of 41. The woman, now wearing a neat cardigan and skirt, oddly like a uniform, answered. He explained his presence. "Whatever Mr. Littleton says," she said.

"How's Hazel?"

Her manner grew less brisk. "Tired. She was ill last night and it's left her shaken."

"I'm sorry. Will you tell her I was asking for her? My name is Freddie."

She assured him she would. Again he got the ladder around the back and up. He was standing near the top, hammering at the flashing just to make a noise, feeling like an idiot, when below him the study window slid open. He climbed down a few rungs.

"How are you?" he whispered.

"Not so good."

"That's what the woman said. I'm sorry. Can I help?"

"Not today." Her eyes filled with tears. "I have to get my strength back. I'm all muddled and upset."

"Call me," he said. "Anytime."

Jonathan had stayed with Hazel for several hours. Gradually, without ever fully recovering consciousness, she shifted from the comatose state that followed a seizure into a deep and speechless sleep. In the morning she woke only when the hammering started. He came into the study to find her gazing out of the window at the roofer. "He's fixing Mrs. Craig's roof," he explained, and offered to run her a bath. Hazel trembled—was she having another seizure?—and edged towards the door.

In his daydreams he had imagined their lovemaking would transform her back into the woman who had lured him away from half-eaten meals and half-watched films and once, on a June evening in the garden, had drawn him down onto the grass. But for the rest of the morning Hazel assiduously avoided him. When he came into a room, she left or stared at a book until he left. By the time Bernadette arrived, he'd been glad to go to work. He was tired of feeling as if a huge hand were squeezing his chest every time he entered a room. Where would she be without him?

At the office he sat at his desk, emptying his in-tray and enjoying the round robin of his colleagues' praise as they dropped off files and memos: how wonderful he was to Hazel, how devoted. No accident that he dallied, fielding a late phone call, sending one more e-mail, until the last possible moment. He arrived home to find Bernadette buttoning her coat. Before he could excuse his tardiness, she was gone. He was still hanging up his own coat, bracing himself for the evening ahead, when the bell rang.

Hoping for a brief reprieve—a canvasser, perhaps—he opened the door and discovered Maud. In the last twelve hours she had vanished from his mind. Now he stared, doubly amazed by her presence and by his own forgetfulness, while she explained that she'd spoken to Bernadette on the phone. "I brought soup. After last night, I thought something simple would be fine."

"Last night," he said, then realised she meant the imaginary supper with Steve and Diane.

And somehow they were outside embracing over her ten-speed, her tongue searching his. Only when she pulled away, asking him to hold the groceries and flowers, did it occur to him how easily Hazel could have seen them entwined in the square of light.

In the hall Maud propped her bike against the radiator and reclaimed the flowers. "White irises," she said. "Can you put them in water?"

As he started towards the kitchen, he heard her voice from the living-room and, lower, Hazel's. Christ, he thought, I shouldn't leave them alone, but when he carried in the flowers, one glance at Hazel sent him backing out of the room, muttering about work. Upstairs, he tried to imagine the worst-case scenario, each woman admitting their lovemaking, and drew a paralysing, shining blank.

Surprisingly, he managed to begin a report and indeed became so engrossed that the knock at the door made him start. "Hazel feels crummy," Maud said. "She's gone to bed." And he knew nothing had changed, or not in that way.

"Did she take her medicine?"

"Yes." She stepped closer. "I need to talk to you." Then, seeing his gesture of alarm, she added, "Not here."

"Shall I phone you?" In his desire to avert the present danger, he heard himself sounding almost eager.

"Yes, call me at the shop."

"I will, tomorrow. But are you leaving? No soup?"

"I think I'd better." She gave him a meaningful look, though quite what her meaning was, he hadn't an inkling.

A blade of light across his face woke him. After Maud's departure, he'd fallen asleep on the sofa, watching a film on TV, and when he stirred, long after midnight, had simply reached for the rug and remained. The spare-room bed offered no particular temptation, and joining Hazel did not bear consideration. Now, blinking away the wisps of a dream—he'd been bicycling along a river—he felt curiously well rested.

Half an hour later, bathed, dressed, coffee beside him, he sat at the kitchen table, paging through his beekeeper's diary. In a few weeks it would be St. Gregory's Day, when, by tradition, the spring flowers opened and the bees emerged. A year ago he'd found most of the bees in his middle hive dead. *Need to restock middle hive,* he read. *Try a Buckfast Queen?* Unbidden, the terse entry recalled the rest of that day. He'd come into the house upset—he should've been more vigilant, given the bees more food—to be confronted by Hazel holding one of his old cheque books. "Who is S.B.?" she had asked. When he admitted the truth, something had happened between them as startling and irrevocable as Flopsy's disappearance.

But now, he thought, irrevocable no more. All that was needed was for him to join Hazel in amnesia. Last year, after hours of argument, he'd retreated to the middle hive and begun, furiously, to search the frames for the old queen. As if sensing his murderous intent, somehow she eluded him, hiding amidst the workers and drones. He'd been stung half a dozen times before giving up. A week later, he spotted her on the first attempt, killed her, and installed the new queen.

No need, he thought, for replacements this year. Closing the diary, he turned to the files he had brought home. He was studying the estimates for a garden fence demolished, according to the owner, by last November's gales when the phone rang.

"Sorry to call so early," said a brusque voice, Alastair, his boss. "I need to know your plans for returning to work."

Jonathan was about to explain how they'd just missed each other at the office yesterday, how even now, at quarter till nine, he was hard at it, but Alastair had already jumped in. "Two afternoons a week is not exactly full time."

On the television, which he'd forgotten to turn off, a woman raised a hand towards the sky. Jonathan felt a tingling of alarm. "Hazel still can't be left alone," he said.

"That's too bad, though, strictly speaking, not our problem. In the circumstances we've been remarkably generous, all this time off for an ex-girlfriend."

Jonathan stared at the phone, aghast. To hear such words when, only a few yards away, Hazel lay sleeping, put everything in jeopardy. "We're getting married," he managed, "on March nineteenth."

"Super. At the risk of sounding like a schoolmaster, I'd say if Hazel's well enough to get married, then she's well enough for you to come to work. What we've given you is discretionary leave, and our discretion is at the end of its tether. You heard about Tim?"

Of course. Several people yesterday had mentioned Tim's accident, a fall from a climbing wall, two months in a neck brace, and he'd made sympathetic noises, not stopping to consider how this might affect his own situation. "Frankly," Alastair continued, and now Jonathan could hear the fatigue beneath the brusqueness, "I can't cope. Being out of the office every day is wreaking havoc with my schedule. You know how time-consuming these site visits are. Tim was due at a house in Finsbury Park this afternoon, and I hate to cancel so late. The case has dragged on for nearly a year."

"What about the paperwork?"

"We'll messenger it over. Is this a yes?"

"Give me half an hour to see if I can find anyone to sit with Hazel."

"That would be great," Alastair said, and hung up.

Jonathan gazed at the television, where a plane was taking off. Just when everything was settling down, this new wild card. If at all possible, he should go to Finsbury Park. He remembered Hazel bucking beneath him. Then he pictured a suitcase, a taxi. She was a woman who ran away, had before, might again. He eyed the white irises on the mantelpiece and for a befuddled moment considered taking her to Plantworks. Why was it, he wondered, that doing exactly the same thing with two different people could be so wrong. Was there a philosophical principle that covered that?

Into his mind came the nurse's sister. Bernadette was only free two days a week—besides, the agency fees were dear—but Charlotte might be available. He was reaching for the phone when he thought to consult Hazel; the illusion of choice often seemed to cheer her. He took the stairs two at a time and hurried into the bedroom. Hazel was sitting up in bed, holding her book like a missile. "Do you want breakfast?" he faltered.

"I'm not hungry."

In a little over a fortnight, he reminded himself, we'll be married. He clenched his fists and summarised the situation. "I was going to ring Charlotte, if that's all right with you."

"Fine." He was almost out of the room when she said his name. "Jonathan." He turned back. "Did something happen the other night?"

"Why would you think that?" Oh, bad answer, wretched answer. Blood hurtled into his face.

"Something in bed," she persisted.

"Hazel, darling, I've no idea what you're talking about. Of course, I'm longing for us to make love again, but only when you're better, when you want to."

He tried to shape his mouth, his eyes, into what might pass for a smile, gave up, and rushed from the room. This was terrible. She loved him, she had to love him, he'd saved her life. How could she look at him like that, without a flicker of affection? Anyway, she couldn't know. Late in the night, while she was still unconscious, he had washed away the evidence.

Charlotte stared resentfully at the driver's dull brown hair flopping over his jacket collar. For god's sake, she thought, get a ponytail. She herself wore the same clothes as the night before, like the old days, and here she was already on the streets, along with an astonishing number of other people. Surely they didn't all work in hospitals or film production. "Am I your first trip?" she said.

"I wish. I've been to Heathrow twice and done a maternity-ward grand prix. Things just quieted down."

He had a voice like a cheese grater. Imagine having this yob as your midwife. "Have you ever had a baby in your taxi?" she said, eyeing the grey seatcovers.

"You mean delivered one? Not yet, touch wood. Unless you're about to change my luck." He gave a quick leer over his shoulder.

"Absolutely not." So much for her baggy black jumper. She sat back and, although it wasn't clear he noticed, refused to say another word until they pulled up outside the obstreperous wooden door. The dishy Jonathan appeared, and she made an empty-handed gesture. In fact she had ten pounds at the bottom of her bag, but people often confused inclusive and exclusive sums; he might be less generous later if she paid for the taxi now.

While he dealt with the driver, she examined the walls of the hall, bare save for tiny scraps of wallpaper. Like Bernie, she thought, Jonathan was not quite as orderly as he pretended.

"Thanks for coming on such short notice," he said. "How long can you stay?"

She stole a glance from under her lashes. He had that glossy, newly shaved look and seemed taller than before, though perhaps that was just the suit. She started to say she had to be at the school by three, then remembered today was Rory's day for the rug-rats. "As long as you need me," she said, and, not wanting to sound too pathetic, added she had plans for the evening. He assured her he'd be back by six.

The door closed and he was gone before she realised he hadn't given her a phone number. Stupid bugger. Bernie always left a list as long as her arm and the rug-rats were healthy as kings. What if Hazel started ranting and rolling her eyes?

The sound of television drew her into the living-room but she found the machine twittering to vacant chairs. Down the hall, the kitchen too was empty. What a nice, bright room, with none of the clutter that she herself seemed to generate simply by breathing. If she and Walter had got a house like this, might he have stayed? When they met he'd been sleeping on a friend's sofa, and her bed-sit had struck him as sumptuous; a year later he'd claimed their one-bedroom flat in Kilburn was palatial. But people changed, got older, wanted more. Maybe Walter, for all his talk of bourgeois crap, had been looking over her shoulder, his eyes wide with greed.

Through the glass door at the end of the kitchen the garden rippled seductively. Later. For now she put on the kettle and returned to the hall. "Hello," she cried, pitching her voice up the stairs. "Anyone at home?"

A figure appeared, ghostly in pyjamas. "Who is it?"

"Me, your reader. Would you like a cup of tea?"

For a few alarming seconds Hazel swayed, then she collapsed on the top stair and buried her face in her hands. Charlotte perched on the stair below. Nice carpet, she thought, patting Hazel's knee. "There, there. You'll be better soon. Nothing like a good cry."

After several minutes of platitudes, she persuaded Hazel back to bed and went to make tea. By the time she returned upstairs, Hazel was teary but composed. Charlotte balanced herself and the tray on the edge of the bed. "Who chose the colour for the kitchen?" she said. Then, seeing Hazel's frown, "Sorry. Is that in the part you forget?"

"No. We painted the kitchen the year I moved in. It's later that things get foggy."

"Can't Jonathan help?"

"Not so you'd notice."

"Maybe he's afraid you'll remember something you don't like about him."

"What makes you say that?" Hazel was pleating the sheet back and forth between her fingers.

"I'm just guessing. It must be nice to have your side of the story be the only one. Don't you have friends you can ask?"

A blush crept into Hazel's face. "I was abroad for so long," she said, sounding calmer. "France and India. Most of my London friends, I don't remember. And Jonathan keeps saying I'm too ill to have people round."

Charlotte had a flash of sympathy. Hadn't she and Hazel suffered similar fates? Everything fine one minute, and the next in smithereens. But Hazel had someone waiting to pick up the pieces. That was the difference. "Well," she said, and at the same moment Hazel said, "Jonathan knew about memory palaces. They started with a Greek poet."

She described how Simonides had gone to supper with his patron. Charlotte listened attentively. Family life was having a dismal effect on her conversation. Last week at the Trumpet, she'd even told Louis an anecdote about the rug-rats.

Simonides recited his new poem. The other guests applauded, but the patron peevishly announced that he would pay only for the verses praising him. A little later, a servant brought the message that Simonides was wanted outside. In the courtyard he found a man waiting—in some versions two men, the twins Castor and Pollux. While they spoke, the roof of the banquet hall collapsed, killing everyone. Simonides identified the mangled corpses not by jewellery or clothing but by remembering where each guest was seated. "And that was how they got the idea," said Hazel, "that space was a way to order memory."

Not so stupid, then, thought Charlotte, to have sealed off the bedroom after Walter left. Quickly she began to calculate her finances. If Jonathan was as good as his word and stayed away until six, that was forty pounds. Plus—she added, reaching for the biscuits—all she could eat. At Bernie's there was often, at least with the things she liked, an unpleasant sense of rationing. She was about to go and investigate the fridge when Hazel spoke again.

"Actually I was hoping you might help me with this memory stuff."

Charlotte felt her scalp tighten. Reading was okay. Drawing was okay. But who wanted to wade around in the sewers of the past? Shouldn't everyone be afraid of what they might find amongst all that piss and shit? She began to stammer out excuses. What about the book on India or a game—Snap, or Snakes and Ladders? "I've been practising with my nephew and niece. Scrabble?"

She stopped, conscious of Hazel's imploring gaze, and went over to the window. For tuppence ha'penny she'd have burst into tears herself. She stared out at the sunlit garden, a bushy tree and the flower beds with their sprouts of colour. Beyond the lawn were three grey mounds, some sort of sculpture, perhaps.

"Charlotte," Hazel said, "I wouldn't ask if I wasn't desperate."

Charlotte swallowed. She remembered her sister saying the same word, and if Bernie had meant it, Hazel meant it twenty times over. I can always stop, she thought, I can walk away and leave everything that happens in this house right here. "Okay." She turned her bedazzled gaze back to the darkened room. "Though I don't see how I can be of much use. I hardly know you."

Shyly Hazel explained her idea. She wanted Charlotte to interview her and write down the answers. "What should I ask about? Your work? Jonathan?"

Hazel's clear blue eyes washed over her. "Both, everything. Imagine you're writing an exposé, or the authorised biography."

. . .

So they began. Quite soon Charlotte was enjoying herself, as if playing an intriguing role, halfway between psychiatrist and detective. She learned how Hazel and Jonathan had met, when a librarian brought Hazel the books Jonathan had requested. "He was reading about bees, and we started talking. I told him that in India honey is one of the few foods that can be freely exchanged between castes." Presently they agreed to go for a drink. "I was twenty-eight and felt I had nothing to show for myself. So to have this man hang on my every syllable was lovely. He asked wonderful questions—about India, my travels. And he told me about his bees.

"We'd been going out for a few months, three or four, when I started having trouble with my landlord, and Jonathan suggested I move in. We were in love, but we wouldn't have lived together so soon otherwise."

"Did he live here with someone before you?" Charlotte asked.

"Suzanne. She moved out the spring before we met. That was one of the ways Jonathan and I were compatible. I'd had my share of men. It would've made me nervous to be with someone inexperienced."

I wish I were like you, Charlotte was about to say, then she saw Hazel's face. "But there is something, isn't there?"

"Oh, I hate this. Yes, when I come to Suzanne there's a chasm, a shadow."

"Perhaps something Jonathan told you? Or you ran into her? People don't stay in exact compartments." News about Walter still filtered back, even though she did her utmost to avoid it.

Hazel pleated the sheet twice, three times, and at last shook her head. "No, I can't. I can't get hold of it."

Fearing more tears, Charlotte reverted to the less frustrating questions about jobs. Hazel described teaching ESL, working at Plantworks, her early steps in journalism. "Because I'd lived abroad, I started getting foreign pieces—articles about an Indian novelist living in London, French education, things like that."

Gradually they filled in a picture. Jonathan with his sensible career. Hazel with the interesting, erratic work. The two of them going on walking holidays in the Dordogne, Tuscany, the Lake District.

"Were you faithful?"

Hazel let out a gasp of laughter. "I was going to say of course, but how would I know? I could have screwed twenty Dutch sailors end to end and I wouldn't have a clue." She shook her head. "I do remember that Jonathan was jealous from the start. At first I thought it meant he was paying attention. After a while, though, when he got upset every time I worked late, it was a bore. I used to wish I really was having a fling."

"He does seem like the jealous type."

"Why?"

Again Charlotte wished she'd kept her mouth shut. "Well, he's very intense, and—" she hesitated—"last time I was here, I'm almost sure he was eavesdropping on our conversation."

"He spies on me," said Hazel matter-of-factly. "And he always answers the phone. Sometimes I hear him making excuses, as if I were still at death's door."

"Why didn't you get married?"

Hazel shrugged. "I'm not sure, but we are in a few weeks."

"You're getting married? To Jonathan?" For some reason Charlotte couldn't keep her voice from shrilling.

"He saved my life," Hazel said tonelessly. "He loves me."

She's scared shitless, Charlotte thought, and caught herself. Exaggerating as usual, Bernie would say. Hazel was convalescing, out of sorts, no big deal. "That's enough for today," she said briskly. "How about a fried-egg sandwich? Where shall I put these?" She held out the notebook and pen.

"You keep them. I don't have a place for papers."

"But what about your work? Surely you must have a desk, files."

She spoke unthinkingly, but the effect of her words was immediate. Hazel stood up and motioned her to follow, first to a room at the back of the house. A desk with a computer stood in front of the window, bookshelves lined one wall, a narrow bed stood against another. "Jonathan's study," said Hazel. "He showed it to me the first time I came to supper."

Charlotte nodded and ran her finger along a line of books. Here, after all, was her area of expertise. You didn't get this kind of layering of papers and dust in under six months. Together they moved along the corridor to the spare room where the furniture could be counted on one hand. A bed, a built-in wardrobe, a chair in front of the window, and to the left a bookcase, its shelves bare save for half a dozen paperbacks. No pictures, no clutter.

Charlotte wandered round the bed. In the carpet by the window she discovered four indentations. She beckoned Hazel over. "Maybe you used this as a study and stopped once you got an office at work? It looks as if someone had moved out and the room was waiting to be turned into something else."

When Hazel clutched her arm, Charlotte remembered the seizures. "Why don't you come back to bed? You don't want to be rushing around."

She watched uneasily while Hazel moved the chair to face an imaginary desk in front of the window, and sat down. Was she about to witness one of those Hollywood scenes: the victim recalls the long-ago crime? But Hazel's amnesia was the result of an accident, not some kind of malice.

She swung around. "I did have a desk here. I can remember writing, editing my interviews."

"When did you move it?"

Hazel gripped the edges of the chair. "Last year, sometime during the last year. Oh," she exclaimed, turning back to the window.

Over her shoulder Charlotte saw a young man with a crest of dark hair and a ragged backpack walking down the street. As they watched, he stopped, made a circle, and walked on. "It's the Tourette's boy," said Hazel, as if Charlotte would know what this meant. "He frightens me."

"Is he dangerous?"

"I don't think so, or at least only to himself." The boy, after a scant thirty yards, was circling again. "I'm afraid I could end up like him—completely separated from normal people."

You, Charlotte wanted to say, you've nothing to worry about. You could grow an extra head and still be normal. "Come," she said, "take a bath while I make us sandwiches."

chapter 14

That she came downstairs instead of waiting for him to bring her breakfast was unusual; that she was fully dressed, more so. But, absorbed in the newspaper, only half-awake, Jonathan offered juice and cereal without registering these danger signs. Since her damning question, he had been the one to leave rooms and seize a book. If she brought the matter up again, he planned to say Hogarth had warned him that paranoia was a possible side effect of one of her pills. I saved your life, he would remind her. He was sinking back into the financial news, having given her a bowl of muesli and the arts pages, when she said, "Where is my desk?"

"Your desk?" He made the mistake of looking up.

"Yes. I'm a journalist, I write articles. I must've written them somewhere."

The important thing was not to hesitate. "We sold it. You said it wasn't large enough and you wanted a new one. Don't you remember?" he added. That usually brought her to heel.

"And where is the new one?"

"On order. I'm sorry, I keep meaning to phone and chivvy

them." He made a little gesture suggesting, modestly, how overworked he'd been these last few weeks.

Hazel clutched her spoon. "I don't believe you. The room is stripped. You call it the spare room, not my study—and there're no books, no papers. I haven't worked there in months."

Shut up, he wanted to say. None of your fucking business. "You moved everything to your office. If you feel up to it, I thought we might go shopping later. Get ourselves some new togs for the big day. You always complain you don't have enough dresses."

"Jonathan, I'm a freelance journalist. I don't have that kind of office." Then, almost pleading, "Why won't you tell me the truth? I might've lost my memory, but I haven't lost my mind."

He recognised the tone: his mother asking if he couldn't come home for his father's seventieth birthday; Suzanne asking if he didn't want the baby. He glared across the table, his brain bursting with confusing impulses. I'm in charge, he thought. I don't have to answer. He got up, as if to get something from the fridge, and went straight through to the living-room. But alone with the cheese plant, he was afraid of being cornered. He rushed out again to climb the stairs to his study: his papers, his computer, his window. He closed the door, turned on the computer, and, on second thoughts, left the door ajar; he didn't want to be ambushed. As the screen went through its paces, he thought, In two weeks all will be well. The wedding rings he'd ordered would be waiting on Monday.

But why hadn't she believed him? Yesterday, in Finsbury Park, the man had fidgeted and cleared his throat in such a way that Jonathan had credited every word of his improbable story about the immersion heater. If only he'd listened to Maud. She'd warned him this would happen but, day by day, he'd been reluctant to upset the delicate balance. Now he must sit Hazel down and throw the bomb himself so it would explode exactly where he wanted. Maybe he'd even tell her that the other night, after a good-night kiss, she'd kissed him back and they'd ended up making love—a mutual act that subsequently, because of her seizure or medicine, she'd imagined into something else. Her beloved, a rapist? And afterwards, how wonderful, no need to be afraid. They could visit Steve and Diane, friends or colleagues, whoever they pleased.

He was staring blankly at the computer screen when the front door opened and closed. An office messenger, at this hour? Then, he was on his feet, scrambling down the stairs and—no time for keys—propping the door open with the mat.

The street was empty save for a woman with a bag of shopping, an elderly black man in a grey suit, three youths in baggy trousers, and a woman pushing a pram. No Hazel in either direction. He looked again to make sure she hadn't been hidden by a lamppost or car. For a few seconds, all he could think was that the paving stones had swallowed her up. He crossed the road to the blare of a horn, then ran to the nearest corner.

She was standing, talking to the bitch next door, wearing her winter coat, a dark green scarf, and, incongruously, her grubby blue trainers. No bag, though. She looked like a woman out for a stroll, save for the way she gripped the nearby garden wall.

Jonathan paused to catch his breath. "Hazel," he called. "Your parents are on the phone. I told them you'd ring back, but Nora said it was urgent."

"Oh." She glanced at him, cheeks flushing and instantly paling. "Thanks." And then, to Mrs. Craig: "It was nice talking to you."

She took a step, another, away from the house. Shit, he was thinking, when Mrs. Craig intervened. "Come, dear. Let's walk together." Taking Hazel's arm, she steered her homeward. Jonathan fell in behind, playing heel-to-toe, triumphant. So much for managing without him. She couldn't even make it to the corner alone.

Inside, he closed the door and allowed himself a moment of respite, leaning against the thick, comforting wood while Hazel continued into the living-room. Of course, the phone. When he followed, she was holding the receiver, looking perplexed. "I'm sorry," he said. "I did lie. Twice. Once in the kitchen, and just now. I didn't want Mrs. Craig to know we were having a row."

She replaced the receiver and curled herself into a corner of the sofa.

"Hazel, forgive me. I've been worried sick, and it makes me say the stupidest things. I keep thinking you're not well enough to hear the truth. You don't know how frightening it is—" he paused—"when you have seizures."

Her shoulders sank. Whatever spark had driven her to flee was being extinguished. "What was the first lie?"

"I've been meaning to tell you for weeks. When you were still in hospital, Maud and I talked and we decided it would upset you too much and—"

"Jonathan, tell me."

He blurted out the story they'd concocted: how he'd been overwhelmed at work, ignoring Hazel, the handy sublet. All his fault, each and every difficulty. He pushed on, not daring to check her reaction. After the accident, of course, he felt terrible.

"Thank you," she said at last. "I wish you'd told me sooner. I remember back at the hospital, I sensed something was wrong—the four of you saying 'home' in such a strange way."

"I'm sorry." He crossed the room, light-footed with contrition, to kneel beside her. "We were trying to protect you."

"So I ought to be specially grateful that you're taking such good care of me."

Her voice was small and forlorn, and suddenly his play-acting was genuine. "Hazel, I was barking. Work got on top of me. Two of my cases were in court, I'd lost the company a ton of money, I was worried about being made redundant. And it didn't help that you move in such glamorous circles."

He held out his hand, hoping she'd take it, their first voluntary touch since her seizure, but she ignored him. "I can understand," she said. Then she broke off. "No, I can't. I can't understand systematically lying to another person. You even asked me to marry you without telling the truth."

"I'm sorry." Grovel. Lick that dirt. "I was planning to, every day. I never knew where to start. I was afraid you'd think I didn't love you. As soon as you were hurt, I realised what . . ."

He saw her eyes, the muscles in her neck. "Hazel, take it easy, relax. Here, lie down. Let me get the rug."

But she was gone. No bad thing, he thought, as she slipped to the floor, heels drumming. "Boris," she said. "Where is my book? Where is it?"

When Maud arrived that evening, Hazel was still lying next to the armchair. Together, they got her to her feet and half carried, half dragged her up the stairs. She seemed not to know who they were or where she was, but once in bed, she said, to Maud, "Don't go."

Jonathan withdrew, saying he'd make hot milk. Back in the kitchen, he thought, Sod it—he was fed up barging in where he wasn't wanted—and began to pace the hall. Why, in her delirium, had she said Boris's name? From now on, he'd work harder at reminding her of their happy life together. Without him, she'd still be at Plantworks or teaching foreigners.

At the sound of footsteps, he hurried into the living-room and flung himself in an armchair. "Everything all right?" he said.

Maud sat down in the other chair. "Not everything. But Hazel seems okay. I gave her her eight o'clock pills."

"Thanks. Would you like a drink?"

"Please."

When he came back, a glass of wine in each hand, she appeared to be watching the television; as he approached, though, he saw her eyes brimming. "Cheers," he said. "I took your advice today, finally."

"My advice?"

"To tell Hazel about the flat, our ups and downs. You were absolutely right. I was an idiot not to do it sooner."

"What did she say?"

"She was upset, but mostly that I hadn't told her." He tried to remember if she'd asked anything about the flat. "I don't know if she really took it in."

"Before the seizure," Maud said.

He hadn't seen the sequence in quite that light. "Well, she'd been overdoing it. She escaped this morning. Fortunately she ran into Mrs. Craig at the corner."

"So you're keeping her prisoner." Maud examined the arm of her chair with fixed attention.

"Of course not. This is her home."

"But you and I don't 'escape' when we leave the house, do we?"

Once again he got that scary feeling about Maud. He stared at her shadowed eyes, her full mouth. What was in it for her? He hadn't a clue. "Shall we get a take-away?"

"You didn't phone."

For a moment he couldn't think what she meant, then recalled her request to meet. "I'm sorry." He explained about Alastair, his suddenly hectic schedule. "We can talk now," he offered. With Hazel comatose, even that seemed safe.

Maud drained her glass and, still scrutinising the chair, stood. "Not tonight," she said. "I have a feeling I might fall apart and behave badly."

"Maud."

"What?"

If he knew, if he had the faintest notion what she was asking for, he might've answered. All he could do was raise his
empty hands.

Outwardly, Freddie was in his usual position, sprawled on the
couch, a cup of Earl Grey beside him, the *Herald Tribune* open
across his chest. Inwardly, everything was changed. The couch
was no longer a place of hibernation but the headquarters of his
campaign to save Hazel. He tried to recall Mrs. Craig's words.
Hazel had been so angry she could hardly speak. She had moved
out. Then he thought of what Hazel herself had told him on his
second visit.

The *Tribune* slid to the floor. Somehow, Littleton was taking
advantage of her problems. Or did the seizures keep her captive? He remembered visiting a friend in Santa Monica. One
minute they'd been hulling strawberries at her kitchen table;
the next, she dragged him into the doorway and made him
crouch down, arms around his head, while the berries rolled to
the floor and the books tumbled from the shelves. What scared
him was not the earthquake so much as his own absolute lack
of premonition; he'd always believed the world would give
him the signals he needed. No wonder Hazel couldn't leave
when, at any moment, she might be felled by her own personal
earthquake.

He jumped up, so filled with insights that he had to
share them. "Felicity," he said when she answered the phone,
"remember the roof I was doing for Trevor in Highbury? The
woman who was sick?"

"Hold on a minute." He heard the receiver being set down,
then the little surge of it being lifted again. "Who's ill?"

He'd forgotten how brisk she could be at work. *Quarter to*

six outside Warren Street tube. Order me a prawn korma. That was
the limit of her conversation while she sat at her desk, helping
immigrants apply for welfare. "This woman I told you about,
the one who lost her memory and has seizures."

"Is she having one now?"

"No, no, I'm at home. I just—"

"Freddie, can we talk about this later?"

He hung up and wandered into the kitchen. The puppies
squealed and wriggled, nature's way of stopping him from putting them on the barbecue. He picked up what he thought was
Virginia, looked more closely and recognised Georgia's crooked
ears. She licked his hand with tiny, warm, wet slaps. Four hundred quid. Unbelievable. He'd give ten, twenty tops. Ounce for
ounce, she compared favourably with certain drugs. No question, there was something weird about buying and selling a
living being, even a dog.

He put her down squarely on all four paws, as Mrs. Jackson
had stressed, and she started scuffling with Connecticut. One of
the things Felicity used to say she admired was his talent for living in the present. All this talk about the past and the future,
she said, goes right by you. He protested that he liked her stories about the suffragettes, the riots. But not, she pounced, the
personal stuff. Watching her cat-and-mouse smile, he'd felt a
door close between them. It wasn't fair, he knew, but that she
didn't sense what he so carefully concealed made her seem more
distant. Didn't she realise he had a secret?

As Agnes gave a warning growl, he pictured the room of
heads. Mr. Early, that was who he needed to talk to, not Felicity. He went through his roofing papers until he unearthed
the Vulture Video flyer on which he'd written the details of
their first phone call. Only when he heard Mr. Early's voice—
"Freddie, how are you?"—did he understand the oddity of

what he was proposing. I'm treating him like a priest, he thought, or a shrink. "I wanted to ask you something," he said.

"I'm all ears."

"I don't mean like this."

"Oh, I see. In person, as they say." Complete silence followed. Anyone else would have asked why, or expressed irritation. "How about tea?" Mr. Early suggested, as if entirely at his own inspiration. "Would four o'clock suit?"

"For me?" said Mr. Early. "Why, thank you, Freddie. Daffs are my favourite spring flowers."

At the sight of the green-skinned buds in his host's pale hands, Freddie felt the meagreness of his offering. They'll open tomorrow, the man at the flower stall had assured him, puffing disconcertingly on a stogie.

"I got us some cakes, too. Kiplings' Bakewell Tarts."

Mr. Early again expressed thanks, and led the way inside. Freddie concentrated on the room of heads. Somehow he believed the conversation would go better in their presence. His heart crashed as they turned towards the kitchen, then recovered as Mr. Early said, "Let me put these in water and make the tea. If it's all right with you, I'd like to keep working. It doesn't mean you won't have my undivided attention. My hands have their own brain, like those dinosaurs."

While Freddie arranged the tarts on a plate, a nice piece of Limoges, Mr. Early installed the daffodils in a crystal vase and made the tea. "If you could carry the flowers," he said.

The room was even more crowded than last time and the tang of glue was gone. In the centre of the worktable sat a box of what Freddie at first took to be centipedes; on closer inspection, eyelashes. "Where should I put these?" he asked, hoisting the flowers.

"On the mantelpiece. No, how about the table by the window? It's cooler."

Soon they were seated, tea poured, tarts served, Mr. Early at his worktable doing something intricate with an ear, Freddie beside the fire. "Well," said Mr. Early, and Freddie would've bet a hundred bucks he was going to ask the purpose of his visit, but this was London, not Cincinnati; Mr. Early was enquiring about Agnes.

After Freddie's brief summary, he said, "Splendid," and reached for a small brush. "I'm working on a consignment for Glyndebourne. Have you ever been? They did a gorgeous *Marriage of Figaro* last year, though you had to sell your granny to get in. I'm hoping for some free tickets this time around."

He continued to talk, about his assistant who'd fallen in love and the radio interview he was doing next week. Watching his nimble fingers bend and flex the material, Freddie found himself casting back to the story of the two designers. Surely there was no way Mr. Early could tell a lie. Anybody would see the shadow through his smooth pink skin.

"So?" said Mr. Early, when the second cup of tea was poured, and Freddie understood that even here some explanation was required. He stood up and carried his cup over to the rows of heads. A sly-eyed woman with full, pouting lips regarded him quizzically. The bee-stung look, he thought, surprising himself. "Do you ever pretend they're alive?"

"Not exactly. I often name them, but that's to keep them straight. Isn't that right, Lavinia?" Mr. Early gave the head he was holding a shake.

"I know someone who's in trouble. I don't know how to help."

"Oh," Mr. Early sighed crisply, "helping. Not my subject. Can one person ever help another? Often I think the answer is a resounding no."

His hands never hesitated; it really was as if they had a sepa-rate brain. Just for an instant, though, Freddie wondered if his host was vexed. But now that he was launched, he couldn't stop. He spilled out the story of Hazel, so far.

"Let me see if I've got this right," said Mr. Early. "You've met a woman who as the result of an accident has lost part of her memory, and you're convinced that she's being held captive by the man she used to live with."

Put like that it seemed crudely melodramatic. "She's obvi-ously not happy with this guy."

"From what you've told me"—Mr. Early reached for a clamp—"you'd scarcely expect her to be singing 'The Sound of Music.' Even if the two of them go at it hammer-and-tongs, that doesn't necessarily mean anything. People have the most unusual arrangements, domestically speaking."

He swivelled the head a hundred and eighty degrees and turned his attention to the other ear. He sounded like Felicity, Freddie thought: cool, analytical, entirely failing to grasp a cer-tain mysterious level of life. And suddenly, the knowledge was as tangible as the sly-eyed head, he understood that he wasn't in love with Felicity, and that pretending was turning him into a jerk. Hadn't she told him, in twenty different ways, that she wanted to have kids? His mother, several thousand miles away, was right: Felicity did not have his heart. The revelation was strangely calming.

He returned to his seat and made a second attempt. "I know it's weird, but suppose she's being kept against her will and she's too sick to get away. What then?"

Mr. Early's hands actually paused. "Then, I don't know. People who are ill do need to be taken care of. Has she men-tioned wanting to leave?"

Freddie thought back to their last conversation, him dan-gling on the ladder, Hazel in her bathrobe. What had she said?

That she wasn't feeling too hot, was a bit muddled. "Not really, no."

"Well . . ." Mr. Early's hands were moving again.

"I see what you're saying—I'm sticking my nose in where I'm not wanted. Still, there are times a person might need rescuing without knowing it."

"Indeed there are."

Freddie stared at his glowing head, disappointed. He had thought Mr. Early would have the answer, yet here he was as wishy-washy as everybody else.

His host looked up with a small smile. "Freddie, be reasonable. I'm not going to tell you to kidnap some woman from a house in Highbury. Your willingness to be a knight in shining armour is splendid. But right now, it doesn't seem there's anything to be done. Not until Hazel asks." Using a razor blade, he began to trim the earlobe. "Helping other people is admirable, but maybe the person who needs help is yourself."

Freddie perked up. Finally, Mr. Early was sounding like his old self, and just then the phone rang. He cooed and exclaimed, asked after the health of his caller, and dictated a shopping list. Vaguely listening—"the feathers have to be blue"—Freddie wondered if Mr. Early ever left the house, and with that thought came another. Since he wasn't a father confessor, just an ordinary, busy guy, why was he giving Freddie the time of day?

"I'm sorry," said Mr. Early, hanging up. "I hate to do that when I have company, but I need the materials first thing."

"Couldn't you get them yourself?"

"Given how much I make per hour, no."

"I was wondering," said Freddie, "why you put up with me."

"You Americans, there's no stopping you." He leaned back, scrutinising Lavinia. "There's a mirror in the hall. If you want the answer, stop and look on your way out."

. . .

A piece of ice slid down Charlotte's back when Bernie told her what she'd done, but thanks to the several drinks she'd had at the Trumpet—courtesy of Bill, a TV repairman and a real doll—only one. "I already have a job," she grumbled. "Two: child care and reading to your patient. I don't have time to traipse all over London trying out for some crappy play."

"Yes, you do." Bernie was at the sink, rinsing dishes, her remarks punctuated by the rush of water. "The play sounds perfect for you. I can help you rehearse your party piece or whatever you do on these occasions, and what's more I'll give you a beta blocker so you won't get the shakes."

"How do you know I get the shakes?" Further speech was curtailed by the sight of her cereal bowl, still sitting on the counter from that morning, a little circle of reproach; she hastened to retrieve it.

Bernie took the dish from her. "Anything with more brain cells than an amoeba," she said, deftly inserting the bowl into the dishwasher, "would guess that the reason you mess up these auditions is because you're nervous."

Charlotte retreated to the table. She had been out most of the day, enjoying her old freedoms, going to the coffeehouse, visiting her favourite charity shops, although with her clean clothes it was harder to justify purchases, and later taking the bus to Kilburn and the Trumpet. Everything had been perfectly satisfactory—she'd timed her return for after the rug-rats' bedtime—and then she was greeted by Bernie waving a piece of paper. Guess what? Renee had phoned with a message about auditions for a new play in Battersea, and Bernie had taken it upon herself to phone back and assure them of Charlotte's presence.

"They still remember how good you were in that play last

year," she said, wringing out a dishcloth. "The woman I spoke to was very keen you should come."

"That's just what they say to get you there. Then they mow you down like cannon fodder. Besides, Battersea is miles away."

"Less than an hour, door to door."

Charlotte watched Bernie's ponytail swishing as she wiped the counter. How could she explain that one moment she had everything under control, was driving down the road straight towards her destination, and the next a roadblock loomed and she was on some mysterious detour? For a while after Walter left, she had turned her grief into art. She believed if she acted well enough, if she got glowing reviews, if everyone said how brilliant she was, he would have no choice but to come back. Together they would open the door to the empty bedroom, make love on the floor, and, giggling like teenagers, go out to buy a new mattress.

That belief had sustained her through the rest of the Ibsen run, and the play Bernie'd seen in Battersea. Then, at a party Ginny had dragged her to, a last night at the Royal Court Theatre, there he was: large as life, breathing, palpable. Without stopping to think, she pushed her way across the room. "Charlie!" He bent to kiss her cheek, and the next thing she knew he was introducing her to the tall, fair woman at his side. "Hi," Kerry said. "Walter's told me so much about you. Heard you were great in *A Doll's House.*"

Charlotte had backed away, people parting before her, as if she carried a leper's bell. Out in the street, her memories stopped. Did she go home, or visit someone, or pick up a man in Victoria Station? She had no idea. Twenty-four hours vanished, and the following night the ASM had to shove her onto the stage and prompt every speech. The next audition she'd gone to, she blacked out in the toilet.

Now her sister thought she could fix all this with a pill.

Beam me up, Scotty. Charlotte found herself remembering Hazel and the missing desk, nothing like the way memories surfaced in plays and films—as if the person were giving birth to something horrific. What would it be like, she wondered, if she lost all memory of Walter? Woke up in an empty flat with a room she never used and no idea why? Just for an instant, she thought, This is better.

Bernie sat down across the table. "You know," she said, "I'm not completely oblivious to your feelings. Sometimes I even envy you. I mean, I care about Rory and we'll probably get back together, but if it weren't for the children, I'd let him go. The way you feel about Walter is how we all hope to feel. None of this late-twentieth-century nonsense: if one person doesn't work out, move on to the next."

The salt shaker needed filling and the pepper grinder had a smear. Two pink butterfly barrettes lay beside the pepper, and Charlotte kept her eyes fixed on them. *I must, I must, develop the bust.*

Bernie was talking again. "You don't need to ruin your life to prove you love Walter. Why not show him what a fool he's been by acting well? He can't take that away from you, Charlie."

Which showed how stupid Bernie was, for hadn't Walter already done so? Still, the remark about envy echoed in her ears. Was it possible she had something her sister wanted? "Okay. I'll give it a shot. Maybe your pills will do the trick."

And Bernie, for once, was perfect. She didn't gloat or go smug. In fact she said something so surprising that Charlotte, momentarily, forgot her own distress. "I wouldn't recommend them if I hadn't found they helped."

At the sight of her face, Bernie laughed. "What did you think? Because I'm a nurse I can get drugs at the drop of a hat? I need a prescription, like everyone else."

She opened a bottle of wine and they made a plan, what Charlotte would wear to the audition, how Bernie would get a neighbour to collect the children, and it all seemed manageable. Why was I making such a fuss, Charlotte wondered. In her narrow bed she recited Puck's speech:

> Through the forest have I gone,
> But Athenian found I none
> On whose eyes I might approve
> This flower's force in stirring love.

Now there was a part to die for.

Next morning everything went smoothly. Bernie woke her as she left, and Charlotte emerged to find the prescription bottle on the table: *Take one about half an hour before. You'll be fab.* She bathed and dressed in the clothes they'd chosen, a black skirt and light-grey jumper. Then she was out of the house and walking to the tube. The first edition of the *Evening Standard* was on sale at the station. The train came almost at once and she got a seat. She turned to the horoscopes. *Taurus: The winds of change are coming. Let them blow. Keep a good eye on financial matters today.*

She was at the theatre twenty minutes early, as she and Bernie had planned, and backtracked to a café to buy a cup of coffee and take her pill. One is plenty, Bernie had said; you don't want to lose your edge, just for the world to lose its edge. More of the paper and, a whole five minutes early, trotting over to the theatre. Did she feel any different? She looked at the passing shops, the parking meters, a pillar box. The pillar box seemed a touch redder, but everything else was the same.

The woman who greeted her had a Glasgow accent—another good sign, thought Charlotte—and in the waiting room she saw that the half-dozen people clutching newspapers or books were all strangers. Opening her own paper, she felt inexorably patient. She could sit here all day if need be. But if she should be called upon to move, if there was a next thing to do, that was fine too.

The door opened, closed, opened, closed. Two more for the gladiators. She didn't look up until a voice said, "Charlie, is that you?" Into the chair beside her plopped Cedric.

She held tight to the paper, but it was no use; the familiar tang of his aftershave fell over her like a noose, and she knew she was done for. She should've left right then, folded her newspaper and walked out. "Hi," she said. "Fancy meeting you here."

"I was going to say the same. Who would've thought you had time for poor little Battersea with all your movie deals?"

"Excuse me, I must get some water."

In the corridor, she fumbled the pills out of her bag and dry-swallowed two. She recalled a woman she'd met at a party telling her about taking acid; she'd run round the park to make it kick in more quickly. Now Charlotte stumbled up and down the stairs, twice, then went to the ladies' and held her hands under the cold tap for as long as she could stand.

Of course he was still there, his eyes fixed on the door. There were other empty chairs, several, but she couldn't not sit beside him.

"So what are you here for?" he said.

"I don't know," she said vaguely. "I got a message."

"Ah, from your agent, perhaps. I'm hoping for some sort of peon's position, under-ASM. Wouldn't that be a hoot, us working on the same show?" He crossed his legs and stared admiringly at his right foot, shod in immaculate black leather. "Louis told me you've got all your possessions in rubbish bags in his cellar. Maybe someday we'll have a rummage."

We, Charlotte thought. Who is this mythical we? But she didn't say that, or at least she didn't think she did. Instead she went all Noël Coward—darling, she must concentrate now, for one teeny moment, a drink soon, very soon—and raised the paper so close to her face that a photograph of two teenage brides separated into a mass of dots. I'll count them, she thought, beginning with the veil of the bride on the left. *Two, four, six, eight, one, three, five, seven.*

Her name was called and she was on her feet. "Good luck," smirked Cedric. "Not that you need it."

She did not deign to reply. Everything seemed distant, including her own chilly limbs—and Cedric, Cedric was no more than a piece of thistledown waiting to be blown away. Puff, he was gone.

Inside the theatre, various people descended upon her. The director shook Charlotte's hand and launched into a fluent speech; she had beautiful braids. The play was set in the East End and used the background of the Mosley marches in the thirties to dramatise more recent problems of immigration. "There's a mother and daughter. The mother works in a local sandwich shop, and her livelihood is threatened by the immigrant family who open a shop next door."

"Like Jonah," murmured Charlotte.

"I beg your pardon?"

"Nothing."

"We'd like you to do a couple of scenes, one when the mother first meets her opposite number, the mother of the immigrant family. And at the beginning of the second act, when her white boss puts pressure on her about the new neighbours."

She was on stage, the lights blazing, a sheaf of pages in her hand. Words came from her mouth, gestures from her body. She moved in and out of the lights and at last, the pages gone, climbed down into a dark silence out of which the director finally spoke.

Later she described to Bernie how the ASM, reading the immigrant mother's part, kept missing her cues. "She couldn't tell when I'd got to the end of a sentence. Just a flat line of speech, no heartbeat."

"Why in the world did you take three?" Bernie said for the twentieth time. "I should never have given you the bottle."

Again, Charlotte tried to explain about Cedric. "But I could see, before he showed up, that they would help. One put me on quite a cosy plateau. Don't be upset. There are other auditions. Now, thanks to you, I know I can handle them."

No point in mentioning that two more of the pills, wrapped in tissue paper, lay in her purse, beside her library card: a small umbrella against the next rainy day.

chapter 15

Freddie was raising the knocker when he saw the note: WEL-
COME. PLEASE ENTER QUIETLY. SHOES! Inside was ample evidence that his fellow students of the Golden Road had heeded
this last request. The row of grubby, down-at-the-heel footwear
made him recall his visit to the shoe museum in Northampton.
The whole history of feminism is here, Felicity had claimed. On
the one hand, she gestured at a jewelled slipper, women forced
to lead useless, ornamental lives; on the other, she indicated a
factory worker's clog, working like animals. Men too, he had
said, pointing to a coal miner's boot. But even the poorest man
had someone to boss around, said Felicity. We were the slaves of
slaves. At which point he lost it. However poor, a freeman was
no slave. You're right, she said, briefly penitent, and began to
discuss how industrialisation had affected women. Now, he
thought, setting his boots beside a pair of running shoes, surely
she would understand Hazel's situation.

Entering the living-room was like leaving London. The air
smelled of lavender, the photo of the guru again had an offering
of white flowers, and a dozen people were lying on their stom-
achs, holding their ankles and rocking. Freddie found a space

near the window and joined in. After a minute or two, he managed to keep time to the mournful drumbeat.

"And now," said Mrs. Craig, whom he hadn't seen, lying near the guru, "let's try this the other way round."

He had come to talk to her, but exercise by exercise grew more absorbed until, during the final meditation, he drifted off. He woke to someone rubbing the balls of his feet. Mrs. Craig, wearing baggy purple trousers and a white T-shirt, cut short his apologies. "The class is meant to leave you relaxed. I often wish I taught in a commune or a boarding school where people could go directly to bed rather than back out to the streets. So how's your spine?"

He stood up and twisted from side to side. "Better," he said. Although he hadn't felt in particularly bad shape before, his whole body did now feel loose and vigorous. "What do I owe you?"

"Five pounds."

"Is that the top of your scale?"

"The bottom." She pressed her palms together.

"Here." Freddie held out a ten-pound note. "I have a sliding scale for roofs, and I charged you near the top."

"Do you mind putting it in the basket by the door? It's a little superstition of mine, not to handle money directly."

Freddie eyed her with renewed admiration. Stooping to the basket, full of five- and ten-pound notes, he said, "I'm here under false pretenses."

"That's all right. I told you you didn't need to believe for this to work."

"No, I mean I have an ulterior motive. I came because I wanted to ask you about Hazel."

Behind him the door swung open and the silver cat stalked in, gave him a yellow-eyed stare and continued across the room to weave around his owner's ankles. Mrs. Craig, busy with the combs in her hair, ignored him. "I ran into her the other day," she said. "She was better than when we had tea, though still shaky."

"Did she say anything?"

"We'd barely exchanged greetings before Jonathan appeared."

She bent to fondle Lionel, and Freddie asked if they could sit down for a minute. He hoped for a cup of tea or some root infusion, but Mrs. Craig just floated onto the nearest cushion and looked at him expectantly until he did the same. Telling her was easier than Mr. Early. She knew the cast of characters. And when Freddie got to the point, that he was afraid Jonathan was keeping Hazel against her will, Mrs. Craig nodded. "Now that you mention it, our meeting in the street was quite charged. He was so tense, there were sparks coming off him—and she wasn't glad to see him, either."

"I want to help her."

Like Mr. Early, Mrs. Craig seemed nonplussed. "What did you have in mind?"

He'd pictured Hazel in this room, seated on a cushion while Mrs. Craig fed her beetroot and Lionel offered his feline attentions, but her slight stress on "you" did not encourage such revelations. "I want to be sure she's living there because she wants to, not because he's somehow tricked her."

"And if she isn't?"

"Then I'll take her wherever she'd like to go."

Mrs. Craig regarded him thoughtfully. "Hazel may not have many alternatives. She can't be alone, and there's no family besides her parents."

"She can always stay with me."

"Mightn't that be like exchanging Broadmoor for Wormwood Scrubs?"

Freddie felt his jaw sag. "You think I'd keep her locked up? No way. She'd have keys, cash, she could come and go as she pleased."

Mrs. Craig patted the air. "Forgive me. People do tend to assume the worst of a man offering hospitality to a woman."

"Oh, you mean the sex business. No problem. I have a girl-friend." He smiled. "If you knew Felicity, you'd understand I don't normally think women need rescuing."

"What do you want me to do?"

There was something witchy about this woman, for sure. He tugged at the tassles of his cushion. "I wondered if you might go over, to see how she's doing."

"And should I say I've spoken with you?"

"You're the best judge of that. I don't want to add to her problems."

"Good answer. I'll pop round when the time feels right. Meanwhile, maybe you should have a chat with Felicity."

More witchy behaviour, for hadn't he suggested that Felicity was already on board? Mrs. Craig rose in her effortless fashion and, followed by Lionel, left the room. Perhaps, Freddie thought, that was something he'd learn later on the Golden Road. Kneeling to retrieve his boots, he saw the basket with its crumpled pile of money still by the door. Pigs could fly before this would happen in Cincinnati.

"Out," said Felicity, "of the fucking question."

She had listened to the story without a single interruption— a bad sign, he now recognised. "I thought you'd been acting funny these last few weeks. If you want to leave me for some-one else, go ahead, but don't expect me to pull the trigger. God, Freddie." She heaped biryani onto her plate. "It's so sleazy. We spend all this time talking about how society uses women, just discards them when they don't look a certain way, and you pretend to be so sympathetic. Then you meet a pretty woman and that's it. Bye-bye, principles. Bye-bye, Felicity."

He'd heard her angry before, plenty of times, but never this note of self-pity. As she helped herself to raita, he remembered the early days of their relationship, her arm in a sling, her stories. I should tell her, he thought, that I don't have what it takes, but the need to enlist her help with Hazel overshadowed the demands of truth.

"Felicity, this isn't about love. This is about a person who happens to be in trouble. I was sure you'd be glad to help. You're the one who taught me how many women are in abusive relationships, how hard it is for them to leave. What if I stayed at your house, and you stayed at my flat with Hazel?"

At the next table, two men and a woman were squabbling. "Rabbit," the larger man said loudly.

Felicity cracked a papadum. "We live in a big city, in the twentieth century. If this woman's in trouble, there are plenty of people who can help."

"Who?"

"Social services. Or call rape crisis and they'll give you advice."

Freddie imagined himself phoning offices. If he couldn't convince Mr. Early or Felicity, how was he going to convince a stranger? "Listen," he said, "maybe I'm completely off the wall. All I know is that Hazel is sick and confused and even her next-door neighbour agrees there's something weird about the setup. If you were in that state, wouldn't you be pleased to know you had a place to stay, no strings attached, for a few days?"

"Don't try to manipulate me," said Felicity between mouthfuls. "Forget about this woman. Let's try to sort out why things are so difficult between us."

"But I promised. I told her if she needed help, I'd be there, anytime."

"You're not a fucking boy scout, Freddie. You already have a promise—" she tapped her chest—"to me."

Just like him, to have said something and forgotten. He tried to think of recent vows. At Christmas, he dimly recalled, they'd discussed her moving in. Where would you work, he'd asked. At the kitchen table, Felicity said. When he pointed out how awkward that would be, they'd gone back and forth about practicalities until Felicity concluded it was probably best for her dissertation if she remained in Bethnal Green. But promises? He didn't remember any promises.

Now she put down her knife and fork and leaned across the table. "I hate ultimatums. But if you go ahead with this woman, our relationship will change."

"Hazel, her name is Hazel." He had the same desperate feeling he'd had at Lourdes when there weren't enough stretcher bearers and he didn't know who to help first.

She stood up with an expression that contained so many others that he couldn't begin to list them. His mind was working furiously—wait, he wanted to say, don't go—but his mouth remained closed. Felicity watched him for a few seconds longer. Then she put on her jacket, picked up her bag, and walked out of the restaurant, her silence more frightening than any outburst.

Jonathan's first thought, when he saw Mrs. Craig on the doorstep, was that the roof was acting up. He knew he should have waited for Trevor; idiotic to think a Yank could tell the difference between Welsh slate and Spanish.

"Sorry to disturb you," she was saying. "I wondered how Hazel was doing."

"A little better every day."

Mrs. Craig smiled and nodded until it dawned on him that she was in fact asking to see Hazel. He was about to offer the usual excuses—ill, tired—when he thought, what the hell. After all, he never saw her these days. Since their last conversation and her subsequent seizure, they divided the house between them like strangers.

In the dark bedroom she didn't answer his hello, but peering around the door he caught the glint of her eyes. "Mrs. Craig is here."

"Oh, good." She reached for the light.

Waiting for the kettle to boil, he rummaged for the herbal tea Mrs. Craig had firmly requested and chose blackberry over camomile because the box was prettier. Upstairs, she was sitting cross-legged on the bed. As he came in, she and Hazel both stopped talking. For a moment he was tempted to pull up a chair. Why should he let them drive him away? Then, moving a magazine to make room for the tray, he caught sight of the monitor, lying next to Hazel. Surreptitiously he switched it on, flicking the volume to high.

"Call if you need me," he said, and hurried downstairs to retrieve the listening device from the mantelpiece.

"How do you feel?" Mrs. Craig was saying. "You look rather—" a sweet sound interrupted her words, as if a tuning fork had been struck—"frayed around the edges."

"That day I met you in the street, afterwards I had a seizure. A bad one."

Their voices emerged from the monitor only a little mossy. He positioned himself in the armchair below the bedroom. Why hadn't he thought of this before? He'd always yearned to know what Hazel said and did in his absence, the unseen tree in the forest seen at last.

"Oh, I am sorry." He suddenly appreciated Mrs. Craig's excellent diction. "How are you now?"

"Terrible. It was the first time I'd been out alone since the accident. I wanted so badly to prove I could manage."

"And you did. Like everything else, though, you have to begin slowly. Where were you going?"

"Anywhere. I couldn't bear to be under the same roof as Jonathan a minute longer. My skin crawls when he comes near me."

Crawls, he thought. He stared at the aerial roots of the cheese plant, dry, hairy, searching for something they would never find.

"I have a tricky question to ask you."

What was the old busybody after? He should never have let her in. Anxious not to miss a syllable, he raised the monitor to his ear. Then Hazel must've made some gesture of assent. "You know the man who fixed our roofs, Freddie Adams? He's worried that you're living here because of some kind of confusion."

Freddie, thought Jonathan, but his spurt of indignation was lost in Hazel's reply. "He's right," she said. "I just found out that I'd moved into my own flat before the accident."

Was Mrs. Craig nodding, trying to interrupt? At any rate, Hazel rushed on. "I can't tell you what a relief it is. For weeks I've had the feeling things weren't quite right between Jonathan and me, but no one would come clean. It was driving me mad."

"I'm sorry. I've been a poor friend. He didn't make me feel very welcome when I came to tea."

He fought the impulse to run upstairs crying "Fire! Fire!," drag Mrs. Craig from the room, and hurl her into the street. I already told Hazel the worst part, he reminded himself.

"Jonathan I can understand," she was saying, "in some

warped way. The person who baffles me is Maud. She stone-walls, says she has no idea what I'm talking about. That I mustn't excite myself. Please, will you tell me what you know?"

In her clear voice Mrs. Craig embarked on her version of their history. Hazel moving in, delicious meals, interesting excursions, articles gradually accepted. "Your job brought out the worst in Jonathan. You used to complain that he'd interrogate you if you were even a few minutes late. Once you said it was like living with a detective."

That damn humming.

"And last spring you found out about Suzanne."

"The Suzanne who lived here before me?"

"Exactly. They broke up when she got pregnant and she had the child on her own. Apparently Jonathan hadn't bothered to tell you. That was what upset you, that he didn't seem to think it was important."

During a long pause, he twisted the volume into a roar of static, out of which Mrs. Craig's voice leapt—"Don't upset yourself"—followed by hushing sounds.

"And then I moved out," Hazel said hoarsely.

"In the autumn. I'm not sure why."

"Jonathan said it was because he was busy, overworked."

"Maybe. You were so angry you could hardly speak."

For a few seconds, the blood seething through his veins, he didn't notice the absence of voices. He fiddled with the volume, turned the power on and off, all to no effect. He was halfway up the stairs when the bedroom door opened.

"Jonathan," Mrs. Craig said brightly. "I was coming to see if we could get some more tea."

She knows I was listening. "How's Hazel?"

"A little tired." She smiled. "I won't stay much longer."

No, she doesn't.

She returned to the bedroom and he retreated to the

kitchen. Now who's paranoid, he thought. When had that bitch been interested in anything besides auras and massage? And, of course, her garden, a haven for his bees.

"Camomile compresses are marvellous for that," she was saying as he carried the tea into the room.

Bending to retrieve the empty mugs, he spotted the monitor face down on the floor. No danger. One of them had accidentally knocked it off the bed. He'd been imagining they were as clever as he was. Boldly, he turned to Hazel. "Have you invited Mrs. Craig to the wedding?"

"She was just telling me," Mrs. Craig said. "If I can rearrange things, I'd love to come." She explained she'd offered Hazel half a dozen massages as a present—"Most beneficial for restoring inner balance"—and Hazel announced she was going for the first session tomorrow.

He flung out of the room. Suzanne, for christ's sake, she knew about Suzanne. He'd hoped never to utter that name again, but mightn't it be for the best, one less secret between him and Hazel? And now he knew what to emphasise, his deep feelings about having a daughter, the anguish of the decision, etc., etc. Downstairs rain was streaking the kitchen door, pattering on the leaves of the elderberry tree. Damn, he thought; then, why not? Being in the house was intolerable, and the bees could survive a sprinkle. Retrieving the veil and smoker, he stepped into the garden.

At the hives, he lit the smoker and gave two puffs into the the nearest hive. He was debating a third when it occurred to him that he hadn't heard a word about the wedding through the monitor. Distracted, he pried off the lid. Before he could blink, he was stung twice, on the nose and the chin. Checking his hair, he pulled on the veil and gave several fierce puffs. In recent years he'd prided himself on using as little smoke as possible. Now the bees seemed to guess his rage. Even after the second dose they continued to erupt, trying to penetrate the veil. When two more managed to sting him, he pumped smoke into the hive. At last they quieted; he began searching the wax sheets for the long cells indicating an extra queen, but his hands were shaking so severely, the stings ached so sharply, the rain fell so drearily, that soon he gave up and returned indoors.

Since Walter's departure, Sunday was Charlotte's least favourite day of the week, most of her normal haunts closed and British family life in full swing. But at Bernie's, it was noticeably less of a dog and could even be mildly pleasant. This afternoon they'd gone for a walk along the canal and she'd served a high tea of macaroni cheese, which the rug-rats devoured. Now they were in bed, Bernie was ironing, and she was sitting on the sofa, skimming an article about the Redgraves—she'd once been in a play with Corin—when Bernie made an announcement. "I've been waiting all day." Her iron hissed over a blouse. "Rory's moving back in."

"Oh." Charlotte clutched the newspaper. "Great."

"I thought you'd be pleased. You were the one who kept telling me to take him back."

"I am pleased. It's just . . ." She folded the paper so that the pages all lined up. "I've got used to the four of us, being an aunt. I'll miss that." And it was true. Day by day, her old free-doms seemed less alluring. For the last few weeks she'd been helping Oliver with his class play, a pageant about the early Britons, and she'd taught Melissa to waltz and fox-trot. She was even daydreaming about staying longer, perhaps until the autumn, which would give her a chance to really get back on her feet. Though Bernie was a pain, she wasn't an automaton. She had desires, fears; she simply repressed them better than most people.

"We'll miss you too." Bernie reached down to draw a new

red garment, Melissa's, from the basket. "How soon do you think you can leave?"

"Leave?" Her first thought, absurd in retrospect, was that she'd forgotten to pick up something from the shops.

A little cloud of steam rose as Bernie tackled a sleeve. "Well, we're pretty squeezed here, and once Rory's back he can collect the kids, all of that."

"You mean you want me to move out? But what about our agreement? That piece of paper you made us sign. I rented my flat until the end of June." She struggled to keep her voice calm. Suddenly she wondered if Bernie had been at the pills; that would explain her steady ironing, her icy demeanour. It isn't that she doesn't care about me, Charlotte thought. I'm far away, a small object on a distant planet.

"Yes," said Bernie, "we did have an agreement, including a default clause. I think it was your suggestion that, with sufficient notice, we could change our minds."

Surely not, but Bernie was setting the iron on end, going over to the desk and—amazingly—producing the paper. She sat down beside Charlotte and pointed out the sentence: *We are both at liberty to alter these arrangements as long as we give the other proper notice.*

"But where will I go?"

"You've got loads of friends." Bernie patted her arm. "I'm sorry. I've liked having you here, but the kids need their father. I hate for them to shuttle back and forth, even for an extra day."

Here it was, thought Charlotte, shrugging off her hand: the invincible argument, always more important than anything or anyone else. God damn the rug-rats.

Only as she neared the garage at the end of Mr. Early's street did Charlotte wonder if she should have phoned. But how ridiculous now that she was a hundred yards away. Besides, two in the afternoon was a perfectly respectable hour for a visit, not as if she were trying to scrounge a meal; and she'd bought a bunch of half-price tulips. Reassured, she lifted the dolphin knocker. A damp smell rose from the small front garden. Spring, she thought, stepping back down the mosaic path. From the gate she saw lights in the upstairs room where, a few weeks ago, she and Mr. Early had sat by the fire. A piano was playing. She cocked her head, trying to ascertain the source, and lost it to a passing car. Two boys strode by. "In Corinthians," the taller one was saying, "God offers . . ." Charlotte gazed after them. For as long as she'd lived in London, a poster in the tube had advertised a church near the Elephant and Castle; she could picture the curly-haired woman and the boy in a suit both finding religion.

She knocked a second time, more vigorously, and retreated again to the gate. As she took the final step, a dark shape flitted by the window. Any moment the door would swing open with a flurry of apologies—I was on the phone, I was frying an egg— and she would launch into her speech: personal assistant, house-keeper, dogsbody. Surely he had room for her. After all, she was giving nearly a week's notice. *If you could move out by this week-end,* Bernie's note on the kitchen table had said.

No light, no footsteps. Once more she raised the knocker— a single, timid tap—and then, without waiting, she laid the tulips on the step and ran down the street.

Not until she was on the 43 bus, breathing hard, did Char-lotte allow herself to consider that her eyes might have been playing tricks; no one had stood at the window. What she'd seen was the shadow of a cloud, the huff of a curtain, but not a person, and certainly not Mr. Early refusing her entrance. His warm welcome last time, the whisky, the midnight feast, showed how absurd that was. No, like Bernie, he simply left the lights and a radio on for security.

But where now? She tried to summon the image of a single person who would be unequivocally pleased to see her. Melissa galumphed across the playground: Auntie Charlie, Auntie Charlie. Worse than useless. The Trumpet was out of the question and so was Ginny, who would either want her to buck up or point out what a fool she'd been. Brian? With luck he'd be in his office, trying to sell some hapless person a flat in Bermondsey. She could go and drink watery Nescafé and tell him theatre gossip between his important phone calls, but that wasn't going to ease her mood, let alone solve her own housing crisis. The bus was nearly at the Angel when she thought of Jason.

Now, if only she still had his card. Her normal system of conservation had broken down under Bernie's influence. With apologies to the woman beside her, Charlotte delved into her bag. On and on, down and down, and yes, nearly at the bottom, here was a crumpled rectangle with, praise be, both office and home phone numbers and the office address, which Jason had intimated was close to Baker Street. That it was some distance away made Charlotte happy: a destination. She would change at King's Cross and go along the Euston Road, or maybe via Holborn.

The glass doors wouldn't budge. She tried first the right, then the left, before knocking. At last, the young man at the reception desk—she was sure he'd been aware of her struggle all along—raised his head; his voice crackled out of the speaker. "Do you have an appointment?"

"Yes, with Jason."

"Jason Holmes or Jason Needham?"

"Needham."

At a clicking sound, the right-hand door yielded and she stepped into the carpeted room. Nice, she thought, sniffing the warm air.

"What did you say your name was?"

"Charlotte, Charlotte Granger. I may be a little early, so please tell him I'm happy to wait."

As she spoke, she drifted across the room and leaned over the counter, giving the young man her most intense smile. Idly she picked up a programme schedule, checked the clock and pretended to study it. What would Jason say? She hoped for a whoop of pleasure and a request for her company in some cosy studio with a sign on the door: AUTHORISED PERSONNEL ONLY.

"Take a seat," the man said, and she did, as far away as possible to emphasise her secure conviction in Jason's welcome.

Now, which was his programme? She looked more closely at the schedule: *Art Watch? News from Nowhere?* She heard her name, the receptionist talking on the phone. Finally, he motioned her towards a phone at the end of the counter. "Line two."

Charlotte picked up the receiver, heard the line fizz, and pressed a button. Suddenly her ear was full of noise, which she recognised as the show playing on the radio in the reception room. "Jason?" she said cautiously.

"And now we have a young American writer, a former stockbroker and Wall Street errand boy—"

"Charlotte, hi. Great you stopped by. This is a crazy time. We're on the air and we have to figure out the second part of the show."

"Can I—?"

He was still talking. "Give me your number and I'll call you when I'm done."

"What about a drink? My treat. I can wait." The voices echoed around her, disconcertingly stereophonic.

"Sorry, what did you say?"

She repeated her offer.

"No, no, I'll be at least a couple of hours."

She tried to say that was fine, she'd be happy to take a little snooze on the couch, but he didn't seem to hear. "Give me your number," he repeated and, once the digits were out of her mouth, hung up.

On the pavement again, she was staring bleakly at the bookshop across the street when something made her turn: the receptionist, still with the phone to his ear, was watching her. Propelled by his snotty gaze, she trotted briskly to the corner and came to a halt in front of an old-fashioned linen shop. TWO FOR £5, read a sign next to the tea towels. SPECIAL! £9.99, claimed the pillows. What in the world am I going to do, Charlotte thought. A passing woman gave her a curious look. Raising her hand, she discovered her face was wet.

She couldn't have said how long she stood there, or what— a footfall or a voice—made her glance up at that particular moment. With no surprise, she recognised Jason, in his leather jacket and black jeans, and his companion, almost identically dressed, with hair the colour of butter. Laughing, talking, they turned the corner and were gone.

chapter 16

The crack grew like a tree, an oak or a sycamore, something thick-trunked and leafy, splitting the brick from below ground level, forking into thinner, increasingly erratic branches as it rose towards the second storey. Jonathan counted off the glass strips, installed across the fissure last autumn to measure movement and now all broken. Beside him the owner of the house, a forensic scientist named Gerald Finch, hunched gloomily forward to finger a smaller crevice. "Ever since this started," he said, "I've been having dreams of my teeth falling out."

As he spoke, Jonathan glimpsed his own teeth, splintering and breaking, an image he'd dreamed last week, or the week before. He ran his tongue tenderly over his molars and copied the numbers from the strips onto the form. "The movement has definitely continued. We now have the measurements to complete your earlier report."

"Measurements?" Mr. Finch said bitterly. "None of my windows or doors close, the ceilings are threatening to come down, my children's marbles and cars run willy-nilly to one side of the room. The question is how much it's going to cost, who's going to pay, and whether it's remotely possible that this whole business can proceed at faster than glacial pace."

Jonathan suddenly caught the man's *r*'s. "Are you Scottish?"

"Perth. Yourself?"

"The Borders, near Hawick. I was stung," he added, feeling the need to explain the swellings on his nose and chin.

"Scott country."

"Almost, but not quite."

"Could be the claims adjustors' motto." Mr. Finch gave a little laugh and aimed a kick at the base of the crack. His appearance, Jonathan thought, was the opposite of his name: tall, burly, broad-shouldered. "Sorry, I don't mean to take it out on you. I'm sure you're a perfectly decent chap who'll file the proper forms and whom I'll never hear from again. We'd planned to move last summer, for the schools, but no one will make us an offer until we get this sorted. Do you have kids?"

"No."

Mr. Finch nodded, as if the denial had confirmed all his suspicions. "Tell me, as one Scot in exile to another, is there anything I can do to speed this business along? My dad used to dish out the whisky. If it would help, you're welcome to my entire stock: a bottle of Glenfiddich and the dregs of some Dewar's." He smiled, revealing two rows of excellent teeth, and settled back into gloom.

Jonathan had a vision of walking him down to the local, buying him a dram, and telling him everything. Last autumn, my girlfriend moved out after a row. A few months later she had an accident, lost part of her memory, and moved back in. I'm taking care of her, and we're going to get married. The only problem is she's fallen victim to delusions; every day she "remembers" something else about me she doesn't like. Now she leaves the room when I enter and refuses to discuss our wedding plans. Ghastly, Mr. Finch would say. Appalling.

The front door flung open and a red-cheeked boy in tartan trousers yelled, "Dad."

"Alex, I'm busy. Ask Mummy." Then, to Jonathan, "I'm putting you on the spot."

"No problem. What you can do is get the estimates. You need three, in writing. I'll file my report this afternoon, then it has to be okayed. That happens at a meeting on Wednesday. Call this number on Tuesday, ask for Alastair Stevens, and tell him what you've told me. He's from Edinburgh, so it wouldn't hurt to stress your origins. Phone back on Thursday and, whatever you do, don't lose your temper—Alastair tends to put people who blow their stack to the back of the queue. Keep phoning until you get an answer."

"Thank you." Finch turned with outstretched hand. "My whisky is yours. And if you ever need advice in forensic matters, which I hope you won't, I'm your man."

Driving back to the office, Jonathan thought that with luck, by this time next year, Mr. Finch's children would be able to roll their marbles in both directions. I'm not a terrible person. People like me. A bus lurched past in a smear of exhaust. But not the ones I want or need to. Hazel, Hazel, Hazel. For a few seconds, the surrounding vehicles disappeared; he guided the car to the kerb and rested his head against the steering wheel.

"Are you okay, lad?" A traffic warden with a burgeoning white moustache was peering in the window.

"Something in my eye."

"Short of being struck blind, you can't stop here." He stepped back. "Try the car park second on the right."

Jonathan blew his nose and, for form's sake, peered in the rearview mirror. His eyes, at close range, did have a dull, unhealthy look, the whites laced with blood. Was there really a problem? Some invisible worm eating away inside of him, like a wax moth devouring the honeycomb? But the presence of the warden, still standing nearby, precluded further examination. As he pulled out behind a motorbike, Jonathan remembered Maud's demand for a meeting. Perhaps they could have a drink after work this evening. Almost anything seemed preferable to going home.

In his car opposite Plantworks, he watched the late customers emerge with bunches of flowers wrapped in shimmering paper. The apology trade, Maud called it, those last-minute purchases made to head off disaster or put a dodgy evening on a more secure footing. How often had he brought Hazel flowers in their years together? Frequently at first, but only sporadically after she moved in, when the bouquets she brought home from Maud's had seemed to render such gifts superfluous. Probably a mistake, he thought, gazing at the miniature orange tree in the window, its fruits glowing like tiny lanterns, to neglect the romantic gestures.

After ten minutes, maybe fifteen, a slight, androgynous figure stepped out of the shop, paused in front of the window display, and sauntered towards the bus stop: Grant, Maud's assistant and the best wreath maker, she boasted, north of the river. Surely she would follow soon.

The car radio nattered on about fox hunting, the pros and cons. As with the teeth that morning, Jonathan felt a fragment or premonition surfacing. The last time he saw them, nearly two months ago, Steve and Diane had talked about foxes and the dwindling supply of lion shit. That was the evening, he recalled, of the amazing day when Hazel had opened her eyes and he had begun to hope. He rubbed his hands against the growing cold. Five more minutes, he promised, and he would let Maud know he was here. "It's easy to romanticise the fox," the announcer claimed, "as a beautiful, wild animal. But foxes, by their very nature, are wanton killers." The shop door opened, and there she stood. At first he barely noticed that she wasn't alone. Then, when Maud stepped to one side, he recognised Mrs. Craig's shining hair.

He was out of the car, fury spewing through him. "Maud!"

She turned and something clattered to the pavement. He caught the glint of metal and bent to retrieve what became a pair of secateurs. As he straightened, he found himself looking into the familiar face of the roofer.

"Jonathan," Maud said. "Is Hazel all right?"

With the hand not holding the secateurs, he grabbed her wrist. "What's going on?"

She made a small sound.

Someone tapped him on the shoulder. "You're hurting her," the roofer said.

"Take your fucking hands off me." After all his restraint, it was a relief to be shouting at last, but he did let go of Maud.

"Jonathan?" Mrs. Craig stepped forward. "You seem upset. Has something happened to Hazel? Can we help?" She was regarding him with her usual calm demeanour, arms outstretched, as if to offer support.

Steady, he thought, steady. Grabbing people, shouting on the pavement, wasn't going to help. "Hazel's fine," he said. "I need to talk to Maud."

As he moved towards the shop, he heard the roofer and Mrs. Craig, almost in unison, ask if she was all right and Maud say of course. "Don't worry about Jonathan," she added. "He's just overwrought."

In the cool, sweet-smelling shop, he shivered. A bird-of-paradise winked at him, and the buckets of spring flowers—

daffodils, narcissi, tulips, irises, freesias, lilies, baby's breath, roses, anemones—made him think of his bees. This would be their Eden, so many blooms so close together. But no, their ideal was singularity, one species at a time.

He heard footsteps, the door being closed and locked. "What the hell do you think you're doing?" Maud took the secateurs from his hand. "You can't storm around, behaving like a wild man."

Over her trousers and pullover she wore a striped butcher's apron with a row of pockets. The stark shop lighting made her skin creamier and her eyes darker. Or perhaps that was anger. "I'm sorry," he said. "I was waiting for you, and when I saw Mrs. Craig, I panicked. What was she doing here, and with the fucking roofer? Everything's getting in such a muddle. Hazel keeps finding out more and—"

"Jonathan, not everything is about Hazel."

Something soft lay beneath his right heel: a pile of clippings, leaves, flower stalks, ready for the dustpan. "But," he started and, at the sight of her lips tightening, stopped. He imagined the secateurs stabbing into her cheek, her breast. "Is there anywhere we can sit down?"

She led him through the shop to a small office lined with counters and filing cabinets. Seated, they were almost knee to knee. Jonathan pressed back in his chair, a fruitless effort to increase the distance. The silence quickly passed from possible to bearable to impossible. Maud was staring at him, and he was suddenly conscious, again, of his stings.

"How do you feel about me?" she said.

If she'd spoken in Urdu, or demanded the formula for a complex protein, her question would have made more sense. "I'm fond of you. Very fond." *More,* he thought desperately. "You've been marvellous with Hazel. I admire your energy, your—" he groped—"business acumen." He waved at the rows of labelled files, the Interflora directories, the fax machine. No, wrong, still not enough.

"What about what we did on the living-room floor?"

Christ. "That was wonderful." Their knees were virtually touching. If only he could stroke her breasts, stick his tongue down her throat, but his body, from toenail to forehead, was beyond movement, as if the winking bird-of-paradise had shot curare into his veins. "Maud."

Her eyelids dipped. In the silence he heard ticking: her watch. Again he thought of his bees, and the faint noise of the hives in winter.

"You don't have any idea, do you, what this is all about? It's not very complicated." Her voice cracked, then steadied. "I love Hazel. And unfortunately, I'm in love with you."

Lunch, a sour memory, rose in his throat. He swallowed and swallowed again, no longer hearing the watch, breath, traffic, any sound save his own bubbling disgust. How could she? At the same time, all the bewildering twists and turns of the last two months fell into a straight line. She trapped me like a fly in her sticky web.

Maud raised her eyes, and it was his turn to drop his gaze. "I know it's hopeless," she went on, speaking more quickly now. "You feel about Hazel the way I feel about you but, as you say, you're fond of me. Which is better than nothing."

Briefly, curiosity eclipsed disgust. "How can you stand it?"

"What choice do I have?" she fired back. "It would be nice if the world were a binary operation, either/or, but it doesn't work like that. You love Hazel, and you find me attractive. One ought to make the other impossible. Instead the two coexist side by side. If I sat on your lap right now, you'd get a hard-on—even though you hate what I'm saying."

Involuntarily, he glanced down. His head was swimming

with the sense of everything changing from black to white, round to square, earth to fire. "I always thought you disapproved of me," he said.

"I was worried Hazel might guess—you know how intuitive she is—and last autumn, after she left you . . . well, I got my hopes up. It drove me mad, the way you'd suggest we meet and then all you'd talk about was Hazel. As if you'd do anything not to be with me." From the front of the shop came the door rattling, one last desperate customer. "Did something happen the other night?"

"The other night?" An arrow parted the clouds.

"When she had that massive seizure. She seemed to be getting better. Then suddenly she was right back in the thick of it."

He babbled about setbacks, side effects, new medicine.

Maud watched. "I'd been wondering"—her tongue slid over her lower lip—"if you might've forced yourself on her."

After the headlines of the last few minutes, her tone was so quiet, so casual that it took a moment for her meaning to reach him. She's mad, he thought, edging his chair back the final inch, absolutely barking.

Before he could protest, Maud was speaking again. "Ever since then she's been in a terrible state. She keeps asking me to tell her the truth."

"What do you mean, 'state'?"

"She says she's afraid of you. She doesn't want to marry you, but she doesn't know what else to do." She leaned forward and, before he could protest, took his hands in hers. "I don't think it's going to work, Jonathan. And even if it does, so what? I left my husband while he was at the pub. Marriage doesn't come with a lifetime guarantee anymore."

He pulled free of her grasp. "You don't understand." He glared at the row of files: ACCOUNTS PAYABLE, SUPPLIERS, DEVELOPMENT, PROMOTION. "Hazel loves me. When she came to, I was the one she recognised, not you. Her illness makes her confused. I've messed things up between us—once, twice—but this time I'm going to do everything right."

"Like make love with me?" Again her tongue slid over her lips.

There was nothing he could say: damned if he claimed it was a momentary lapse, damned if he didn't. I should've accepted Finch's offer of a bottle, he thought. "What did Mrs. Craig want?" he said. "And that roofer?"

"Let's get out of here. Who's minding Hazel?"

"The nurse's sister. I called from the office and asked her to stay late."

"Is that okay? Apparently Hazel didn't show up for her massage, and no one answered the door. That's why Mrs. Craig came round. She was worried and couldn't remember the name of your company. The roofer gave her a lift."

"Hazel probably just forgot. Everything was fine when I phoned a couple of hours ago. Charlotte said they might go for a walk. If there was any problem, she'd call Bernadette."

Maud stood; he did too. In the small room her breath touched his face. She looked so sad that, for the first time since he seized her wrist, he found himself thinking not of Hazel or himself but of her. What had he done to deserve such devotion? Nothing. Poor Maud. It was a cruel, cosmic joke.

He followed her back into the shop, the buckets of flowers on one side, the ficus and ferns, ivies and cyclamens on the other. "Do you need to put things away?"

"No, all done." She moved a couple of buckets closer together. "You know, once I was sitting on your sofa, checking through recipes, when you came and sat down beside me. . . . That was all it took."

"Oh, Maud," he said gently.

When Jonathan rang that morning, Charlotte had begun by refusing in spite of his offer of extra pay. I have plans, she said, and it was true. Given the crisis with Bernie, the debacle with Jason, the last thing she ought to be doing was rushing all over London, babysitting. Then he put Hazel on the line—Please, I know you're madly busy—and Charlotte melted. Here was someone who wanted, even needed her.

At the house Jonathan greeted her with a twenty-pound note. "In case you want to pop out to the shops," he had said and, as she took the money, brushed her palm with his fingers.

The gesture was so startling, so intimate, that for a moment Charlotte thought she'd dreamed it. Then he banged out of the front door, and she knew she hadn't. Was he coming on to her, or something more sinister? She folded the note into her purse and headed upstairs.

Hazel was seated on the bed, fully dressed; no weeping in the pillow today. Is he gone, she asked, getting to her feet. At the kitchen table, she produced a list of some sort and poured out a fantastic story.

"Wait a minute," said Charlotte. "You're saying that last spring you discovered Jonathan had a child with an old girl-friend which he'd forgotten to mention. Then, in the autumn, you moved into your own flat, taking your desk, and that's where you were living when you had the accident."

Hazel nodded.

"And Jonathan pretended you'd been living here all along."

"Exactly. Remember what you said about how he might like his version of the past to be the only one."

"So where is the flat?"

"I was hoping," Hazel said, "you'd help me to find out."

This took two phone calls, one to directory enquiries and the second to the listed number where a man answered, and said that of course Hazel could come over to collect a jacket. "His name's Daniel," Charlotte announced triumphantly. "Any time before four is fine."

Then, seeing Hazel's face, she shepherded her onto the sofa. "Read to me," Hazel whispered, and she did. She was finishing the chapter on water rationing, when the phone rang and she had to summon all her actorly skills at the sound of Jonathan's voice. An emergency at the office, he claimed. She could feel Hazel listening as they negotiated an extension of her day. Bollocks, this was going to push her over the edge. But, hanging up, she discovered Hazel galvanised rather than upset. Let's go, she said. In the taxi the air tightened as if they were approaching a crucial audition. Charlotte knew she was hoping that the flat would bring back everything, good and bad, from the missing years.

If anything, the reverse occurred. Hazel showed no signs of recognition as they neared the house. Upstairs, she wandered from room to room, saying, "This is mine, I bought it in Bombay," or "Here's my desk," but of her life in the flat not a single detail returned. Charlotte joined with the tenant, a dishevelled academic with juglike ears, in trying to cheer her. Rome wasn't built in a day, Daniel said, and offered to start looking for new digs.

In the taxi on the way home, Hazel began to tremble. Is this a seizure, Charlotte asked apprehensively. No, Hazel said, this is rage. Back at the house, however, she had become curiously subdued and insisted on Scrabble. Later they ate supper in the living-room and Charlotte, on a whim, lined the bay with all the candles she could find.

When Jonathan arrived home, even later than he'd promised, it was clear that the pub had played a part in his emergency, but she could scarcely complain. She'd opened a bottle of wine at supper only to learn that Hazel wasn't drinking and then, on impulse, while Jonathan was phoning a cab, she'd lifted a second bottle from the wine rack into her bag. She could feel its satisfying weight in her bag now as the cab trundled down the Liverpool Road.

"Seventy-four?" the driver asked, his first words since she'd slid into the back seat. "Here we are."

She stepped out of the car and—somehow the pavement wasn't where she expected—grabbed the door to steady herself.

"All right?"

"Brill."

A Coke can lay at her feet, and a strange spiky object which on second glance Charlotte recognised as an umbrella. Then the taxi drifted away and she was standing alone in the deserted street singing,

> "Sail bonnie boat like a bird on the wing
> Over the sea to Skye.
> Carry the lad that is born to be king
> Over the sea to Skye . . ."

What came next? Bernie would know, Dad's favourite song.

She began to rummage for her keys. After five minutes she set the Chardonnay on the doorstep and sat down to continue her search. Later this would seem like the one small sign of prescience: by not ringing the bell she had refrained from ratcheting Bernie's wrath a notch higher. Ah, here they were, safety-pinned together, tangled in what proved to be a spring onion. She leaned back, the step above jutting into her spine. Smothered in clouds, the moon was hanging over St. Pancras. She would make her peace with Bernie. That was what the wine was for, a glass each and here's to you and Rory. She was sorry she'd taken umbrage. Just the shock. Not to worry. As Bernie said, forget Cedric, forget Jason, she had loads of friends.

She drew a deep breath—*I must, I must*—and rose to her feet. Yes, she felt better. The brief rest, the dank air, the glimpse of the moon, had revived her. The key turned smoothly on the first attempt. Inside was a line of black bags. Bernie must be making one of her periodic trips to the Oxfam shop. Typical, Charlotte thought. What else did you do to celebrate your husband's return? She peered into the nearest bag and saw a black cardigan, not unlike one she owned. She stepped farther into the hall, lured by the next bag, and then, feeling a draft, went back to close the door.

No radio, no TV. Could Bernie already be asleep? Forgetting the bags—she'd check them out in the morning—she looked into the kitchen, then the living-room. She almost dropped the bottle when she saw her sister seated in an armchair. "Hey, Bernie, I thought you'd gone to bed. Would you like a glass of wine? Mr. Littleton gave me a bottle. Chardonnay—a good year, he said."

Bernie moved not a muscle. Was she practising for Madame Tussaud's or trying some kind of relaxation technique? "Is that where you've been?" she said at last.

"Yes, taking care of Hazel. She sends her love."

"What about Melissa and Oliver?"

"It's Wednesday. Rory collects them."

"No, I said in my note that he couldn't this week."

Charlotte felt her cheeks go scarlet. "What note? Mr. Littleton rang this morning to ask if I could come. Then all kinds of things happened and he had to work late. You're the one who told me Hazel can't be left—"

"Don't give me this crap. You didn't think about Mel and Oliver for one second. They flew out of your tiny, self-centred brain. Who cares if they wait in the playground, watch all their friends leave, and listen to their teacher ringing around to find someone, anyone, who will care for them. Rory had a meeting, I was at the dentist's. Finally, the teacher reached their old child minder. Melissa cried for three hours."

"I'm so sorry." She wrung her hands. "Oh, Bernie, I didn't forget. I don't know what happened, but I didn't get your note. I love Melissa and Oliver. I'd never hurt them."

"Charlotte, I left it for you on the table on Monday, about our plans for the week. I know you got it. I found it in the rubbish later. If I had my way, you'd never speak to the children again, but Rory convinced me it would be better if you phoned tomorrow to apologise. Explain that you won't be seeing them for a while. Unfortunately, I've allowed you to become part of their lives and you can't vanish without a trace. Your things are in the hall. Call a taxi and get out."

"What things?" She sank into the nearest chair. Something jabbed her thigh; she removed a fire engine and set it on the floor.

"I blame myself." Bernie no longer bothered even to look at her, staring fiercely at the silent TV, where two men in wellingtons tramped across a ploughed field. "I knew you were hopeless about everything—men, work, money—but I thought the children were different. I couldn't believe you'd take out your neuroses on them."

Everything, thought Charlotte. Bernie's words whizzed past like stones. Meanwhile, inside her skull, her brain shuffled and hopped, a toad waking from a long winter. She knew what had happened; after reading the part about her moving out, she'd crumpled the rest of her sister's note unread, into the bin. Still, there must be something she could say or do to make this right. Didn't one hear, almost every week, about parents leaving their kids in supermarkets and playgrounds? Nothing terrible had happened and, for god's sake, it wasn't as if she'd been out gallivanting. What had Hazel said after their trip to the flat? I couldn't have managed without you.

Bernie came over, held out her hand. "Keys."

Her palm was the colour of a seashell. Charlotte didn't dare to meet those eyes so exactly like her own.

"I remember the first year of your training," she said, "I came to see you. It was awful being at home without you, and I'd decided to run away and find a flat of my own. You had an exam the next day, anatomy, so you made me quiz you on the bones of the hand and the foot, metacarpals and metatarsals. Afterwards I got into bed, a mattress on the floor, and told you what I'd been thinking and you said, Don't do it, it'll mess up your whole life if you quit school now."

Not a shell, the breast of one of their father's homing pigeons.

"I believed you. I caught the bus home next day and I stuck it out. Everything I knew about the future, about being an adult, came from you. Mum and Dad didn't have a clue. You were the one who came to my shows, who read the reviews, whom I brought Walter—"

Something stung her cheek. Her sister's pale pink palm had slapped her. "Un-fucking-believable. On top of everything else, you're drunk." She picked up Charlotte's bag, and within a moment extracted the keys and slipped them into her pocket. "Stand up."

No question, now, of tears or no tears; they poured down her cheeks. She was blubbering like Melissa, saying, "Please, please, please." Bernadette had grabbed her arm and was dragging her towards the door.

"Mum, what's happening?"

Through her tears Charlotte saw a pyjama-clad figure. Her arm was suddenly free. She reached down into some deep part of herself. "Hey, Ollie, I'm showing Bernie this part I've got in a play. A woman gets awfully upset so I'm practising crying— boo-hoo-hoo. I didn't mean to disturb you."

Bernie was moving across the room. "Come along, Oliver. Back to bed."

Charlotte sank back into the chair and searched for a handkerchief. Could one drown in tears? Presumably. All it took was for the lungs to fill with liquid, any liquid, and you were gone. Ah, here were the tissues she'd bought for the audition. She blew her nose. Thank god for Oliver. Surely now Bernie would see she was trustworthy. Everyone made mistakes, even nurses. The important thing was to learn from them. On the television a boat appeared. *"Sail bonnie boat like a bird . . ."*

"Get up. I've called you a taxi. They'll be here in five minutes." Bernie was shaking her. "Come on."

In the hall the door was open and Bernadette had already begun to carry the bags into the street.

"What about my toothbrush? My shoes?"

"All here. If by any chance I've forgotten something, I can always post it to you."

"Post it?" Was her sister bonkers? She picked up a surprisingly heavy bag—of course Bernie would've crammed everything in—and carried it down the steps to join the others on the pavement. Only three more bags and Bernie was hailing the cab, coming slowly down the street.

The driver climbed out. "Looks like a midnight flit."

"Can you open the boot?" Bernie said.

She and the driver packed the car as Charlotte watched distantly. The moon had shed its veil of clouds and rode free. Bernie was beckoning towards the open door. Then Charlotte remembered the Chardonnay; whatever was happening next, she might need it. She ducked back inside, pursued by Bernie's cries, recovered the bottle, and stumbled down the stairs. Without looking at her sister, she swept into the cab.

"Where to?" said the driver.

chapter 17

"She wasn't being straight with us," Freddie said. "As for him—" A sudden noise made him look back at the shop, from which he and Mrs. Craig had so recently emerged; on the door of Plantworks, OPEN clicked to CLOSED.

"As for him," Mrs. Craig concluded, "porkies flying."

"Porkies?"

"Pork pies, lies. Shall we?" She pointed towards the nearest pub, a hundred yards down the street, and Freddie fell in beside her. His limbs felt oddly light, as if his whole body had been engaged in that childhood game when you press your hand against a wall, step back, and your arm floats up of its own accord. If Littleton had manhandled that woman, the florist, for one more second—well, he didn't know what he might have done.

Following Mrs. Craig into the pub, Freddie recognised the kind of place he normally shunned: fake wood panelling, imitation brass rails, copies of twenties posters, everything save the customers out of a kit. "What can I get you?" he said, hoping the coins in his pocket amounted to a drink or two.

"A half of bitter, please."

She smiled and moved off towards an empty table while Freddie stepped to the bar. He'd have bet fifty bucks she was into white wine. Or something healthy: maybe orange juice to rebalance the system. Up a tree again, he thought, ordering her bitter and after a moment's dithering—he'd have liked an o.j. himself, but the price in pubs was loony—a half of lager. His pockets disgorged six pounds and twenty pence. Plenty.

"Health and strength." Mrs. Craig raised her glass. "Well, I feel thoroughly ticked off."

Ignoring her toast, Freddie asked what about Hazel. Should they phone the police, or the hospital? And the nurse, did Mrs. Craig know her last name? Mrs. Craig made a humming sound. Her hair was pinned on top of her head, and he glimpsed a purple pullover under her coat. "Freddie, I'm sure Hazel's fine. Maud certainly didn't seem worried. Or at least not about that. What worried her was our nosy questions. I just didn't think how it would look, our showing up out of the blue and accusing her."

Here it comes, thought Freddie, the British obsession with appearances: Chamberlain and his stupid umbrella. Better to starve, better to watch your best friend writhe on the rack, than to risk embarrassment. On the slenderest of evidence, he'd assumed Mrs. Craig beyond such concerns. A sudden growl— it sounded like Agnes—startled him. Glancing around, he spotted a small brown-and-white dog gnawing a bone under a nearby table. "We didn't accuse her," he countered. "You said we were concerned because Hazel hadn't made her appointment. That's pretty legit."

"At least we could've pretended to want a plant." She drank some bitter. "The anemones were lovely."

Anemones at a time like this. "A few porkies on our side," Freddie said firmly, "weren't going to change the bottom line, which is that for some reason Littleton doesn't want us talking to Hazel like a normal person. And the florist, Maud, is in his camp." Underneath the table, the dog snorted and banged his bone against the floor. "What should we do now?"

"Wait."

Freddie's gaze blurred until all he saw was the terrier's head snapping back and forth, breaking the neck of a rat or a rabbit. "That's how hundreds of people get messed up every year. We're not the police"—he turned back to Mrs. Craig—"and we don't have to convince a jury."

"Why do you think Hazel wants to leave?" She made the humming sound again. "To most people, Jonathan's a saint. Standing by her in spite of their difficulties, taking time off work to nurse her."

"He just went ballistic," Freddie exclaimed. "In Cincinnati, the way he grabbed Maud would be assault."

"He's very quick tempered, always has been, but that's not a crime. Hazel knows we're here. It's up to her to come to us."

Shades of Mr. Early, thought Freddie. Did all middle-aged Brits share this belief that you never helped anyone until they begged? "What if she can't?"

Mrs. Craig lowered her glass. "You're in love. Aren't you?"

He fingered his remaining coins. Heads, yes; tails, no. "Would you like another?" he said.

The streetlight in front of the house had shrunk to a dull cinder, and inside the only illumination came from beneath Kevin's door. For a moment Freddie was tempted to sit down in front of that golden thread and await whatever it was you waited for when your life had fallen apart. Instead, muscles aching as if from a long day on a steep roof, he groped his way upstairs. What he had told Felicity was true; he was a nothing kind of guy. All this activity had pole-axed him.

At the door to the apartment, he closed his eyes and nudged the key into the lock. As a locksmith he'd learned to listen to the clicks and hesitations that marked the passage round the cylinder. This particular key always hit a snag at three o'clock, where a slight jiggle was needed to get it moving again. Eyes still closed, Freddie stepped inside and caught the faintest whiff of the cleaning products he had used that morning, in an attempt to control the pups' miasma. They were squealing now, a regular coven of banshees.

"You'll be lucky," he muttered. Opening his eyes, he found the flat in darkness. In his haste to meet Mrs. Craig he must've forgotten to turn on the lights. He moved towards the switch and barely kept his balance.

The Yellow Pages lay on the floor amid a pile of books. As he went from room to room, Freddie discovered the emptied bookshelves were just the start: the kitchen was a mess of plates and food; his newly washed clothes carpeted the bedroom; in the living-room, the cushions were scattered. A burglar, he thought, taking revenge for his lack of computer, or kids getting their kicks. But he was on the third floor and the lock, he was sure, had been okay. He was bending to retrieve a pillow, when from the kitchen came an especially loud outburst.

Agnes was sitting with her forepaws on the edge of the pen. "What happened, girl?" he asked, stepping over two broken plates.

She pushed her nose damply into his hand. He stooped to pat the puppies, first Virginia, then Connecticut. As he reached for Georgia, he grasped the problem. Arkansas was gone.

Dumbfounded, Freddie leaned back against the table. Recent events rolled over him like eighteen-wheelers. Why was he always the last to learn the news about himself? He would have sworn on the head of his mother that he was simply helping the sick, playing stretcher bearer to Hazel's seizures, but Felicity had been right all along. He hadn't pulled the wool over anyone's eyes but his own.

With some faint hope that the puppy might have escaped, he turned to search the room and caught sight of a sheet of paper propped against the peanut butter. On the top line, neatly printed, was one word: *Paris*.

The candles shimmered against the dark glass. Hazel, calm and beautiful, sat on the floor. She's back, Jonathan thought. My beloved. He had, after the usual song and dance about money, got rid of the actress; now, at last, they were alone. He crossed the room to kneel on the other side of the Scrabble board. "Piano," someone had made. "Pot." Idly he studied Charlotte's letters: Z A U A B S O. "Saab," not allowed. "Soba," maybe.

He could still taste the Scotch he'd drunk with Maud, the second a double, which had meant driving home with tedious caution. Then, of course, nowhere to park, so he shuffled into a space round the corner. Other women had loved him but none so ardently, so secretly. As he locked the car, he had a sudden flash of understanding: that was why she'd sublet Hazel's flat. Nothing to do with being businesslike; she simply wanted access to him. In the grip of these revelations he barely noticed his progress until 41 came into view.

Lights flickered at the living-room window. My house is on fire, he had thought, hurtling down the pavement. Before his eyes the flames leapt into an all-consuming blaze. Smoke snagged the back of his throat. Who would you save?

A few more strides and his vision had separated into its parts. The bay was lined with candles. As for the smoke, the neighbours opposite were indulging in their new wood stove. That damned actress. A curtain could catch in an instant. Or Hazel. No longer running, not even walking, he had recalled the morning, two years ago almost to the day, when a sleeve of her nightdress caught in the cooker. He had smothered the flames with his jacket and square by square, throughout the spring, used the nightdress in his smoker.

When Charlotte greeted him in the hall, he had burst out with his fears. She smiled as if at a compliment. "They're quite safe," she said. "Glass can't burn because it's slow-moving water. In old windows, the bottom is always thicker than the top."

Was she drunk? wondered Jonathan, resisting the urge to examine the nearest window. With her vivid lipstick and eye-liner she certainly looked different than this morning; her blouse, unbuttoned, offered a tempting glimpse.

He had gone to his study to call a cab. When the doorbell rang, he returned downstairs and found Charlotte embracing Hazel. At the sight of the two women, their arms around each other, Charlotte's dark hair mingling with Hazel's fair, some-thing had swarmed up in him, an unexpected, unnameable emotion. "Don't keep the driver waiting," he had said.

"Base," he thought, if he could find an E. Better still, "abase." For the first time since the accident, Hazel was wear-ing a sleek dark skirt and black top. Why was she all dressed up? What had made her miss her massage with Mrs. Craig?

But when he opened his mouth, the question that emerged was neither of these. "Do you remember," he said, "the night I showed you the dances of the bees?"

Hazel frowned. He could almost see her searching the foothills and valleys of the cortex, unwilling to admit defeat.

People had known for centuries, he explained, that bees pass along information about where to find nectar, but no one could figure out how. "In the twenties, Karl Ritter von Frisch, a Bavarian, finally discovered it was by dancing. I must've been drunk because I remember prancing round the room. First I did the Round Dance, for when the nectar is near the hive, then the Wagtail Dance, for when it's farther away." He laughed, at once rueful and delighted, and reached for her hand. "You're cold. Shall I turn up the heating?"

"No."

"Cold hands, warm heart. I'm sorry I'm late. I had to see Maud." Hazel's fingers twitched. "She told me something extraordinary."

"Did she dance for you?"

"In a manner of speaking." He laughed again before he could catch himself. Promise you won't tell Hazel, Maud had said, leaning in his car window. My lips are sealed, he said, and kissed her. "You know how I always used to think she disliked me? Quite the contrary."

"I don't understand."

"Maud is in love with me." He couldn't suppress the note of triumph. "She just pretended," he hurried on, "not to be able to stand me, so you wouldn't guess—so that neither of us would guess—what she felt."

"Maud is in love with you?"

He nodded. In the candlelight, Hazel's face was grave. "You could've knocked me down with a feather, but it makes a kind of sense. Not because I'm Valentino, but all that hostility and disapproval—it's a lot of emotion to squander on someone you don't give a fig for."

"She's in love with you?"

He squeezed her hand, gently rubbing her cold fingers between his warm ones. "Maybe I shouldn't have told you? She is your friend."

Her hand slipped from his grasp. "I don't think so," she said quietly. "I think she was my friend years ago, not now. Do you love her?"

"Who?"

"Maud. Do you reciprocate her affections?" She pushed a T across the board.

"Absolutely not." He shook his head. "She's been great since your accident. Before that, though, in the old days, I never understood why you liked her."

"So," said Hazel, releasing the T, "let me see if I've got this straight. Last autumn you and I have a major row. I move out and get hit by a car. You and Maud, for some mysterious reason, decide to pretend that you and I are, were, and always will be happy as Larry. You secretly sublet my flat, instruct other people to stay away or keep quiet, and count on gratitude to prevent me from investigating my doubts." She stared at him steadily, until there was nothing in the room save her eyes, the whites shining around the pupils. "True or false?"

Both, he wanted to say. Neither. Just when he thought he might have to tell her everything, he managed to pull his gaze away. The taller candles he knew by their clear, steady flames to be beeswax. In the Middle Ages, monasteries often kept hives partly in order to make the altar candles. His palms itched furiously. The bees signalled their intention to swarm by building a new queen cell; her skirt, her tunic. Some keepers clipped the queen's wings after the nuptial flight, not him. Everything I did, he thought, I did for love.

"True," he said. "But not the whole truth."

She nodded gently, almost approvingly. "What was the row about? Was it to do with Suzanne?"

"No," he said, and at once thought, *idiot.* Suzanne—with her earnest opinions, her sensible skirts and flat shoes—could be negotiated. "I'm sorry about Maud," he repeated. "It's not as if it makes a difference."

"Jonathan, what did we quarrel about?"

None of your effing business.

"You know, my memory's coming back. In a few days or a few weeks, I'll remember for myself. You might as well tell me."

She leaned against the sofa, arms folded. In the past he'd always been able to outwait her; now her patience filled the room. He stared at the Scrabble board: a few words—"zoo," "pot"—were still intact. What if he told her, told her everything, couldn't they make a seamless union between past and present, then and now? He let the sentences unfurl in his mind.

All last spring and summer, ever since she found his cheque book, they'd had rows. Then in September she applied for a job in Brussels. Jonathan's first intimation was when she came home, and announced that the interview had gone well. He didn't understand—after all, she did several interviews a month—until she explained. But what'll happen if they offer it to you, he said. I'll live in Brussels, she said. You can always visit, once I get settled.

Rage had foamed inside him. How could she do this? Apply for a job abroad, without even talking to him. Nowadays, she'd said, I don't think it's any of your business. Her calm torched his fury. She watched contemptuously as he broke a chair, pounded the bathroom wall.

Oddly, or perhaps predictably, once he'd stopped thrashing around, they were easier together than in several months. She listened to him talk about his bees, he asked about her latest article, they collaborated on the cooking. He lulled himself into believing there wasn't a job in Brussels; or that there was, but she hadn't applied; or that she had applied, but was wholly unsuitable. One evening, walking along the towpath near Noel Road, he dared to bring it up again. I'm glad you decided against pursuing the Brussels business, he said. What's that, said Hazel, pointing at a grubby white pyramid rising from the middle of the canal. Fifty yards closer, they recognised a mattress, mostly sunk beneath the brackish water.

I can't imagine who dumps these things, she said. They told me I'd have a letter by the end of the month.

After that, it was easy. He watched the letter box like a warrior bee guarding the entrance to the hive. The second post was tricky until he got into the habit of dashing home at lunchtime. Eleven days later it arrived, the envelope clearly marked.

Dear Ms. Ransome,

It is with great pleasure that I write to announce our unanimous decision to offer you the position of sub-editor in our Brussels office. The terms would be as we discussed at the interview, the standard salary plus . . .

Without delay he had climbed the stairs and switched on his computer.

Dear Ms. Charlewood,

Thank you for your letter of the 22nd. I am honoured that you decided to offer me the post of sub-editor. Unfortunately since our meeting an unexpected family situation makes my going abroad impossible at this time. I apologise for any inconvenience this may cause.

He had posted it in the pillar box at the end of the street and stopped for a dram at the Lord Nelson. In the bottom of his glass he found the flaw. If Hazel got no letter, she would phone Ms. Charlewood. He started back to the house, then remembered the office computer, on which he could construct a facsimile of the letterhead.

What he hadn't counted on was the grapevine. A fortnight later, a friend of a friend ran into Hazel at the pub and mentioned how disappointed the editors were by her refusal. Too late to do anything, though; their second choice had already signed the contract.

It all made sense, he thought now. His failure to recognise his own feelings in the early stages, his mishandling of the Suzanne business, Hazel's sudden intoxication with worldly success, a few pieces in the *Guardian* and she thought she was Hunter S. Thompson. And, more recently, the strenuous, complicated efforts he'd made to protect their relationship. He studied her slender ankles beside the Scrabble board and longed to pour out his explanations and apologies in a sweet, unalloyed, golden stream, and have her hear them exactly as he intended. But it was Hazel who broke the silence.

"Look!" she said.

Following her gesture, he saw something quivering at the tops of the windowpanes. The glass, he thought: just as the actress promised, the glass is on the move. As he drew near, however, he saw that what was moving was not the pane but the putty, warmed by the candles, expanding and bubbling beneath its layer of paint. One by one he snuffed out the flames.

Freddie woke, standing in the hall, holding the phone. "Mr. Adams," the receiver was saying, "is that you?"

"Who is this?"

"You fixed my roof, I fixed you meals. Donald Early."

Unmistakable, yet somehow different. In his voice was a wisp of embarrassment, or maybe shame. "I was asleep," Freddie offered.

"I am sorry. I'd call back if I weren't ringing to ask you a favour, an odd and unhappily urgent favour."

"Shoot." Freddie shook himself. "I owe you one, if not two."

"All debts are cleared. I have an acquaintance, a former student, who's in trouble. I was hoping you might give her a hand."

Through the kitchen doorway, Freddie saw the frying pan lying upside down beside a pile of rice. He could barely keep himself afloat. Anybody else would sink him for sure. "What sort of hand?"

"Oh, this *is* embarrassing. I'm about to put her in a taxi. She should be with you in a few minutes. I only answered my door because I was expecting my assistant and instead, there stood Charlotte, Venus of the rubbish bags. Well, you'll see. She just needs a sofa for a couple of nights. Her sister's thrown her out."

"Why send her to me when you've got room for a family of ten?"

Mr. Early cleared his throat. "My candidate for the most excruciating sentence in the English language is 'I need you,' when I am the addressee. Whereas for you, forgive me, I sense it may be your favourite."

From beside Freddie's left foot a man in a red shirt brandished a power drill, the *Reader's Digest* manual of home improvement. "Which of the designers," he said, "were you?"

"Freddie." Mr. Early laughed. "I was the one who got the job. Surely that's obvious. I was trying to make myself sound wicked and interesting; also to warn you. I'm like a primitive organism, even more ancient than the dinosaurs—I'll stop at nothing to preserve my world. I'd better let you go, however. Answer the doorbell or not, at your peril. I'm still in your debt."

Freddie stepped into the living-room, drew the curtains,

picked up a lamp. If this doesn't beat all. He didn't know whether he was coming or going, but he did know if the door-bell rang he would answer. To that extent Mr. Early was right. He was a different kind of organism, more primitive or less, he couldn't say. But his sense of self came from others. Left to his own devices, he was a formless blob.

chapter 18

"I should warn you," the man said, leading her up the dark stairs, a bag in either hand, "things are kind of a wreck."

Charlotte nodded, blindly. She was still stunned at the speed with which first Bernie, then Mr. Early, had thrown her out. The latter had opened his door with alacrity, but at the sight of her his smile had dimmed and, once she started to fetch her bags, faded altogether. He hadn't even allowed her to take off her coat, just a quick whisky in the hall while he made a phone call. When his assistant, Ray, showed up a few minutes later, she'd guessed the recipient of Mr. Early's smile. She refused to lift a finger as Ray loaded the bags into yet another cab. Wanker, she thought, glaring at Mr. Early. Pathetic old poofter. How dare he treat her like some underling, some extra. And now this American was apologising for the state of his flat, which probably meant, if he was like most people she knew, three teaspoons lying in the sink or, tut-tut, a newspaper spread open on the sofa. Spare me.

But as she entered Freddie's hall, she tripped over what turned out to be a phone book, and when she recovered her balance and took in her new surroundings, on all sides the balm of disorder met her gaze. For the first time since moving to Bernie's, Charlotte felt at home. "What's that noise?" she said.

"The dogs. They'll settle down in a minute. Let me get the rest of your luggage."

Luggage. What a lovely, dignified term for her flock of bags. "I can help. There are so many."

Freddie smiled. In the unlit hall she had missed his skin, lustrous as an aubergine, his smooth, high forehead and dimpled chin. "You must be tired. Stay here and put your feet up. The couch is free, sort of."

Alone, Charlotte wandered into the kitchen. My, my, she thought, taking in the mess of broken china, pots and pans, various foodstuffs. This was beyond disorder; a vigorous tantrum, more likely. She set the Chardonnay beside a jar of peanut butter and, tiptoeing from one island of linoleum to the next, knelt beside the enclosure. The larger black dog sniffed at her outstretched hand and waddled away. The puppies, however, piled up without restraint. They licked her fingers, wagged their entire small bodies, fixed her with their melting eyes. She lifted the nearest one onto her lap.

"Be careful how you put them down," said Freddie from the doorway.

"They're adorable. What do you mean?"

"You have to set them on all four paws else their legs get damaged."

Then he was gone. She gathered up a second puppy, and the third. One chewed her hair; the other, with excited yips, attacked a button of her blouse. Charlotte nuzzled their warm, black fur. This beat rug-rats any day.

Twenty minutes later, the pups were back in their pen and she and Freddie were on the sofa with mugs of tea. She could smell the slight, pleasant tang of his sweat: all those bags, all those stairs. "Sorry about the mess," he said. "Let me explain. I just came home, and while I was out a friend got mad and kidnapped Arkansas."

"Arkansas?"

"One of the puppies."

She knew what he was telling her was important, upsetting even, but Mr. Early's whisky, on top of the wine at Hazel's, rendered her stupid. "Awful," was all she could muster. Suddenly she noticed she was sliding towards Freddie's shoulder. Wait a minute. She'd met him only half an hour ago. Swaying back to the vertical, she said, "This is very kind of you."

"No problem." He sipped his tea. Charlotte did the same. Lacking his shoulder, she allowed herself the small luxury of slipping off her shoes and curling her feet beneath her on the sofa. "I don't mean to be a doofus," Freddie said, "but what's wrong that you need a place to stay?"

Doofus! Weren't Americans wonderful? "I fucked up."

"Tell me about it," he said, so clearly meaning "Me too" that she did. Not the version she'd hastily concocted for Mr. Early—torn between two good deeds, a woman taken ill and the rug-rats, her sister going berserk because she chose the former, etc.—but the one that had actually happened: the unexpected morning phone call, the drama of Hazel finding her long-lost flat, Bernie's missing note.

"This woman, Hazel, where does she live?"

"In Highbury, off the Holloway Road." Why was he leaning forward, his voice sharp with interest?

"And does she have seizures?"

"Sometimes."

He stood up, paced to the door, back again, gave an absurd little jump, and finally knelt in front of Charlotte and took her hands. "You must think I've gone nuts."

He explained how he'd met Hazel through work, and her

next-door neighbour taught some kind of class. Charlotte let his words wash over her—such coincidences were commonplace—and focussed on his hands. "So what happened today," he was asking, "when you went to Hazel's flat?"

"Her lodger let us in, a quite nice one-bedroom in Kentish Town. We had a cup of tea."

"And? Did her memory come back?"

Something's going on, thought Charlotte. She started to push her way through the veils of alcohol, the pleasure of his touch. "No. She recognised stuff, furniture, pictures, but she didn't remember being there at all. She got rather upset."

"Shoot." He let go of her hands and resumed pacing. "Where is she now?"

"Home. Are you okay? You seem a bit flustered."

Freddie pulled himself back inside his amazing skin. "Sorry. I just know the setup between Littleton and Hazel isn't on the level. He's taking advantage of her."

Charlotte remembered the occasions on which she'd caught Jonathan gazing at Hazel. "He loves her. I mean, he may still be taking advantage, but he is crazy about her."

"You say that as if it's some kind of excuse." He bounced from foot to foot. "I think we should go over there."

She stared up at him. What exactly was he proposing? That she leave his cosy sofa to traipse over to Hazel's, once again an unwanted guest? She recalled her glimpse of Jonathan earlier that evening: his grumpiness about the candles, his brusque payment. "If you don't mind, I'll sit this one out. Find my toothbrush and get settled. Do you have any blankets?"

"No," he said, not meaning the blankets. "Black boys don't prowl around alone at night, even in London. Please say you'll come. All you need to do is walk to my van. I'll do the rest."

In the face of his urgency there was only one answer. "Can we have scrambled eggs when we get back?"

"Sure. And I'll wash the pan." He held out his hand, the palm nearly as pink as Bernie's, in a gesture Charlotte recognised from American films. "Deal?"

"Deal," she said, searching for her shoes.

Jonathan began to lob sentences through the tendrils of candle smoke. "We did make mistakes, Maud and me. You have to understand what it's like. Hogarth claims the seizures have no single cause. Often, though, after we have a difficult conversation, you foam at the mouth. Surely you can see how that makes me feel."

Hazel gave no sign, either by word or gesture, of seeing anything. He fanned away the smoke, trying desperately to think of additional arguments. A detail from an epilepsy pamphlet he'd read at the hospital came to mind. "You probably don't realise that the seizures affect your short-term memory. You often lose a couple of hours preceding them. I did tell you, more than once, that we'd had our quarrels."

It wasn't working—she was getting up—but he rushed on. The main thing was not to mention the job, those letters. Blame himself for everything, not that. "Of course I should've told you about Suzanne, but you were so strident about women's rights. It was as if my opinion, the man's opinion, was irrelevant."

At last he had her attention. She paused, crouching, to look at him. "You have a daughter."

"Suzanne has—" he began and then, as she made a slight pushing motion, quickly said, "Yes."

"And you've never met her?"

"No."

"Why not?"

He drifted over to the cheese plant. Now was the moment to deliver his well-rehearsed anguish. "I'm not sure." Do the puzzled frown. "At first it was mostly my fault. I wasn't very persistent. You and I were just getting to know each other, and I didn't want anything to come between us. Then—"

"Don't do that."

He released the leaf, what remained of it, and dropped the green fragments into the pot. "When I did ask to see her, Suzanne wouldn't let me. Either I had to be a full-time father or nothing. All she wanted was my money." Hazel raised a hand to shield her yawn. "I can see how engrossing this is."

"Jonathan, it's hard to be interested, except in a pathological way, when my first reaction is to wonder whether this really happened. When you told me about Maud, I knew you were telling the truth. You blurted it out. Just now I could see you calculating every sentence. If what you're saying about Suzanne is true, that's rotten. Frankly, though, I wouldn't bet a fiver either way."

He ought to explode with righteous anger—that was what people did when falsely accused—but he could only listen, mesmerised, as she gathered momentum.

"I was describing to Charlotte the day we met at the library. You were wearing a shirt with tiny red and black checks and you asked me about India, about tutoring those rich kids. You told me about your bees. I loved how passionate you were, and that you didn't take yourself too seriously. Later, over dinner, you talked about your dog, Fluffy."

"Flopsy."

"Flopsy. It never occurred to you that your parents had lied. I found that so—" she spread her fingers—"so touching. You know Plato's theory, the original whole divided, the halves striving to be reunited. I had the idea that was us. I'd been living on impulse for nearly a decade, and you'd had your shoulder to the grindstone. You could teach me how to live the examined life, I thought, and I could teach you the reverse. It seems funny now, but I blamed myself when our relationship started to unravel."

If the brain has cells like a honeycomb, thought Jonathan, little wax chambers, row after row, waiting to be filled and capped, now his were brimming.

"Maybe," she said, and finally she was looking at him, "you didn't do anything with Suzanne I wouldn't have done, but I would never have kept it secret."

"You know"—he took a step towards her—"for all your principles about tolerance, you aren't very forgiving. No one gets a second chance. Not me, not your parents, not even my parents with their stupid fib. Anything dodgy, you run for the high moral ground."

"What do you mean?"

For a moment, the interest in her voice made him want to laugh. Wouldn't ninety-nine people out of a hundred rather talk about their own bad behaviour than another person's virtues? "You said our relationship unravelled." She gave a small nod; he did like her hair longer. "If I had to pick a single occasion when matters took a wrong turn, it would be the night you proposed to me and I panicked. I've regretted that a million times, I've apologised from here to Timbuktu, but you never listened. I had my chance. I blew it. End of story."

"Boris told me the same thing, that I hold grudges." She stopped, and from the way she cocked her head he knew she was chasing some distant memory. "No." She sighed and moved towards the door.

"Now we have a second chance." Two halves, she'd said, seeking a whole. "That's what your illness has given us, the ultimate second chance."

She was doing what she always did, walking away.

For the second time that evening, he grabbed a woman's wrist. Hers was thinner than Maud's.

"I met Daniel today."

"Daniel?"

"My tenant."

His palms itched, his eyeballs no longer seemed to fit. In his grasp, Hazel's bones squeezed together. "You can't imagine"— her voice wavered—"how strange it was to be in this flat and see my books, my pictures, my desk, the sort of washing-up liquid I always buy, and to have not the faintest recollection of ever setting foot there.

"When I try to recover the past," she went on, "where most people have a window, I have a wall."

Suddenly he found himself remembering that snowy evening, her eyes rolling back in her head as she walked, endlessly, into the living-room wall. And then he was holding her, shaking, trying to contain her despair and his own jubilation. The letters were gone, dead and gone. His arms were around her, and she was neither crying nor shouting nor pushing him away. Soon, nothing could come between them.

Charlotte regarded the van's uninterrupted windscreen with pleasure. She could not remember the last time she'd ridden in the front of a vehicle and so high up. "Here we go," said Freddie, but for a minute or two the engine coughed and hesitated. When it finally caught, he turned to her. To thank her again, or give her a hug? No, something about a seat belt.

She was still disentangling the loop of material as he leaned across, his arm pressing gently against her chest, to straighten the belt and snap the buckle into place. I've only known him for an hour, she reminded herself. But could compatability be measured chronologically? Bernie had thrown her out after more than thirty years, and Walter bolted after five.

"You should have air bags," she said. "Why do you have a van? How old are you?"

He was back-and-forthing to get out from between the adjacent cars. "To carry my tools. I fix roofs. Didn't I tell you that's how I met Hazel? They had a problem with the flashing on the back party wall." He edged into the street. "Thirty-five."

After the van's balky start, their progress was remarkably smooth. As they turned onto the main road, Charlotte had a pleasing sense of Freddie beside her, shifting gears at precisely the right moment. "I'm thirty-three," she said. "Do you have a girlfriend?" A pub where she'd once done a Pinter play flashed by. Something warm lay beneath her fingers; glancing down, she discovered her hand resting on Freddie's thigh.

"I did. Felicity, but I have the feeling she's history. Or I am. She's the one who stole the puppy."

"If she ditched you, I think you're history. Am I asking too many questions?"

They slowed down at a red light. "Too bloody right," he attempted in cockney, then switched to American. "Well, we're roommates, so can I ask you a question?"

Here it comes, she thought, whisking away her hand: the dreary interrogation. How long are you staying? When's the last time you acted? Where's your boyfriend? The road ahead was jammed with cars. People going home from a night on the town, seeing *Les Miz* or *An Inspector Calls,* and what was she doing? Trundling along on some tedious errand, with an American stranger. Even his shambolic flat was less reassuring now that she knew this Felicity was responsible. "I suppose," she muttered.

"I just wondered about Hazel, whether she ever mentioned me?"

Was it possible, she thought, that Freddie had a pash? He shifted down, and she dismissed the notion. He was like her, worried about Hazel, caught up in the drama of her amnesia. As if neither of them need notice, she put her hand back on his thigh. "Not that I recall, but there's no reason why she should. Either I'm reading to her or we're working on her memory. You know she and Jonathan are getting married in a couple of weeks?"

Only the seat belt saved Charlotte from meeting the windscreen. She found herself staring down at a white mini.

"Married?" said Freddie.

"Good you made me wear the belt." She pointed at the dumpy car. "Don't worry. We didn't hit them."

The mini bounded forward, apparently unaware of its narrow escape, and again they were moving.

"What do you mean, 'married'?"

"That thing people of the opposite sex do at the Town Hall when they exchange rings." She giggled. "Though maybe the flat will change that. Hazel was pretty upset."

"Shit."

Looking around, Charlotte saw they'd missed their turn. "We can do a U-turn at the lights," she said soothingly. Although at this point, her initial reluctance to leave the sofa had vanished; she would happily drive all night. They could go to Scarborough, where she'd once done a summer season, and watch the sun rise from the clifftops. Only two hundred miles.

But Freddie was already signalling, apologising. "I've had a peculiar day," he said. They passed a school, a stark playground, and here was Hazel's street of neat two-storey houses and leafless trees. Why did that woman ditch you, she was about to say, as he pulled over. Later.

The engine was still creaking when a spaniel came down the street, trotting so purposefully from one pool of lamplight to the next that the appearance of a woman in a raincoat, holding the lead, was a foregone conclusion. Head down, she passed within a yard of the van, oblivious to its occupants. "Strange," Charlotte said, "she didn't see us."

Freddie agreed. "I've noticed that before," he said. "In a pub, you can get someone to turn around with a quick look. Once you're in a car, you can stare to your heart's content. Thanks for doing this," he added. "You must be bushed."

"As a matter of interest, what are we doing?"

"I want to walk by, check out the house, make sure nothing weird is going on. I know——" he tapped his temple——"you're thinking the craziness is located right here. But I'm positive Hazel's in trouble. She shouldn't be marrying this guy, not when she's sick. Whatever I can do to help, I want to. Does that sound totally insane?"

"It sounds——" if only she'd known someone like this last year——"nice."

They climbed out of the van and eased the doors shut. Upright in the cold air, Charlotte realised she was still a little drunk and whispered as much to Freddie. "No problem," he whispered back.

Gone were the candles, though she could make out their white shadows in the window, and so were all the downstairs lights. Upstairs, a diffuse glow indicated a lamp. They walked slowly along the opposite side of the road and back again. They were standing by a tree two doors down when a clicking sound heralded the spaniel and its walker. This time, as she drew near, the woman glanced at them apprehensively and hurried along.

Freddie's cheerful "Good night" had her almost jogging. "You see," he said, shaking his head, "why I needed your company."

Charlotte pointed over at the house. "It looks like they've gone to bed."

"Where do they sleep?"

"Jonathan's in the spare room, that window there. Hazel's room overlooks the garden."

"Let's check out back."

Before she could argue, Freddie led her through the gate and round the bay. Waiting for him to open the side door, somehow he knew where the key was, she had a pang. This was actually trespassing, whereas they could stand in the street all night long. Not quite, she thought, remembering the evening she'd run into Walter at that party. She had left the room, it was true, but then she had gone back in and asked Ginny to get his address. Tell him I have some post for him, she'd said. Five minutes later, Ginny handed her a slip of paper and Charlotte took a taxi to the house, somewhere near Clapham Common, and waited on his garden wall. Mercifully, not every detail returned. She could hear Walter shouting, still picture the waif-like policewoman who had told her to try hot milk and a bath.

Out of the darkness, something grazed her cheek. She gasped.

"You okay?"

"Fine." As she pushed the branch aside, she imagined herself once again on Freddie's sofa, a puppy in her lap, describing her encounter with the law. He might tease her or sympathise or call Walter a son-of-a-bitch, but for reasons she couldn't define, Charlotte knew he would think none the worse of her.

"That window?" he asked.

"Yes." Only a few days ago she'd stood there with Hazel arguing the pros and cons of memory. She turned, looking for the sculptures, and spotted them at the bottom of the garden. Of course, she thought, walking over the grass, not sculptures, beehives, three of them. Those red marks on Jonathan's face the other day were stings. She put her hand on the nearest hive to feel the warmth.

Freddie had trailed her. "Look," she said. "Jonathan is a beekeeper."

"Come on, Charlotte. We don't want to disturb them."

As they drew near the house, she saw a pale figure standing at the window, in the gap in the curtains. Beside her, Freddie made a little sound. But could Hazel see them, she wondered, both in their different ways dressed in black? She raised her hand and waved. Nothing happened for half a dozen breaths, then the figure stepped back and the curtains closed.

Only when he put his arm around her and said "Let's go" did Charlotte realise that the noise she'd been hearing was the chattering of her own teeth. In the van, he started the engine and turned on the heat. "Sorry," he said. "I should've lent you a jacket."

"At least we saw her."

"She looked so sad."

"She did, but you can't be sure. If I wanted to play a sad woman in a movie, one way I'd do it is to stand at a window and gaze out into a dark garden, pretending to have thoughts too deep for words, while really I was fretting about the leaky dishwasher."

"Well, that's acting," Freddie said. "Are you getting any warmer?"

On the Holloway Road they joined the shoal of black cabs pouring back into town. Charlotte began to count and, once she'd got to twenty, in both directions, asked why Felicity had dumped him. They passed a row of shops, eight more cabs.

"Too many reasons," Freddie said at last. "Because I'd rather sit on the couch than earn money. Because I'm historically unenlightened. Because, finally, I couldn't fool either of us any longer." He rubbed his hand over his head. "What about you?"

"Me?" The traffic of Highbury Corner engulfed them. "I used to live with Walter. He's an actor, too. One day I came home from the theatre and he'd done a bunk, taken his clothes, possessions, most of our furniture. He didn't even leave a note."

"I'm so—"

But she couldn't stop now. "I've been a disaster ever since. I can't act. I haven't earned tuppence. I mess around, pretending to be busy. And the worst thing, the very worst, is that I know he isn't worth it. He drank too much, he was sarcastic, he was stingy. But as soon as he left, *voilà*—the love of my life." They were slowing down. "Are we home?"

"Nearly." Freddie was turning to her, his gleaming, eloquent face bending towards her. "I'm sorry," he said. "I'm so sorry." He pressed his forehead against hers as if his sympathy, the whole fluent current of his goodwill, could pass from his cranium to hers; and somewhere, far behind her eyes, wherever she'd stored the pain of the last year, a small, clear light sparked.

chapter 19

The bottle of oil, deceptively whole, dripped steadily. A bag of flour cracked open in Freddie's hands. As for the rice, it was a total loss, heaped beside the frying pan. For a moment, staring at his floured palms, his anxiety about Hazel vanished. All this mess and Arkansas, too. "Boy," he said, "Felicity sure was thorough."

Charlotte nodded. "Do you have a beater?"

"Who knows?" He moved uncertainly toward the cutlery drawer, and she said not to worry, she'd use a fork.

In stolen glances, he noted how quickly she seemed at home; probably something to do with being an actress. She showed him how to crack eggs one-handed, a skill she'd mastered for a cookery show, while he made the toast and tea. Once the food was ready, he started to clear the table but she stopped him. "Let's eat in the living-room. It's cosier."

He carried in the mugs of tea, went back for his own plate, and returned to find her sitting cross-legged in the same corner of the couch as before, shoes on the floor. Her eyes, bloodshot earlier, were clear, and he could see that the tipsiness she had confessed to outside Littleton's was fading. He took his corner of the couch. Now, at last, he could ask if Hazel and Jonathan were really getting married. Like dog and cat, mermaid and human, it struck him as a completely unnatural union. Whatever happens, he thought, this shouldn't. "Excuse me—" he started, but Charlotte was butting in.

"Have you ever been to Los Angeles?"

He told her about his last visit to Santa Monica, the earthquake sending the strawberries to the floor. "Crikey," she said, "then you really would be history. Actually, I'm more interested in movie stars than tectonic plates."

"Movie stars are a dime a dozen. I saw Dustin Hoffman at an Indian restaurant. Michelle Pfeiffer at a bookstore." By the time he finished his list, she was mopping her plate and swallowing the last mouthful of eggs. His heart was doing a kind of tortured flip-flop. If Charlotte hadn't been with him tonight, he would've fetched his ladder and climbed up to talk to Hazel, make sure she was all right. But if Charlotte hadn't been there, he reminded himself, he would never have risked going into the garden. At the far end of the couch she yawned. Maybe he should wait, hold off questioning her until morning. "Let me take that," he said, reaching for her empty plate.

"We can clear up later." She licked her fingers and set her plate beside his on the floor. He felt a twinge of disloyalty; Felicity had always insisted on doing the dishes right after a meal. But then he pictured Arkansas, whimpering, alone. Tomorrow, he promised, they would get the puppy back and sort out Hazel. All he needed was a chance to have a decent conversation with her. Surely Charlotte could help to arrange that.

"Why do you live in London?" she asked. "Everyone here wants to go to America."

From the street below came the sound of heavy footsteps, a neighbour making a last pass with a dog or coming home from the pub. Freddie stared at the crumpled *Herald Tribune*, the gas fire, the floor lamp with its faded pink shade. A year ago Felicity had asked the same thing and he'd reeled off his standard answer, no problem. But something about this crazy day—his conversation with Mrs. Craig, the glimpse of Hazel, Charlotte's miraculous arrival and her own confession—had opened him up like a can of sardines, all his thoughts and feelings, stretched head to tail, side by side, undeniable. Some deep wrong would be done if he didn't at least try to answer this woman honestly.

Slowly, dodging and weaving past the tiny hands, he explained what had happened after graduation: the awful jobs in Silicon Valley, his escape to Paris and Lourdes, the drifting which year by year took him further from his contemporaries and compounded his fear of disappointing his parents. "My going to Stanford was like you guys going to Oxford, a big deal. They were sure I'd made it. Now, as long as I'm over here, they don't have to deal with the fact that I'm not some big-shot professor or lawyer." Her eyes were fixed on him. "And I guess I don't, either. Living in a foreign country is a kind of disguise. All people see when they look at me is an American in London."

In the silence, the heavy footsteps returned. Dog, thought Freddie. Everything depended on his keeping absolutely still. Let me answer again, he wanted to say, but if he so much as moved a muscle, he'd start crying like a baby.

"If you want to be truly invisible," said Charlotte, "try being an actor. I'm so busy playing other people that no one even notices who I am. And when I fail, well, it's especially ludicrous. I'm failing at something that doesn't matter anyway, a kids' game of make-believe."

"I bet you're terrific."

Charlotte studied her nails. "No," she said, gently. "Okay in the right role, far from terrific. At least I used to be."

Open mouth, he thought, insert foot. "You must be

exhausted. Let me show you the bedroom. It's a mess, but at least the sheets are clean."

"Where will you sleep?"

Suddenly, for once, she was entirely still. Throughout her arrival, the drive, the meal, and their conversations, Freddie now realised, she'd been in constant motion, not fidgeting exactly, but always making little accompanying gestures—a lift of an eyebrow, a crook of a finger. Only a jerk, he thought, could resist such an unmistakable invitation.

Side by side they lay on top of the duvet. He kissed her cheek. "Should I be doing this?" he whispered, and kissed her again. "I'm doing it." Someone was trembling. Charlotte, he thought, but his own limbs were shaking, too.

She lay on her back, her small, straight nose pointing toward the ceiling. "I haven't made love," she said, "in nearly a year. I think I've revirginised myself."

"We don't have to."

"We do," she said. "Can't you feel it?" In the faint light he saw her face, set and solemn.

"Let's get under the covers." As he heard his own suggestion, dread seized him. He felt something but not, he knew, what Charlotte meant. With Felicity this had been easy, in the beginning. She'd made clear that what they did in bed meant no more than a meal or a movie. When he told her he was Catholic, she'd said, too Catholic for this? and held out a foil package. Later, the complaints started. All my friends assume I have a great sex life, she said bitterly. You know me, he tried to joke. I just can't stay awake. How could he tell her he had confused Lourdes and love?

Now, fully dressed under the duvet, he felt his limbs grow languorous, and Charlotte's hand warm and damp in his.

"What about Felicity?" she said. "Is this too soon?"

"Felicity's been leaving for a while." Then, lord knows why, he offered a statement misleading on more levels than he could count. "Whatever you and I do, there's only the two of us in this bed." And, in some amazing way, his remark did succeed in banishing Hazel; now it *was* only the two of them. He propped himself on one elbow. "Will it scare you if I take off my jeans?"

Charlotte pulled away. At first he didn't know what to think, then saw she had taken his question as an invitation. Side by side, they arched their backs. "Do you have any siblings?" she asked, bending to lay her leggings beside the bed.

"James. He's a doctor in Illinois."

She made a little noise. "My sister's a nurse."

"You know"—he reclaimed her hand—"I think I met her once at Littleton's. Ponytail, efficient-looking."

"That's Bernadette. Did you think she was pretty?"

She slid her bare leg between his, and the shock emptied him of speech. "Yes," he finally managed, "though not like you."

"She drives me mad." Charlotte's voice was slow and dreamy. "She can be so self-righteous. I mean, throwing me out of the house this evening, like Goneril and Regan." Her leg pressed against his thigh. "From her perspective I've been a loser for years. She has the steady job, the husband, the kids. In one way all that lets me off the hook. In another it makes me seem even more of a ne'er-do-well."

He buried his face in her neck, breathing in the sweet, complex odour of her skin. Everything she said could just as easily have been spoken by him.

Nothing was magical or effortless. He undid her blouse, each button sliding out of its neatly stitched hole a marker on their journey, then removed the rest of his own clothes, except for underwear. Lying down again, he wished he could say, let's stop now; sleep and dream and wake up together. But he knew Charlotte would splinter into a hundred pieces, that she'd been hurt and hurt over and over, and that for him to turn aside now, for any reason, could spell nothing other than rejection.

She counted his ribs, traced his nipples and biceps, her fingers quick and slow, caressing and calibrating, never venturing below the waistband of his underpants. And he touched her as best he dared, her shoulders, her smooth stomach, but not yet her breasts.

"Why do you think," she said, stroking his collarbone, "you've turned out like this, so different, so far from home?"

So she hadn't bought his answer on the couch, or not completely. Here was his second chance, no sooner recognised than blown. He muttered something about growing up Catholic.

"Freddie." She patted him as if he were a small boy.

The words, never spoken before, came together as simple and stubborn as a stack of slates: measure one, then the next; fasten one, then the next. His last year at Stanford, a party near Santa Cruz, a house out in the woods.

"You can't imagine how beautiful it was, all these giant redwoods, and when you leaned back in the hot tub you could see the Milky Way. It got late. I'd only had one beer. The friends I'd come with weren't ready, and I decided to leave anyway.

"I remember coasting down the driveway, without the engine to keep from spoiling the quiet. In the woods I could see glinting eyes—skunks, raccoons, I guess. Near the main road, near the ocean, the mist started, wisps drifting in and out among the trees. At the intersection I pulled out and started north. The mist came and went, clouds and patches, but never for more than a few yards. I was doing sixty, maybe sixty-five, when I passed a car parked on the shoulder. A second later, this guy stumbled out into the road.

"His name was Roy Harper, a guitar maker. White, drunk,

twenty-nine years old. His body flew forty feet off the road and landed against a tree.

"Everyone said it was an accident, that there was nothing I could've done. But I was driving, breaking the speed limit and daydreaming—about what I'd do after graduation, about going to the beach the next day. If I hadn't gone to that party, if I hadn't left early, if I'd been paying attention . . ."

Charlotte put her hand on his heart and leaned over, her hair falling around his face. "Hush," she said.

> "Look how the floor of heaven
> Is thick inlaid with patines of bright gold.
> There's not the smallest orb that thou behold'st
> But in his motion like an angel sings,
> Still quiring to the young-eyed cherubins."

She pushed back her hair. "Lorenzo, in *The Merchant of Venice.* It's what made me want to be an actor, that plus people telling me not to show off." She shrugged off her blouse and did something that made her underwear disappear. "I'm so sorry."

Her mouth opened into his, her hand was slithering past his waistband, and—Freddie couldn't quite say where or how—the dread was gone. When he touched her, she was waiting.

chapter 20

Jonathan lit the cardboard on the second attempt and closed the smoker. In the late-afternoon sunlight the worn brick houses of his neighbours seemed part of a kinder, happier city, and as he headed for the hives, the blunt roar of jets—some days, for no apparent reason, Highbury lay on a flight path to Heathrow—bisected the assorted radios and TVs playing in those golden houses. From a nearby garden he heard a rustling, then a decisive snip. When he had a moment, he must ask Mrs. Craig's advice about replanting the herbaceous border to benefit his bees. After the scene outside Plantworks, it would be good to have a neutral topic of conversation.

The hives, too, glowed in the sun, but already the shadows were lengthening; rain clouds were massing to the west. In fact it was far too late to be handling the bees. A few hours ago, most of the workers would've been out foraging on one of the first warm days of the year, whereas by now they were back inside, clustered around the queen. But he had arrived home to find Bernadette even more businesslike than usual. I should tell you, she'd said, putting on her jacket, that my sister is no longer living with me. And when he asked how he could reach Charlotte, she claimed to have no idea. Then Hazel, reading on the sofa, kept turning the pages determinedly. The only possible solution was to visit the hives.

He puffed smoke into the hive nearest the house and, indecisively, into the other two as well. While waiting for the bees to grow gorged and sleepy, he tried to decide which one to work on first. That was something, something else, he'd never succeeded in conveying to Hazel, that each hive had a distinct personality; not simply what Maud had called a binary operation, docile as opposed to hostile, but a whole range of complicated, conflicting traits.

He eyed the first hive, whose inhabitants had responded so fiercely to his last visit. He had only to visualise the four supers, filled to the brim by summer's end, to be reminded that their aggression was combined with excellent nectar-gathering. The bees in the middle hive, with two supers, were unreliable, given to making large quantities of propolis with which, once the hive was sealed, they jammed up the frames; they probably would try to swarm several times in the course of the summer. The third hive, although he had changed the queen last year, remained disaster prone. In January he had found a dead sparrow wedged near the entrance, and twice he'd had to fight off a wax-moth invasion. The bees, however, behaved admirably: the latest queen laid vigorously from May to November, and the hive required less feeding over the winter than either of the others.

Now, bending down at the entrance to the third hive, he saw several winged corpses, then a whole drift of bodies, from darkest brown to clear golden. He scooped up a handful. They weighed nothing, all their instinct and purpose hollowed away to wingless husks. He remembered reading Hazel a passage in which Pliny the Elder described hives made not of reeds or bark but of transparent stone—mica, they'd speculated. And suddenly, as if the bees were speaking to him, whispering a question with their frail wings, a voice in his head said: What if you're wrong? What if Hazel's contempt conceals not its opposite but the same emotion, only more so, magnified a hundred times? What if she actually hates you? He hurled the dead bees towards the wall. Most of the tiny bodies floated down, featherlike, within a couple of feet of where he stood. A few crossed over into Mrs. Craig's garden.

He was putting the smoker on the shelf by the kitchen door when he realised he was not alone. Gooseflesh rose on his arms. Against the sink leaned a motionless figure.

"You bastard," Maud said.

On the second attempt he managed to get the veil on its hook. "Maud," he said, striving for normality. "You startled me. Can I get you a drink?"

"I must have been mad. For months I've helped you, aided and abetted you. In exchange I asked one thing, only—"

"Keep your voice down."

She took a step towards him, and involuntarily he stepped back. "That's all you care about, isn't it? Your precious Hazel. She's next door having a massage, so don't worry. We're alone. Why the fuck, Jonathan, why did you tell her? You promised you wouldn't."

He longed to clap his hand over her mouth, to throw her to the floor, drag her out of the house. She would lie in the gutter until someone—the Tourette's boy, perhaps—found her. I mustn't, he thought, lay a finger on her. He shoved his hands into his pockets and, for additional safety, sat down. The answer was obvious: he wanted to show Hazel how lovable he was— look, Maud loved him—and trustworthy: here he was telling her of his own free will. Surely Maud could understand that. As for his promise, any promise to her was glass on the floor, dust in the wind. From some drunken session years ago came Alastair's voice. When in doubt, apologise. Bitches, clients, bank managers, they none of them can resist a chap saying he's sorry.

"Sorry," he muttered. "I don't know what came over me." For fear she would read the anger in his eyes, he fastened his gaze on the Amnesty calendar.

"Hazel told me," said Maud.

She leaned back, arms folded, as if to allow him to assimilate some potent fact. Well, he was thinking, of course.

"What happened in the autumn," she continued. "Her job offer, the—"

"Don't." He leapt to his feet. Even to utter the words in the house seemed fatal. They would leave a trace Hazel couldn't help noticing.

"And," Maud went on, not flinching, "I know that Hazel doesn't remember. It's the piece of the puzzle she keeps searching for, that would make sense of everything: the flat furnished with all her possessions, her nagging sense that something is out of joint, her antipathy towards you."

He sank back into the chair. She was draining the honey from his cells, the marrow from his bones.

"So," she said mockingly, "until I met you, I thought bee-keepers were elderly men in Oxfordshire villages. Laurie Lee and all that. It does seem bizarre, keeping bees in North London."

She moved away from the sink; her feet crossed the lino-leum to the back door, returned. "Bizarre," she repeated. "You're in your own little world, aren't you?"

Raising his eyes from the calendar, he saw she had donned the veil. All pretence between them was over. "What do you want?" he said.

She sat down across the table. Through the thin mesh, her

face was both vivid and distant. He smelled sweetness and a film of smoke. "You can't have two queens in a hive, can you? I want what I can't have. I also want what I can have. You're a bright boy. You'll figure this out."

Her voice changed, the mocking quality gone. From behind the veil she spoke with unabashed urgency, as if that scanty protection enabled her to drop the guises of irony and anger. "Sometimes I think I'll wake up one morning and this grotesque feeling will be gone. My life would be so much easier, and so much emptier. There's no good reason you fell for Hazel rather than me, or why I succumbed to you rather than some other bloke. One of these days, one of us will get off the merry-go-round—I'm betting on Hazel—but meanwhile, here we are."

She pulled off the veil, leaned across the table, and kissed him. For a few seconds, he resisted, then fury got the better of him. He opened his lips and thrust his tongue into her mouth, ground his face against hers.

"You mean that one?" At the sight of Felicity's house, each brick outlined in white, Charlotte felt immediately better. "What colour is the door?" she said. "Green?"

"Blue." Freddie unrolled his window and leaned out. "I thought I might hear him."

Staring at what must be the living-room, Charlotte spotted the ubiquitous paper lampshade and a poster bearing a well-known admonition to Sisterhood. She would've liked to rest her head on Freddie's shoulder, but he was still dangling out of the window. After making love they'd fallen asleep, and when they woke long after dawn, he had leapt from the bed, announcing he was due to help someone called Trevor. Except for tending the dogs, Charlotte spent the day on the sofa, drinking tea and reading old newspapers, pretending to catch up on peace in Ireland, famine in Africa. In reality her mind was occupied with the more pressing matter of talking Freddie into letting her stay. Would he mind having her name on the answering machine?

At dusk came a key in the lock and Freddie's voice. From the way he stooped to pick up the Yellow Pages, Charlotte had understood that he was tired and then, as he put the book back on the shelf, pissed off that it was still on the floor. Suddenly she had a dismaying picture of the kitchen. Bollocks, she thought frantically. Busy? No. Work? Not likely. Poorly? Yes, that was the business with Freddie. Plead a headache. Better yet a migraine, more serious, less like a hangover. As he started to ask a question, something about Hazel, she let her smile vanish and her shoulders droop. At once he became nicely sympathetic. Told her to lie down while he called Felicity. If she wants the dough from Arkansas, he'd said, fine, but he's too young to leave Agnes. Charlotte agreed; she could not help identifying with the unmet puppy, hustled from pillar to post. Felicity was out, but one of her roommates said she'd be back by nine. So here they were, for the second night in a row, seated in the van, waiting.

Charlotte reached in her bag, drew out an orange, and began to peel it. "I was in a play once about a woman who kidnapped her daughter, but I don't know what happens in the case of a dog."

"I think this would be categorised as theft. In Cincinnati I'm sure I could sue for emotional damage—at least to me, if not Arkansas."

"You're not damaged." She handed him half the orange. "Anyway, Felicity doesn't have any money, does she?"

"Thanks. That never keeps my fellow citizens from litigation." He pointed. "There's one of her roommates, Nicole."

A tall woman with a backpack was approaching the house.

She inserted a key, leaned a shoulder to the door, and, finally, pushed her way inside. "Drove me nuts, that lock," murmured Freddie.

"Could we ask her about Arkansas? Make a pre-emptive strike?"

She longed for Freddie to hold her hand again or squeeze her thigh; he hadn't even kissed her in the hall. Now he simply gave her a look. "That would put Nicole in a weird position, and me too. How's your head?"

So that was why he was so distant. "Better, much better. The fresh air helps." She swallowed the last segment of orange and licked her fingers. "Aren't you scared, though, of seeing Felicity?"

"Totally. The truth is, she can be pretty intimidating. While the rest of us are bumbling around, she knows exactly what she wants."

"Like my sister. *Oh.*"

"What is it?"

"You asked about Hazel? I just realised, now that I'm not with Bernie, she won't be able to reach me."

"Well, we'd better stop by and—" He broke off and opened the door. "Here we go."

Charlotte assumed he meant the woman in the yellow oil-skins, but she walked on, leaving a small figure with a mass of springy hair standing before the house. Remembering her own last encounter with Walter, Charlotte slumped in her seat. As Felicity commenced the battle of the lock, Freddie greeted her from a respectful distance. Although he towered over her, his entire posture indicated that he didn't plan to take advantage of his size. He stretched out a hand, spread his arms—the gestures of pleading, Charlotte knew too well. Felicity looked down at the key and said something, still without turning around. Perhaps she feared her resolve might vanish if she saw his face.

On their way over Charlotte had asked if it wasn't hard to drive again. And how, Freddie said. I didn't get behind the wheel for ten years. That was another reason not to be in America. Here it seems okay, because everything's on the wrong side anyway. He had paused to change gear. Do you think you'll act again? This was the question all her friends asked—Bernie, Cedric, Brian, Ginny, Jason, Mr. Early, even Bill, the TV repairman—but somehow, on Freddie's lips, the effect was quite different. I don't know, she'd said. It's all I've ever wanted to do. He smiled. Lucky you.

Now Felicity was pounding on the door while Freddie kept talking from his respectful distance. Presently the door opened and, across the street, Charlotte heard it slam. She was tempted to rush over and throw her arms around Freddie. He stood there waiting. I'll count to a hundred, she thought, and then, come hell or high water, I'll go and help him.

At nineteen, the first drops of rain rolled down the windscreen. At thirty-one, a man jogged past wearing a reflective vest. At fifty-six, a pizza-delivery scooter chugged by. At seventy-two, the door opened. Charlotte caught the barest glimpse of a lighted interior, Felicity's dark hair. Once again it slammed shut. Freddie remained rooted to the pavement. Watching him, Charlotte knew that she couldn't rescue him, that somehow he had to find it in himself to turn away from the house, from Felicity, and walk back across the street. She closed her eyes.

Before Charlotte could question him——she was exclaiming over the squirming Arkansas—Freddie announced he was off to the corner store, to get a paper for the floor. Probably there was one in the back of the van, but he needed a few minutes alone to recover from Felicity's thunderbolts. In their early days, she'd told him about her last boyfriend, a lecturer at the LSE; what a jerk, Freddie had thought. Now he felt a wave of solidarity with his predecessor. The two of them would hang side by side in Felicity's rogues' gallery.

"What do *you* want?" she'd snapped.

"Felicity, I'm sorry."

"And I suppose you think that makes everything better." She began to list, in painful detail, his many shortcomings.

He was about to interrupt—what's the point of an autopsy if you already have a diagnosis?—when a remark of Charlotte's came back to him. I knew it wouldn't change anything, she'd said, describing her last encounter with Walter, but I couldn't stand that it was so easy for him. Felicity, he thought, as he pushed open the shop door, certainly understood that impulse.

The newspapers, not surprising at this time of night, were almost gone, but they had an *Evening Standard,* nice and thick. Moving on to the fridge, he chose a pint of milk and a bottle of Lucozade. Might perk Charlotte up, though already she seemed better than when he'd arrived home to discover her pale and wan, the flat still in chaos. He went over to pay.

Two women talking across the counter turned to include him. "Someone got caught in the rain," said the customer.

"Darling, have you got far to go?" chimed in the shopkeeper.

"Just round the corner." He remembered asking Felicity why, in the land of the stiff upper lip, shopkeepers were so effusive, all "love" this and "darling" that. Sales talk, she'd said. They think you'll buy more.

Outside the rain was picking up. The phone would be ringing tomorrow, people complaining about their gutters and bays. And a good thing, too, he thought, with all these mouths to feed.

"You can have the money," he'd told her, "but he isn't ready to be weaned."

"You never gave things between us a chance," Felicity

hissed back, and he realised this would be their final encounter. Why else was she spouting clichés?

"You're great," he had said, joining in. "I didn't deserve you." Which made even Felicity wince. She rushed inside and reappeared with Arkansas. "Every penny," she had said, slamming the door again.

He dodged a pothole, already filling with water, and glanced across the street; the door was shut, the living-room curtains closed, the house, each vivid brick of it, sealed against him. His legs slowed as he contemplated all he'd lost. For the last year, Felicity's vigorous opinions, energy, and ambitions had shaped his days and nights, and now there wasn't even a chance of friendship. Like Mrs. Craig, she'd seen right through him. And what the heck was he doing with Charlotte, anyway?

When he reached the van, she opened the door. "Lucozade," she said. "Great."

"How's Arkansas?"

"You're wet. So far, so good. He's got sharp teeth."

"Let's put him on the floor."

He spread the *Standard* at her feet and set the puppy down. Arkansas whimpered, scratched the paper, and started to chew Charlotte's laces. Freddie closed the door, feeling the rain on his face. He saw himself at the playground in Cincinnati, sitting at the top of the long, glittering slide, heading inexorably to— where else?—the couch. He saw Roy Harper flying through the air. I'm sliding, he thought, can't help it. Only Hazel, with her luminous gaze, could save him. Then—he had no notion how—he was in the driver's seat, the engine knocking slightly from the cheap gas. Sometimes it seemed almost blasphemous, the way machines became one with you.

"Freddie, are you all right?"

Charlotte's shadowy face was indecipherable, but not her hand on his arm, the affection in her voice. The dread, the dread had made him do it—and her too, so now what? The answer hovered over the lighted dashboard. They must find Hazel. Charlotte had appeared at his door as an ally.

"Felicity wasn't at all like what I expected," she said.

"Tell me." He leaned over to fasten her seat belt. "Once we're out of here." At the first intersection he turned, without consultation, towards Hazel's. "What about her?"

Charlotte hesitated. "For some reason I thought she was black."

"She is, at the other end of the spectrum from me. In America it would be weird, her passing without meaning to. Here it's pretty much a non-issue."

"And all those operatic gestures—flinging her arms, tossing her head. Once, I couldn't quite see, but I think she even stamped her foot, like someone in a fairy tale." They passed a fish-and-chip shop with a line outside. "Was she okay about the dog?"

"I guess." He felt her watching. "Not really. Even though I promised her the money, she was still mad."

"Amazing," Charlotte exclaimed. "On the steps of that church three women were wearing kimonos and carrying umbrellas. Arkansas was a connection between you. Now it's gone."

"Were they Japanese? She doesn't want any connection. As far as she's concerned, I'm lower than a dog turd."

Something landed on his shoulder: Charlotte's head. "Freddie, you're so myopic. No, they were dumpy white women. I'm sure they're a good omen."

"Omen," he repeated, and suddenly he was back on the sidewalk outside Plantworks with Maud and Mrs. Craig. One minute they were talking, more or less cordially. The next, Littleton showed up, eyes flashing. And a few hours later, he'd glimpsed Hazel, forlorn at the window. She can't marry him, he thought. Whatever it takes. For an instant he wished Felicity were sitting beside him. How she would rant and rave at Littleton, blow his arguments out of the water. "Excuse me," he said. Leaning forward to wipe the windshield, he managed to dislodge Charlotte.

Hazel returned from Mrs. Craig's, trailing the fragrance of lavender. "Where's Maud?" she asked and barely seemed to register his reply that she'd had to leave.

"Oh well." She blinked slowly and gave a small yawn. "I'm going straight to bed after supper."

In the half hour since Maud pedalled away, Jonathan had been rehearsing his counterattack: she'd finally gone off the rails, shown herself so vicious and untrustworthy that he'd told her not to come again. But there seemed no immediate need to deliver it. Perhaps Hazel had already forgotten her indiscretion. He noticed that her back was straighter and, mysteriously, her breasts fuller: could massage accomplish all that? The crescent of desire Maud had etched on the evening waxed. "I picked up some haddock," he said, "and new potatoes."

"Probably from Cyprus." She raised her arms over her head. "Can I do anything?"

"Keep me company," he ventured, and to his delight she pulled out a chair and sat down.

She fingered the edge of the table. "You know, I do feel much better. Maybe we needn't worry so much about my being alone. Mrs. Craig was saying she's home a lot, if you're out and I need something."

"That's very kind of her." He rinsed the potatoes under the tap. Beneath the dirt their skins glowed with pearly light. She was talking as if everything was all right, as if, finally, she accepted their relationship. What a fool he'd been, trying to keep the flat secret. Did he think this was some spy film? No wonder Hazel had been furious. But fury, he knew, could pass.

He put the potatoes on to boil and set Hazel to slicing tomatoes. "I checked the bees while you were with Mrs. Craig. They're already foraging in two of the hives."

"Isn't that earlier than last year?"

"Ten days. We had that cold snap last May, just when they ought to get started." He held out the fish. "I thought I'd fry it in lemon and butter. How does that sound?"

"Delicious. Shall we open some wine?"

"But you're not drinking."

"I wasn't planning to go mad, but a glass would be nice."

So there was wine and food and the narcissi Maud had brought—pheasant's eye, Hazel called them—and Hazel smelling of lavender. How could he help himself? Over supper they reminisced about the summer Steve and Diane had rented a house in Lewes and they'd gone down to celebrate the solstice. The fish made Hazel think of it. Steve had cooked mackerel for supper, she said, clearly pleased with her recall, baked with lemon and peppers. Afterwards, under a burly sky, they had climbed onto the Downs and walked across the short thistly grass past the Roman temple until, from a windswept ledge, they were gazing down on the roofs of Glyndebourne. Later, at the station, the platform had been swarming with people in evening dress carrying ugly plastic picnic coolers. Jonathan had been proud of Hazel in her flowery dress and trainers.

"Would you like something else?" he asked. "I got a nice piece of Camembert."

She shook her head. "I'm afraid the wine has done me in."

"Did you take your pills?"

"Earlier." She carried her plate to the sink. In the doorway, looking down the hall, she paused. "We did love each other, didn't we?"

Before he could correct her tenses, she was gone.

He washed the dishes, then forced himself to remain at the table, leafing through a biography of Brother Adam, the famous Dorset beekeeper. Last time, he admitted, had been premature—she had been far from well—but tonight was perfect. She no longer needed help with the stairs, and what else was her parting remark but an invitation? He raised his glass to Hazel, and emptied it.

After putting the chain on the front door, he tiptoed upstairs. Her room was reassuringly quiet. He undressed in the spare room and on impulse—why not give her a little longer?—decided to take a bath. As he ran the sandalwood soap over his arms and legs, he thought, this time I'll tell her that I love her. I won't let the words go unspoken, not even for a few more hours. Bathed, he approached the basin. When he and Hazel were first together, he had shaved nightly; now, swishing the razor in the water, watching his reflected face lose its shadow, he remembered the passion and ingenuity of those early, hopeful days.

He came to her naked and found her asleep in pyjamas.

"Hazel," he whispered, slipping beneath the duvet. She stirred and he kissed her neck. He removed her pyjama bottoms and she shifted helpfully from side to side; perhaps being in hospital had habitualised her to such activities. He sighed at the touch of her. Feeling her flesh against his own, he thought, this is enough, I'll sleep with my arms round her, breathe in her breath. And for a few minutes, it was. Then desire flared again.

He reached between her legs, his fingers moving over the coarse hair. At first, when he felt the cord, he thought it was some part of the pyjamas left behind. Of course. So her breasts really had been fuller. Perfect. Hazel, the old Hazel, had always been particularly receptive at her time of the month. How indignant she had been when he told her that menstruating women were believed to have a bad effect on the bees. Carefully he looped his finger round and tugged. Nothing. He felt a twinge of panic. What if it got stuck, or disintegrated? He pulled again, steadily increasing the pressure. All at once the pressure was gone but Hazel was waking. Quickly he dropped the tampon over the side of the bed and reached for the lubricant.

"Hazel, I love you. We're making love. This is what you want, now that you're well."

He was over her and, proud of his skill, inside. She was looking up at him. He could see her eyes in the gloom. "Jonathan," she murmured.

"Hazel." He bent to kiss her, moved into her, drew back. "Darling."

Suddenly, as if she had been dreaming with her eyes open and only now was fully awake to what was happening, she was screaming. "Stop it! Stop it! Stop it!"—words a child might say.

He was in the foothills, close to that final ascent but still in control. God, how sweet.

"No." Her hands pushing at his chest. *"Stop!"*

Her voice beat on. He forgot the meaning and thought of the sound, the screaming urgency, so like that of sex. Closing his eyes, he moved with the rhythm of her cries, adjusting to the rise and fall. Briefly another noise caught his ear, a vague scraping sound, neighbours in the street outside. He bore down, entering a space where neither time nor history existed.

Hazel's hands kept pushing against him as he pressed deeper and deeper, further and further, into that region of bliss. He was there, almost there. "I love you," he said.

chapter 21

Jonathan felt cold air on his back, a touch on his shoulder.
Then, incomprehensibly, hands were gripping him. He was out
of Hazel, lifted off her, and pulled upright onto his knees.
Someone—he caught a whiff of orange—was holding his arms.
But I chained the door, he thought. We're about to die. He
imagined the press of metal against his spine, a knife skimming
his throat. The light came on and he glimpsed that the hands
holding him were black.

"He's hurt her," said a man's voice. "She's bleeding."

For a moment, in a daze of fear and fucking, Jonathan
thought so too; his cock was crimson and the sheet bloomed.
Hazel herself, pyjama jacket open, pale bare legs drawn close,
was crouched against the pillows, her eyes fixed on him. "Stop
it," she whispered.

"No," said another voice. "It's the other kind of blood."

Incredulous, he recognised the actress and then, from
the black hands and American accent, the roofer. His heart,
so recently hammering out the rhythm of love, ricocheted
between terror and anger. He had been on the very edge, at
last, of fusing with Hazel; minute by minute, movement by

movement, she had been growing closer. Now she was further away than ever. "Let me go," he said, trying to pull free.

The roofer's grip neither tightened nor loosened. Jonathan wondered if he had indeed struggled or spoken. This is not a dream. A drop of bloody liquid fell from the tip of his cock onto the sheet below.

"Hazel," said the actress, "it's all right. We're here, Charlotte and Freddie."

Jonathan stared at her. She was wearing her usual coat and black leggings, but in some mysterious way she looked entirely different. As she dragged the duvet from the foot of the bed, he registered the change. From the word go, Charlotte had made it clear she fancied him, all those fluttering eyelashes and flirtatious smiles as they haggled about money. Now she stepped past him as if he were a twelve-stone parcel, and bent to wrap the duvet around Hazel. Then the bitch passed him again. From his back came a grating noise. Of course, that sound a few minutes or centuries ago had been the window opening.

A switch turned in his brain and Jonathan grasped the full indignity of his position: naked, still partly erect, in a room full of strangers. The man, the roofer, was motionless; why didn't he speak? Once again fear flickered at the edges of Jonathan's consciousness. Was it possible his first apprehension had been correct, that this was a life-threatening situation? The newspapers were always reporting that most violent crimes occurred between people who knew one another.

"Let go of me," he cried again. "I'll report you for breaking and entering with aggravated assault."

A swift jerk was the only response, and he was lifted off the bed until he was standing. The roofer yanked his arms back even more tightly, like a prisoner's. Meanwhile, Charlotte bent to pick something off the floor. The pyjama bottoms.

"Here." She handed them to Hazel and, the final violation, climbed onto the bed beside her.

My place, thought Jonathan. "For god's sake, this is an outrage." He didn't even bother to try to wrest free. "Let me get a dressing gown and we'll sort this out."

Again he had that eerie sense of not having actually spoken; his words seemed to reach no one. For a distracted second he stared, uncomprehendingly, at a tattered red object on the floor. The tampon. All that blood, the blood that was meant to bring them together, squandered. "Hazel, I don't know what's going on here, but tell your friends they're making a mistake."

"You're the one making the mistake," the roofer said over his shoulder.

"How did you get in?" Jonathan couldn't help asking.

"Ladder."

"You raped me," said Hazel. Under cover of the duvet she'd pulled on her pyjama bottoms. At the head of the bed she and Charlotte sat side by side, facing him, like judges.

"Hazel, we were making love. The pills make you paranoid—I told you, Hogarth told you, they might—and you started to panic, but you wanted me, you've always wanted me."

"No." She was clutching the duvet. "You want me. Maud is the one who wants you." Charlotte nodded, as if somehow privy to the whole story.

"You know, at the hospital," Hazel continued, "when I didn't recognise my parents? I could still tell they were important in my life, that I loved them. I can't remember what went wrong between us, but that doesn't matter anymore."

She fell silent. For a few, hopeful seconds he thought she might be having a seizure. He watched her eyes, the muscles in her neck. Please, god, let it come.

Then her hands stopped thrashing, and when she spoke

again her voice was steady. "For weeks I've had this stranger wandering through my brain. He's pale, with colourless eyes and lank hair. He wears a dark suit and a white shirt, like a student or a waiter. Every time I pick up a book, or eat an apple, or try to sleep or look out of the window, he shows up. I've done my best not to recognise him, to send him away—why should I want to smash up my whole life?—but he won't leave. The truth is, I *don't* love you. That's all that matters. And you know it, too. Why else would you keep me here against my will?"

Before he could answer, she turned away. "Get him out of here," she said. "Please, Freddie."

If I live to be a hundred, he thought, I will never forget this moment. Over Littleton's head he watched Hazel and saw her blue eyes, their white haloes, staring at this man, this creature, he had in his grasp. And Charlotte beside her, mirroring, underlining, her expressions like a chorus.

This had to be one of the strangest nights of his life. First the scene with Felicity, then coming to leave a note for Hazel and hearing her screams through the mailbox. He'd run for the ladder, set it up at her bedroom window, which was ajar, thanks to the British obsession with fresh air. All he had to do was slide it open and scramble inside. Luckily, Charlotte had followed. Without her, the whole situation might've gone ballistic.

He tightened his grip on Littleton and started to frogmarch him towards the door. He resisted for a couple of steps, then seemed almost eager to get out of the room.

Charlotte led them into the spare room and closed the door. The men were alone. Freddie faltered. What could he do with a naked white guy? Tie him to the bed? Littleton also seemed confused. This time when he asked to be released, he even said "please." Freddie let him go and stepped back.

Littleton just stood there, arms at his sides, cock limp. How hairy he was, a river of hair from chest to groin and, beneath the hair, the flesh tinged with blue. He's cold, thought Freddie, and was about to suggest clothes when Littleton had the same idea. He grabbed a robe from the end of the bed, a navy-blue terry-cloth number, pulled it on, and meticulously knotted the belt.

The garment seemed to restore him to his true asshole self. "I want you out of my house," he said. "Immediately."

For a few minutes, caught up in the strangeness of the events, Freddie had forgotten to be angry. Now rage spurted into his throat. This man had imprisoned Hazel, had hurt her. He stepped forward and punched Littleton in the jaw. Though the blow was inept, his junior-high boxing lessons twenty years past, he felt bone beneath his knuckles. Littleton reeled back onto the bed.

Freddie was bending over him, arm raised for a second punch, fist tingling, when he heard, through the closed door, the women going into the bathroom. "Jesus Christ," he murmured, not sure if he was swearing or praying. He's turning me into him. Since the night Roy Harper hurtled through the air, Freddie had fled confrontation, used his strength to play the peacemaker and done his best to live without harm. Until now.

He had to get away from this monster. He rushed out into the hall, slamming the door behind him as if to seal off some deadly contagion, and clung to the bannister, shaking. Now what? If only he could see Hazel.

Suddenly he remembered the ladder. A task, a little fresh air might do the trick. "Littleton," he called, "I need to go get something. If you try to lock me out, I'll call the cops from Mrs. Craig's and smash a window. You got that?"

Silence.

Freddie eyed the door. Should he look inside? No, he never

wanted to see that man again. Besides, what could he do in two minutes? He called to Charlotte, telling her where he was going. "Okay," came her muffled reply from the bathroom.

He blocked the front door open, and felt better as soon as he stepped into the street. Quietly, he unhooked the ladder and carried it round the house. He was strapping it on top of the van when a yelp caught his ear. Opening the door he smelled pee— Arkansas had been making good use of the *Standard*—and the yelping crescendoed. When Freddie picked him up, the puppy's whole body was shivering. Why can't I do one single thing, he thought, without messing up? But as he hurried back across the street he noticed an amazing fact: he *was* doing something. For better or worse, he had left the couch.

Jonathan sat up to make sure the footsteps really were descending the stairs. Safely alone, he sank back on the bed. An hour ago, half an hour ago, all had been well in his world; Hazel his, the wedding in a matter of days, his mistakes forgiven, his job secure, his hives mostly flourishing. And now . . . His jaw throbbed. Even the walls seemed whiter and barer by the second. How had his life come to such a pass that a man was fixing his roof one week, bursting into his bedroom the next? When Adams released him, his impulse had been to knee him in the balls, but an instinctive calculation had warned him that he was giving away at least three inches and a couple of stone on the roofer.

He squeezed his fists against his eyes, conjuring a warm darkness. Steady, lad, steady. Nothing was irrevocably lost, only one evening in a lifetime of evenings. First get dressed, then evict the trespassers, settle Hazel down and make sure she got a good night's sleep. Wasn't there some Valium at the back of the bathroom cupboard? His clothes lay at the end of the bed, where he'd neatly folded them an eternity ago. Still he did not move. You're wrong, whispered the bees. I don't think it's going to work, said Maud. Colourless eyes, lank hair . . . but that was not to be borne.

The sound of the front door made him jump. Like a character in a farce, he scrambled into his clothes: underwear, trousers, socks, shirt, pullover, shoes. Now to get rid of these scum. If they weren't gone in five minutes, he would phone the police.

In the hall, the roofer was talking to Charlotte. "I was worried he'd catch cold," he was saying. "Maybe you can find a T-shirt or something to wrap him in."

"He'll cheer Hazel up," Charlotte said. Then she caught sight of him. "Mr. Littleton."

"Good evening." Absurdly, he found himself nodding as if to invited guests. "I must ask you both to leave."

"Not a problem," said Adams. Beneath his accent, Jonathan heard the note of contempt. "We'll be out of here as soon as Hazel's ready."

"Let me make myself absolutely clear. In five minutes I'll call the police." His mouth was moving automatically, but his mind was babbling: was the fucker seriously suggesting that Hazel was going with them?

Charlotte reached for whatever the roofer held in his arms and returned to the bedroom. Jonathan took a step forward and, catching the roofer's eye, stayed put. All the brightly lit shame of the last few minutes came back to him. This man had seen him as no one ever had, save his lovers. But no, Adams was the wrongdoer, he and Charlotte. He scratched his palms. From the bedroom came voices and—was it possible?—laughter.

He glanced over, wondering if the American had heard it too. "I've never been very keen on your native land," he said, "but it does have a certain appeal that if you behaved like this over there, you'd be dead on the floor."

"Or you would, though I'm totally anti-NRA."

Jonathan stared at his study door. Why hadn't he phoned the police while he was alone? It was like the letters about Hazel's job. He always overlooked something.

Adams intercepted his gaze. "Go right ahead," he said, waving towards the study. "From our point of view, the sooner the cops get here, the better."

Before Jonathan could reach the phone, however, the bedroom door opened and, astonishingly, a small black puppy emerged. Charlotte followed, and Hazel, dressed in the clothes she'd worn earlier.

She neither looked nor did not look at him. He didn't even have the reassuring sense of being ignored. Rather, he had ceased to exist. "Hazel. What's happening? What's going on?"

He stepped towards her, arms outstretched. Her face, he could see, was still flushed with lovemaking. One of the buttons of her cardigan was in the wrong hole. "What's going on?" he repeated. "Hazel, I love you. Talk to me."

She kept walking towards the top of the stairs, and it was Charlotte who turned to face him. "Mr. Littleton, Jonathan, you don't seem to understand—"

Reaching to shove the bitch aside, he collided with the roofer. "Hazel, stop, wait," he shouted, fists whirling, legs kicking, head butting. And she was drawing farther away as she and Charlotte hurried down the stairs. Adams blocked his path. Jonathan hit him in the shoulder, he kicked his shins, yet Adams stood there like a wall. Then, as Jonathan aimed for his diaphragm, the roofer jumped.

Once again Jonathan found himself helpless in his grasp. But just for a second, he thought, the fucker's bloody terrified, which made no sense at all. "Let me go, you stupid bastard," he screamed.

A blast of cold air rushed over them. A moment later Charlotte called, "Freddie, we're set."

With a jolt, Jonathan was free, sprawled on the landing outside his study.

Adams was going down the stairs, two or three at a time. Jonathan leapt to his feet to rush after him and, halfway down, tripped and nearly tore the bannister out of the post. He'd fallen over the puppy. Launched by the toe of his shoe, the small black animal tumbled down the remaining stairs. He stepped over it and dashed into the street, in time to see a van, ladders on top, turn the corner.

When he came back into the house, Mrs. Craig was seated on the bottom stair, cradling the dog. "I'm afraid it's dead, poor beast. May it travel safely." She made a humming sound and raised the small body three times, as if commending it to some unseen being. Then she looked up at Jonathan. "I couldn't help hearing the noise," she said, "and the door was open."

As she went to close it, he leaned against the wall. The cold of the bare plaster pressing through his shirt and pullover was the only sign he was still alive.

Back on the stair Mrs. Craig began to speak. "You know how I hum? Some people find it irritating. I learned it from my mother. She died when I was two and a half. It's the single most important event in my life, and however hard I try I can't remember her, not the tiniest thing. Yet I hum like her. I have her hands. I inherited her love of gardening, her inability to keep accounts." She paused as if to review a much longer list.

"Hazel didn't really forget," she went on. "Even though she lost the words, she still had the attitudes, the postures. I felt that today when I was doing her massage. You thought you could win her in the body, but that was always the first place you were going to lose her."

"Did you call those two?"

"Freddie and his friend? No. I think they just came by on a hunch. Freddie got it into his head that Hazel needed help. That's all he's trying to do, believe it or not: help her."

She rose to her feet. "I'll take him, shall I?" she said, lifting the puppy. "That way you won't have to see Freddie again." As she opened the door, she gave him a final glance. "I'd suggest an extremely stiff drink."

Jonathan could not have said how he got from the hall to the living-room, or how long he rested his forehead against the cold windowpane. When he returned with a glass of Scotch, he wandered over to the cheese plant. Suddenly he remembered that snowy night, driving to rescue Hazel, how he'd hit something—a dog or cat—and driven on. And he was right to do so. Every second had counted, if he was to save her. Later, at the hospital, he'd seen the neat, white feet of the dead man. He bent down and poured a dribble of Scotch into the soil around the plant. I like dogs, he thought absurdly. With amazement he saw that the clock on the mantelpiece said twenty past ten; the way he felt, it ought to be two in the morning.

Setting his glass aside, pulling with one hand, steadying the stem with the other, he began to tug the pot towards the door. On the wooden floor of the hall, it was noisier but easier. Outside, on the cement, it made a grinding sound—loud enough, his mother would've said, to wake the dead.

He pushed it against the gatepost. Should he fashion a sign: TAKE ME? Surely that was obvious. A couple of leaves were damaged, but basically the plant looked as it had always done: loathsome. He was standing there, amazed by its ugliness, when a figure stopped beside him. The Tourette's boy.

"Would you like the plant?" he asked. "I'm giving it away."

"No," the boy said. "Thank you. It's too big for . . ."

The rest of his reply vanished as he bowled off down the pavement. Thirty yards away he stopped and did his little circle dance. If he were a bee, thought Jonathan, that would mean nectar near the hive. Go forage.

And suddenly he was running down the street, his feet thudding on the pavement, and doing what he had longed to do for days, weeks, months: hurting someone. He punched the boy as hard as he could below his backpack. His fist connected in exactly the right place, sinking into the soft mass of the kidney. With a scream, the boy collapsed to the kerb.

chapter 22

They were all sitting in the front of the van, Hazel in the middle, thigh to thigh with Charlotte, and Charlotte herself half off the seat, pressed against the door. When Freddie had jumped in and turned the key, the engine had given a nervous cough before catching. Appalling if it hadn't, Charlotte thought, to have Jonathan pounding on the doors, threatening to smash the windows. Once, in her father's pub, she'd seen two men come to blows; the assailant was a regular, and for years afterwards she had summoned his face whenever she needed to enact rage or anger. Now she had a replacement.

None of them spoke as they drove past the school and onto the main road; only the late-night shops and restaurants were still open. For a few seconds, in the bedroom, Charlotte had forgotten herself. She'd been watching Freddie, his fierce, glowing face, and her gaze had drifted to Littleton's cock only to find, when she looked up, his eyes flicking over her. Unbelievable. After that she resolutely avoided looking at any part of him—disdain was one of her talents—but she couldn't help noticing that he did have a nice body, which, like his odd smile, made him seem scarier. Poor Hazel.

As they passed a showroom full of plump, shiny new cabs, Freddie let out a whoop and Charlotte found herself saying, "We did it!" Although what they'd done exactly, she wasn't quite sure.

"How did you know what was happening?" Hazel said.

As Freddie began to explain—they'd come by to leave her a note—Charlotte felt something slippery underfoot. The newspaper. Bollocks. She was about to blurt out the news when Freddie shifted gear and, as Hazel pressed against her even closer, she heard the gasp of her breathing. She needs to be home, Charlotte thought, safe in bed. No point in turning back now. She would take Freddie aside when they reached the flat and tell him, quietly, that they'd left Arkansas behind.

"I can't thank you enough," said Hazel. She was leaning forward, clutching the dashboard. "I felt as if I were being smashed into a hundred pieces."

Charlotte kept expecting her to ask how she and Freddie knew each other, but Hazel seemed to think that was perfectly natural. And in fact, perhaps even more than Mr. Early, she was responsible for bringing them together. Their fairy godmother. She had a vision of the two of them sitting in Freddie's kitchen, miraculously clean and tidy, and her telling Hazel the whole story, beginning with Mr. Aziz—no, beginning with Walter, or maybe even earlier, going right back to the pub, her ill-matched parents and bossy sister, how her impersonations had made the customers laugh like drains. One New Year's Eve, her father had set her on top of the bar to act out Goldilocks and the Three Bears. Her Daddy Bear had brought the house down.

"The thing I don't get," Freddie was saying, "is how he thought he could get away with treating you like this."

"He calls it love," said Hazel. "You heard him."

"But"—Charlotte sensed Freddie navigating between

delicacy and curiosity—"he must've known you didn't love him."

"He did and he didn't. After all, I did and I didn't. He saved my life—and by some trick of fate, he saved the life he wanted, the one in which I still cared for him and didn't remember his bad behaviour."

Charlotte reached behind Hazel and tapped Freddie's shoulder. When he glanced over, she gave a little shake of the head. "Enough," she mouthed. He regarded her blankly before turning back to the road.

Time for her to take charge. "What an amazing play this evening would make," she said. "The ladder, Jonathan out of his mind at being interrupted, the way you took him to task, Hazel. Fantastic. With the right actors, you'd be able to hear a pin drop in the theatre."

Neither Freddie nor Hazel said a word. She was speculating about possible playwrights when the familiar white building on the corner, a Chinese restaurant offering both karaoke and Elvis nights, came into view. And then Freddie was pulling into a parking space between a butcher's van and a little Fiat, the same place from which they'd extricated the van a mere two hours ago. He turned off the engine and for a moment none of them moved. Hazel hung on to the dashboard; Freddie sat with his hands on the wheel; Charlotte perched on her shred of seat. She longed to be alone with Freddie, climbing the stairs arm in arm to bed. "Well, here we are," she said brightly. "Home."

She scrambled out and reached up to help Hazel. How hot her skin was. Had she been resting her hand on a heating vent, or was she getting a fever? Before she could ask, Freddie exclaimed, "Arkansas! We forgot him."

"I know." Charlotte nodded towards Hazel, meaning we have to take care of her first.

But Freddie stood there, scowling over their heads in the direction from which they'd come. If he had looked like that, Charlotte thought, when she rang his doorbell, she would've got right back into the taxi and driven off to kingdom come: Ginny, Brian, Cedric, any place but here.

"This is bad," he said. "I don't trust Littleton."

"But what can he do," said Charlotte, "besides ignore him? Arkansas won't starve overnight. At least he's warm and dry. Come, we need to get inside."

"I have a bad feeling." Freddie's gaze returned but not, Charlotte realised, to her. "I know who that man is," he said. "The man with the suit and the colourless eyes. He's Littleton's shadow, his devil shadow."

Why is he talking to Hazel, Charlotte thought, and so strangely? "Let's go in," she said again.

"Yes," said Hazel. "It just took me a while to recognise him."

"You poor baby," said Freddie.

Charlotte looked down to make sure her feet were still touching the pavement, and when she raised her eyes, for a moment, the woman standing beside her was not Hazel but Walter's blond bimbo.

"Watch out for the bicycles," said Freddie, ushering them into the dark hall. "My flat's on the third floor."

"Second," Charlotte corrected.

He led the way upstairs. Bringing up the rear she felt rather than saw Hazel's steps slowing. Half an hour ago, a quarter of an hour ago, she would've taken her arm and asked if she was all right. Now, after the exchange in the street, she had to bite her tongue. Hurry up. Hurry up. All she wanted was to be in bed with Freddie. And where the hell was Hazel going to sleep? Why had they brought her here, rather than dropping her off with friends? She's my employer, Charlotte reminded herself. And in Freddie's case, not even that.

Inside, pandaemonium reigned. The pups yelped, Agnes barked, Freddie apologised. Charlotte moved towards the kitchen, meaning to quiet the dogs.

"I need to sit down," Hazel said.

Charlotte turned in time to see her fall to the floor, not the practised pratfall of the actor or the soft droop of a faint but a terrifying keeling over, like a statue toppling from its pedestal. "Oh, my god. What's the matter?"

"She's having a seizure." Freddie was on the floor. He managed to get hold of Hazel's head and wedge it between his knees. Then he bent forward to take her wrists. "Can you get her legs?"

But Charlotte couldn't. The spastic jerking, the frothing of the mouth, the eyes rolling back, the weird sounds—it was unbearable. "I'm sorry," she said. "My head's killing me."

In the kitchen, the dogs were going wild. She scooped up the nearest puppy and held it while she filled the kettle, doing her best to ignore Agnes's barking, the cries of the other two pups, the terrible noises coming from the hall, the pounding of Hazel's heels, and, amidst this din, Freddie's voice: "Baby, you're safe now. Just relax. Hush. Let it go."

How calm he was, she thought, all that practice at Lourdes.

"Who will pay?" Hazel cried. "Who will pay?"

Charlotte found the teapot and a box of Typhoo. "First heat the pot," she said to the puppy. "A teaspoon each and one for the pot. The water should be almost but not quite boiling so as not to bruise the leaves. Pour swiftly before the oxygen is boiled away."

"Hazel, sweetheart, you're safe now. I'll take care of you."

Sweetheart. Suddenly Charlotte was back at Mr. Littleton's, in the bedroom, seeing what she'd failed to notice at the time—

Freddie with his far-from-colourless eyes fixed on Hazel in an expression full of yearning. The pounding was slowing, growing weaker.

"Allow to steep for five minutes. Pour milk into clean cups, add tea. Whenever possible use porcelain—"

"Charlotte." Freddie stood in the doorway. "What's your sister's number?"

"My sister's number?"

"Yes, the nurse."

The man who had referred to her black bags as luggage, who had pressed his forehead to hers, who had said "I'm so sorry," had disappeared. Like opening a favourite book and finding every page blank. I must say exactly the right thing, Charlotte thought, but she had no idea what that might be. A shrill squeal made her look down at the puppy writhing in her grip.

"Charlotte, for Pete's sake. Tell me the number. I need to know whether to phone an ambulance, or take Hazel to the hospital."

"It's awfully late to ring Bernadette. She's on early shifts this week. We can call—"

Freddie's hand rose, not exactly a threat but a reminder that such possibilities existed in the world. Before she knew what she was doing, she repeated Bernie's number and he was gone.

"Ms. Granger," she heard as she dumped the puppy back in the pen, "your patient Hazel Ransome just had a seizure. . . . No, this isn't Mr. Littleton. . . . She seems calm now, as if she were in a deep sleep."

Whatever he said next was lost in the gush of water as Charlotte rinsed the mugs. Moving on to their plates from last night, she realised she'd forgotten his admonition to set the puppies down on all four legs. She stacked the plates in the rack and then, rubbing her hands on her coat, stepped over to the table. Next to the peanut butter and the Chardonnay, Freddie had emptied the pockets of his work clothes: a handkerchief, three ten-pound notes, and a pile of change. Charlotte took the money, even the coppers, and slipped the Chardonnay back into her bag.

In the hall, Hazel lay unconscious and Freddie was bent over the phone, writing down whatever Bernadette was saying. He didn't look up as Charlotte stepped past him and Hazel. Fortunately her body wasn't blocking the door. Down the dark stairs and out into the dark street. Now what? No moon tonight. No valley of lost things. She looked at the house number, and at the corner stopped to check the name of the street. There, she would be able to reclaim her luggage, tomorrow or the next day. She passed the Chinese restaurant. *I must, I must . . .* Who should she telephone first?

Bernadette had clearly been asleep, but once she grasped the situation became reassuringly efficient. "Keep her warm and make sure she can't hurt herself," she instructed. "Where is she now?"

"On my floor," he'd said, looking down to where Hazel's head lay a few inches from his feet. Saliva flecked her chin.

"I'm afraid I missed your name."

He considered mentioning their one meeting, but introduced himself only as a friend of Hazel's. Was there anything else he should be doing?

"Cover her with a blanket," Bernadette said, then listed Hazel's medicines. "Try to make sure she takes them in the morning. You may find," she added, "that she wakes up disoriented, but that should pass in a few hours."

He replaced the receiver and knelt down. With her arms

flung wide, her legs outstretched, Hazel occupied most of the hall. Not for a moment, even to the most casual observer, could she have passed for dead. She was breathing heavily, right on the edge of snoring: little volleys, a pause, then another volley. Though she seemed comfortable on the floor, no way he'd leave her there. He squeezed her hand and, after a few seconds, unmistakably, she squeezed back.

Only then, as he moved to make the bed ready, did it dawn on him that Charlotte was gone. While he was writing down the names of Hazel's pills, she had crossed the hall, opened the door, stepped through it, closed the door. Seeing the unmade bed, he remembered her bending over him. *Look how the floor of heaven is thick inlaid. . . .* I fucked her, he thought. He tried, as he smoothed out the bottom sheet, to tell himself she had left of her own volition, popped out for more Lucozade. Who was he kidding? He'd done what everyone else had done, what he never intended to do: driven her away. For a moment he wondered if he should phone Mr. Early, then he understood: so long as she didn't show up on his doorstep, Mr. Early wouldn't give a toss.

"Please, Hazel," he whispered, "wake up soon."

She showed no signs of doing so, however, as he carefully carried her to the bed. After removing her shoes, he climbed in beside her, fully dressed, and endeavoured to put his arms around her—he wanted to begin at once, telling her every-thing—but Hazel tossed and moaned. Her elbow hit him on the side of the head. "Don't, Jonathan," she exclaimed. "Stop it!" and he was forced to retreat.

Was that his mother calling? *Frederick Lewis. Get in here!* What was this blue thing? In the dim light, the hardness of the floor and his relationship to it, became apparent. He had spent the night beside the bed, using a blue T-shirt as a pillow. Cautiously he pulled himself up and peered over the edge of the mattress.

Empty.

In the kitchen, Hazel had taken over where Charlotte left off, washing dishes at the sink. "Good morning," she said. "I hope I didn't disturb you."

Freddie shook his head. Her hair was damp and her face, when she turned to greet him, had lost its brittle flush. She was wearing one of his sweatshirts. "How are you feeling?" he managed.

"A little shaky. I had a seizure, didn't I? I hope it wasn't too awful. I could feel it coming, but there was nothing I could do. Then your damn dogs woke me up."

"Damn?" he said stupidly.

"Collies and guide dogs are okay, but pets? Forget it. I can't stand it that most dogs in Britain are better fed than most children in India. Would you like some tea?"

"I'll just go and wash."

She doesn't like dogs, he thought dumbfounded as he squeezed toothpaste onto the brush. Hadn't he, a couple of weeks ago, considered giving her a puppy? This was not going the way he'd imagined. He'd pictured himself up hours before Hazel, getting everything spick and span, then her waking up, sweet and befuddled. He'd bring her tea in bed, maybe oatmeal, and sit beside her to talk and hold her hand.

Back in the kitchen she had set the table, made tea. "Toast?" she offered.

"I'll do it," said Freddie. "You seem so . . ." He trailed off. Less than twelve hours ago this woman had been huddled in a bloody bed, ranting at her former lover, and here she was doing his washing up.

"Yes," said Hazel. "I'm surprised myself, after yesterday." She sat down. "Tell me again what happened."

Simplifying where need be—Charlotte was a friend of a friend, and yes, she'd gone home; they'd been out late retrieving Arkansas—Freddie described the events leading up to her seizure. "And now," he said, raising his mug to her, "we're in sunny Dalston."

He hoped she might turn those amazing eyes upon him, give one of her brilliant smiles, but while it was true she was looking at him, her expression was closer to a frown. "I still don't quite get why you and Charlotte climbed in through my bedroom window. I'm profoundly grateful, but it does seem odd, leaving a note in the middle of the night. Why not phone in the morning?"

Helpless, Freddie gave a little shrug and got up to make more toast. Only with his back to her could he utter the crucial sentence with anything remotely like calmness. "You're welcome to stay here as long as you like."

"Thanks. Obviously I've got a lot to figure out."

"I have extra keys," he persisted, "and money. I could fetch your things when I pick up the puppy."

The toast popped, and he carried the slices by their edges back to the table.

"I have to be careful today," said Hazel. "The seizures often come in waves. What I'd like to do is make a few phone calls: Mrs. Craig, my tenant, Charlotte. With any luck I'll be able to move back into my flat fairly soon, and I was hoping Charlotte might stay for a week or—"

He would never have predicted that the ringing of a phone could be so welcome. "Freddie," said a voice he recognised but couldn't place, "how's Hazel?"

"Who is this?"

"Sorry, Mrs. Craig. Am I ringing too early?"

"Not at all. Hazel's fine."

"Well, that's the main thing." She made her humming sound. "Listen, I have something sad to tell you. Your puppy fell down the stairs at Jonathan's—who knows how—and broke its neck."

Still holding the phone, avoiding the place where Hazel had collapsed the night before, Freddie sank to the floor. The little hands were back, stroking his arms and legs beneath his clothes, reminding him. I am a bad person, he thought. Forget America, forget the accident. I was cruel to Felicity, I used Charlotte, I hit Littleton, I did my best to deceive Hazel, to sneak into her affections, like a wolf into the fold. He stared at the floorboards, scarred and riven with dirt, the knots watching him. He could remember now, he was almost certain, stumbling over something as he rushed down the stairs. Dogs, he thought. India. She's a stranger.

Soft sounds came from the receiver. "I have a corner of the garden," Mrs. Craig was saying, "where several of my cats and their victims cohabit."

"Fine, whatever."

"I'm sorry," she said again. "I hope I'll see you soon at the Golden Road. Can I have a word with Hazel?"

He rose raggedly to summon her. "Oh, good," she said. They changed places.

Freddie remained standing inside the doorway. A few feet in one direction, Hazel spoke cheerfully into the phone; a few feet in another, Agnes was squinting at him over her empty bowl. Fire on the mountain, said her cocked ears. Famine, famine. Wash the floor, he thought, feed the dogs, finish my toast. He took a step back, another, then across the threshold and out of the room.

Hazel didn't look up as he appeared in the hall. "I have my pills," she was saying. "Charlotte brought them."

Freddie kept moving. He passed the black bags, lined up against the wall. His destination came into view: the faded pink upholstery of the couch.

Jonathan was putting the sheets in the dustbin when the doorbell rang. In another country, another century, he might have hung them from the window to advertise the triumph of love over virginity. Now he stuffed the bloody banners in among the fish wrappings and coffee grounds. On his way to the door, he stopped to wash his hands, using dishwashing liquid, rinsed and dried them. The only person he wanted to see would not be standing on the doorstep. What else mattered?

"Do you live here?"

A man of about his own height, wearing a shabby green cardigan and brown trousers, regarded him sternly. Over his shoulder Jonathan saw the cheese plant, still unclaimed. Hazel's mother had polished the leaves, one by one, and they glinted in the bright light. "Yes," he said.

"Lee Davies. Could I have a word with you?"

"Concerning?" Who the fuck was this? An angry client? But they could never get his home address. An irate neighbour? Maybe the bees had stung someone. He got ready to apologise and offer a gift of honey. Mr. Davies—his face, anyway— seemed unscathed. With his straight dark hair falling in a fringe, rather narrow eyes, and high cheekbones, he had an Oriental aspect.

"Concerning my son."

He stepped forward, and Jonathan yielded. In the hall he hesitated between the kitchen and the living-room before leading him into the former. They would sit at the table, as if

conducting an interview, rather than pretending the friendli-
ness of armchairs. He moved the newspaper, gestured the man
to take a seat. "I have to leave for work in a few minutes."

"He's in hospital," Mr. Davies said. "My son is in hospital. He didn't come home last night. He wanders a lot, round
and round, but he's always home by eleven." What was dis-
turbing, Jonathan realised, was that the man's face didn't
move, save for his mouth; his eyes and forehead remained
immobile. "Finally I went searching for him. It took nearly two
hours—I passed him once on the other side of the street, without seeing him—but at last I found him, a few yards from
here."

Christ. The Tourette's boy. Jonathan had forgotten all about
him. Keep calm, he told himself. Steady. He just wants information, witnesses. "I'm sorry. Of course I've seen your son
walking around—I always say hello—but not last night. There
are some punks round here, glue sniffers. Maybe one of them
decided to have a laugh. I hope he'll be better soon."

"He told me," said Mr. Davies, still unmoving, still in the
same tone, "the man with the plant had hurt him."

For a giddy moment Jonathan thought Mr. Davies might
be about to kill him. And then that he might be about to kill
Mr. Davies. "But . . . I . . ."

Mr. Davies, however, was speaking again. "His kidneys are
bruised, and there's some internal bleeding, but they think he
should be all right in a week or two. Physically, at least." He sat
back with his arms folded. "If you touch him again," he said
conversationally, "you'll be sorry."

He stood up and, as if completing an everyday household
task, emptied the dish rack filled with the plates and glasses
from last night's dinner onto the floor. In a cascade of glass and
china and cutlery he walked out of the room.

.   .   .

Jonathan reached for Hazel's calendar where it lay on the table. Many of the days were marked in her untidy handwriting— names, hospital appointments, groceries, medicines—but in the odd blank spaces he began to write: *Call George and Nora. Call Bernadette. Call Adams. Talk to Mrs. Craig. Buy sheets. Clean kitchen.*

All along he'd been looking in the wrong direction, trying to make time stand still, to re-create the past, but everything in life taught the opposite. A single hive changed from year to year; at the height of summer a bee lived a scant six weeks, its wings torn apart by constant nectar gathering, whereas in winter it might survive for as long as four months.

Suddenly, as if the thought of winter had alerted him, he noticed how cold the room had grown. Ignoring the fragments underfoot, he went to investigate and discovered that Mr. Davies had left the front door wide open. His first instinct was to slam it shut, but something made him pause. Standing on the threshold, Jonathan searched the street for what it was that had altered in the familiar landscape. The cheese plant was gone. In the brief interval between Mr. Davies's arrival and now, the plant had been carried off, he could only assume, to a good home.

He stepped back and closed the door, slid the chain into place, and, taking the keys from his pocket, applied both the upper and lower mortice locks. The bolts slid home with a solid, satisfying stiffness. He was tired of people coming and going without permission.

Back in the kitchen he fetched the dustpan from beneath the sink and—even in the midst of such disarray he was pleased by his practicality—pulled on his beekeeper's gloves. One by one he picked up the shards of china and glass. First Hazel's plate, then his, first Hazel's glass, then his. After collecting everything he could see, he bent to check for the wink of glass and caught the last splinters. There. He carried the dustpan outside to empty on top of the sheets, then clapped his gloves together. The sparrows fussed out of the elderberry tree.

Inside he crossed out *Call George and Nora. Call Bernadette. Call Adams. Talk to Mrs. Craig.* Irrelevant, all irrelevant. Only one thing was necessary now, the thing he should've done first, and would have if it hadn't been for the seizures, the hospital, her parents and Maud, his own deep confusion about second chances and, he had to admit, a certain shame about his slip-up of last autumn. *Talk to Hazel,* he wrote.

ACKNOWLEDGMENTS

The John Simon Guggenheim Memorial Foundation and the MacDowell Colony were generous in giving me time and money to work on this book.

My heartfelt thanks to the friends who made suggestions on the manuscript at various stages: Tom Bahr, Jennifer Clarvoe, Carol Frost, Yusef Komunyakaa, Ann Shuttleworth, Susan Brison, Kathleen Hill, and Camille Smith offered invaluable advice. Once again I am profoundly indebted to Andrea Barrett.

I am grateful to Amanda Urban for her dazzling expertise and Gary Fisketjon for his fabulous editing.

My thoughts about memory and forgetting were shaped by some wonderful books, especially *The Human Brain* by Susan Greenfield, *Memory's Ghost* by Philip J. Hilts, *The Mind of a Mnemonist* by A. R. Luria, *The Anatomy of Memory* by James McConkey, *Searching for Memory* by Daniel L. Schacter, *The Memory Palace of Matteo Ricci* by Jonathan D. Spence, *The Art of Memory* by Frances Yates, and of course the *Confessions* of St. Augustine.

FOR THE BEST IN PAPERBACKS, LOOK FOR THE

In every corner of the world, on every subject under the sun, Penguin represents quality and variety—the very best in publishing today.

For complete information about books available from Penguin—including Puffins, Penguin Classics, and Compass—and how to order them, write to us at the appropriate address below. Please note that for copyright reasons the selection of books varies from country to country.

In the United Kingdom: Please write to *Dept. EP, Penguin Books Ltd, Bath Road, Harmondsworth, West Drayton, Middlesex UB7 0DA.*

In the United States: Please write to *Penguin Putnam Inc., P.O. Box 12289 Dept. B, Newark, New Jersey 07101-5289 or call 1-800-788-6262.*

In Canada: Please write to *Penguin Books Canada Ltd, 10 Alcorn Avenue, Suite 300, Toronto, Ontario M4V 3B2.*

In Australia: Please write to *Penguin Books Australia Ltd, P.O. Box 257, Ringwood, Victoria 3134.*

In New Zealand: Please write to *Penguin Books (NZ) Ltd, Private Bag 102902, North Shore Mail Centre, Auckland 10.*

In India: Please write to *Penguin Books India Pvt Ltd, 11 Panchsheel Shopping Centre, Panchsheel Park, New Delhi 110 017.*

In the Netherlands: Please write to *Penguin Books Netherlands bv, Postbus 3507, NL-1001 AH Amsterdam.*

In Germany: Please write to *Penguin Books Deutschland GmbH, Metzlerstrasse 26, 60594 Frankfurt am Main.*

In Spain: Please write to *Penguin Books S. A., Bravo Murillo 19, 1° B, 28015 Madrid.*

In Italy: Please write to *Penguin Italia s.r.l., Via Benedetto Croce 2, 20094 Corsico, Milano.*

In France: Please write to *Penguin France, Le Carré Wilson, 62 rue Benjamin Baillaud, 31500 Toulouse.*

In Japan: Please write to *Penguin Books Japan Ltd, Kaneko Building, 2-3-25 Koraku, Bunkyo-Ku, Tokyo 112.*

In South Africa: Please write to *Penguin Books South Africa (Pty) Ltd, Private Bag X14, Parkview, 2122 Johannesburg.*